The Blue Wolf

WEATHERHEAD BOOKS ON ASIA

WEATHERHEAD EAST ASIAN INSTITUTE,
COLUMBIA UNIVERSITY

INOUE YASUSHI

THE BLUE WOLF

A NOVEL OF THE LIFE OF CHINGGIS KHAN

TRANSLATED FROM THE JAPANESE BY

Joshua A. Fogel

COLUMBIA UNIVERSITY ♛ NEW YORK

This publication has been supported by the Richard W. Weatherhead Publication Fund of
the Weatherhead East Asian Institute, Columbia University.

Columbia University Press wishes to express its appreciation for assistance
given by York University toward the cost of publishing this book.

COLUMBIA UNIVERSITY PRESS
Publishers Since 1893
New York   Chichester, West Sussex

Translation copyright © 2008 Joshua A. Fogel

Library of Congress Cataloging-in-Publication Data

Inoue, Yasushi, 1907–1991.
    [Aoki Ōkami. English]
    The blue wolf : a novel of the life of Chinggis Khan / Inoue Yasushi ;
translated from the Japanese by Joshua A. Fogel.
        p.   cm. — (Weatherhead books on Asia)
    ISBN 978-0-231-14616-6 (cloth : alk. paper) —
    ISBN 978-0-231-51791-1 (electronic)
    1. Genghis Khan, 1162–1227—Fiction. I. Fogel, Joshua A. II. Title. III. Series.

PL830.N63A86   2008
895.6'35—DC22

                                                                        2008002981

Columbia University Press books are printed on permanent and
durable acid-free paper.

♾ This book was printed on paper with recycled content.

Printed in the United States of America

c 10 9 8 7 6 5 4 3 2 1

References to Internet Web sites (URLs) were accurate at the time of writing.
Neither the author nor Columbia University Press is responsible for URLs
that may have expired or changed since the manuscript was prepared.

DESIGN BY VIN DANG

Contents

Translator's Note

WHAT GREAT FUN IT HAS BEEN translating Inoue Yasushi's (1907–91) epic novel, *Aoki ōkami* (The blue wolf)! The Japanese original was published in ten serial installments in the renowned cultural journal *Bungei shunjū* from October 1959 through July 1960, then published in book form by the journal's parent publishing company, Bungei shunjū shinsha, in 1960, by Shinchōsha in 1964, and by numerous other presses thereafter. To give an idea of its enormous popularity in Japan, Shinchōsha put the novel through its forty-seventh printing in 1987, and it still appears to be in print and available through online book-ordering services in Japan. Indeed, an *Asahi shinbun* report for February 28, 2007 indicates something of the extent of the novel's popularity: during a state visit to Japan by the president of Mongolia, the topic of *Aoki ōkami* came up in conversation with the Japanese emperor and empress.[1]

Many of Inoue's other novels and travelogues have been published in English translation over the past forty years, including *The Roof Tile of Tempyō, Confucius: A Novel, Dunhuang, Flood, Journey Beyond Samarkand, The Tea Ceremony, The Izu Dancer and Other Stories, Lou-lan and Other Stories, The Hunting Gun, The Counterfeiter and Other Stories, Wind and Waves, Shirobamba: A Childhood in Japan*, and most recently *The Samurai Banner of Furin Kazan*. One element of his work that has made him popular among ordinary readers as well as specialists in East Asian studies—a rare accomplishment—is the simple fact that, recognizing that he was a novelist and not a scholar of Chinese and Inner Asian (and, of course, Japanese) history and culture, he frequently consulted with leading academic historians about the subject matter of his works in progress. For example, his novel *Dunhuang* concerns the years in the Tang dynasty (618–907) just prior to that famous cave's being sealed with many hundreds of manuscripts inside, only to be discovered at the dawn of the twentieth century; Inoue sought advice from Fujiwara Akira (1911–98), a specialist on Dunhuang manuscripts. For *Wind and Waves*, a novel about the Mongol subjugation of Korea, which was virtually enslaved at the time of the failed conquest missions to Japan, he consulted with Okada Hidehiro (b. 1931), one of postwar Japan's best known Mongolists. And in writing *The Roof Tile of Tempyō*, about several Japanese Buddhist acolytes in the early eighth century who make the pilgrimage to China with one of the periodic embassies from Japan to pursue their religious studies, during which several members strive wholeheartedly to convince the great monk Ganjin (C. Jianzhen, 688–763) to return with them to Japan, he sought the advice of Andō Kōsei (1900–70), a specialist in Nara-period Japanese history who wrote a number of books on Ganjin and other aspects of Sino-Japanese religious history in this early era.[2] One Japanese Mongolist wrote me that, in his estimation, and perhaps exaggeratedly, Inoue was a genuine "literary giant" (*bungō*), whereas other, more prolific historical novelists, who appeared frequently in the mass media, were merely "mass market authors" (*taishū sakka*).[3]

Does this attention to historical accuracy and authenticity make Inoue's novels more readable or simply more satisfying? Explanations for his works' popularity with the Japanese reading public must take into account these concerns as well as his writing style. Inoue has mastered a style that is simultaneously crystal clear—often about events and customs that are anything but familiar to an ordinary reader—and conscientious about historical and cultural detail. This is no mean feat and should not be underestimated—usually an author must dispense with one or the other, often sacrificing history to tell a good story.

Over the course of his career, Inoue won numerous literary prizes in Japan, such as the Akutagawa Prize in 1949, and his name was frequently mentioned as a candidate for the Nobel Prize for literature during the long period between its presentation to Kawabata Yasunari (1899–1972) in 1968 and to Ōe Kenzaburō (b. 1935) in 1994, the only two Japanese to win this highly coveted award. Few authors of historical fiction, in which Inoue specialized, have received the Nobel.

As he explains in his own afterword, Inoue was drawn to write about Chinggis Khan precisely because there were areas of his character that historians had not explained or simply could not explain. Enter the historical novelist who need not be tied down by the hard-and-fast pull of facticity or the silence from documentation. Where the historical record dries up, the novelist takes over. Inoue wanted to get at the source of what drove Chinggis psychologically to virtually endless conquest and colossal mass murder. Needless to say, we have no contemporary documents describing the Great Khan's psyche—indeed, for much of the history retold in this novel, the Mongols were preliterate.

This direction might lead one to write a novel of utterly no use whatsoever. Imagine a comparable novel about Napoleon or Hitler, both mentioned by Inoue in his afterword, that explained their penchant for conquest as based on a single psychological source. Many readers might reject it out of hand; at best, it might attract those drawn to monocausal explanations of great events or people. Inoue does manage to penetrate the character of his fictional Chinggis without either completely demonizing him or idealizing him; there is similarly no effort to explain away any of his obviously monstrous behavioral traits by invoking some form of historical relativism. And where the facts are available, Inoue sticks to them. I give but one example. There is a famous story—recounted every year in East Asian survey courses around the world—of Chinggis's plan, once he completed his conquest of the state of Jin in north China, to depopulate the entire area and turn it into a massive pastureland for the nomadic Mongolian people; he is said to have been dissuaded only by the intervention of his aide, the Khitan nobleman

Yelü Chucai (1190–1244), who makes repeated appearances in the novel. This story would have made great copy in *Aoki ōkami*, but to his credit Inoue makes no mention of it, presumably because it has no basis whatsoever in fact.[4]

The enduring popularity of Inoue's psychological take on the driving force behind Chinggis Khan, the conqueror, is attested by the nearly four-and-a-half-hour television drama based on the novel, entitled *Aoki ōkami, Chingisu Kan no shōgai* (The blue wolf: The career of Chinggis Khan). Appearing initially in four installments on Asahi TV in 1980, it was directed by Morisaki Azuma and Harada Takashi, and it starred Katō Gō in the title role.

On a far grander scale than the small screen, however, is the release on March 31, 2007 of a major motion picture shot entirely on location in Mongolia, putatively to commemorate the 800th anniversary of the founding of the first Mongolian state: *Aoki ōkami, chihate umi tsukiru made* (The blue wolf: Till the end of land and sea). The story is based both on Inoue's novel and on a more recent novel by Morimura Seiichi entitled *Chihate umi tsukiru made, shōsetsu Chingisu Kan* (Till the end of land and sea, a novel of Chinggis Khan).[5] The blockbuster was directed by Sawai Shin'ichirō, a veteran screenwriter and director, and runs over two hours.[6]

As Inoue was periodically aided by experts in various histories, I too was fortunate enough to have recourse to the assistance of specialists. Although there have been Mongolian, French, and three Chinese translations of this novel, I assiduously did not consult them until the copyediting stage of production. The modern Mongolian rendition is beyond my abilities in any case, but I did not want to be unduly influenced by the French or Chinese translators' take on the events portrayed. In matters concerning Mongolian toponyms, ethnonyms, and other proper nouns, I frequently consulted with Christopher Atwood of Indiana University. Despite considerable attention by highly trained specialists over the years to many of the details of early Mongolian history, rendering these proper nouns is no mean feat. Like all living languages, Mongolian has changed over the eight centuries since Chinggis lived, and chronolectal difficulties only added to the problem. Chris's advice made it possible for me accurately to romanize the terms I was reading in Japanese syllabary form. If I have done this correctly, it is all to his credit; where I have failed, it is because I misunderstood or mistranscribed one of his renderings. For the Central Asian terms that appear in the latter chapters, I have relied (at Chris's advice) on John Andrew Boyle's (1916–78) translation of the Persian historian Ata-Malik Juvaini's (1226–83) *Genghis Khan: The History of the World-Conqueror.*[7] My only addition to Inoue's original text are the (rather simple) names of the chapters; in the original they were merely numbers.

I do not know if Japanese read more historical fiction than Anglophones, but I do know that the percentage of historical novels translated from Japanese into English (vis-à-vis all novels rendered from Japanese into English) is much lower than their comparative numbers in the original language. For example, only two historical novels by Chin Shunshin (b. 1925) and only three or four by the most prolific of all, Shiba Ryōtarō, have appeared in English-language editions. Like films with historical themes and personages, historical novels can be used in teaching with great efficacy, but only if they are approached critically. They help us to imagine the inner workings of historical actors in a way that less accessible academic works cannot. But they are novels, not chronicles. One should no more confuse the Napoleon and the Mikhail Kutuzov (1745–1813) of Tolstoy's *War and Peace* with the real men than the men and women surrounding John F. Kennedy (1917–63) with the characters in Oliver Stone's (b. 1946) film *JFK*.

Enjoy, enjoy.

Joshua A. Fogel

NOTES

1. See www.asahi.com/national/update/0228/TKY200702280361.html. Thanks to one of the anonymous readers for Columbia University Press who brought this to my attention.

2. *Tonkō* (Tokyo: Iwanami shoten, 1981), English translation by Jean Oda Moy, *Tun-huang: A Novel* (Tokyo, New York: Kodansha International, 1978); there are also German, French, and Chinese (three times) translations. *Fūtō* (Tokyo: Kōdansha, 1963), English translation by James T. Araki, *Wind and Waves: A Novel* (Honolulu: University of Hawai'i Press, 1989); also French and Chinese translations. *Tenpyō no iraka* (Tokyo: Chūō kōronsha, 1957); English translation by James T. Araki, *The Roof Tile of Tempyō* (Tokyo: University of Tokyo Press, 1975); also French, German, and Chinese (three times) translations.

3. Personal e-mail communication from Nakami Tatsuo, August 24, 2002.

4. See two fine books by Sugiyama Masaaki: *Yaritsu Soꝫai to sono jidai* (Yelü Chucai and his age) (Tokyo: Hakuteisha, 1996) and *Dai Mongoru no sekai, riku to umi no kyodai teikoku* (The world of Mongolia, an immense empire of land and sea) (Tokyo: Kadogawa shoten, 1992).

5. (Tokyo: Kadogawa Haruki jimusho, 2000), two volumes.

6. As of this writing, the film has not come to North America, and I have not seen it. From an assortment of Web sites, including one launched solely for the film itself (www.aoki-ookami.com), the following roles will be played by the following actors: Temüjin (Ikematsu Sōsuke); Chinggis Khan (Sorimachi Takashi); Yisügei (Hosaka Naoki); Ö'elün (Wakamura Mayumi); Qasar (Hakamada Yoshihiko), Jamugha (Hirayama Yusuke); To'oril Khan (Matsukata Hiroki); Börte (Kikukawa Rei); and Qulan (Ara, a young Korean actress in her first major role).

7. (Seattle: University of Washington Press, 1958).

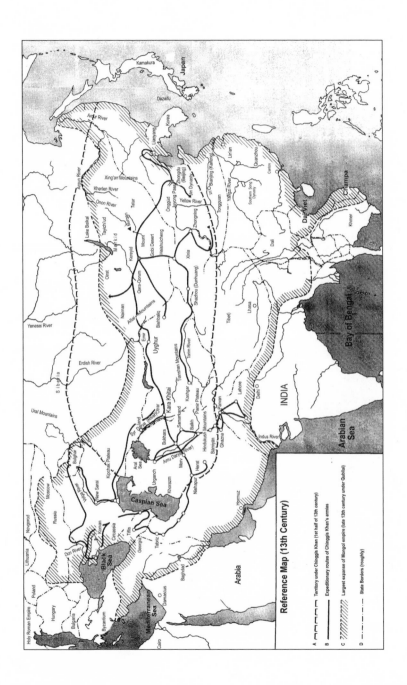

Reference Map (13th Century)

A   [   ]   Territory under Chinggis Khan (1st half of 13th century)

B   ———   Expeditionary routes of Chinggis Khan's armies

C   //////   Largest expanse of Mongol empire (late 13th century under Qubilai)

D   –·–·–   State Borders (roughly)

Japan

Kamakura

Dazaifu

Korea

Liaoyang

Amur River

Argun River

Xing'an Mountains

Kherlen River

Onon River

Talar

Lake Baikal

Taychi'ud

Markid

Burgan

Mount

Kereyid

Onggud

Juyong Pass

Zhongdu (Beijing)

Jin Dynasty

Yellow River

Buqing (Kaifeng)

Linian

Quanzhou

Canton

Champa

Gobi Desert

Heishuicheng

Zhongxing

Tongquan

Yangzi River

Southern Song Dynasty

Dai Viet

Khmer

Oirat

Qara-Qorum

Xixia

Shazhou (Dunhuang)

Dali

Bay of Bengal

Yenesei River

Naiman

Altai Mountains

Emir

Beshbalik

Uyghur

Erdish River

Lhasa

Tibet

S i b e r i a

Kara Khitai

Tianshan Mountains

Tarim River

Kashgar

Pamir Plateau

Ural Mountains

Syr Darya (River)

Samarkand

Balkh

Panjan

Lahore

Delhi

INDIA

Bukhara

Hindukush Mountains

Bamiyan

Ghazna

Indus River

Amu Darya (River)

Aral Sea

Khiva

Ulgench

Merv

Nishapur

Herat

Arabian Sea

Kipchak Plateau

Volga River

New Sarai

Khorazm

Hormuz

Moscow

Russia

Bulghar

Novgorod

Arabia

Lithuania

Poland

Holy Roman Empire

Hungary

Bulgaria

Byzantium

Konan

Circassia

Tiflis

Georgia

Tabriz

Don River

Black Sea

Baghdad

Mediterranean Sea

Cairo

Damascus

Caspian Sea

The Blue Wolf

Earliest Years

THE YEAR WAS 1162. A baby boy was born in the chieftain's yurt in
a settlement of the nomadic Mongols who lived in the grassy plains
and forests by the Amur River, which, along its upper reaches, splits
into the two tributaries of the Onon and Kherlen rivers. The mother
was a beautiful young woman still several years shy of twenty by
the name of Ö'elün. As was often the case, at this very time the men
of the settlement had all left to launch an attack against the Tatars of
a neighboring area, a tribe with whom they had long been fighting.
Thus, the only people then residing in the several hundred Mongol
yurts were old people and children.

Ö'elün dispatched an old servant to report the birth of her son to
the camp of Yisügei, her husband, who was several miles away from
the lineage at the time. After the messenger had departed, Ö'elün
put her ear to the face of her newborn. The infant had rolled over
in his raggedy swaddling. The fingers of his left hand were wrapped
around hers so tightly that the women who had just delivered him
could not unpeel them. With the instinctive tenacity of a mother
attempting to ascertain for herself that the four limbs of the child
to whom she has just given birth were all in good working order,
Ö'elün tried her best to remove his left hand clasping her tightly.
This required considerable attention, without the least violence.
When she managed to separate her hand from the child's, Ö'elün
heard the roaring wind rush by above the yurt. Like a solid object

but with the volume of a rushing, mighty river, the wind was blowing east to west, and it seemed to shake the earth's very axis. When it ceased blowing, Ö'elün remembered the height of the pitch-black night sky above the yurt in which she was lying on her back. Countless stars studded the sky, each glistening before her eyes with its own icy light. When the next wind swept over her, though, it was like a black cloth embroidered with the stars came howling, and the stars scattered in all directions, ultimately leaving only the roar of the wind enveloping heaven and earth. While the wind was blowing or the starry sky hung over the roof, Ö'elün invariably was taken with the feeling of her own utter insignificance, lying there alone in her humble yurt.

This very sense of insignificance and powerlessness amid the vastness of nature was surely to be found somewhere in the heart of each of these nomads who, possessing neither fixed houses nor designated plots of land, moved in search of grasslands and owned no soil on which to live sedentary lives. Wherever they went and whatever else they might have been thinking about, in the end this inevitable feeling was like a spell cast over them. For Ö'elün that evening, there was still another, even stronger reason for her feeling of forlorn loneliness. Ö'elün could see an even higher sky through the roof of the yurt that night, and the force of the night wind causing the yurt to sway felt that much wilder.

Having just become a mother, Ö'elün was now troubled by two things. First, would the baby to whom she had just given birth possess the full physique sufficient to satisfy her husband? Second, would the infant have as acute powers of sight and smell as his father to fully satisfy Yisügei?

Ö'elün was able to rid her mind of one of these two concerns. The baby, apparently of his own volition, opened the little fingers of his hand that he had until then entrusted to her palm. He firmly grasped a blood clot the shape of a deer's anklebone, as if he were holding some sort of military decoration.

Beyond this, Ö'elün had no other worries. From the features of her newborn, one could derive no proof or confirmation that he was the son of Yisügei. In some ways he resembled Yisügei, and in others he did not. By the same token, he certainly did not look like another man, which would have been cause for Yisügei's distress. In a word, the boy looked like no one at all in particular. That is, except for one person—he did resemble the mother from whose womb he had just emerged.

Ö'elün had no idea whatsoever what Yisügei's feelings would be when he learned of the birth. Throughout his wife's pregnancy, Yisügei had remained taciturn and expressionless, as brave men of his lineage always were. Joyous or angry, he would not allow his inner feelings to be visible to anyone other than himself. Ö'elün would be able to learn her husband's first words when news of the birth reached him. It would not have been altogether out of the ordinary were he to utter, "Kill him!"

The old servant dispatched to Yisügei's camp returned to Ö'elün's yurt the next evening. He reported to the young mother that Yisügei had selected the name Temüjin for the boy. When she heard this, for the first time since she had given birth, Ö'elün looked relieved, for at least she now knew that her husband did not bear anger such that he might wish to curse the newborn child. Aside from this, however, everything remained unclear, for according to the old servant the meaning of the name Temüjin could be construed by Ö'elün in any way she wished.

"When I reached Master Yisügei's camp, he was in the midst of enjoying a victory celebration after merciless fighting with the Tatars. To the side of the campfire were two enemy leaders who had been taken prisoner and were tied up. It seemed to be the middle of a drinking bout, and one of the prisoners was dragged out and beheaded on the spot. As if to commemorate this triumphal celebration, it was the wish of Master Yisügei to give the newborn child the name of this Tatar chief."

Thus spoke the elderly servant. To be sure, a name taken simply to commemorate a military victory posed no problems, but when she tried to come to terms with the fact that it was the name of an enemy chief who had been decapitated, Ö'elün could not repress a certain disquiet. And she remained confused as to whether Yisügei was happy or enraged at the birth of his son. In any event, this infant boy who as yet had no clear sense of who his mother and father were was given the name Temüjin and thus was fated to be reared as the eldest son of a leader of a Mongol lineage.

For the next few days, Ö'elün suffered with a high fever due to postpartum illness, vacillating between life and death. When the fever subsided and it eventually became clear that she would live, the first thing her frail eyes caught sight of was her husband, Yisügei, taking their baby son, Temüjin, up in his arms.

Ö'elün had become Yisügei's wife about ten months earlier. Born into the Olqunu'ud lineage, she had been taken captive by a young man of the Merkid lineage and carried off to a Merkid settlement. En route she was again taken, this time by Yisügei, by the banks of the Onon River and hence became his wife. She had been raped over a dozen times by the young men of the Merkids, and although she gave birth only after becoming Yisügei's wife, there was no way of determining for sure that the boy was his biological son.

Ö'elün continued looking at the profile of her husband holding Temüjin. Commonly called Warrior Yisügei, he was feared by other tribes for his famed courage and valor. From the intrepid look on his face, she could not detect so much as a fragment of his inner thoughts, but the fact that he was embracing Temüjin in his large arms gave Ö'elün cause for relief. And this sense of relief gradually changed into a powerful emotion she herself could not even explain clearly, as tears bathed her cheeks.

A number of nomadic peoples were encamped at various sites on the terrain north of the Great Wall of China where the Mongols lived at this time. The land was obstructed on the east by the Great Xing'an Mountains and on the west by the Sayan, Altai, Tannu-Ola, and Tianshan ranges; to the south it bordered China at the Great Wall and the Western Marshes across the immense wasteland of the Gobi Desert. And the north, bounded by the region around Lake Baikal, was engulfed in the endless no-man's land of Siberia. Six rivers streamed through this immense plain surrounded by great mountain ranges, deserts, and uninhabited wilderness. The Onon,

Ingoda, and Kherlen flowed together, formed the Amur River, and poured out into the Sea of Okhotsk. The Tula, Orkhon, and Selengge rivers all flowed into Lake Baikal. These two water systems both began in the central portion of the high plains, and their basins formed the grasslands and forest regions. From time immemorial nomadic peoples had risen and fallen here. With this area as a base of operations, the Xiongnu, Rouran, Orkhon Turks (Tujue), and Uyghurs had all attempted to extend their influence southward, the only way out. Thus, Chinese statesmen over the centuries had no choice but to construct the Great Wall and prepare for invasions from these nomads to their north.

It was unclear just when the Mongols had moved into this region, but in roughly the eighth century they, together with other settlements, fell under the domination of the Turks, and in the middle of the eighth century they became subject to the Uyghurs who replaced the Turks. From the ninth century, they were under the control of the Tatars who supplanted the Uyghurs. After the collapse of the Tatars, though, a number of unrelated peoples who differed in hairstyles, skin color, and customs formed their own villages and spread out here and there around the vast grasslands. Through the years, they lived fighting constantly over domesticated animals, women, and grasses.

In the middle of the twelfth century, when Temüjin was born, besides the Mongol people there were the Kirghiz, Oirat, Merkid, Tatar, Kereyid, Naiman, and Önggüd ethnicities living on this Mongolian plain. The Mongols and Tatars were trying to gain supremacy over all the settlements, and that meant incessant small-scale fighting. Temüjin was born in the midst of the battles between these two peoples.

In addition to fighting between different ethnic groups, there was repeated and often fierce fighting within the same group over collected booty. The Mongols were divided into a number of lineages, each with its own independent settlement, which were prone to vie with one another. The Borjigin lineage to which Yisügei belonged had long effectively functioned as the main family line of the Mongolian people, and from it someone had eventually emerged as the *khan* or ruler who controlled all the Mongol groupings. The first khan was Temüjin's great-grandfather, Qabul Khan, who brought a certain unity, albeit imperfect, to the Mongol settlements, which had been in a state of chaotic disorder, and he put in place a system for other settlements that proved to be of benefit to all. Although the second khan was Hambaghai of the Tayichi'uds, in the following generation leadership returned to the Borjigin lineage with Qutula, Yisügei's uncle, as khan. At present, Yisügei was the fourth khan.

Temüjin was therefore raised in the tent of the chief of the Mongolian people on the great Mongolian plateau. Two years after giving birth to him, Ö'elün bore Qasar, and two years after that Qachi'un, both boys. Thus, at age four Temüjin had two younger brothers. His father also sired by another woman a boy one year his junior by the name of Begter and another boy two years Begter's junior by the name of Belgütei, thus giving Temüjin two more younger brothers. Temüjin was reared together with all of his younger male siblings, as Yisügei treated his five sons equally, not doting on or showing particular favoritism to any one of them. The same was true of Ö'elün. She never distinguished between the three sons she had borne in her womb and the two children born to another woman. And just as her husband showed no favoritism toward Temüjin, Ö'elün too showed none toward any of the children she and her husband had produced. This was particularly perspicacious on her part.

When Temüjin was six years old, Ö'elün gave birth to another male child who was given the name Temüge. The six-year-old Temüjin was considerably bigger physically than other boys his age and considerably stronger, but he was a quiet child who rarely spoke. Although he quarreled with others very infrequently, when he did so it was with great resolution. He would always listen silently with his eyes glaring whenever someone would speak to him abusively, and when he saw that that person had nothing further to say, he would suddenly, without so much as a single word, attack him. He might throw the person to the ground and from horseback pelt him with stones, or he might ram the person's head into the sand and trample him underfoot—his methods were decidedly violent. There was something brutal in the manner of his assault, as Temüjin possessed, in the eyes of the adults who came to stop him, a bizarre disposition lacking many of the charms associated with childhood. On such occasions, the adults were under the illusion that Temüjin was the same age as they, and they would always reprove him as one castigates an adult.

These instances aside, though, Temüjin was just a quiet, unobtrusive lad. Being the eldest child, he had to allow his mother to look after his younger brothers. He thus had little opportunity to rest at Ö'elün's knee or wrapped in her arms. Yet he was no different from other children in his desire to spend time close to his mother.

The first time Temüjin heard stories of ancestors in his lineage and the traditions about them, he was seven years of age. He had a distant relative, an elderly man by the name of Bültechü Ba'atur. The term *ba'atur* was an appellation meaning "brave," indicating that in his youth this man had undoubtedly been a valiant warrior. Now, however, he was a gentle old man, fond of children, who had grown a white beard over his cheeks and chin. He retained a stunning memory, and when on occasion relatives gathered in Yisügei's yurt, he regaled them with tales of their ancestors through the ages. As if he had known all of these men from the past personally, he described in intimate detail their facial appearances and even their dispositions. No one listening ever lost interest.

Whenever a group of men gathered around, Bültechü Ba'atur always faithfully drew out—as if he were tracing it with string—what he had crammed inside his head. While a portion of what he recounted was remembered by the majority of those assembled, no one else could tell a story like Bültechü, and it was hard to imagine that anyone else could keep such extraordinarily long stories stored inside his mind as he could.

When Bültechü was about to launch into one of his tales, people would often try to be the first to jump in from memory.

—There was Batachiqan and his son was Tamacha, and Tamacha's son was Qorichar Mergen, and Qorichar Mergen's son was A'ujam Boroghul, and A'ujam Boroghul's son was Sali Qacha'u, and Sali Qacha'u's son was Yeke Nidün, and Yeke Nidün's son was Sem Söchi.

In this way one might enunciate the names of one's ancestors who had been the heads of the family. If one became confused, another might pick up the lead and continue the genealogy.

—Sem Söchi's son was Qarchu, and Qarchu's son was Borjigidai Mergen; and Borjigidai Mergen had a beautiful wife by the name of Mongoljin Gho'a, and they had a son by the name of Toroqoljin Bayan; and Toroqoljin Bayan had a beautiful wife by the name of Boroqchin Gho'a, as well as a young servant named Boroldai Suyalbi and two fine steeds named Dayir and Boro.

Even one with the best of memories would usually find himself stymied at this point in the tale. Thereafter—that is, from Toroqoljin Bayan (meaning Toroqoljin "the rich"), the tenth-generation head of the family with his wife and two horses and young servant—the number of offspring proliferated, and all of a sudden the names of the people that one had to commit to memory expanded like the branches and limbs of a overgrown tree, necessitating that one wait for the likes of Bültechü with his astonishing memory. When others couldn't recall anything more, he would smile in apparent satisfaction, his face wrinkled by age, and slowly begin to speak. And of course, what Bültechü actually had to say was more than just a simple list of the names of the heads of the Mongol families through the ages. His tone often went as follows:

"Toroqoljin Bayan and his wife Boroqchin Gho'a were a very happy couple. Because they were so very amicable, they produced a son with a single eye. Thus, they gave him the name Du'a Soqor or 'one-eyed' Du'a. This eye was placed right in the middle of his forehead, but it was an extremely efficacious eyeball, for he was said to be able to see—although it surely sounds like a falsehood—to a distance three days' journey away, perhaps as far as 250 miles. After Du'a Soqor, Dobun Mergen (Dobun 'the sharpshooter') was born, and both developed into high-spirited youngsters. On one occasion the brothers went out hunting. Du'a Soqor surveyed the plain and saw in the distance a fine young woman. She seemed as though she might be married. He said: 'Since she should be passing this way tomorrow or the next day, let's snatch her up when she arrives and she'll make a fine wife for you, Dobun Mergen.' Although Dobun

Mergen did not, in fact, do this, the following day when she arrived at that place, she turned out to be a young bride amid a small group of people. The young men drew their bows and brandished their spears, preparing to attack them. Such were the circumstances by which Alan Gho'a (meaning the 'fair' Alan) became the bride of Dobun Mergen. The two soon produced two sons, Bügünütei and Belgünütei, who were to become, respectively, the ancestors of the Bügünüd and Belgünüd lineages. Well, then, Dobun Mergen now had Alan Gho'a as his wife, but regrettably he died, leaving behind his young wife and two young sons. Alan Gho'a continued to raise the boys, and in succession produced three more sons. Although she had no husband, she gave birth to several children. That said, Alan Gho'a was a chaste woman, and never had she committed a sin. How then were the births of these children to be explained? Just before she became pregnant each time, light from a corner of heaven shone down, entered a hole in the roof of her yurt, and touched the white skin of her body. Thence were born Bügü Qatagi, Bughatu Salji, and Bodonchar Mungqaq (Bodonchar 'the fool'), and they were the progenitors, respectively, of the Qatagin, Salji'ud, and Borjigin lineages. Thus, the blood of the beautiful Alan is mixed with the light of heaven in the bodies of those of us Borjigins who come together and form the line descending from Bodonchar Mungqaq."

Bültechü went on to recount in detail and with vibrancy the generations of brave warriors and military prowess that followed Bodonchar. There were ten generations from Bodonchar to the present head of the lineage, Yisügei, and many things had to be described, but it would be impossible to relate the entire story in a single evening.

The only story that left an impression on the seven-year-old Temüjin was that of Du'a Soqor. If the other parts of the tale did not elicit much interest, it was probably because he did not fully understand them. Temüjin was even more fascinated when, at some great meeting of all the Mongol families, a number of elders responded in chorus, as if in prayer, to Bültechü's oral transmission, in the open space before their yurts, of the origins of the Mongols. In particu-

lar, it was the content of the phrases of their prayer that intrigued
Temüjin:

—There was a blue wolf born with a destiny set by heaven.
There was a pale doe who was his mate. She came across a wide
lake. They set up camp at Mount Burqan at the source of the Onon
River, and there was born Batachiqan.

These were the short phrases that were begun by the chorus, and
soon thereafter they were absorbed into intricate ceremonies. The
oral tradition had it that through the mating of the wolf and doe the
initial ancestor Batachiqan was born, and whenever this tale was recounted, it evoked extraordinary emotions in the hearts of all Mongols, whether they were of the Borjigin or the Tayichi'ud lineage.
Everyone believed the story. It told of a great lake far to the west
and a rampaging wolf that crossed it at the orders of his deity and
took the graceful, beautiful doe as his mate. Mount Burqan was a
peak everyone knew well. Wherever they moved their yurts, Mongols were raised nearly every day from birth with an adoration for
Mount Burqan.

Temüjin was profoundly moved by the story of the blue wolf.
Satisfied that he was himself a descendant of the wolf and doe, he
firmly believed that the tale did not refer to another lineage, and as
a result those of the other lineages had declined to a debased state.
In short, Temüjin felt great pride that the blood of the wolf and doe
coursed through his veins.

Hearing this strange chorus of elders, including Bültechü, singing was the most important event of Temüjin's youth. The meaning
of the words they sang, of course, was difficult for the seven-year-
old to comprehend and was explained to him by his mother, Ö'elün.
While the elders were intoning these words, though, Temüjin was
visualizing an immense, ferocious wolf and an elegant, lovely doe.
The wolf had an acute eye, one that could see even farther and more
accurately than Du'a Soqor, an eye that grasped everything within
its purview and would not let go, and that feared absolutely nothing.
The cold light in his eye held both the spirit of attack ready to confront anything and the powerful will to make anything he desired
his own. His physique was made entirely for attack. His sharp ears

could pick up sounds hundreds of miles away; all of the flesh and bones of his body were solely dedicated to the objective of slaughtering the enemy. When necessary, his tenacious limbs could dash through snowy wastelands, race through strong winds, climb over peaks, and leap through the air.

Attending this wolf was a doe of slender build covered in magnificent fur. Her chestnut coat was dotted with white specks, her mouth covered with white fur. Unlike the wolf, she possessed delicate eyes, but she moved them incessantly, giving her whole body a nervous edge, as she tried to protect the mate she loved from his enemies. The doe served the wolf with her great beauty, and served him as well by never relinquishing her vigilance for so much as an instant. To the least stirring of the leaves of a tree in the wind, she inclined her long face alertly. While she lacked virtually anything of an aggressive nature, her defensive posture was unsurpassed.

These two entirely different living things both provided enough beauty to enchant the young Temüjin's mind. And from these two marvelous creatures was born the first human ancestor: Batachiqan. Over the course of many years, the blood of the wolf and the doe had continued to flow in the bodies of many of his ancestors, and now it flowed in his own.

After he learned this story, no matter what tale Bültechü recounted—and Temüjin came to know them all himself—none captured his mind as fully as this one. Although he would hear Bültechü numerous times retell the story of the blood of the beautiful Alan Gho'a mixing with the light from heaven into the body of the Borjigin lineage, compared to the tale of the wolf and the doe that he had relayed with such pride, it struck Temüjin as dull and without any charm whatsoever. The fact that members of the Borjigin lineage were superior to other Mongol families by virtue of this heavenly light was, of course, not something that saddened Temüjin, but the tale of the blood of the wolf and doe, which was distributed equally among the entire Mongol population, was on a far grander scale in his mind. Supporting it was a stage with the far greater breadth of all Mongols upon it.

In the spring of the year that Temüjin turned eight, Ö'elün gave birth to one more child, this time a girl, who was given the name

Temülün. At the time of her birth, Temüjin was overcome with a deep emotion that included troubling doubts unlike anything he had experienced before about the blood of the wolf and doe flowing in Temülün's veins. Certainly that blood flowed in the bodies of his younger brothers, Qasar, Qachi'un, and Temüge—and, for that matter, in his half-brothers, Begter and Belgütei. He had not the least doubt that their veins carried it, but in the case of his younger sister Temülün he harbored a sensation he couldn't quite comprehend.

The bewilderment that had stricken him unexpectedly when she was born was the result of a different eye applied by the eight-year-old Temüjin to seeing a female, something common among most adults and children. A female probably bore the blood of the doe within her, but it was inconceivable to him that she also had the blood of the wolf. At one point, Temüjin questioned his mother, Ö'elün, about this, and she replied:

"What difference is there between males and females? All Mongols, be they men or women, carry on the blood of all their ancestors."

As far as Temüjin was concerned, his mother's answer was altogether insufficient. He found it impossible to think of females in the same way that he did males—if they were knocked down, they would immediately stagger and fall; if beaten, they would immediately collapse into tears. He found the idea of being together with them odious. Was it possible that the weak who did not go into battle inherited the blood of the wolf that had crossed the lake to the west at heaven's command?

Temüjin never played with girls, and with the exception of truly important matters never listened to them. This was less a belittling of the weak than it was antipathy or indignation taking root in his eight-year-old mind at the notion that the frail shared the same blood of the Mongol people.

From this time on Temüjin began to adopt a policy of always checking his surroundings with his own eyes. Although he was growing more rapidly than other youngsters, this taciturn, wild lad was maturing spiritually no less than they.

Temüjin tried to learn many things and in fact did learn a great deal. While there was no reason to expect any changes in the conversations between his father, Yisügei, and his mother, Ö'elün, as far as Temüjin was concerned, things were completely different. From their conversations, Temüjin acquired knowledge of the family line and history of their Borjigin lineage, the position occupied by the Borjigin line within the Mongol people as a whole, and—more widely still—what place the Mongols held among all the residents of the Mongolian plateau. From the conversations of men and women in the settlement and from the words and deeds of villagers at small meetings of the settlement and at larger meetings of the entire people, the youngster absorbed these many pieces of information as a sponge soaks up water. Temüjin's mind and body were always on the move from his youth through adulthood.

First of all, Temüjin knew that within the larger Mongolian group the Borjigin lineage to which he belonged was not likely to advance smoothly with the Tayichi'ud lineage from his father's generation forward, and that this was causing friction on many fronts. Originally, the Tayichi'uds belonged to the Borjigins, but they had become independent when Hambaghai became the second khan, established their own settlements, and took the ethnonym Tayichi'ud. Between the two, one might say, there was a main family–branch family relationship.

From the time that Yisügei became khan, though, the children of Hambaghai had gradually extended the influence of the Tayichi'uds and were gathering under their own umbrella many other Mongol lineages. At present, a good number of them would probably not follow orders issued by Yisügei. All of the internal Mongolian troubles were rooted in this.

In addition to the Tayichi'uds, there were any number of other lineages within the larger Mongolian grouping. Whether they were subservient to the Borjigins or to the Tayichi'uds, on the surface the entire Mongolian people were united with Yisügei as their khan. But in fact, they were divided into two camps.

Besides this internal situation, there were also incessant small disputes with other peoples that kept Yisügei busy on a daily basis. The most powerful among these other groups were the Tatars, a people with whom the Mongols had long been on bad terms. From ancient times, the biggest issue on the Mongolian plateau had been structuring a unified confederated body of peoples. For the nomadic groups living on the same Mongolian plateau, such a confederation was absolutely essential not only for living together in peace but also for dealing with the neighboring states of the Jin dynasty, the Xixia, and the Uyghurs. The Jin bordering them on the plateau across the Great Wall was most desirous that such a confederation not be created. Should the numerically small groups scattered across the plain come together to form one great force, this would be a wholly unwelcome event. Whenever it witnessed the circumstances necessary for the formation of a confederation on the plateau, the Jin state intrigued to nip it in the bid, causing rifts and rivalries among the various ethnic groups on the plain.

The first four khans of the Mongol people—Qabul, Hambaghai, Qutula, and now Yisügei—were all thoroughly determined to create such a confederation, but were always obstructed by the Tatars, who joined in with the plotting of the Jin. Qabul had been nearly poisoned to death by a Jin emissary; Hambaghai was taken by a Tatar escort to the Jin and there executed; and Qutula and most of his six brothers had lost their lives fighting against the Tatars. In other words, Temüjin's great-grandfather and his grandfather and great uncles had all been killed in combat against the Tatars.

In the warfare at the time of Temüjin's birth, Yisügei had been able to launch a major assault against the Tatars for the first time, and a state of relative tranquility had been preserved thereafter between the two peoples. The dispute between them, however, was certain to flare up again sometime as long as the Jin was working behind the scenes.

The young Temüjin knew that both the Tatars and the Jin state were enemies of the Mongol people. The name Tatar and the name of the great state of Jin on the far side of the Great Wall were both etched in his mind as ghastly, diabolical appellations.

On one occasion, while drinking wine in his yurt, Yisügei blurted out:

"I won't die, so help me, until we attack the Tayichi'uds and the Tatars."

At the time, Temüjin thought it suspicious that his father had not mentioned the third name of the Jin. When he said as much, Yisügei said, laughing:

"Launching an attack on the Jin is an enormous undertaking. Even if we were able to rally all the peoples living on the Mongolian plain right now, our numbers would not reach 200,000 troops. By contrast, the Jin has an army dozens of times as large, every soldier with a weapon so fine you can scarcely imagine it."

He then went on to discuss how, after concluding the fighting with their enemies, they would face the Jin on the southern side of the Great Wall and the Song state beyond the Jin, farther south. Their people formed cities on sites surrounded by immense walls. They constructed houses out of earth and wood from which they never moved. Each person had a specialized job: merchants built shops and sold their wares; farmers plowed the earth and produced agricultural crops; bureaucrats traveled between offices and handled all manner of affairs; soldiers spent their time training for battle with weaponry. Within these city walls were large temples and government offices built of stone and rising into the sky.

Temüjin wondered if such lands, which were like figments of his imagination, really existed. He wanted to know more and more, and he asked his father all sorts of specific questions, but Yisügei had not seen any of this with his own eyes and was thus unable to speak in any more detail about it.

At some point later, Temüjin asked Bültechü about the states of Jin and Song. He assumed that Bültechü, who knew everything, would be able to fill him in. The old man with the fine memory prefaced his response with:

"They're despicable places!"

Then, not touching on what Temüjin really wished to know, he told the lad as proof of the Jin's foulness the story of Hambaghai Khan, who had been put to death by its men.

"Hambaghai Khan was taken captive by the Tatars and escorted to the king of the Jin state. There he was somehow nailed to a wooden donkey and then, while still alive, had his skin peeled off and his body chopped up into small pieces. Hambaghai Khan was a stouthearted man, and at the time of his death the servant who had accompanied him was sent home to report on what had transpired: 'You must take revenge for me on this enemy, even if you wear down all ten of your fingernails and then lose all ten fingers.' The servant ran off, returned home, and conveyed everything. Everyone cried. Your father cried. I cried."

This servant had by now passed away, but a few years earlier, while in his mother's lap, Temüjin had seen the diminutive elderly man. To the extent that he was somewhat familiar with this man, the tragedy of Hambaghai Khan now struck the young boy with its verisimilitude and profound, unalleviated gloom. That his father, Yisügei, had given up seeking revenge upon the Jin state, a great land beyond his reach, was vexing to Temüjin. For him, this Jin state was at once an immense, unknown place about which he often dreamed and that he wanted to see just once and an implacable enemy that had earlier murdered their khan. It was a state that, even were he to lose ten fingers and ten fingernails, had to be fought by way of retaliation.

In the summer of the year Temüjin turned nine, his father, Yisügei, took him on a trip, at the request of his wife Ö'elün, to her own hometown, an Olqunu'ud settlement, to find the girl who would be Temüjin's future bride. This was Temüjin's first journey into scenery altogether different from what he had experienced in his first nine years. To be sure, the Mongols moved their dwellings to various sites with the seasons, but they were always in the foothills of Mount Burqan along the shores of the Onon and Kherlen rivers, within a limited radius determined by natural conditions. All that Temüjin knew until then were the dense forests comprised of the same kind of trees and grasslands all the same color. On this trip, however, there unfolded before his eyes thoroughly dissimilar topography and surroundings. A row of a dozen or more men mounted their horses, and they led as many camels laden with food supplies. The row of men followed the Kherlen downstream into a valley luxuriantly overgrown with trees, midway through left the river and crossed the grasslands, climbed up hills with numerous rocky crags, and advanced through gravel and desert sands. Lakes were scattered here and there, and Temüjin found every day's itinerary pleasing. Because it wasn't a rushed trip, the men fished and hunted birds and rabbits en route.

Before they reached the village from which Ö'elün had come, an unexpected incident disrupted their journey. While they were passing between the two mountains of Chiqurqu and Chegcher, they met a group traveling with Dei Sechen, leader of the Unggirad lineage. It was the first face-to-face meeting of the leaders of these two families, but they were immediately able to speak frankly with each other. When Dei Sechen learned of the goal of Yisügei's group, he encouraged them to change their plan of travel to the Olqunu'ud village and instead come to a settlement of his own Unggirad lineage.

"I have taken a liking to your son Temüjin," said Dei Sechen quietly as he bent his solid torso back a bit. "Happily there is a girl named Börte, and they will surely be a well-matched couple in future." Yisügei was favorably impressed by this easygoing leader of another family, and he had oftentimes heard that the Unggirads were quite wealthy. He quickly accepted the invitation. It was never a losing transaction for the Mongols to establish a marriage relationship with the Unggirads.

When their conversation came to an end, the two groups joined together and, changing direction slightly, headed toward the grasslands in the southern foothills of the Xing'an range. Among the various peoples on the Mongolian plateau, the Unggirads held terrain closest to the Great Wall, which put them closest to Jin culture just on the other side, so they enjoyed the highest cultural life of the residents of the plateau.

The Unggirad pastureland was far better than that of the Mongols. The gently sloping grasslands continued as far as the eye could see, and a large number of sheep and horses had been put to pasture there. Dei Sechen's yurt was incomparably larger and more lavish than Yisügei's. All of his personal effects too were polished and fine looking. His storehouse was full of animal hides and varieties of pelts. As for items he had acquired, it seemed, in exchange for these hides and pelts, both Temüjin and his father were overwhelmed. He had lacquered furniture, finely crafted weapons and armor, and magnificent ornaments—also ivory and jade. Temüjin was forced to confront the fact that, by comparison, their own Mongol yurts were humble and shabby.

Börte was ten years old, a year older than Temüjin. Yisügei liked her the moment he set eyes on her, and Temüjin found her lovely, a girl with a large build who had grown up quickly. There was a luster to her white skin and light brown hair. Ever since he was a little boy, Temüjin had heard of the people known as "white Tatars," as opposed to the "black Tatars," but not until this trip to the Unggirads did he discover it was not simply a rumor.

After entertaining Yisügei's party for three days, Dei Sechen hoped that Temüjin alone would remain behind for a time so that he might become closer to the Unggirad people. In this instance as well, Yisügei readily consented to Dei Sechen's proposal. Although Temüjin was heavyhearted about living with an alien group of people, when he realized how much knowledge he could acquire by doing so, he obediently followed his father's wishes and remained in Dei Sechen's yurt. Eventually Yisügei's group headed back toward the foothills of Mount Burqan, while Temüjin from that day began an entirely new life with a new language and new customs.

From the autumn of his ninth year until the spring of his thirteenth, Temüjin lived under Dei Sechen's roof. He showed no interest at all in Börte, the young girl destined to be his future wife, but he did demonstrate an extraordinary interest, for one so young, in everything to do with quotidian Unggirad life. The Unggirads had a small number of young men specially trained to defend against raids by other peoples. They could manage a horse and manipulate a bow with extraordinary dexterity. Almost every day they trained at deployment over the grasslands and practiced drawing their small bows while on horseback so as to protect their flocks of domesticated animals from marauders. At Dei Sechen's request, Temüjin joined one of these armed bands.

The most important thing Temüjin acquired during this period of time spent with the Unggirads was knowledge of the great state of Jin. At times, merchants from Jin who had crossed the Great Wall came by camel to their settlement. He learned all manner of things about Jin that he never could have attained had he remained along the upper reaches of the Onon River. What struck Temüjin as most awe-inspiring was that the Jin state and the Song state beyond it were each unified under a single ruler whose soldiers moved in concert with his orders.

In the spring of Temüjin's thirteenth year, a young man some thirty years of age by the name of Münglig, a blood relative of Yisügei's from their Borjigin settlement, came as the latter's express messenger to meet Temüjin at the Unggirad village. It was not clear what Münglig actually said, but he noted that Yisügei had not seen Temüjin for quite some time. Although Dei Sechen wasn't entirely satisfied with such an abrupt suggestion that Temüjin depart, he permitted the boy to return home on the condition that he would soon retrace his steps back to the Unggirad village.

Temüjin and Münglig rode their horses across the plain day and night. En route he learned from Münglig of the death of his father, Yisügei. As was the custom of a traveler on the road, Yisügei had attended a banquet of one Tatar lineage and fallen victim to a plot: his cup was filled with poison. He rode his horse for three days in great pain, making his way back to his own yurt, but at last did not survive. Yisügei had spent his entire life fighting his archenemies, the Tatars, and had launched a massive assault on them from which his people had gained twelve or thirteen years of peace, but his ultimate fate was to fall prey to their revenge.

When Temüjin learned of this from Münglig, he felt less a sadness at the death of his father than a flaming indignation. When Yisügei had fought against the Tatars thirteen years earlier and won a great victory, he ought not to have let them remain as they were. He should have rooted out what would become the fundamental cause of this latest incident. Every male should have been put to death, and every female child should have been assimilated into his father's settlements as lowly servants. As a result of his failure to take these measures, naturally enough, his father had learned a divine lesson.

The thirteen-year-old Temüjin returned to the Borjigin base, a settlement that compared far less favorably with that of the Unggirads and that appeared to be sunk into even deeper wretchedness because of mourning for Yisügei. Temüjin and Münglig walked their horses slowly among several hundred yurts. It was still, with no sign of life in any of them. The lad finally dismounted in front of his own dwelling and entered. Suddenly, close to the entrance, he saw his two younger half-brothers, Belgütei and Begter, grown so big he would not have recognized them, standing before him. How was it possible for not a single shaft of light to enter through a hole in the roof and for the interior to be floating in such a dark, melancholy atmosphere? Temüjin stood by the entrance momentarily until his eyes adjusted to the darkness inside. Gradually the image of his mother, Ö'elün, seated before him and surrounded by his four siblings, came more clearly into view.

"Your father, Yisügei, has died. From now on, you will have to stay here as the family pillar." Temüjin heard these first words from Ö'elün and remained silent. Then, as if just becoming aware of something, she added:

"Call Münglig in." Ö'elün seemed to be planning to thank Münglig for his trouble, but Belgütei, standing at the entrance, said:

"Münglig's already mounted his horse and left."

These words appeared to surprise Ö'elün for a moment, but checking to see if Belgütei's words were accurate, she stood up and walked out of the yurt. Eventually she returned, gathered her seven children together, and said to them:

"From this day forward, only those living here are our allies. We must go on living by putting our efforts together."

It had been several days since Yisügei's funeral ceremony, and Ö'elün had yet to shed a single tear. According to Temüjin's eleven-year-old brother, Qasar, the source of their mother's tears had already withered away.

In a short period of time, Temüjin learned much startling information from his mother and brothers. First, as expected, with Yisügei's death, effective power moved into the hands of the Tayichi'uds, which caused rumblings among the Borjigins and provided the opportunity for almost everyone to move over to the Tayichi'ud side. Second, accordingly, Yisügei's successor as khan was clearly to be selected from the Tayichi'uds. Third, out of their pent-up jealousy, Yisügei's various concubines had ostracized his primary wife Ö'elün and unilaterally carried out the ceremonies honoring the spirit of Yisügei, an action tantamount to societal expulsion. Fourth, even those close to the Borjigin lineage were avoiding Ö'elün more with each passing day, and in the past two or three days they had disappeared altogether. Finally, although the people of the settlement had been accustomed to convening almost daily meetings, all of a sudden no one called on the now powerless Ö'elün or her family to participate.

Temüjin listened to all of this in silence. He now understood why, when he had entered the village a while earlier, it was so quiet that it seemed as if no one was there. It was the time when they were meeting and handling various matters. Temüjin now realized why his family was in such a situation.

There was no one among the Borjigins with the influence or clout to lead the entire lineage after Yisügei's death. That such a person did not exist was due to Yisügei's not having prepared such a man for the position. This practice was not limited to the Borjigins; it held in the Tayichi'ud and other lineages as well. The people of a settlement came together around a single powerful person and were thus unified, but when the man died, they had to seek out another powerful man to rally around so as to protect all of their interests. This pattern had repeated itself numerous times in the history of the Mongol people. It was the very nature of a group that lacked organization.

Furthermore, the fact that the heirs of such a power holder should fall into miserable circumstances after his passing was simply the nature of things. Resentment of pressures brought to bear by such a powerful person necessitated the venting of heretofore smothered indignation against his heirs. "Do not suck out only the sweet juice"—this was an expression frequently used among the Mongolian peoples in many different circumstances, which may be understood as perfectly natural. To their way of thinking, it was the will of heaven that forced all men to be treated equally.

Temüjin reflected on the situation of Dei Sechen of the Unggirad people, with whom he had spent three and a half years. Although they too lacked organization as a group, accession to the position of leader was restricted to people in the family of Dei Sechen, which retained its effective power in the form of wealth. Dei Sechen had become wealthy from his various relatives, and he had not wished to separate from his future son-in-law Temüjin because he had no male heir.

Temüjin glanced around the inside of the yurt in which his father had so long lived as chief of the Borjigins. It was somewhat wider and taller than those of other settlements, but it differed in no significant way in its interior cramped feeling. Even if particularly expensive items were all crammed together, it didn't mean that they were plentiful. Objects plundered from other peoples were quickly distributed equally, and the chief received no special portion. In short, they had no classes, and thus they had no particularly wealthy or impoverished among them—everyone was equally poor.

In a cold tone of voice containing a measure of anger, Temüjin said to Ö'elün:

"Everything as expected, following the normal path." These were not the words of a youngster. It was the voice of a young man bearing the responsibility of a family head after the death of his father. Temüjin continued:

"The Tayichi'ud gang is probably not going to leave us alone. Like water finding its own level, our family's misery will probably only become more wretched before it is resolved."

When his mother heard Temüjin's words, her tears began to gush forth once again from the source Qasar had just said had already dried up, and she continued sobbing until finally her wellspring had truly run dry. After she had been crying a long time, Begter and Belgütei took their bows and went out to hunt, Qachi'un and Temüge went off to play, and at some point five-year-old Temülün fell asleep.

Temüjin saw to his side only his brother Qasar standing and, like him, quietly gazing at their mother. Then, as if issuing a manifesto, he said to Qasar:

"From this day forward, you're going to be my trusted retainer. Never violate any order I give you! In return, I will recognize that within this family you are second only to me in power and authority. If we quarrel with Begter and Belgütei, we need to cooperate to oppose them. And if I fall, you shall take over leadership of this family in my stead."

When she heard Temüjin, Ö'elün stopped weeping and raised her head slightly, but then soon reverted to her earlier posture. Temüjin sought a definitive response from Qasar. His normally composed face dizzier with agitation than that of his more mild-mannered brother, Qasar replied:

"So be it! I shall comply with your decision."

Temüjin also felt stirred up. For him this vow was extremely solemn, exceeding in its gravity any moment since his birth. To help his weak mother and support the family, Temüjin established an order in his isolated and unaided family, laid out a system, and established strata. His determination was rooted in his sense of responsibility that he had to continue supporting them, but one thing further was his new vigilance toward his two half-brothers, Begter and Belgütei, who over the three and a half years of his absence had grown big and strong, as if to defy him. When he entered the yurt after this period of absence, Temüjin had seen his two younger brothers face to face, but the impression he had received was certainly not of loving blood relatives. He sensed in them less brethren than enemies.

As Temüjin predicted, yet worse circumstances soon struck them. One morning about two months later, there was some sort of uproar outside the door to his yurt, and Temüjin was aroused from sleep to step outside. In the dim light of early dawn, he saw several hundred men and women hard at work folding up their yurts and packing away their household effects on horses and camels. The whole settlement was on the verge of moving. At some point Te-

müjin realized that Ö'elün was standing at his side. She was dumb-
struck, incapable of speech.

Temüjin left his mother, walked over to the neighboring yurt,
and asked where they were heading. The man he addressed replied:
"We're moving to new pastureland on orders from the Tayichi'ud
chief."

Although there was nothing the least bit odd about the settlement moving, as summer was drawing near, that they were following orders from the Tayichi'ud chief and that this information had
not been conveyed to Temüjin's yurt were serious issues. Temüjin
soon realized that he and his family were being ostracized and abandoned. With no khan yet selected, it would have been normal to
consult Temüjin, as Yisügei's eldest son, on all matters concerning
the movement of the settlement. Not only was there no word of
parting communicated, but his family was on the verge of being deserted here and now.

Although Temüjin virulently attacked this behavior verbally, everyone held him in disdain and ignored what he had to say. When he
began to walk back in the direction of his own yurt, his body trembling in anger, he saw the figure of his mother, Ö'elün, sitting astride
a white horse, holding a banner adorned with the hair from the tail
of a white horse. She was raising a distinctive banner, symbol of the
khan's power, and attempting to prevent the villagers from unilaterally moving to new pastureland. Temüjin knew full well that his
mother's action would have no effect. He neither backed her up nor
moved to stop her.

When he returned to his yurt, he stood in front of it for some
time, observing the confusion of activity among the villagers. His
mother stopped her horse at the southwestern corner of the settlement's center. From time to time, the horsehairs on the banner she
was holding aloft fluttered in the high breeze as if they had been
tossed up into the air. At a distance the banner appeared small.

Eventually small groups of camels and horses placed here and
there in the center of the settlement all began moving without control. There was one group comprised of the occupants of two or
three yurts. They had abandoned the land they had become famil-

iar with over the past half year and disappeared beyond an incline sloping abruptly from where Ö'elün was holding her banner. The banner in her hands was effectively marking the exit for groups setting out from the center of the settlement. The people and animals that had filled this area gradually decreased in number until all that remained was the yurt of Ö'elün and her children.

When the last of the groups vanished beyond the slope in the land, Temüjin saw Ö'elün approaching from the center that had suddenly been completely emptied. Still holding the banner aloft and riding her horse, Ö'elün looked ashen. From such extreme tension, she had a fervent expression on her face, such a look of courage and beauty as he had never before seen in her.

"Münglig has gone too, as have Jamugha and Sorqan Shira," she said as she dismounted, enumerating one by one each of the men who had been on intimate terms with Yisügei. Among the names was that of Bültechü Ba'atur, the elderly man with the great memory.

That evening the oldest member of the Borjigin lineage, Charaqa (father of Münglig), rode over to them on horseback. He was injured, tumbled from his horse, and immediately fell unconscious. His wound was severe, a spear having been thrust into his back. Although the circumstances were unknown, Ö'elün and her children pulled Charaqa into their tent and looked after him.

After two or three days, Charaqa with great difficulty was finally able to say something. He described how he alone had to the bitter end raised objections to the abandonment of Ö'elün and her children; even after the villagers had begun departing, he had gone around trying to persuade prominent figures among the Tayichi'uds not to do this. At that time, one of the Tayichi'ud leaders, by the name of Tödö'en Girte, said:

"The deep water has run dry. The bright stone has crumbled. Yisügei is dead. How dare you chatter like this!?" No sooner had he spoken than he plunged the spear in his hand into Charaqa's back.

Old Man Charaqa lived for three more days, drank only water, then died. The tears he had been unable to shed at the time of his father's death, Temüjin now cried upon the death of this lone brave man among the Borjigins. Ö'elün worried while Temüjin wailed. He deeply regretted the fact that he had no means of repaying the fidelity that Charaqa had shown his family whose fortunes were now in such decline.

Thereafter, life for Ö'elün and her children deteriorated to an appalling state. She and her seven children, with Temüjin the leader, had but one tent and a small number of sheep and horses. Also, because the tent stood by itself all alone, they had no one to trade with for food and clothing.

Having abandoned her and her family, the Borjigins had united with the Tayichi'ud lineage and built a new settlement on the grassy plain along the lower reaches of the Onon River, a few days' journey away. The ruler of the Tayichi'uds, Targhutai, had also acceded to the position of khan of the Mongolian people, but nothing of this had reached Ö'elün or her children.

To stave off starvation, Temüjin did not allow anyone to play. Almost every day, Ö'elün took baby Temülün with her farther and farther up the Onon River to pick wild herbs and pushed deep into the mountains to gather wild pears. In the small field in front of their tent, she grew leeks and shallots. Each day the six sons divided up the work and went out into the pastures to drive the sheep. If they had a moment's break, they would fish or hunt.

During this period, Temüjin worried most about the fact that his half-brothers, Belgütei and Begter, were always going off together and disobeying his orders. They resembled each other like two peas in a pod, with robust builds, fierce strength, and coarse temperaments.

In the spring more than a year after Yisügei's death, Temüjin repeatedly clashed with his two younger brothers. His full brother Qasar had sworn an oath of allegiance with him and remained obedient, but he lacked power and was meek in temperament. Thus, when it came to confronting his two half-brothers, Temüjin really had no subordinates he could rely on. His other two brothers, Qachi'un and Temüge, were only ten and eight years of age, respectively, not yet old enough to be depended upon as allies. Temüjin had been deprived of much booty by his two younger half-brothers. When they came and confronted him directly with demands that he knew were unjustified, he had no choice but to acquiesce.

On one occasion, Temüjin had gone fishing with Qasar, and Qasar caught a fish called a *soghosun* or dace, which had a strange, shiny light on its body. Upon seeing it, Belgütei and Begter quickly contrived to seize it from Qasar. A ferocious struggle broke out between Qasar, who did not want to relinquish the fish, with Temüjin supporting him, and the two half-brothers. In the end, the shiny dace fell into the hands of Belgütei and Begter.

Temüjin complained of this incident to his mother. Ö'elün grimaced sadly and said:

"Why are you behaving like this? You're fighting with your brothers. Why aren't you seeking revenge against the Tayichi'uds? We have no friends other than our shadows now and no whip other than a horse's tail."

Their mother's words pierced Temüjin to the heart, but they also revived his antipathy toward the Tayichi'uds and strengthened his resolve never to leave Begter and Belgütei to their own devices, as he had until that point.

The following morning, Temüjin called to Begter outside his tent and rebuked him for his recent actions, bidding him to reform his ways. Before he knew what had happened, though, an argument broke out between them.

"You are not the son of Mother Ö'elün," said Temüjin. "What gives you the right to make the gentle Ö'elün even sadder?"

"It's you who aren't the son of Father Yisügei," replied Begter. "Belgütei, Qasar, Qachi'un, Temüge, Temülün, and I are all his children, but only you are different. I know it! Everyone in the settlement knew it. You're the only one who doesn't. Merkid blood flows in your veins. You just used Ö'elün's body to be born into this family—that's all."

"What are you talking about?"

"You may think it's a rumor and no more, but go ask Mother. Your mother, the woman who gave birth to you, she knows all this better than anyone. If you can't stomach asking her yourself, then ask yourself the question. Father Yisügei didn't love you at all. Did it ever occur to you to wonder why?"

Temüjin understood Begter's words the moment he heard them, for he had held so very much pent up inside him for a long time. It was like a mighty rainstorm pounding around his ears.

"Why are you speaking such nonsense?" said Temüjin, rejecting Begter's every word. His voice had lost its resounding echo necessary to coerce an interlocutor. He didn't believe Begter's words, but he was indeed sharply hurt by them. They were the final blow to Temüjin.

"From this day forward, I obey nothing you may command me to do. I do not recognize you as my elder brother. I bear the blood of Yisügei and shall be giving the orders in this tent."

He spit out the words, turned away from Temüjin, and walked off. For a short while, Temüjin watched Begter's back after his grand declaration of resistance and his departure. All of a sudden, the feeling exploded in Temüjin's mind that he could not let his younger half-brother go on living. One who would disturb the peace under their roof and defy him personally had to be eliminated, no matter who he was.

Temüjin called on Qasar and ordered him to check where Begter had gone and inform him. When Qasar returned shortly thereafter, he reported that Begter was guarding nine dappled-gray horses on a mountain not far away.

Seizing his bow, Temüjin ordered Qasar to do the same, and the two of them left the tent together. When they reached the foothill of the mountain, Temüjin confided in Qasar his determination to slay Begter. Qasar's countenance momentarily changed color, his eyes opening wide in astonishment, but when he learned that this was to be Temüjin's command, he swore to cooperate.

Attacking Begter from two sides, the brothers climbed opposite slopes of the mountain. They simultaneously fixed arrows in their bows and aimed at Begter, who was then standing on the peak. When Begter noticed them and figured out what they were trying to do, he dropped to the ground abruptly and declared in desperation:

"So, you intend to kill me. Then shoot away, as I have no recourse! Qasar, you shoot your arrow first. I'll probably die. I don't want to die from the arrow of a Merkid."

Begter may have finished speaking or he may not have, as both Temüjin and Qasar let arrows fly. Hit in the chest and in the back, Begter staggered weakly and stopped. One after the next, they shot arrows at him. All of Qasar's hit his abdomen in front; all of Temüjin's struck him in the rear. Looking like a hedgehog, Begter dropped dead.

When they arrived back at their yurt, Ö'elün immediately asked them in a stern tone of voice unlike any she ordinarily used:

"What have you just come from doing? What's that look on your faces?"

Temüjin said that Begter was on the small mountain, but was not likely to be coming back. Ö'elün's face was transformed in the twinkling of an eye; she let out a groan and scowled at Temüjin.

"You've killed one of a small number of your allies—like a dog chewing its afterbirth, or a panther rushing into a cliff, or a lion unable to stifle its rage, or a serpent swallowing animals alive, or a large falcon dashing at its own shadow, or a *churaqa* fish swallowing silently, or a camel biting at the heel of its colt."

At the point, Ö'elün ceased speaking, or, to be more precise, her agitation took the words away from her. Eventually, though, she continued in an even more impassioned tone:

"You have killed. You have killed an irreplaceable ally—like a wolf injuring its head and mouth, or a mandarin duck eating its young because it cannot keep up with them, or a jackal attacking if one moves his sleeping spot, or a tiger not hesitating to capture its quarry, or a wolverine rushing off recklessly."

Ö'elün ceased speaking at this point and collapsed onto the ground. Temüjin did not know that a person could become so profoundly incensed. Given the virulence of her manner of speech, she clearly had collapsed in anger, like a rainstorm raging so fiercely one does not even realize when it has stopped.

Until that moment, Temüjin was not the least inclined to allow Begter's accomplice, Belgütei, to go on living, but his mother's

anger made him reverse his murderous designs. He whispered to
Qasar:

"We're going to let Belgütei live."

Having now lost his partner, Belgütei was someone who might,
as their mother had said, be an important ally. Qasar was dumb-
founded at their mother's expression of fury, but when he caught on
to Temüjin's words, this loyal family supporter offered:

"Belgütei does have some good attributes. When he takes a vow,
he never breaks it."

At their mother's demand, Temüjin and Qasar buried Begter's
corpse on the small mountainside.

Ö'elün visited the site almost every day for some three months.
For his part, Temüjin did not believe he had erred in his actions.
Since Begter's disappearance from the scene, life in their yurt had
become immeasurably more peaceful. Not a single verbal argument
had broken out among the brothers. In his accomplice's absence,
Belgütei had become a changed, mild-mannered young man. As
Qasar said, once he made a promise, no matter what transpired, he
would always abide by it.

After Begter's death, Temüjin remembered the final words out
of his mouth even with the passage of time. They seemed to follow
him everywhere, as if replicating the tenacity of Begter's rancor itself: "Qasar, you shoot your arrow first. . . . I don't want to die from
the arrow of a Merkid."

Countless times these words came back into Temüjin's mind. In
the final moment when Begter realized that he could not escape, he
thought to say something spiteful, but it was nonetheless a feeling
that had gotten under Begter's skin.

In addition, Temüjin always remembered the words that Begter
had used to assail him that same morning. Was he was not the son
of Yisügei but of a Merkid man? What would it mean if his mother
was Ö'elün, but his father was not actually Yisügei? And what did
Begter mean by saying that Yisügei never loved him?

Amid the many words that Begter had hurled at him, those that
left the deepest scars in Temüjin's mind were his final words, that
Yisügei did not love him.

From time to time, when he wasn't entirely sure, Temüjin would find himself recalling in precise detail every single word and deed that his late father had said or done to him. Even in Yisügei's few words and trivial actions—such as how he moved his eyes—Temüjin tried to detect some kind of meaning. This sort of work inspired spiritual isolation and intense physical fatigue. An exhausted Temüjin thought that possibly there had been something different in the way Yisügei behaved toward him as opposed to his other children. Once he began thinking along these lines, Yisügei seemed altogether a different man from the one Temüjin had known when he was alive, and cast an immense eerie shadow.

The more he brooded over this, the more his having been entrusted from age nine to the Unggirads took on a completely different meaning. Perhaps it had been his father's intention to get rid of him to this alien lineage settlement. He had returned home only because of his father's death, but had his father been alive, would he have had to remain abandoned forever in that village near the Xing'an Mountains?

From around the time he turned fifteen, Temüjin became not only reticent but also more sullenly taciturn, rarely speaking to anyone. He and his younger brothers fortified their solid physiques tirelessly cultivating the leeks and shallots their mother planted, but the young leader always seemed to find himself alone, sitting inside their tent.

Unfortunately, Temüjin was not near anyone who could have alleviated his doubts. Were he to ask his mother, the whole problem might have been cleared up immediately, but he was not willing to ask Ö'elün about the secret of his birth. He thought he might again touch the frenzied rage that she had shown when they had killed Begter. It appeared as though the words he had uttered to her contained something that goaded her heart and might again put her in that maddened state.

As far as Temüjin was concerned, there was nothing particularly cruel in the hypothesis that Merkid, not Mongol, blood was coursing through his body. He simply had to be Yisügei's son. If he were not, then he would have no connection with Grandfather

Bartan Ba'atur or Great-grandfather Qabul, or earlier with Tumbinai Sechen (Tumbinai "the wise"), or with Bai Shingqor Doqshin
before him, or much earlier with the brave Qabichi, or with Bodonchar Mungqaq (son of the fair Alan and light from a corner of heav-
en), or further back still to Du'a Soqor (the man with one eye) or
Toroqoljin Bayan, or back many generations to Yeke Nidün, Sali
Qacha'u, or all the way to the first Mongol Batachiqan—and, pursuing this chain all the way back, to the latter's father, the blue wolf
that crossed the large lake to the west, and his mother, the pale doe.
No trace of such a doubt could remain.

When Temüjin contemplated the possibility that he bore no relationship to the wolf or doe of highest antiquity, he was overcome
by a feeling of utter hopelessness, as if all had turned black before
his eyes. Ever since he could remember from his earliest youth, he
had lived within the transmission of the Mongol origins. Having his
body now deprived of Mongol blood meant denying this entire past
as well as any future. Temüjin now no longer knew what he had been
living for, nor for that matter what he would live for in the future.
Was there neither a drop of the wolf's nor a drop of the doe's blood
in his own? Was he, then, unrelated to those two beautiful creatures
that had spawned so many brave men, capable archers, and sagely
figures? Qasar, Qachi'un, Temüge, and the weak female Temülün,
as well as his half-brother, Belgütei, all carried Mongol blood—did
he alone not share in this heritage? At his wits' end, worried sick
day in and day out, Temüjin would always forcibly thrust aside his
suspicions as empty speculation unworthy of consideration. For,
right or wrong, he had to be a member of the Mongolian people.

In the summer of his fifteenth year, Temüjin had an unusual
experience. At this time, his yurt was set up on grassland on the
right shore (as one went downriver) along the middle reaches of the
Onon River. One day he was returning home from the pastureland
when he caught sight of a destitute man walking at the far end of the
plateau. Since he had been separated from his own settlement, Temüjin would see another person at most two or three times a year.
Moved by an urge for companionship, Temüjin cautiously rode his
horse over in the man's direction. Unexpectedly, the man was a

Borjigin known to Temüjin. In his youth, Temüjin remembered, he had played with the man's children in their yurt. "Hey, you're Yisügei's son," he said with emphasis. "Absolutely, you're Temüjin." In a short period of time, fifteen-year-old Temüjin had grown into a fine young man. As far as he was concerned, this man was one of the lineage who in anger had abandoned his mother and siblings, but Temüjin also felt in this shabbily dressed, haggard little man looking up at him a yearning to meet up with members of his lineage, and thus he bore him no ill will.

"How are you supporting yourselves?" asked the man. Not only was it incomprehensible that they could survive alone in their yurt, completely isolated from the settlement, but also it was beyond his comprehension that Temüjin could grow into such a stalwart youth. Temüjin learned from this fellow that the members of the Borjigin lineage who remained under Targhutai Khan of the Tayichi'uds had not fared well at all.

When the man finished speaking and was about to depart, Temüjin, from an emotion even he could not suppress, called out to him unthinking:

"Wait!" Temüjin thought that perhaps the man could help unravel the secret of his own roots by which he had long been haunted.

"I am Yisügei's son? Go on, say it," called Temüjin to the man, who was looking back over his shoulder. For a moment the man was confused by this extraordinary question, but after a while he answered nebulously:

"Well, certainly."

There was a stern look on Temüjin's face when he finally spoke once more:

"Not everyone knows this. Only Mother Ö'elün does. But what can I do? My mother was abducted twice by a Tatar. My younger brothers are Yisügei's sons, but I don't know whose son I am, because Borjigin and Tayichi'ud women were all taken by force once or twice." Temüjin was speaking in utmost seriousness.

"Uhuh, I see. Well, your mother did come to us when Yisügei snatched her from a Merkid, so if your father's not Yisügei, you'd be a Merkid, right? So, be the person you want to be. Anyway, you've

got to wait until you're fifty to know for sure. Truth be told, everyone learns who their parents are when they turn fifty. Merkid people
age fast and they're all thieves. Kereyids have receding hairlines and
are all miserly."

"Are they Mongols?" said the youngster with an expression of
incomprehension.

"Mongols become wolves," said the old man.

Temüjin didn't know precisely what it meant to become a wolf,
but didn't question him further. Becoming a wolf—as opposed to
ageing fast and stealing or have a receding hairline and being stin-
gy—struck him as something qualitatively different. There was in
the expression "to become a wolf" something that registered with
Temüjin—vague, to be sure, but nonetheless something that had
been with him from early on—and it was connected, it seemed, with
the secret of Mongolian blood. In this sense, the answers offered up
by this ragged old Borjigin man seemed accurate. Any other way of
putting it could certainly not explain the issue of blood.

Although Temüjin had been unable to unearth any of the essential details of his birth, he was resigned to it and let the man go. Now
all that he could think about was becoming a wolf at age fifty.

As he reflected on it, he thought that it was better to have met this
Borjigin man than not. On his way home after leaving the man, Temüjin vowed that he would never ask his mother about the identity
of his father. To shoot the arrow of such a question at Ö'elün would
not only embarrass her but also sadden her—it offered not a single
positive result. If his mother were to tell him that his father was
a Merkid, what could that possibly mean for him? Everything that
now supported him would be completely rent asunder. By contrast,
if he were to learn that his blood was indeed that of a Mongol, it
would be merely a consolation. Ö'elün surely knew what was proper to say and what was not. Most important, as the shabby old man
had said, was that he, Temüjin, believed that Yisügei was his father
and that accordingly he had inherited Mongolian blood.

When Temüjin reached home late that night, he reported having
met an old man of their lineage that day. He told his mother and

siblings that the Borjigin people were not, in this man's assessment, doing at all well.

"Just a little more patience," said Ö'elün. "When you all become full-fledged adults, the Borjigins will come scrambling to our side."

Although he said nothing, Temüjin had no interest whatsoever in waiting until he reached his majority to launch an attack on their enemies, the Tayichi'uds, and regain the Borjigin settlement and bring it back together as before. His was not an easygoing manner. Temüjin could afford to lose no time in becoming a wolf—not only for the Borjigin lineage and for Ö'elün and his siblings, but also for himself. No becoming a thief or a miser! No hair turning light brown or going bald! He could never resemble another line's appearance in any way. And Temüjin had to become a wolf. That would definitely prove that he was the son of Yisügei and that Mongolian blood coursed through his veins.

2

The Merkid
Massacre

AFTER THE MISFORTUNE OF BEING abandoned by all of their
other kin, Ö'elün and her children lived for two years in their small
yurt in the northern foothills of Mount Burqan. Temüjin was now
sixteen. Physically, he was considerably stronger than his father
Yisügei had ever been, even in his most formidable years, with a far
more robust build. Insofar as there was nothing pressing to attend
to, he remained taciturn to the point of only rarely speaking, but the
entire family had taken shape around him and in this way lived har-
moniously. In any business matter or family affair, Temüjin had ab-
solute authority and gave all orders. If there was a matter not to be
decided solely by himself, he would consult his fourteen-year-old
brother, Qasar, as Temüjin had decided that Qasar was his second
in command within the family.

Qasar still had the dependable nature he had borne since his earliest years. Thoroughly cautious about everything, he continued to
work as Temüjin's trusted advisor. In those matters in which Temüjin sought his view and he himself did not have a fixed opinion,
he would not give Temüjin an immediate response, but went and
consulted with his half-brother, Belgütei, who was roughly the
same age, and the two of them hammered out a position that they
brought to their older brother. Belgütei had an extraordinary physique surpassing even that of Temüjin, though he possessed a number of rougher aspects as well. He was not particularly scrupulous
about little matters and somehow had developed a certain gentle-

ness about him. Therefore, more than Temüjin himself, he was beloved by twelve-year-old Qachi'un, ten-year-old Temüge, and their
youngest sibling, eight-year-old sister Temülün. Ö'elün and her
children may have been a poor and isolated family, but the seven of
them—with Temüjin at the core—managed to live in peace.

Mother Ö'elün's position within the family was special. Temüjin
never consulted her on anything but used his own judgment for all
decisions. On occasion, she might put in a word or offer her own
opinion. In such instances, Temüjin listened attentively to what his
mother had to say, but he never allowed his own view of things to
be influenced by it. Opinions were for gleaning information only.
To be sure, Temüjin never slighted or ignored his mother. She was
his greatest concern. He always saw to it that she received the best
pieces of meat, and when unusual items such as bedding or clothing came into his possession, he made sure to give them first to her.
When it came to the business of running the household, though, he
allowed her no voice at all. Ö'elün's only options then were to be
an advisor or a critic. Thus, no matter what she might have wished
to do, without the approval of Temüjin, she could not so much as
move some bedding around.

This method of operations adopted by Temüjin was highly pru-
dent. If Mother Ö'elün had meddled in every matter and tried to
alter things even a little, the family would never have functioned
well. Even though Belgütei was a half-brother and Ö'elün loved
him just as much as she did her other children, a distinctive relationship between the two of them had not been snuffed out. As before,
Belgütei was a stepchild for Ö'elün, and Ö'elün was a stepmother
for Belgütei. So Ö'elün always failed to demonstrate a fair proportion of love for Belgütei, and to that extent he always bore his own
suspicions regarding her.

The complexity of relations among the brothers did not end
there, though. Temüjin himself was in precisely the same position
as Belgütei. In his heart of hearts, he had not fully extinguished the
idea that he might not be Yisügei's son. He would have to bear the
doubt once hurled at him by Begter, whom he had killed, all the way
to the grave. Like his four siblings, Qasar, Qachi'un, Temüge, and

Temülün, he had certainly been delivered of the womb of Ö'elün, but his father was a different matter. And although they were all born of the same mother, perhaps there were different allotments of love. This was an issue of subtle complexity that defied Temüjin's imagination, but it nonetheless tortured him to no end. If he took control in all matters away from his mother, he believed, everything would move along smoothly.

Ö'elün was not the least bit disconcerted by this mode of behavior on Temüjin's part. She was thoroughly cherished and treated with great affection by her children, and indeed, as a mother, was even pleased that all such matters would be handled under Temüjin's leadership. The full trust she enjoyed in her six children shone in her eyes.

Just as Temüjin would on occasion take some time to himself and sit in a corner of the yurt, deeply engrossed in his own thoughts, Ö'elün too would now and again take time to indulge in her own private thoughts, which would never be divulged to anyone. These were never long periods, in fact quite short, but once in a while she would abruptly fall into such a secret abyss. Who did Temüjin really resemble? Was it Yisügei or Chiledü, a male member of the Merkid lineage?

Ö'elün herself did not know which of these two men had sired Temüjin. She assumed that when he grew up, she would be able to judge based on whom he resembled more, but Temüjin did not resemble either one—neither when he was very young nor at any time until the present. If she pressed her search for clues, at times, such as when he slightly stooped his large frame to enter the tent, his physical carriage seemed to resemble that of Yisügei. Although it happened only once, one evening when a fierce windstorm was blowing, while rain was pelting the outside of the tent, she heard Temüjin's voice assiduously directing his younger brothers to reinforce weak spots in the yurt lest the wind blow it away altogether. Ö'elün sensed Yisügei's presence on this occasion too. Temüjin's voice shouting out orders reached Ö'elün's ears intermittently as she stared out from the entrance into the darkness with its violent wind and rain.

By the same token, though, there was something about Temüjin's nature that did not resemble Yisügei. In his strength as a warrior fearless of death itself, Yisügei had still possessed a certain gentleness, a human virtuousness, a weakness whereby he would abruptly withdraw his own point of view in favor of another's. This weakness had earned him the admiration of many of his relations and enabled him to retain his high position without any significant trouble among the more powerful households. One could not point to a quality of this sort in Temüjin's makeup. He had a coolness— perhaps better dubbed a heartlessness—absent in Yisügei, and he possessed a strength of will such that, as soon as he articulated his opinion on something, under no circumstances would he ever relinquish ground to anyone.

Temüjin, though, no more resembled the Merkids. Merkid men were small in stature with a nimbleness in appearance as well as in body, but Temüjin was much larger on the whole. What his face and torso lacked in similarity to the Merkids, so too did his nature.

Only once, though, did a telling incident transpire. When Temüjin was involved in the murder of his younger half-brother Begter, he suffered relentless rebukes from his mother. On this occasion, he stood silently, offering not a word in his own defense, but at the time Ö'elün had unconsciously placed before herself none other than the young Merkid named Chiledü. He had come one night like a sudden squall, snatched her from the Olqunu'ud people, raped her without a word emanating from her mouth, and then over the next few days assaulted and continued to violate her. And now, there he was. His actions were all linked by a craving to make whatever he wanted his own with no preconceived method in particular.

Although Ö'elün had become enraged when she learned that Temüjin had killed Begter, the harsh words that continued to pour from her mouth, as if she were in a trance, were due to the fact that in her mind, this savage Merkid youth was standing there. Directly before her was not Temüjin but Chiledü.

When her excitement abated and she regained her composure, Ö'elün pondered one scary thought. Perhaps it was fine if Merkid blood ran in Temüjin's veins, but she had shunted to the side her own position as Temüjin's mother. That event had without a doubt left a scar in Ö'elün's own heart.

In the summer of the year Temüjin turned sixteen, an incident occurred that shook the lives of these descendants of the Borjigin *khan*s at the roots. Targhutai, leader of the Tayichi'uds, commanding a force of 300 men, launched a surprise attack on Temüjin's yurt.

At some point, Temüjin foresaw this coming. About a month before it happened, a Borjigin man living an utterly wretched existence at the Tayichi'ud camp appeared unexpectedly at Temüjin's tent. Although he had been hunting nearby, it seemed clear that his visit was purposely occasioned both by curiosity about how Ö'elün and her children were faring and by feelings of homesickness for old faces. While properly speaking, he was an accomplice of the hated enemy who had abandoned them, because he claimed that he was visiting specifically out of worry on their behalf, any animosity Ö'elün and her family might have harbored toward the man dissipated. He placed a third of his game before them and quickly departed, but during this short visit he did inform them that the Tayichi'ud leader Targhutai bore evil intentions toward Temüjin. When a group of his fellow family members gathered in the first month of the year, Targhutai reportedly had said, while drinking wine:

"The chicken's feathers are spreading. The lamb too is growing up. Before it's too late, we shall put an end to the life of Yisügei's little brat. If his wings are allowed to spread as if flying in the sky and his step allowed to grow sturdy as if running across the desert, then he may come to pose a serious problem."

Because of this, Temüjin knew that an attack was impending. He set to making preparations for it, constructing a fortified hut out of tree branches in a nearby forest and in the evening assembling their sheep and horses around the yurt.

It was late one night in early summer when the moon was shining brightly. Hearing an unusual cry from the animals, Ö'elün and her children woke all at once. When they left the tent, they saw arrows that had fallen among the livestock. Temüjin led his family

across the field and then ran toward the forest that was home to the
fortified hut. The Tayichi'uds unleashed a volley of arrows from
horseback, and from far down a broad slope he could see horsemen
advancing toward him.

Temüjin had not foreseen an attack by such a large detachment.
He had thought that this was a matter for a small group and that at
most fifty or sixty men might come surging in with swords drawn.
He had completely miscalculated and was unsure what to do. He
found refuge for his mother and three siblings too young to fight—
Qachi'un, Temüge, and Temülün—in the fissures of the precipices
in the woods. Then, with Qasar and Belgütei, he holed up in the
fortified hut and exchange arrow fire with the attackers.

Victory in this fight, though, was determined from the start. With
only a few arrows remaining, Temüjin ordered his two younger
brothers to take their mother and younger siblings and escape deep
into the forest to save their lives.

"They've launched such a large assault because they want all this
grassland for themselves," he said. "If you manage to escape, head
straight north of Mount Burqan and don't come near here again."

To save his brothers, sister, and mother, Temüjin alone was left
to shoot his final arrow from the hut in the woods. He then mounted
his horse and rode off to the foothills of Tergüne Heights, hidden
deep in the woods.

Temüjin spent three days in the forest. Were the Tayichi'uds still
looking for this fugitive? On a number of occasions he heard the
whinnying of horses. On the fourth day, Temüjin attempted to lead
his horse out of the forest, but for some reason his saddle attached
to the horse's girth separated from it and fell to the ground. Highly
inauspicious, he thought, and returned to spend another three days
in the forest. He then tried once again to leave, but this time a white
stone roughly the size of a yurt blocked his way out, and he abandoned the idea and lay concealed there for yet another three days.
With no food, on the verge of starvation, Temüjin decided for the
third time to make his way out of the forest. The immense white
boulder still obstructed his path. He attempted to circumvent it, but
there was no solid footing to be found.

Again, Temüjin felt this an unpromising omen, but he realized that if he remained there, he would likely starve to death, so he boldly crossed over the rocky precipice and left the forest. No sooner had he emerged from the trees than Temüjin was apprehended by Tayichi'ud men who spotted him. They tied him up and brought him to a new Tayichi'ud colony not far away on the banks of the Onon River.

Laden with a large piece of timber across his shoulders and with both hands shackled to it, Temüjin was walked into a village of several hundred scattered tents. Many were the faces of Borjigin men and women there whom Temüjin recognized. With expressions of mixed feelings on their faces, they cast their eyes on his half-naked figure with rippling musculature like a stone, the now splendidly grown son of their former khan, Yisügei. No one addressed him. As Temüjin had learned from the two men he chanced to have met earlier, his fellow Borjigins had fallen on bad times, and he now saw that this was not simply a rumor. All of them, men and women alike, stood silently before their squalid tents.

Temüjin sensed that the leader of the Tayichi'uds lacked the will to kill him. Had he so intended, Temüjin thought, then he would surely not have led him before a group of his own people. Whatever he might have been planning, that would have done more harm than good. Temüjin reasoned that he would probably have to endure torture for a number of days, then be released from his shackles, enticed into the Tayichi'ud camp, and compelled to swear allegiance to it.

That night Temüjin was forced to stand in an open area at the edge of the settlement. Only one person stood guard over him, while the rest of the population assembled in an area in front of the chieftain's tent and held a banquet. With one section of the piece of wood strapped to his shoulders, Temüjin struck this guard, and as soon as he saw that the man had collapsed on the ground unconscious, he quickly escaped. The moon was bright that night. Temüjin could see the strange shadow he cast on the ground with the large piece of timber still attached to his shoulders, and instinctively he began running along the bank of the Onon River. When he reached the point of exhaustion, he was able to conceal his body and the burden he carried in the verdant overgrowth by the river.

It wasn't long before Temüjin knew that the Tayichi'uds had learned of his escape and were shouting among themselves to find him. Voices could be heard from the riverbank and from the extensive grassland that abutted it. On a number of occasions, human voices and footsteps passed close to where he was hiding. Fearing that he would eventually be found, Temüjin slipped deeper into the slimy overgrowth.

Suddenly a voice overhead called out:

"There is fire in your eye and light in your face. With that weight on your shoulders, the Tayichi'ud leader envies and fears you. Stay quiet where you are, and we won't tell anyone."

Temüjin had been holding his breath with his half-naked body in the water. He had a faint memory of this hoarse voice. It was surely that of Sorqan Shira. When his father, Yisügei, was alive, this man had frequently come to visit their family, but he was solemn and never laughed, and for that reason none of the children ever took a liking to him.

After he had hidden there for a long time, Temüjin's fear of being discovered by the search party dissipated, and with the wooden burden on his shoulders, he crawled up from the water's edge. His arms, tied up and extended horizontally for such a long period of time, had utterly lost all feeling. Temüjin realized that in his present shape he was unable to escape anywhere. He was unable to swim in the Onon River, and he could not cover much ground by walking through the night. Dawn was now fast approaching.

Temüjin reasoned that the best plan might be to slip into the tent of Sorqan Shira, who had earlier passed him by. Although this course of action entailed dangers, once he decided on it, Temüjin again concentrated on being inconspicuous and headed back toward the Tayichi'ud settlement.

Sorqan Shira's household, when he was one of Yisügei's subordinates, made a living by producing *kumis*, fermented mare's milk. Temüjin remembered how Sorqan Shira would work late into the night pouring fresh horse's milk into a large vat and then churning it. Imagining that he still pursued the same livelihood, Temüjin walked around the village late that night listening for the sound of milk being churned. He was finally able to find the right tent.

Stripped to the waist, Sorqan Shira was aided in his work by his two sons, Chimbai, who was Temüjin's age, and Chila'un, who was two years his junior. He was stirring the liquid in the large vat with a stick. When Temüjin came inside their yurt, Sorqan Shira was gravely surprised.

"Why in the world did you come back here?" he asked. "I told you to hurry back to where your mother and younger brothers were." His expression was one of genuine consternation. Then, his elder son Chimbai, who was short and had protruding eyes and a large head, said in a surprisingly mature tone of voice:

"What's done is done—he's here. There's no looking back now. We have to help him." He said it as if admonishing his father. Then his younger brother, Chila'un, with a squint in his eyes, opened them wide, though without a clear focus, and approached Temüjin, speaking neither specifically to his father nor to his elder brother: "We once received from Temüjin the nail of a small deer's hoof." Although but two years younger than Temüjin, he barely came up to his shoulder and was unmistakably the shorter of the two brothers.

Initially Temüjin had no idea why Chila'un had walked over in his direction, but he soon realized that one of his shackled arms was free. Until Chila'un had completely unbound Temüjin, Sorqan Shira had a dour expression on his face and stood up straight beside the large vat.

Chimbai removed the fetters from Temüjin's body and threw them in the fire. A girl of about ten years in age named Qada'an appeared out of nowhere. She looked like her older brothers and was very short.

"My clever daughter," said Sorqan Shira, ordering the girl with the face of a young child, "never tell any of this to another living person. I am putting the care of the eldest son of Yisügei in your hands." His countenance effectively said that there was no other choice, things having reached this pass. Qada'an quickly brought some food and gave it to Temüjin, and without saying a word she urged him to leave. When he followed her out of the tent, Qada'an led him around behind it to a cart piled high with wool and pointed to it. Her father had called her clever, and indeed she seemed to be very resourceful.

Temüjin quickly crawled into the wool. When he finished eating the food she had given him with only his face and hands exposed to the night air, he buried himself entirely, unable to see anything outside. With his entire body now wrapped in wool, Temüjin was sweltering, but an overwhelming exhaustion soon plunged him into a deep sleep.

The following day Temüjin hid in this place all day. Only at nightfall, at Chimbai's signal, did he crawl out. A mare with black mane and light brown coat was waiting for him. It bore no saddle, but large leather bags hanging on either side of the horse's torso were filled with roasted lamb.

"This horse has borne no offspring, so there's no need to return it," said Chimbai, as he passed Temüjin a bow and two arrows. When Temüjin was about to depart, Sorqan Shira came out and said to him:

"You've exposed us all to grave danger. Listen, my little immortal friend, you must never say anything about us—ever! Now, go quickly."

Highly attentive until he had left the settlement, Temüjin made his horse walk slowly, and as soon as he was beyond the village he rode off at a dash. In retrospect, he realized he had narrowly escaped by the skin of his teeth. Rather than thinking about his own close brush with death, Temüjin was absorbed in the thought, as he rode off, that gathering all the Borjigin people under his leadership as in the era of his father would not be that difficult a task.

For the next few days, Temüjin walked around the northern foothills of Mount Burqan in search of his mother and siblings. He had learned in the Tayichi'ud settlement that they had not been apprehended, so they were surely hiding out somewhere in this area.

One day as Temüjin was walking upstream along the bank of the Onon River, he passed its point of confluence with the Kimurgha Stream and climbed Qorchuqui Hill on Beder Promontory. At the foot of the southern slope of this hill, he spied a small tent. When he approached and looked inside, he found Ö'elün, Temüge, and Temülün. Qasar, Belgütei, and Qachi'un had gone into the mountains that morning to gather food. Only eight horses—all the possessions this family had—were hitched close to the tent.

The next day Temüjin folded up the tent and moved them three days' journey away to the banks of a lake full of azure water located at the foot of Mount Qara Jirüken. Here was a suitable spot in a corner of the plateau where the impoverished family of Mother Ö'elün could live near the flow of the Sengkür Stream. There were many rabbits and field mice, and the lake and river were filled with fish.

Temüjin had to rebuild their lives at this new dwelling. With Qasar and Belgütei, he searched for the furrows of marmots to trap them almost every day. They ate the flesh and used the pelts to make garments. If they accumulated a good number of them, they could also exchange them for sheep.

One day about three months later, Temüjin and his brothers set off to trap marmots as always, but that evening when they returned home with their heavily laden, short-tailed chestnut horse, they learned that every one of their horses had been stolen. Ö'elün and the younger children had been out looking for food in the hills and were completely unaware of the theft.

"I'm going after them," said Belgütei. With only the chestnut horse left, only one person could go in pursuit.

"You can't do it," said Qasar. "I'll go." In physical strength Qasar was no match for Belgütei, but he was far more accomplished a horseman than his brother.

"You can't do it. I'll go." This time it was Temüjin who spoke, using precisely the same words as Qasar had. He loaded provisions on the horse, armed himself with bow and arrows, mounted, and was quickly gone.

Temüjin drove his horse straight through the night, and the following day he rode around in search of anything that resembled a settlement. Come what might, he had to retrieve those eight horses. They were irreplaceable, the sum total of his family's property. After three full days roaming about the plateau, on the morning of the fourth day Temüjin chanced to meet a young boy milking horses on pastureland. He asked the lad if he had seen eight dappled-gray horses.

"Before the sun rose this morning," he replied, "I saw eight grays galloping along this pathway. If they're stolen, let's give chase and get them back."

He led his black horse out and encouraged Temüjin to change horses, while he himself mounted a fast, light-yellow horse. The boy handled everything with an attitude of confidence befitting an adult, and saying nothing to his family, joined Temüjin in the search.

Until that point in time, Temüjin had never met such an agile youngster. Despite the fact that he made his preparations in no time at all, he had bow and arrows, tinder, and two leather bags with food loaded on his horse. Because there were no covers over the bags, he picked wild grasses en route and cleverly fashioned substitute lids. The dexterity with which he did all this left Temüjin with a good feeling. He was the son of Naqu Bayan, chieftain of a small village, and his name was Bo'orchu.

Temüjin and Bo'orchu rode for another three days, and on the evening of the fourth day entered a settlement of a branch of the Tayichi'uds. They found the eight horses they had been looking for tied up on the pastureland. It was preferable to round up the horses at night and then lead them back home.

Just at daybreak, they caught sight of a dozen or more mounted men coming after them.

"My friend," said Bo'orchu, "take the horses and ride off quickly. I will stay and shoot my arrows at them."

"How can you go to your death on my behalf?" said Temüjin. "I will fight them." As soon as he had spoken, Temüjin turned and fired off an arrow. It pierced the chest of a man at the front of the group who was riding a white steed and trying to hurl a lasso at them. Seeing that the other pursuers had ridden up to their fallen comrade on the ground, Temüjin and Bo'orchu galloped off post-haste, and the other men made no further effort to catch them.

Temüjin made his way to the tent of Naqu Bayan, stayed one night, thanked Bo'orchu for his help, and returned home. Although thrilled at having brought the eight horses back, Temüjin was even happier about the fact that he now knew that there were men in this world who would volunteer to join him in action with no mercenary interest whatsoever—and they were young men his own age. He had never even dreamed such men might exist until then.

After returning to his tent, Temüjin tried on several occasions to say the name of the youngster. Bo'orchu, Bo'orchu—he was, of course, neither a Borjigin nor a Tayichi'ud, but a Mongol. Temüjin could not help but think that he was like this young man Bo'orchu whose veins overflowed with the blood of the blue wolf that came from the West. Bo'orchu in fact did somehow give the impression, in the fearless limbs of his body, that he resembled a wolf. Physically he was certainly neither robust nor big, actually rather slender in appearance, but his muscles were gracefully compact, and he seemed to be always waiting to join in action at the necessary moment with a sense that nothing was in vain.

That year, ten head of sheep came from Bo'orchu's father, Naqu Bayan, on behalf of his only son. Naqu Bayan was extremely pleased that his son had made such a friend as Temüjin.

Temüjin and his brothers spent the autumn making a pasture next to their new dwelling.

The following year Temüjin turned seventeen. His mother, Ö'elün, advised him to go to the Unggirad village to see Börte, the young woman to whom he was betrothed. Ö'elün had offered this counsel several times already, but each time he had ignored it. All he could think of was that this would add another mouth to feed in their already isolated and helpless, poverty-stricken home.

On this occasion, though, now that he was seventeen, Temüjin thought of the matter slightly differently. He was beginning to think that adding one more person might actually be necessary. If increasing the numbers of those dwelling within his own tent would strengthen it, then surely the minds of the Borjigins, who were far from enjoying a happy situation at present, would be moved. And certainly they would recollect past times when they had made Yisügei their khan and gathered at his camp, and they would look forward to such an era returning. Since they had al-

lowed him to gain such knowledge, Temüjin's having been attacked
by the Tayichi'uds and taken captive into their settlement ironically
were positive experiences. Hadn't Sorqan Shira and his three short
children all demonstrated their goodwill? Undoubtedly, the senti-
ment expressed by Sorqan Shira's family was an emotion shared by
all Borjigins.

Now Temüjin thought he would indeed go, just as his mother
was suggesting, to see Börte in her tent. And he would be happy
to receive with Börte the Unggirad men and women—even if they
were disabled and old or maidservants—who were surely to accompany her to her new home.

When he had made up his mind, Temüjin set off on the journey to
the Unggirad village with his half-brother, Belgütei. They traveled
downstream along the Kherlen River for several days. Although
this was scenery Temüjin had seen once before, what unfolded before Belgütei was an altogether new plateau, forests, valleys, and
grasslands. Many times when they camped in the evening, far from
his usual taciturnity, Belgütei talked on and on in great wonder-
ment. What he spoke of was always the extraordinary vastness of
the world before them, the fact that no one was dwelling there, and
why, he wished to know, so many nomads had been unable to build
numerous settlements throughout this wide, uninhabited space.

Temüjin remained silent, listening to this unforeseen volubility
of his half-brother as if it were some sort of pleasant music. It was
all just as Belgütei said. Temüjin also felt the immensity of the Mongolian plain over which he had been galloping with his horse for
some days. The horses, the sheep, the fertile pasturelands—all were
so abundant and beyond one man's capacity to take in hand. Grasslands on which it was easy to pitch one's tent and banks of lakes
and rivers that seemed perfectly fine as sites on which to live were
also abundant. Why hadn't people pitched their tents here? For his
part Temüjin could think of only one possible reason: in the ongo-
ing strife among peoples, each settlement had to have a few days'
distance between itself and all the others. The range over which one
group moved in its nomadic migrations seemed to have been naturally determined as if by a deity in the ancient past. No single lin-

eage was about to move beyond its prescribed range, and if one did so and invaded a neutral zone, this would invite attack by another group who accordingly felt threatened.

Had the various lineages and ethnic groups scattered across the Mongolian plateau dispensed with their mutual animosities and freely opened up new grazing lands, the lives of nomads now living there would have been vastly different. No matter where travelers ventured on this immense plateau, they would always see tents and large groups of sheep and horses. Yurts would be dotting the entire Mongolian plateau, and herds of sheep and horses moving slowly over every slope and valley like clouds drifting across the sky. It was such a fanciful vision he almost wanted to sigh out loud. Could that ever come to be? It wasn't necessarily impossible, was it? If they were to defeat the Tayichi'uds and even finish off the Tatars, then such a proposition was by no means out of the question.

When they entered the Unggirad settlement, Dei Sechen joyously came to greet them. He had heard, but only in the form of a rumor, that Temüjin had been injured in an attack by the Tayichi'uds and presumed him to be no longer of this world. And now the young man, completely changed from four years before, suddenly appeared in front of him all grown up and powerful of build—it seemed frankly unbelievable to him.

That evening they celebrated a great banquet in Dei Sechen's tent.

"The son of the past Mongol khan, having overcome astonishing adversity, has now grown into a mighty young man. And, as he once promised, he has come to take my daughter. I could never break a promise. I gave Börte to this virtually invulnerable young man. Thus, my daughter and those who accompany her must go to the Borjigin yurts in the west, where they will pitch several tents, for Börte will feel lonely in only one."

Dei Sechen made this speech with his own distinctive, rhythmic intonation to the people of his yurt, but so that Temüjin would hear. The eating and drinking went on late into the night. Temüjin had still not seen Börte since arriving, as she had not appeared to take a seat at the banquet.

When the banquet came to a close, Temüjin was led to another tent different from that of Dei Sechen. When he entered, he saw by the light of a lantern Börte dressed in resplendent garb, sitting punctiliously in a Jurchen-style chair from the state of Jin. Just as the four years that had passed had changed Temüjin, so too had they utterly changed this young woman. Börte had a large-framed torso not seen among the Borjigin women. Her breasts and waist were quite fleshy, and it seemed to Temüjin as though her entire body was glowing. Indeed, there was something of a brownish brilliance to her hair and a lustrous sheen to the white skin of her face and the nape of her neck. He could not say if this was due solely to the flickering light of the lantern burning mutton tallow.

Until this point in time, women for Temüjin were merely weak creatures, inferior in every capacity, never able to measure up and be ranked together with men. With Börte standing before him, though, he was gripped by the strange feeling that his view of them was going to be completely overturned. He realized that he was seeing the true face of a woman now for the first time. Still standing by the entrance, Temüjin continued gazing directly at Börte. His mind was sensing an eerie confusion the likes of which he had never experienced before. The woman before him was beautiful and not in the least a weak creature, and her supple body was in no way inferior to a man's.

Eventually, Börte stood up from her chair. The light-blue necklace hanging over her chest made a faint sound as she moved. She stood still, not speaking a word, as she revealed her entire physical form before the man who had become her husband. With swelling, ample breasts, her figure possessed authority and pride.

Temüjin tried to approach her, but his feet would not move in the desired direction. This was his first experience with something placed before him making him hesitate. He had never feared anything and had never vacillated when drawing near anything. What made his feet stop dead in their tracks? What was this beautiful, glowing creature before him now?

Börte moved slightly at this moment, a mere step or two closer to Temüjin. At the same time, a few short words emerged from her mouth, but Temüjin's ears could not hear them. As much as she

approached, he retreated. The space between them remained unchanged from the time he had entered the tent. Then Temüjin noticed that Börte was speaking again. This time he clearly heard his
named called:

"Temüjin, my father said that you were a young man who resembled a mighty wolf, and you are indeed like a young mighty wolf."
Temüjin remained silent. The words he should have spoken did
not come to his lips. Then, after a while, he hurled out unruly language, as if he were confronting a formidable enemy face to face:

"I am a Mongol. As your father said, the blood of the wolf flows
in my veins. Every single Mongol has the blood of the wolf."

"I am an Unggirad woman," replied Börte. "No wolf's blood
flows in my body. But I can give birth to many cubs who will share
the blood of the wolf. My father has instructed me to bear numerous
offspring of the wolf. To suppress the Tayichi'uds, to suppress the
Tatars, and, yes, even to suppress every last Unggirad as well."

Temüjin took in these words as if they were a divine oracle. He
could not imagine that the words uttered by this young woman were
those of a single individual.

Temüjin felt like a kind of boldness, as the blood in his body
grew warmer to the point of overflowing. He then took a tentative
step toward this beautiful young woman given to him now by the
Unggirad chieftain Dei Sechen, a man who had abrogated his own
father-daughter bond of love.

"Börte!" Temüjin unconsciously called out her name, as he was
seized with something like a profound, heartfelt love.

"Temüjin!" Although she too called his name, as if in response,
her tone struck Temüjin as infinitely gentler. He then took another
step, but now Börte backed away. Temüjin did not now hesitate, but
lunged straight in her retreating direction and took her in his arms.

Temüjin spent three days in the Unggirad village. During that
time, the feasting continued day and night. Because his own life
had suddenly changed, Belgütei took on a sullen mood and ceased
speaking altogether. He had nothing to say. The grandeur of the
banquet, of course, from the clothing of the villagers down to the
personal effects in the tents, stunned Belgütei enormously.

On the fourth day, Temüjin and Belgütei, together with Börte and thirty of her attendants, set off from the Unggirad village. Börte's father, Dei Sechen, and her mother, Chotan, joined the group so that they could see her off midway. Unlike the trip there, the return was a bustling procession.

Among all the peoples scattered over the Mongolian plateau, the Unggirads had been most blessed by the culture of the Jurchen (Jin) state. They thus had splendid travel attire. When they passed other peoples' settlements nearby, large groups of onlookers always came together to gaze at them.

Although it involved a bit of a detour, Dei Sechen encouraged Temüjin to go by way of these other villages. His idea was that it would be good to inform them, even if only a little, of the existence of Temüjin's isolated yurt, and Temüjin decided to follow his father-in-law's advice.

When Dei Sechen arrived at the shores of the Kherlen River, he turned back and left the party. Chotan had planned to return with her husband, but she couldn't bear to leave her daughter. She therefore traveled with the group as far as Temüjin's yurt on the shores of the azure lake by Mount Qara Jirüken. After arriving, Chotan spent about ten days with them before returning to the Unggirad settlement.

The single tent inhabited by Temüjin and his family until then would no longer be sufficient. Temüjin moved out of the tent in which his mother and siblings were living and built a new one for himself and Börte. An additional five tents were constructed for the men and women who accompanied Börte as her entourage. Although it might have been called a settlement, it was still no more than an aggregation of a small number of people. At night the light of the fires from these tents shone and illuminated the darkness in which they had been engulfed. At dawn men and women rose and emerged from their respective yurts to go to work.

When Temüjin had become comfortable with his new life, he planned with Qasar and Belgütei to meet at their own tent with Bo'orchu, who had helped him regain their eight gray horses. Temüjin thought that Bo'orchu would surely come in response to a personal invitation. There was, of course, no reason for either Qasar or Belgütei to object, and Belgütei went on the mission to Bo'orchu.

On the morning of the fifth day after Belgütei had left, Temüjin caught sight all the way from beyond the grasslands of a young man riding next to Belgütei on a chestnut horse he remembered, with a blue woolen cloak over it. Showing him proper courtesy, Temüjin ushered this nimble young man about the same age as himself into their small settlement. Bo'orchu had not consulted with his father about coming to join Temüjin, but a messenger from Naqu Bayan soon arrived as if he had been trailing him. Apparently there were special routes known to men like this messenger. If the two young men consulted and over the long term decided to cooperate, then it appeared as though Bo'orchu might do as he wished. These were the words Naqu Bayan conveyed to them. Thereafter, several dozen head of sheep were delivered to Temüjin's settlement from Naqu Bayan's stock.

After consulting with Qasar, Belgütei, and Bo'orchu, Temüjin moved their dwelling site to the broad, sloping side of Mount Burqan. This area included extensive grasslands and was convenient for pasturing animals. In addition, it would be easier to protect their tents from the pounding wind and rain that came virtually every year. With his own new tent, Temüjin lined up the tents of Bo'orchu and Ö'elün at the center of their settlement, and surrounded them with the others' tents.

Temüjin then took it into his mind to welcome to his yurt Chimbai and Chila'un, the two sons of Sorqan Shira who were in the Tayichi'ud village. He would greet these two benefactors who had released him from his shackles and given him shelter in their home, for they had served him as trustworthy followers. Communicating with them was highly dangerous because they lived in the midst of a Tayichi'ud settlement. It was extremely difficult to get word to them. Qasar served as messenger, and he succeeded admirably in his task. He returned with one large-headed short youth and one squinting youngster, each riding a strong horse.

Temüjin greeted the two young men when they dismounted.

"You know your own minds well!" he said. "Surely, your father, Sorqan Shira, was opposed to your coming."

"Father several times tilted his head to the side dubiously," said Chimbai, "as he stirred the fermented mares' milk in a large vat. But I spoke up: 'A messenger has arrived. We have no alternative but to respond.' Then Qasar and I left together."

Chimbai had offered neither rhyme nor reason for his action. He seemed to be the sort of youngster who, having won another man's confidence and trust, was prepared to give his life in response. Thus, having once had his life saved by this young man, Temüjin now could welcome him into his own camp.

"Chila'un," said Temüjin, directing his voice to Chimbai's younger brother. Chila'un turned his unfocused eyes toward Temüjin.

"Once in the past," he replied, "I received from you the nail of a small deer's hoof." Because of this nail, Chila'un had removed Temüjin's shackles, and now he had abandoned his home for Temüjin and come here. Thereafter, whatever Temüjin said, Chila'un seemed ready to reply to without hesitation. Although Temüjin never spoke directly of such things to these two brothers, in their own minds their only choice was to throw their support firmly behind Temüjin.

With the passage of time, tradesmen from various other locales also made their way to Temüjin's camp. Although their numbers were never large, Temüjin gradually gained a certain latitude in his life, and best of all the movements of the various peoples on the Mongolian plateau became known to him.

Temüjin learned that the most powerful man on the plateau at present was the chief of the Kereyids, To'oril Khan. Under his leadership, the Kereyid people were in constant training with the objective of battle. Temüjin had once seen a small group of youngsters in perpetual military practice among the Unggirads, the native group of his wife, Börte. Among the Kereyids, however, all 30,000 men and boys were in training as soldiers. In peacetime they tended their sheep and horses, but as soon as some issue arose, they immediately shed their farm clothes, switched into military garb, and lined up in prearranged military detachments with their weapons in hand.

.

Temüjin admired the Unggirads' practice of protecting pasture-land and tents, but when he heard tales of the Kereyid people, he saw clearly that the Unggirads were no match for them. Temüjin had heard of the reputation of the Kereyid chief To'oril Khan from many different sources. And now he learned that this man harbored ambitions to pacify the other peoples of the Mongolian plateau and become their sovereign.

Temüjin made up his mind to meet this To'oril Khan. It struck him as clearly beneficial on all fronts to get to know the man. Temüjin was now the head of a settlement, albeit still quite small. Were he to show him every appropriate courtesy and seek his assistance, for his part To'oril Khan would surely not take an indifferent attitude toward him. Furthermore, his father, Yisügei, had enjoyed a period of close friendship with To'oril Khan. In his last years, Yisügei had been tied up trying to resolve problems involving his own people and had been unable to visit or meet with To'oril Khan frequently, but the pact the two of them had made as youths would have continued right down to the present without alteration.

Temüjin sounded out his circle of colleagues about going to the camp of the leader of the Kereyids to seek friendly relations. He consulted, of course, with Qasar and Belgütei, but also with Bo'orchu, Chimbai, and Chila'un. He even spoke about this matter with his mother, Ö'elün, and his wife, Börte. Needless to say, no one offered any opposition.

Ö'elün pointed out that he ought to bring with him as a memento for To'oril Khan the very finest possession they presently owned. Aside from sheep and horses, though, there was nothing in Temüjin's camp worthy of the description. Although she had been silent until this point, Börte said:

"I have a black sable robe that my mother brought into this home as a gift." Temüjin immediately agreed that this would do. It was surely superior to anything Temüjin presently had in his yurt.

Together with his two brothers Qasar and Belgütei, Temüjin took the sable robe and went to pay a visit to To'oril Khan at the Kereyid encampment in the forest by the banks of the Tula River. Compared to the Unggirad settlement, that of the Kereyids was far

simpler, with a gloomy atmosphere prevailing. This mood indicated just how poorly off these people were. Many sheep and horses
covered the extensive grasslands, and many were the tents of those
peoples who made a living this way. Temüjin thought he now understood the reason that To'oril Khan, despite having large numbers of lineage members and excellent fighting skills, had not gone
out of his way to seek trouble with other lineages.

At the back of a large tent, Temüjin and his brothers met with
To'oril Khan, a slender man in his fifties with a coldness in his eyes.

"Our father, Yisügei," said Temüjin, "called you *anda*, a blood
brother, and therefore you are like a father to us as well. My wife's
mother brought a sable robe as a gift for her daughter's father-in-
law. Inasmuch as my father is no longer living, I would like to present it to you as my father's equal."

He then placed the present before To'oril Khan, who was extremely pleased. He acted as though he had never before received
such an extravagant gift. His delight aside, though, his words were
harsh:

"You little urchins without a father, you're awfully generous." In
To'oril Khan's eyes, Temüjin and his brothers still did not amount
to full-fledged men.

"In return for this black sable robe, should the opportunity come
in future, I'll gather together your people who've separated from
you. Once I've sworn something, I never violate a vow. You suffered worse in the past, my little chickens, and while you've grown a
bit, you're still weaklings."

Temüjin and his party were ultimately not treated as adults and
had to leave To'oril Khan's camp. For his own part, though, Temüjin never retained any displeasure toward To'oril Khan as a
person. Compared to To'oril Khan, who could mobilize a force of
30,000 men at a moment's notice, the three brothers headed by 18-
year-old Temüjin really *were* little more than urchins, chickens, and
weaklings.

The three brothers rode their horses to a wooded area known
as the Black Forest, where there was a Kereyid settlement, and traversed it. A cool, somewhat severe atmosphere hung over the camp

there, with the young Kereyids who never laughed silently cutting
a path through the forest. The face of every one of the young men
bore a striking resemblance to To'oril Khan with the stern brow and
cold eyes. The people of this lineage, thought Temüjin, had an innate imperturbability.

When he returned to his own settlement, Temüjin noted to himself that the men there should have a facial expression like that of
the Kereyid youngsters. He woke up early the next morning and
spent the entire day working in the pasturelands. When night came,
he mounted his horse and practiced shooting arrows and wielding
his dagger and spear. Qasar and Belgütei, as well as Qachi'un, who
was still young but trying hard to grow up, and Temüge all followed
him. Bo'orchu, Chimbai, and Chila'un, along with a dozen or so
Unggirad men, all followed Temüjin's example.

In equestrian skills no one excelled Qasar, while Bo'orchu was
unsurpassed in mounted archery. Belgütei was best at maneuvering
the large dagger, and the squinting Chila'un was supreme in shooting arrows. No one could match Chimbai in martial arts, but he also
demonstrated exceptional talent in tailing people and seeking out
the movements of others.

Although Ö'elün came into contact almost every day with these
young subordinates of Temüjin, she paid close attention to all
manner of detail and deplored the fact that there were no young
girls with the particular talents of serving girls and maidservants.
The discontent Ö'elün had with life in this camp was twofold: the
absence of such youngsters and the fact that Börte had not given
birth to a child. To Ö'elün's way of thinking, a woman who did not
give birth was not a woman. On this point Börte herself felt deeply
ashamed. As her father, Dei Sechen, put it, she had to bear numerous cubs with the blood of the wolf, who would crush every last
Tayichi'ud, every last Tatar, and even every last Unggirad. This she
wanted to do ever so much.

Of Ö'elün's two worries, she was able finally to resolve the problem of training young people to be attentive servants as needed.
One day an older man by the name of Jarchi'udai came to their
camp, carrying on his shoulders a smith's bellows, accompanied

by a young fellow. Ö'elün knew the old man, and Temüjin too remembered him, for when Temüjin was four or five years old he had left their camp and moved to a place deep in the region of Mount Burqan, where he built a hut and lived a solitary life.

"When you were born," the old man said to Temüjin, "I presented you with fur swaddling in congratulation. I gave you Jelme here, and from that time forward you and he have had a master-servant relationship. But at that time, given that Jelme was only three years old, I kept him by my side, and I have trained him myself until this day. Jelme has now also reached manhood. Please use him as you see fit. Have him saddle your horse or open the door to your tent." And, so saying, he introduced his son to Temüjin.

From that day forward the young man became a member of Temüjin's circle. Three years Temüjin's senior, he was dark complexioned and undistinguished in appearance. A man of simplicity and honesty, he worked faithfully on every task given him. He thus inconspicuously but gently saw to the needs of the maidservants, and soon made himself indispensable to the camp. Jelme was just the sort of young man Ö'elün had been looking for.

Life in Temüjin's tent grew more substantial with each passing day. He worked tirelessly, for there were many necessary tasks to attend to in his own camp: to match the wealth of the Unggirads, his wife's home lineage, with his own, and to replicate the military capacity of the Kereyids, whose leaders had, in his opinion, gained control over their people.

Until he was twenty-four years old, Temüjin worked hard to increase the number of yurts in his settlement. Aside from the fact that his wife had yet to give birth to a child, he had no major frustrations in life. Although the long-cherished desire of his mother and brothers to launch attacks on the Tayichi'uds and Tatars had yet to be accomplished, Temüjin had come to realize that this was not the sort of problem that would be solved quickly or by a youth barely over twenty. Temüjin was young, as were those in his camp.

Temüjin's life now, as it had been around the time he and Börte had married, was not exposed to the anxiety of never knowing when and where an enemy might attack. The Tayichi'uds had no notion that they might eradicate from the earth all descendants of Yisügei once they grew up; and even if they did entertain such an idea, they did not anticipate realizing it.

Temüjin was, however, assaulted by a completely unexpected disaster. It took place one morning when fierce winter weather was imminent on the plateau. A commotion broke out in Ö'elün's tent.

"Everyone, get up quickly," he heard the voice of Ö'elün's faithful old servant Qo'aqchin saying. "I can hear the beat of horses' hoofs and the cries of battle far off in the distance." Ö'elün jumped up first at the sound of her maid's voice.

The commotion quickly passed from tent to tent. When Temüjin emerged in the open area in front of the camp, everyone was already up and out of their respective tents. Night had not yet given way to dawn, and the darkness of the predawn hour hung over them. The reverberation of horses' hoofs shattering the frigid air grew steadily louder as the shouts and wails gradually grew more audible.

Temüjin ordered everyone to mount a horse and find refuge in Mount Burqan. It was uncertain how strong the enemy's numbers were, and in any event, it was clear to him that attempting to ambush the enemy in their camp had serious drawbacks. While leading his own horse out, he kept an eye on everyone else as they mounted up. Ö'elün climbed up on her horse, as did Qasar and Temüge. Belgütei, Bo'orchu, and Jelme were also astride their saddles. Temülün was together with her mother, Ö'elün, and Börte too had mounted her horse. Qo'aqchin took its bridle. All the other men and women had now also mounted. Those without horses clung to the reins of one.

Jelme was at the head of the group, while Temüjin was at the rear, like a sheepherder urging his flock forward. To ascertain who the attackers were and how strong their force was, Bo'orchu, Qasar, and Belgütei separated from the group and rode their horses in the opposite direction.

Confusion erupted when the evacuees tried to leave through the wooden barricade surrounding the settlement, as the black shadows of several mounted soldiers appeared on the slope to the right of the camp. Temüjin entrusted the group to Jelme and then immediately turned his horse in the direction in which Bo'orchu, Qasar, and Belgütei had galloped off, toward the enemy beyond the wooden fence around the settlement. Jumping over obstacles, he rode after them at full speed.

Temüjin was reunited with Bo'orchu and the others, ready to face the enemy with a shield of a few trees growing near the edge of the slope. Although the enemy was not as numerous as they had imagined, they still had some thirty to forty men. They were riding in what seemed like a thoroughly capricious fashion to the bottom of the slope, now galloping off to the east, now to the west, but never coming directly ahead. As if to remind themselves from time to time, they shot arrows in that direction. Because Temüjin and his allies could not see the enemy clearly, it was all a very strange, uncanny experience, like seeing something by its moving silhouette.

When the arrows being fired by the enemy gradually grew more numerous, shouts were heard unexpectedly from an altogether different direction: the north, where the women and children had fled. Quickly Temüjin and his three fellow fighters doubled back to the settlement. When they jumped the wooden fence and entered the site, a group of the women and children who should have been well beyond the barrier by now came rushing back in a state of utter confusion. Jelme's hoarse voice was calling out something and could be heard amid the pounding of horses' hoofs, the shouts, and the screams.

Temüjin ordered Jelme to take the group that had returned back out through the rear gate of the camp, while he turned and headed toward the fence on the northern side of camp, through which the women had earlier tried to escape. Arrows came pouring down like rain. Temüjin, Belgütei, Qasar, and Bo'orchu stopped for a while in their tents, which they used as shields, and fired arrows back. Because the land beyond the fence inclined sharply, they couldn't see the faces of the enemy who were undoubtedly advancing toward them. Then, on the far side of the barrier, gradually one mounted enemy fighter and then another began to appear and then disappear behind it. They showed no sign, though, that they were going to scale the fence and enter the camp. Temüjin and his colleagues for a long time diligently exchanged fire with the enemy. Temüjin did not leave his present location until it seemed to him that the women Jelme had been charged with leading through the back gate were far away, and he continued fighting this unexpectedly vile group who, while pressing them at their settlement, was not moving at them in any sudden attack.

Bo'orchu then came riding toward him and called out: "They're Merkids." Only then did Temüjin learn that his opponents were not Tayichi'uds.

When it became apparent that arrows were now coming at them not just from the east and north but from all directions, Temüjin ordered the three young men with him to abandon the settlement and escape into the mountains. It was useless and highly dangerous to try to remain there any longer. Bo'orchu took the lead and headed toward the rear gate. Temüjin, Qasar, and Belgütei followed in that order. When they cleared the fence, they could see nothing of the women and children anywhere. It seemed that Jelme had led them shrewdly to make good their escape.

As soon as they were beyond the fence, Qasar yelled:

"Scatter!"

And scatter they all did, each steering his horse in whatever direction he sought. Temüjin headed with typical persistence straight for the grasslands to the west, switched directions midway, and rode up the expansive, slow incline at the foothills of Mount Burqan. No more arrows were being shot at him. He could see the minuscule figures of Qasar and Belgütei riding their horses up the slope of Mount Burqan, climbing higher and higher. Only Bo'orchu could not be seen, which somewhat worried Temüjin. Eventually, from an unexpected direction, Bo'orchu appeared as a tiny, skilled horseman.

That afternoon, Temüjin and Qasar, Belgütei, and Bo'orchu were able to rendezvous more or less at the same time. That evening the brigade of women and children led by Jelme joined them.

When he saw Temüjin and the others, Jelme asked:

"Did you see Börte?"

As he explained, when Börte left through the rear gate, she abandoned her horse and got into a black covered cart next to an area of dry grass. Old Qo'aqchin saw that it was drawn by an ox with a dappled design on its haunches. They fell behind the group as a result and separated from the settlement by way of the nearby farmland so as to fool the invaders. Her horse had been injured, so Börte had no choice but to pursue this means of escape.

After he decided on a site for them to pitch camp, Temüjin spent from that night until the next morning riding back and forth in search of Börte, over the slope of Mount Burqan with its outcroppings of trees, grassy areas, and crags. But nowhere was he able to locate a trace of her.

On the fourth day following their ascent of the mountain, Temüjin sent Bo'orchu, Belgütei, and Jelme out on a reconnaissance mission over the foothills. Having thus learned that the Merkids had left the entire region, he descended Mount Burqan at the head of his lineage of men and women.

Only later did he learn that the attackers were a group led by three Merkid men, each with a different surname. News of old Qo'aqchin and Börte was, as before, not to be had. After about a month had passed, Temüjin learned that Qo'aqchin and Börte had been seized and taken prisoner to a Merkid village, where they were presently residing.

When he thought of Börte, Temüjin became insane with anger, but he was not going to offer up another sacrifice, and the fact that he and the others had been able to return to their own settlement did indeed make him happy. Because they had received the protection of Mount Burqan when they had all escaped into its environs, Temüjin decided to offer a prayer of thanks to it.

Since Börte was no longer among them, Temüjin gathered the members of his settlement together before their now deserted camp and had them construct an altar there. Temüjin then said to them:

"Through the grace of this Mount Burqan, we were protected from the Merkids. Because of this Mount Burqan, our insignificant, antlike, licelike lives were saved. Every morning sacrifice to Burqan! Every day pray to Burqan! And pass on this memory through our Borjigin descendants!"

Temüjin then stood facing Mount Burqan. He took the two symbols of authority and hung his belt around his neck and took his hat in his hand. Placing a hand on his chest, he knelt and poured some mare's milk onto the ground. After repeating this nine times, he offered up his prayer.

Bitter times were now come to Temüjin. With Börte kidnapped by the Merkids, all of nature surrounding him seemed completely to change its complexion. What he had to do now was to seize her back. To that end, Temüjin had subordinates who, he believed, would risk their lives for him without regret, but they were so few that it would have been reckless to launch an attack on the large Merkid settlement.

Any number of times, Chimbai with the large head volunteered and went off on spying missions to the Merkid village, but his report upon returning was always the same:

"The Merkids have placed fifty sentinels around the outside of their settlement. Getting inside their camp without being detected by them would be an act even a field mouse couldn't perform."

Judging by Chimbai's report, the Merkids were expecting Temüjin and his men to retaliate and had stepped up their vigilance.

As if this was part of the task assigned to him, Chimbai waited two or three days after returning from his mission and then set out once again to the Merkid settlement. This time when he returned he had much to report on from having entered the settlement. Thus, Temüjin now was even able to gain detailed information about the number of Merkid horses.

Chimbai's most important finding was the fact that the Merkids' surprise attack was not some capricious adventure on their part. In the more than twenty years since Yisügei had taken Ö'elün back from a young Merkid, they had never forgotten this event. As an act of revenge, they had seized Temüjin's young bride. Their plan had been set at the time that Temüjin brought Börte into his settlement, and until the present day they had been awaiting a prime opportunity to execute it.

Several months had now passed since Börte's disappearance from the camp, and with the new year Temüjin turned twenty-five, biding his time—just as the Merkids expected—looking for an opportunity to take his revenge on them. Unlike the Merkids, though, Temüjin was not the sort of man who could wait for over twenty years. If he were to detect an unguarded moment on their part and take advantage of it, he was prepared to do so today or tomorrow, as need be.

Temüjin pushed memories of Börte's glistening hair and the white nape of her neck from his mind. Whenever such a memory floated into his conscious thoughts, Temüjin felt his entire body fill up with a ferocious rage that this youth could not control.

When Chimbai returned to camp from his reconnaissance missions, Temüjin always listened to his report directly, and he never asked any questions. Temüjin was taciturn, but another level of taciturnity had overcome him. So that his face would not show anyone anything of his inner feelings, he had girded himself even more rigidly so that no expression would appear.

There was, however, one exception. When Chimbai completed his report this time, Temüjin moved his mouth slightly. Unable to hear if Temüjin had said anything, Chimbai urged him to speak further. Then, Temüjin quietly muttered:

"How is Börte?"

Chimbai could barely make out these words. He did not respond for a moment. Temüjin then said in a low voice, more clearly than before, "How is Börte?" His eyes were acutely focused on Chimbai's.

Chimbai replied resignedly with only a few words: "She's become the wife of a young man named Chiledü."

When he heard Chimbai's answer, for a moment Temüjin's complexion changed, but he then straightened up and left Chimbai.

This was the first time that Börte's name had been spoken by either man. Temüjin became even more resolutely uncommunicative, always showing a severe expression on his face. And he now never laughed.

After her abduction, Börte's name became completely taboo in the settlement. It was never mentioned by Ö'elün, by Qasar, by his young sister, Temülün, or by any of the maidservants.

About a month after Chimbai had responded to Temüjin's question and blurted out the information about Börte, Temüjin consulted with Qasar, Belgütei, and Bo'orchu on the matter he had been thinking over day and night in the interim: a raid on the Merkid village to recover Börte. All the men would take part, and protecting the settlement would be the job of the women. Until this point, never had any lineage left the care of a settlement in the hands of powerless women, but in this instance Temüjin decided that he would arm the women and have them guard the camp once the men had departed. He wanted to add every male available to the raiding party.

Qasar, Belgütei, and Bo'orchu all agreed. Temüjin had already firmly decided what he proposed to them. His young colleagues knew this only too well. Whether it was reckless of them or not, they had to set a plan in motion now. The men of the settlement—including the older men—numbered fewer than thirty.

Temüjin decided that the planned raid would be some twenty days hence, when the moon was at its slightest. The Merkid settlement was south of Lake Baikal, near the confluence point of the Orkhon and Selengge rivers. Even if they rode their horses slowly, it was a trip of only a few days and one that Chimbai knew well, as he had taken it any number of times.

With that settled, on virtually a daily basis all the dozen or more women—beginning with Ö'elün and, of course, seventeen-year-old Temülün—took up weapons and began their training in how to defend the settlement. Temüjin assigned instruction of the women to Bo'orchu, while he along with Qasar, Belgütei, and an additional number of horses paid a visit to To'oril Khan, chief of the Kereyids, in his village. Temüjin was hoping to borrow from the Kereyid leader some of his superior weapons. Because his men numbered fewer than thirty, he wanted at least their fighting implements to be fine specimens. Their horses were excellent, having borne up under all manner of warfare, but their weaponry was not at all uniformly satisfactory. Furthermore, the women would have to have arms in the settlement, and there were too few of them at present. Temüjin wanted to see that the younger men who were ready to defy death for him had the best weapons and armor that could possibly be made.

Temüjin, Qasar, and Belgütei rode upstream beside the Orkhon River for several days, until they reached the Kereyid camp situated in the Black Forest by the banks of the Tula River. When he met To'oril Khan, Temüjin confided to him all the facts of the case. To'oril Khan looked at the three visitors with the same cold brow and eyes. After thinking for a moment, he suddenly changed his expression and said:

"Orphaned son of Yisügei, do you not remember that I swore an oath to you? In return for your gift of a black sable robe, I said that I would gather your people who had scattered from you. It would seem that that time has come. I shall rally my forces for you, orphaned son of Yisügei. I shall take my army and kill every last Merkid camped south of Lake Baikal, and return your wife, Börte, to you."

To'oril Khan then cut himself off momentarily before continuing in a slower voice, his cold eyes shining even more frigidly than before:

"You little chickens are just starting to grow up now. I am going to offer you a return gift for the robe of black sable. First, with an army of 20,000 men, I shall set out from here as the right hand. You proceed to the base of Jamugha, chief of the Jadarans, who is encamped at the dry bed of the Qorqonaq River, and convey my message to him: 'To'oril Khan is about to mobilize an army of 20,000 and massacre all of the Merkids for the son of Yisügei. Jamugha, you shall go as his left hand, and you set the meeting place and time.'"

Temüjin stared at To'oril Khan in utter amazement. He had never seen a person who could in such a short time make such a momentous decision. His cold mien was suited to the resolution he was coming to.

When he left To'oril Khan's camp, Temüjin had, to say the least, successfully disposed of the matter of borrowing weaponry, the ob-

jective of his visit, so he remounted and headed back to his own settlement. En route the three brothers scarcely stopped to rest. When
they arrived, Temüjin alone remained behind, while Qasar and Belgütei reloaded their horses with bags of food and set off promptly
for Jamugha's base.

Jamugha was a descendant of a brother of Qabul, the first of the
Mongol khans, and thus he belonged to the Borjigin people. He was
about five years older than Temüjin, who knew him by sight. Although he was only five or six years old at the time, Temüjin had
played with Jamugha when the latter came with his father to pay a
call on Yisügei's camp. The image remained in Temüjin's head even
now of this roly-poly, friendly boy who took quickly to strangers.
Even men much older than he found him stunningly precocious, and
the words that came from his mouth startled the adults around him.

From that time forward, Jamugha's family split off from the
Tayichi'ud lineage, to whom they were related by blood, and from
Temüjin's Borjigin lineage. With their own independent camp, they
called themselves the Jadarans. Jamugha expanded their camp re-
markably, so that its importance outstripped that of all other Mongol
lineages, far surpassing the Tayichi'uds. Temüjin had acquired this
information much earlier. Jamugha had sworn an oath of friendship
with To'oril Khan and assumed the status of a younger brother to
him.

On the morning of the fifth day, Qasar and Belgütei, the envoys
to Jamugha, were exhausted to the point that they could barely
move. They left their horses before Temüjin's tent and went in to
relate to him their meeting with Jamugha.

"Jamugha said that he had heard that Temüjin was a victim of
a Tayichi'ud attack, and it pained him deeply. At To'oril Khan's
encouragement, he is now mustering an army, he says, whose sole
gratification it will be to work tirelessly for Temüjin. He said that
they shall presently storm the upper reaches of the Kilgho River,
make rafts out of the green grasses, enter the plateau where the
Merkids are camped, and demolish the tents. And, he said, they will
take the women and children captive and kill all the Merkid men
until the lineage has disappeared."

Qasar made this report while panting from exhaustion. Belgütei then continued in his stead:

"Jamugha said: 'As we set off for war, I shall pour mare's milk on the earth. I shall beat my drum covered with the skin of a black ox. I shall wear stiff clothing and ride my black horse. I shall carry my metal spear and notch a peach-bark arrow in my bow. I shall be waiting for To'oril Khan's troops in the evening ten days hence at Botoghan Bo'orji. Even if there is a mighty blizzard, do not be late for this meeting! Even if the earth should rumble, do not be late! My blood brother, To'oril Khan!'"

Jamugha's words as conveyed by Qasar and Belgütei were immediately passed along to Bo'orchu and from there to To'oril Khan's base in the Black Forest.

Everything was moving along far more favorably than Temüjin had ever imagined. That 40,000 troops were being called up on Temüjin's behalf seemed almost dreamlike. As Temüjin's two arms, two forces were with each passing hour spreading over a corner of the plateau, aimed at the Merkid camp located near the confluence of the Orkhon and Selengge rivers.

Compared to the forces of To'oril Khan and Jamugha, Temüjin's far inferior band of some 30 men made its way to the designated site on the agreed-upon day. The 20,000-man army under Jamugha had already arrived, while To'oril Khan's 20,000-man army came three days late, despite his own firm resolve.

Although it had been fifteen or more years since Temüjin had last seen Jamugha, the latter had lost nothing of the image he conveyed in their childhood. Unlike To'oril Khan, he always had a gentle smile on his face. His plump torso gave the impression of an energetic man about to enter middle age who, to be sure, was a little too heavy. His call to battle, delivered in a high-pitched voice that Temüjin had learned of from Qasar and Belgütei, seemed to have emerged from the mouth of an affable man.

The invasion began the following morning. With rafts made from the green grasses, the army of 40,000 crossed the Orkhon River, formed ranks, and marched forward like floodwaters onto the grasslands where the Merkids had their sphere of influence. One by one they swallowed up the small Merkid settlements.

The Merkids mobilized 10,000 men and pitched camp around their yurts. The decisive battle, though, was over in just a day. Temüjin led several hundred men entrusted to his leadership by To'oril Khan, launching an assault on the Merkids, who were thrown into disarray along the fighting front and sought refuge in their own settlements. Having given up their will to resist, the majority of Merkid forces quietly tried to disappear into their settlements. Temüjin sought out their tents one by one.

In no time at all he located Börte and old Qo'aqchin. They had sought shelter in the corner of a yurt, not knowing that the invasion that had come upon them was Temüjin's strategy for their recovery. When she saw Temüjin enter their yurt, Börte let out a quiet scream of surprise.

Temüjin said not a word to Börte. Entrusting her to his brother Qasar, he quickly returned to the camp on the grasslands where To'oril Khan and Jamugha were. Temüjin thanked his two benefactors profusely for their cooperation.

To'oril Khan and Jamugha then stationed their respective troops at sites about a mile away, but neither of them was especially anxious to depart. This action on the part of these two men struck Temüjin as altogether different from the image they had conveyed before the fighting. They seemed to him to be checking each other in some way.

During this time, a great massacre of the Merkids was taking place. Whether old or very young, all men faced the same fate of being put to death. Almost every day, a line of Merkid men being transported to the execution ground at the dry riverbed traversed the grasslands. The women were assembled on level ground that appeared to be exactly midway between the camps of To'oril Khan and Jamugha. All of their household effects were piled up like a mountain near the same spot.

Temüjin and his small number of subordinates pitched three tents near the settlement from which the Merkids had been emptied and

made their camp there. The stench of dead bodies was everywhere
and flowed into Temüjin's camp day and night.

One day Temüjin received a message from To'oril Khan to come
and take his portion of the divided women and booty. He had not
had the rights to a full share and did not want it. Temüjin thus went
to To'oril Khan's tent and explained himself, but the old Kereyid
chief would not take no for an answer. Jamugha was in agreement
with him on this point. Although it was they who had mobilized the
armies, Temüjin had participated in the fighting, and he had thus
earned the right to share in the spoils, they claimed. Ultimately, Temüjin would not accede to their position and adamantly refused to
receive a share.

Numerous articles of plunder and several thousand women were
divided in the presence of the many troops, with one group going
to To'oril Khan's camp and the other to Jamugha's. Flocks of sheep
and herds of horses covering the grasslands only a few hundred
yards away were similarly apportioned. There were, though, some
things that could not be dealt with: the grasslands, fields, mountains,
and valleys. These were far from the Kereyid camp and from Jamugha's camp. The plateau was closest to Temüjin's small settlement.

If To'oril Khan and Jamugha were to withdraw, Temüjin thought,
he could make this expansive piece of land his own. Of course, even
if he did own it, right now there was nothing he could do with it,
but if the number of those under his command were to increase, he
would surely be able to arrange them in such a way that they served
at innumerable points over the great Mongolian plateau.

Temüjin made Bo'orchu the chief of half of his roughly thirty
subordinates and sent them back to the settlement that was still
being protected solely by the womenfolk. Henceforth, the rest were
permitted to pitch camp in the environs of the now empty Merkid
camp. Although Qasar and Belgütei soon wished to return to their
settlement, Temüjin had no such desire. Until the armies of To'oril
Khan and Jamugha departed, it was not proper form for him to do
so, and there was as well one thing on his mind that Temüjin had
not decided.

What was he to do with Börte? When he had located her, he had merely exchanged glances with Börte. Every day the image of her had floated into Temüjin's mind, though the figure that he saw now was somewhat different from the Börte that had appeared in his mind's eye back at the camp in the foothills of Mount Burqan. She was wearing light green clothing, and her brownish hair and white skin glistened as before, but one spot on her body was different. Her skirt had unusually expanded. It was the night of the great massacre when the Merkid settlement had fallen, but Temüjin had certainly not observed incorrectly. Without a doubt, Börte had become pregnant.

Although he had entrusted Börte to Qasar, Temüjin did not later ask what had happened with her. Qasar had accepted his elder brother's wife into his care, but he made no mention of her whatsoever. This only proved to Temüjin further that he had not erred.

One day Temüjin called for Chimbai to come into his tent. In the instant he looked at Chimbai's face, his mind was settled. He now felt that he had no choice but to ask Chimbai his opinion, and then the matter would be solved probably in accordance with his reply. This was not something that Börte sought for herself.

"Tell Qasar to bring Börte here," Temüjin told Chimbai. Chimbai left immediately, and soon Qasar entered his tent. With a stiff look, Qasar merely said:

"Börte's in a tent two down from here."

Sensing something strange in Qasar's words, Temüjin just left his tent and walked over to the one she was in. Rays of light came down at an angle from the window. Börte was lying in bed. Temüjin then suddenly saw the figure of a baby at her side. Peeping in, he saw old Qo'aqchin stooping forward toward her.

Temüjin approached the bed. Börte appeared weak as she looked up at him. He remained silent as she pointed to the infant with her eyes. A faint smile floated onto her delicate face, and she said something to Temüjin:

"Give him a name, please." These were indeed the words he heard.

"You want me to give him a name?" he said.

"He's your child," she now said with unexpected clarity in her tone of voice.

"I don't know if he's my child or not," said Temüjin, spurning her, to which she replied:

"Where is there any proof that he is not your son?"

She spoke with a firm desperation. For a moment while he himself was unaware of it, Temüjin walked around the inside of the tent. He simply could not sit still just now. There were so many things he had to think over.

"There's no proof whatsoever that he's not your son, is there? I don't know of it, and you don't know of it." Börte's voice entered Temüjin's ears, but he did not accept it. There was no room left in his mind.

Unable to control the confused look on his face, Temüjin stood still. Then, in a slightly dry voice, he said: "Jochi."

"Jochi?" Börte replied with a question. The word *jochi* had the meaning "guest." This was the name that his pained, confused mind selected for the baby Börte had given birth to, a child whose father remained unknown, just as had been true in his own case.

That Temüjin had acceded to her request and given the child she had borne a name meant in effect that he had forgiven her everything. Had he not done so, he would certainly not have gone to the trouble of assigning a name to a child who might have been the son of another lineage. He decided that he would treat this infant his wife, Börte, had delivered as a guest in his home.

For a long time, Temüjin stared at the face of the infant lying beside Börte in bed. Just as he tormented himself over whether or not Mongol blood flowed in his own veins, this child would in future bear such doubts. And just as he would have to prove that there was Mongol blood in his body by becoming a wolf, so too would Jochi have to become a wolf and bear up under the destiny toward which he was necessarily headed.

"I shall be a wolf, and you too are to become a wolf!" said Temüjin in his heart. These were the first words Temüjin offered to his eldest son Jochi. As words of a father to his son in this context, they were said with an unsurpassable, profound love.

Börte remained silent, in no way indicating her will with respect to the name Jochi that Temüjin had given the baby. Was she satisfied? Did she disapprove? From the expression on her face, there was no way to tell what was in her heart of hearts. Eventually, she quietly turned her face toward Temüjin. Although she was still quite weak, her face had a brightness unusual for a woman just out of childbirth. But from the eyes on her bright face, tears were welling up and flowing onto her cheeks in two clear lines.

Temüjin left the baby's side and looked down on the face of the beautiful one for whom he had so long been searching.

"I have sent a messenger to the Unggirads," he said to his wife, for the first time speaking in gentle words. "Your father, Dei Sechen, and your mother, Chotan, were both very happy."

Temüjin's view of women generally at this time was fixed as a stationary concept and was not to change throughout his life. Although he could recognize a woman's beauty, love, and fidelity, he could not believe that such things were constant. Whatever had any value would always be unstable to the extent that women possessed it. And neither his wife, Börte, nor his mother, Ö'elün, was an exception to this rule. There was always the defect that she could give birth to "a guest." If his wife or, for that matter, his mother could give birth to a wolf with Mongol blood, then she could just as easily give birth to a Merkid, a Tatar, or a Kereyid. She was a container that bore a child who strangely and generously accepted the blood of any ethnic group at all. How was it that the wife who loved him and whom he loved could give birth to a child with enemy blood?

Although Temüjin trusted the men under his command for their loyalty, their courage, and their sacrifice, he could not trust women in the same way. There was no basis on which to establish such trust. Once a woman had something, only while she possessed it were her beauty, her love, and her fidelity her own. The men he commanded would never change, even if conquered by and forced to submit to another lineage, but aside from when a man embraced a woman in bed, she was troublesome because he could never consider her his own.

Temüjin wanted to have Börte as his wife forever. To that end he realized he would have to be so strong that no one would ever be able to take her from him.

"From now on, I shall never be more than a moment away from you," he said. "And you shall always remain perfectly faithful."

He did not say that he loved her or that he had always loved her. Such words were powerless and of no value at all. Temüjin merely announced that he possessed her, though this was a confession on his part of his love for her.

3

Overlordship on the Mongolian Plateau

TO'ORIL KHAN AND JAMUGHA kept their troops stationed at their campsites for about one month longer, with no apparent desire to withdraw. Although they had divided up all the women and possessions equally and nothing of pressing urgency remained to be accomplished, there were reasons for avoiding an earlier pullout. Temüjin was from the start suspicious of the attitudes of these two armed forces, but on reflection felt the situation was only natural for people engaged in battle. Had one side departed earlier and borne malicious feelings toward those who remained, there was the strong possibility that they would be attacked from the rear. Thus, both sides wished to avoid taking a dangerous position.

Temüjin learned many an important lesson from these two leaders. To'oril Khan and Jamugha had sworn a blood-brother (*anda*) allegiance in both life and death, but their actions revealed that neither trusted the other in the least. One further thing that caught Temüjin's attention was the fact that To'oril Khan's decision to dispatch troops was in no way motivated by his concern to come to the aid of Yisügei's eldest son and help him succeed. When Temüjin requested arms to be able to launch an attack on the Merkids, To'oril Khan's decision to send his own forces provided a perfect excuse for him to dispatch troops against the Merkids. He had undoubtedly been looking for an opportunity to wipe them out, but just had not yet found a pretext that conformed to the appropriate principles of duty. The wrongful act committed by the Merkids in raiding the tent of the weak Temüjin and seizing Börte could not go unpunished, and returning his wife to the son of Yisügei would certainly not be criticized by anyone. When To'oril Khan sent his troops off, it also had the effect of inciting Jamugha to increase the troops' strength, but even more important was the fact that by adding Jamugha, who belonged to the same Borjigin lineage as Temüjin, he was further legitimizing his own actions. The way To'oril Khan proposed the plan was by no means disadvantageous to Jamugha, and the latter was sufficiently attracted to readily accept. Temüjin only got his wife, Börte, back, but To'oril Khan and Jamugha split the enormous wealth of an entire lineage, each carrying off half.

In this instance, Temüjin thought it advisable to subordinate his own camp to either To'oril Khan's or Jamugha's. There was, indeed, no better way to make his own small settlement rapidly grow larger. Temüjin chose Jamugha. They were both of Borjigin stock, and he reasoned that to stave off further Tayichi'ud depredations, it would be better to rely on Jamugha's protection. In addition, many of those from his father Yisügei's day had fallen under Tayichi'ud control and later thrown in their lot with Jamugha's settlement; in this they shared a certain disposition as well.

Standing between To'oril Khan and Jamugha, Temüjin casually proposed that on the same day both withdraw and move off in opposite directions. Together with Jamugha, Temüjin retreated toward the Qorqonaq Valley of the Onon River, while To'oril Khan headed toward his own encampment in the Black Forest by the shores of the Tula River with Mount Burqan behind him. To'oril Khan mobilized his troops in a rather leisurely manner, while continuing to hunt.

Temüjin and Börte returned to their own settlement halfway up Mount Burqan near the source of the Onon and Kherlen rivers. However, their own numbers had increased by two small people. One was Jochi, and the other was an adorable five-year-old child they had found in the Merkid village wearing a sable hat and footwear made of the skin of doe's feet. His name was Kuchu. Temüjin brought him to his mother, Ö'elün's, tent as a present. Ö'elün's five children were now grown, her youngest, Temülün, having already reached age seventeen, and she was thus exceedingly pleased with this gift of a youngster. All the men of Kuchu's people had now been put to death, making this child alone the sole repository of pure Merkid blood, a small treasure of sorts.

Temüjin soon moved his encampment from the Mount Burqan area to a site in the Qorqonaq Valley neighboring Jamugha's camp. The following day Temüjin swore an anda oath of brotherhood with Jamugha. The ceremony was carried out in an open area above the Qorqonaq Escarpment, with trees on one side. Temüjin placed on Jamugha a golden belt he had seized from an enemy commander in the fighting with the Merkids, and he similarly placed Jamugha on a black-maned horse he had taken in plunder. For his part Jamugha presented Temüjin with a golden belt looted from a Merkid officer and placed him on a white horse that looked like a horned lamb. They both then called out to each other loudly: "Anda!" The banquet that brought the villagers together was begun at the sound of the two men's voices, and it lasted throughout the night. Instruments were played, people sang, and young Merkid girls whose husbands, fathers, and brothers had all been executed danced before the conquerors.

Temüjin took a seat next to Jamugha at the banquet, although he didn't believe that the oath sworn between the two men was of any value whatsoever. Jamugha would use it as long as it could be used, and when circumstances took a turn for the worse, he would discard it like an old hat. Although he had seen Jamugha's kindly face with its unflappable smile during the daytime, it struck Temüjin as altogether different when half of it was bathed in the light of the moon. Something cruelly bitter was beginning to dawn on Temüjin, making even him shudder.

There were many benefits, though, for Temüjin in having forged this anda bond with Jamugha and living in such close proximity. Wool was more easily sold off, and he could increase his stock of horses and sheep as he wished, should he desire to do so. One other advantage that he had not foreseen was the fact that his group of men and women of Borjigin ancestry lived far from the Tayichi'uds, so gradually many more came to join them. The number of yurts seemed to grow daily, with sometimes as many as ten tents joining the settlement at once. Such a phenomenon, needless to say, incurred the enmity of the Tayichi'uds, but Jamugha's presence as Temüjin's anda kept them at bay. Jamugha effectively restrained the Tayichi'ud leader Targhutai from being able to intervene behind the scenes.

Even within Jamugha's camp, there were many who were by inclination more sympathetic to Temüjin. The means by which Jamugha and Temüjin managed their neighboring settlements were altogether different. While Jamugha divided all profit fairly, Temüjin divided his people into various rankings for allocating goods. Each received advantages in proportion to the labor they exerted, and accordingly those who worked hard received a larger quota. While lazy elements in Jamugha's settlement benefited, exceptional young men lost out. For this reason, the numbers of those who pondered moving over to Temüjin's settlement grew steadily.

This was certainly known to Jamugha. When a year and a half had passed since the two men had sworn their anda oath, Temüjin unexpectedly received an invitation from Jamugha to join a hunt. Had he known that this was not hunting season, he might have been concerned, and Temüjin had sensed several days earlier that something unusual was going on in Jamugha's camp.

Temüjin immediately consulted with Qasar, Belgütei, Bo'orchu, and Jelme. All four of them had the same thought, that it would be unwise to accept this invitation, but their views on what had been happening earlier differed widely: "Let's wait for Jamugha to make a move." "If he's misunderstood something, let's dispel it." These and other views were all voiced.

Temüjin invited Ö'elün and Börte in and asked their opinions as well. When they had heard his entire explanation, before Ö'elün so much as opened her mouth, Börte abruptly spoke out, and her tone was sharp:

"We need to move the whole settlement tonight. It may be too late tomorrow morning."

Temüjin remained silent, as did the others. It was not going to be easy to speedily dismantle the settlement in an orderly fashion and abandon the expansive pasturelands that they had gone to such pains to manage. Then Börte looked Temüjin squarely in the face and said:

"I am pregnant."

This was the first Temüjin knew of it.

"I am pregnant," she repeated. "Would you like to name our second child Jochi too?" With Börte's words, Temüjin made up his mind.

Qasar, Belgütei, Bo'orchu, and Jelme all rushed out of Temüjin's tent. In short order the nearly one hundred yurts comprising their settlement were in a state of utter confusion. One by one they finished folding up all the tents, and small groups left one after the next from the Qorqonaq Valley, traveling parallel to the river and headed north. There were flocks of sheep and horses between the tents and the procession was in considerable disarray, but the whole party nonetheless extended in a long, thin line like a string of thread pulled away from the site of the settlement. When the thread from the spool completely ran out, a hundred or more men forming an armed guard mounted their horses and brought up the rear.

The movement continued without stop. When they came upon a settlement en route, the brothers Chimbai and Chila'un rode their horses into the settlement and announced in a loud voice that Temüjin's camp was moving. Their intent was to invite anyone who wished to do so to join them.

When they passed a camp of the Besüd people of the Tayichi'uds, Temüjin finally allowed his men and women a short rest. They entered the Besüd settlement, and all the Taiyichi'uds scattered, leaving every tent vacant. Temüjin saw one young child sitting on the ground in front of a tent.

"What's your name?" he asked.

"Kököchü," the child replied. Although he asked again several times, the word that came back each time was "Kököchü."

"Are you all alone?"

"I'm in charge while everyone's away," he answered.

Temüjin lifted the child who had assumed such a task for several dozen tents in his arms and passed him to Qasar. He was to be given to Ö'elün.

Just as they were leaving this settlement, the light of dawn began to fill the air. With night about to come to an end, three young brothers of the Jalayir lineage joined the tail end of their procession. They took their first respite on the incline of the plateau. Momentarily thereafter, groups of people from small settlements scattered about the area came one after the next to join Temüjin's camp. Some led their horses while others rode in on horseback in small groups. There were parties of women and of the old as well. The great majority of them were distant relations of Yisügei, men and women who had been subordinated to the Tayichi'uds.

The company moved on and pitched camp that evening by the shore of a small lake. Roughly three hundred new people had now joined them. Upon Bo'orchu's investigation, this included people from all manner of different family lines in the region. We have already noted the Jalayirs, but in addition to Mönggedü Kiyan, there were as well men and women from the Targhud, the Barulas, the Mangghud, the Arulad, the Besüd, the Suldus, the Qongqotan, the Negüdei, the Olqunu'ud, the Ikires, the Noyakin, the Oronar, and the Ba'arin lineages.

Leading his suddenly swelling number of followers, Temüjin proceeded the next day toward the Kimurgha Stream. And that day too his party grew in size as they remained on the move. Ögelen Cherbi, the younger brother of Bo'orchu, left the Arulads to join them, and Jelme's two younger brothers, Cha'urqan and Sübe'etei, both left the Uriangqans to link up with Temüjin.

They reached the banks of the Kimurgha Stream that afternoon, and there settled down for a time by making camp at a divide in the terrain where small hills undulated like waves. It was additionally a well-placed site to defend against attack from pursuing troops sent by Jamugha, and it was not at all bad land for pasturage.

From the time they stopped moving until evening, people who had separated from Jamugha and come toward them could be spotted here and there on the hilltops, disappeared in the valleys between hills, and gradually became visible again as they approached camp. One of those who had abandoned Jamugha was a man about sixty years of age by the name of Qorchi of the Ba'arins. He was a miserable-looking old man and was accompanied by people comprising some twenty tents in all.

When Qorchi arrived at Temüjin's camp, he said:

"I've never been apart from Jamugha, and I had no particular reason for it now. Jamugha's always been very good to me. But a divine oracle said Temüjin was going to become king of the entire Mongolian plateau and that I should go to his base. That's why I've come here." This was his way of announcing his arrival. Although he did not appear to be the sort of good-for-nothing person one would want to go out of one's way to welcome, Temüjin nonetheless listened to Qorchi's words with a sense of the man's deep feeling. Only one man had come in the belief that he, Temüjin, was to become sovereign of the Mongolian plateau. The other newcomers to Temüjin's camp had all assembled there so as to make their lives better, to bring some small happiness to their families. Qorchi was different, for he had come in response to a heavenly oracle.

Temüjin stared fixedly at the plentiful wrinkles on Qorchi's face, lit up by the light of the setting sun, as he stood before him. After a while, he responded:

"If such a day does come when I do, in fact, become king of the Mongolian plateau, at that time I shall make you chief of 10,000 households."

Temüjin realized then that he must never forget the crimson redness of that day's setting sun, when he had escaped from the jaws of death at the hands of Jamugha and sought to restore order at his new encampment with its abruptly swollen numbers. And he must never forget as well the face of Qorchi, bathed in the evening's red glow, who had told of the oracle.

Then Qorchi said with apparent disapproval:

"What joy would I get out of becoming chief of 10,000 households? What I'd like, once I've become a chief of 10,000 households, is to be able to freely choose women to my taste from among the beautiful women and girls of the state. Thirty of them would do fine. I'd like to have 30 beautiful women of my own."

"It shall be so," replied Temüjin to this rather lecherous oracle.

Temüjin was very busy for the next few days. The number of people in the settlement had now climbed to over 3,000, and ordinary affairs could no longer be handled in the simple manner that they had been heretofore. Temüjin made Bo'orchu and Jelme leaders of the settlement, and gave them the authority to control and issue orders in all matters. Bo'orchu and Jelme acquitted themselves well in everything. While Bo'orchu skillfully disposed of all matters on the surface, Jelme followed up, straightened things out, and shored up whatever was lacking.

They made camp at this site for roughly one month, and during that time Temüjin brought a number of settlements under his umbrella. A camp of the Keniges lineage came to join them, as did camps of Jadarans, Saqayids, and Yürkins. Temüjin was now able to assemble the more important figures among his close relatives together with their camps. This included: Temüjin's uncle Daritai Odchigin, his cousin Qochar, his elder cousins Seche Beki and Taichu who were brothers, Altan (son of Qutula Khan), and Altan's younger cousin Yeke Cheren.

When he learned that Jamugha had sent no troops after him in pursuit, Temüjin moved his encampment from the banks of the Kimurgha Stream to the northern shore of a starfish-shaped lake by the Sengkür Stream that ran through Mount Gürelgü. The land here was sufficiently spacious for such a large settlement to pitch camp, and the pastureland, which had thus far remained untouched by flocks of sheep, spread out as far as the eye could see.

Upon the pitching of this new encampment, Temüjin was encouraged by his family members to proclaim himself *khan* of the Mongolian people. The year was 1189 according to the Western calendar, and he was twenty-seven years of age. Until then the Mongolian khan had been a Tayichi'ud by the name of Targhutai, but he had lost most of his former followers and had perforce naturally relinquished the position. The Tayichi'uds, the Jadarans of Jamugha who was now an enemy, and a few other lineages would not recognize Temüjin as khan, but that was no different from any other time in the past.

In the era of the first khan, Qabul, as well as in the eras of Hambaghai Khan and Qutula Khan, even when Temüjin's father Yisügei was alive, the Mongols were never a single, unified group. Thus, even if Temüjin were to take the position of khan, a number of camps within the larger Mongolian grouping would certainly fight against this. As far as Temüjin was concerned, though, it was an enormous leap to accede to this station. At the same time, it promised days of fierce struggle with Targhutai of the Tayichi'uds and Jamugha of the Jadarans.

On the day Temüjin became khan, Qorchi came to him and said:

"That divine oracle I told you of may actually come to pass. Now you've become the Mongol khan. The day will certainly come when you'll unify the Mongol peoples, subdue the many other peoples on the Mongolian plateau, and rule as king. And when that day comes, don't renege on your promise to me."

In the spirit of a kind of advance payment of a certain percentage of the reward he would earn on that day, Temüjin said:

"Heavenly oracle! You are henceforth to be separated from military, pasturing, and battle affairs. You are to help Ö'elün and advise her in the rearing and education of her young sons, Küchü and Kököchü."

Temüjin thus gave Qorchi the nominal title of being in charge of the education of these two adopted boys and released the old diviner from all other matters. It was the first official proclamation by which Temüjin exercised his authority as khan.

Temüjin had to put together a control structure completely different from that which earlier generations of khans had built in their settlements. In normal times, the nomadic people grazed and cared for their herds, but in times of emergency they had to be able to quickly transform themselves into a small number of powerful bands.

Temüjin proceeded to organize units of archers and swordsmen, to prepare official messages, and to appoint the appropriate men to such bureaucratic posts as those in charge of military horses, those in charge of vehicles, those charged with provisioning, those who were to rear the horses, and those who tended the sheep. To the two highest positions directly beneath himself in the camp, he named his first vassals Bo'orchu and Jelme, and each of their younger brothers was named to an important post as well.

Temüjin's encampment was now much larger than it had been in the days of his father, Yisügei. He was gradually acquiring strength needed to defeat the Tayichi'uds and the Tatars. His younger brothers—Qasar, Belgütei, Qachi'un, and Temüge—each had their own wives and their own independent yurts. His younger sister Temülün had also married a young man, and they had built a yurt of their own. Being the siblings of Temüjin, they all enjoyed special privileges. Ö'elün, a women now nearing fifty years of age, put her heart and soul into raising the foundlings Küchü and Kököchü. Although he was assigned to an advisory post by her side, Qorchi's duties were slightly altered by Ö'elün.

"I want to have children hereafter with far different blood," she told Qorchi. "No matter how long it takes, make an effort to find clever abandoned children from other lineages."

Although unhappy that his own ideas were not being implemented in the rearing of Küchü and Kököchü, Qorchi became deeply involved in the strange task given him by Ö'elün. Virtually every day, Qorchi remained alone in an empty tent, and while watching the clouds flow by, he kept an eye out for battles fought with other lineages providing an opportunity to gather up some new orphans.

Temüjin was now living with his wife, Börte, his eldest son, Jochi, and his second son born after his having become khan, Cha'adai—a family of four—in addition to several servants. He treated his sons, Jochi and Cha'adai, exactly the same. Just as his own father, Yisügei, had never discriminated for or against him in any way, so he too strictly admonished himself to do so, though he did on occasion find himself staring coldly at Jochi. Even he recognized that the glint in his eye when looking at Jochi was somewhat different from when he looked at Cha'adai.

Börte was aware of these instances as well. On such an occasion, she would turn to Jochi and then, speaking in such a way that Temüjin would be sure to hear, would say:

"Jochi, when you grow up, you'll have to take charge of the fiercest post in battle. You'll have to do what everyone else isn't able to. You'll have to accomplish what even your grandfather, Yisügei, and father, Temüjin, could not. You were born for that purpose. The divine heaven of Mongolia has bestowed you upon the Mongol people."

The blood drained from Börte's face when she said these words, and only the large eyes that constituted her distinctive beauty sparkled brilliantly. What she had said bore precisely the same meaning as those first words spoken by Temüjin to Jochi back in the Merkid settlement: "You are to become a wolf! I too shall become a wolf."

As always, Temüjin took this silent criticism from Börte's eyes and left the scene. "You are to become a wolf! I too shall become a wolf." Temüjin had repeated these words any number of times to himself. Leaving aside the issue of Jochi, Temüjin was still fully aware that his own issue remained unresolved. Most important of all, though, *he* had to become a wolf first. A wolf had limitless ambitions. If everything were to settle down once they attacked the Tayichi'uds, then a number of things would have to be done first.

Until Cha'adai was born, Temüjin slept in the same bed with Börte and Jochi, but after Cha'adai came into the world, Börte slept on a separate bedstead with him, while Temüjin slept with Jochi. Temüjin and Jochi slept facing each other as father and son with exchanging a word, like a father wolf and his cub. Jochi grew to be as intensely taciturn as his father had been as a youngster.

When Temüjin became khan, he sent Belgütei to To'oril Khan of the Kereyids to announce his accession to the position of khan of the Mongols. To'oril Khan then had Belgütei convey his response to Temüjin:

"My anda, my bold son, your becoming khan is an event to be warmly welcomed for the Mongolian people. The Mongols must have a great khan. Furthermore, you must not break your bond with my Kereyid people. Throughout our lives our pact must never come undone. Were this to come to pass, it would be comparable to the death of either a father or a son."

Temüjin similarly sent a messenger to Jamugha. This task fell to Qasar. For his part, Jamugha mentioned the names of Altan and Qochar, who had left his camp:

"Altan and Qochar! You two have estranged me from my anda Temüjin with whom I had gotten along as well as the light of spring. Why did you divide us? You stabbed Temüjin in the waist and me in the ribs. You two are traitors with the hearts of wild beasts! But I shall now cease listing your crimes. It is my fervent prayer that you two have a good heart for and be a friend to anda Temüjin."

These words, pregnant with all manner of intrigue, bore the distinct mark of Jamugha.

In less than no time, four years had passed since Temüjin's accession to khan of the Mongolian people. During those four years, he fully fortified his position as the autocrat of his settlement. In the leisure time from work in the pasturelands, Temüjin saw to it that every man in the settlement had training for battle. There had been a few changes on the Mongolian plateau over these years. All of the lineages and settlements had been assimilated into one of four camps: To'oril Khan, Jamugha, Temüjin, or the Tatars.

Out of the blue, Jamugha led a force of 13 lineages comprising 30,000 troops over Mount Ala'u'ud and Mount Turgha'ud to attack the camp of Temüjin. News of the approaching army reached Temüjin one morning in early autumn, brought by two young messengers, Mölge Tatagh and Boroldai of the Ikires.

Temüjin immediately issued marching orders to everyone in his encampment, and that night he left camp in command of over 10,000 troops heading for the open country at Dalan Baljud. The company continued to increase in number, and when they arrived in the evening of the second day at the open field that he expected to be the site of battle, a force of 30,000 deployed there. Thirty thousand faced 30,000 in battle.

The fighting began early the following morning. Temüjin initially thought that the struggle was lost. The enemy started the fighting, and as expected, each company took up defensive positions. Temüjin found it the same in numerous subsequent battles: his men were strong in counterattacking, weak in assuming the defensive. Bo'orchu, Jelme, Qasar, and Belgütei, all generals under Temüjin's command, displayed strength so fierce on the battlefield that it was scarcely believable, but when it came to waiting for the opportune moment and ambushing the enemy forces, their capacities dropped off precipitously.

At first observation, then, the great battle scene before Temüjin seemed calamitous. Just before it began, he sensed a certain lack of energy in his own camp as a whole. If an army of 30,000 wolves attacked, it could scale any mountain and descend through any valley, but their look as they awaited and deployed for the start of the fighting had a far from superb expression, as if every single wolf in the pack was chained up in some way. Temüjin himself was no different.

The fighting began lethargically, and in short order the hoofs of Jamugha's cavalry came trampling down on all positions. A moment later, Temüjin issued an order to his entire army for a general retreat, and messengers rode rapidly in all directions over the open fields conveying this order.

Temüjin led the 10,000 men directly under his command along the Onon River to a ravine where the topography was extremely difficult to maneuver. Being routed, the entire company now moved with a certain astuteness, as if having recovered its energy. The defeat oddly registered no actual sensation in Temüjin. The same appeared to be the case for Bo'orchu, Jelme, Qasar, and Belgütei.

After returning to his own yurt, Temüjin learned that at the Chinos settlement Jamugha had boiled their kinsmen in seventy kettles, cut off the head of their chief, attached it to a horse's tail, and dragged it away with him.

Although Temüjin had lost several hundred men in the fighting, this was relatively minor for a battle of such magnitude. Several days after the defeat, Temüjin welcomed to his camp a number of people from Jamugha's settlement who had abandoned Jamugha's base for his own. Several of them moved with their entire camps, and they all berated Jamugha's savagery.

Münglig along with seven children was among those who had left Jamugha's camp and joined them. At the time of Yisügei's death, Münglig had ridden out to fetch Temüjin at the Unggirad village. He then turned him over to Ö'elün's care and rode off to the Tayichi'uds. All those who returned to their former service were without exception traitors who had once forsaken Temüjin and his family, but the case of Münglig was slightly different for Temüjin. Insofar as he had trusted him and taken him to be an ally, the blow at the time of his betrayal was enormous.

When he stood facing Münglig, Temüjin compelled himself to stifle all emotion. Looking into Temüjin's face, Münglig anticipated that words berating him would emerge from Temüjin's mouth, but the latter said not a grumbling word to this "traitor." On the contrary, Temüjin offered words of happiness at Münglig's health and compassionately received his seven children whom he brought with him. It was not that Temüjin had warm feelings for Münglig, but Münglig's father, old man Charaqa, had once, when their settlement had withdrawn and left only Ö'elün's yurt, tried to protect the poor mother and her children until the very end, when he died at the hand of the Tayichi'uds.

Entirely out of gratitude to Charaqa, Temüjin pledged to cherish Münglig and his seven children. Calling on Qasar and Belgütei, he ordered them: "Treat the son and grandchildren of Charaqa warmly."

Just as Temüjin had no genuine sense of defeat in battle, Jamugha bore no feeling of victory. Jamugha had routed Temüjin's armies, but he hadn't marched his men any farther thereafter. As before, the Mongolian plateau remained divided among four powers: To'oril Khan, Jamugha, Temüjin, and the Tatars. On the surface nothing had changed, and it seemed as though nothing had been ruptured in the balance among them.

In the three years following his confrontation with Jamugha on the battlefield, Temüjin devoted himself largely to the unification of his camp. All the various Mongol lineages had gathered there, and there was no end to the confusing problems that ensued. What Temüjin worried most about was the fact that his cousins Seche Beki and Taichu opposed him on every issue that came up. They had pitched their own independent tent for the Yürkins and had not accepted Temüjin as their chief, and on occasion they had entertained the ambitious notion of actually replacing Temüjin. Seche Beki and Taichu were not the only defiant elements. His cousin Qochar, his uncle Daritai Odchigin, and Altan (son of Qutula Khan), among others, maintained private agendas, using every opportunity to extend their respective influences.

In his own camp, Temüjin never trusted this group of his "relatives." It was at their prodding that he had been able to assume the position of khan, and in that connection he continued to countenance them, but he knew full well that a time was coming when he would perforce have to expel them. That event, though, was still off in the distant future. For now he had to plan for peace and harmony in his camp and avoid any discord as best he could. They all constituted significant fighting forces that would need to be invested in combat against other lineages. They might have to fight Jamugha at some point, and they might have to fight To'oril Khan.

Four years having passed since the battle against Jamugha, Temüjin was now in the first month of the year in which he turned thirty-five. The young men who had long shared hardships with him had all entered adulthood. His younger brothers Qasar and Belgütei were thirty-three, while his other brothers Qachi'un and Temüge were each about thirty—all in the prime of manhood. Bo'orchu, to whom Temüjin had entrusted so much as his right-hand man, was the same age as he, thirty-five, while his other "lieutenant," Jelme, was thirty-eight.

At the new year's celebration, Temüjin looked around at his trusted retainers arrayed before his tent, and for the first time in his life he sensed that there was something truly substantial in his camp. They were brimming with strength. No matter whose eyes he looked into, he found a courageous Mongol whom he had been picturing in his mind since youth. It was less that they shared the blood of the blue wolf than that each of them *was* a blue wolf. Bo'orchu, Jelme, Qasar, Belgütei, Qachi'un, and Temüge, as well as the short brothers, big-headed Chimbai and squinting Chila'un, everyone there was a blue wolf. It struck Temüjin that they were now wolves who had set up camp and were about to take the field. Their eyes reflected a light that bespoke a piercing ability to penetrate a thousand miles away and a ferocity that revealed a mighty will to make anything at all their own. Bodies built for attack had been stunningly perfected: lustrous torsos magnificent and rigid, limbs with just enough flesh to ride through snow fields and fierce winds, and full fleecy tails like a blade cutting through the air.

Temüjin looked over at a group of the women. Fifty-five-year-old Ö'elün had fifteen-year-old Küchü, the last remaining child of the Merkids, and fifteen-year-old Kököchü, who had the strange destiny to be born in the Tayichi'ud village and raised in Temüjin's camp, waiting upon her. Temüjin had never seen his mother's face so beaming with pride as it was at this moment. As was always her way of expressing it, Ö'elün said:

"Other than me, who can be the eyes to see in the daytime and ears to hear in the nighttime for the children who have no relatives?" She was raising these children who carried the blood of other races with kindness and courage.

To Ö'elün's side was Temüjin's wife, Börte. Börte was attended by Jochi, who was now ten years of age. Actually, in everyone's estimation, it was more the other way around: she seemed to wait upon him. In her own distinct fashion, Börte had for the past ten years raised the people living in her tent strictly and with an extraordinary ardor which, at times, Temüjin found almost eerie. After Jochi, she had given birth in succession to three children: Cha'adai, Ögedei, and Tolui. In such a formal setting, the other three sons were entrusted to female attendants, while she always took the seat next to Jochi. Both Temüjin and Börte were anxious that Jochi become a wolf; they didn't know if it would in fact come to pass, but this was the main trait that was to distinguish him from ordinary children. He was taciturn to the point that people might think him mute—and he never laughed. He had a keen sense of the sounds of the wind outside their tent and of people and animals passing by and was astoundingly able to recognize them.

Just as the boys seated in a row appeared to Temüjin as wolves, so too did Ö'elün and Börte appear to him at the time as pale does. Not only Ö'elün and Börte, but also the girls seated between them and waiting behind them seemed like a group of pale does looking on as the wolves marched off to battle.

"There'll probably be a battle fought this year," said old Qorchi.

"I think so too," replied Münglig, who was accompanied by his seven intrepid children. Qorchi was past sixty years of age, and Münglig was over fifty. Their seniority always entitled them to seats of honor at such gatherings. If a battle did erupt, the opposition would be Jamugha or To'oril Khan. There was no need for a reason to be concocted for hostilities to commence. When someone had the will to fight, his opponent immediately became the enemy. As a group, most were of the view that Jamugha was more likely to be the opponent should fighting break out.

As these two old-timers would say, it seemed to Temüjin that the group of wolves here assembled should take to the field this year to topple the enemy. Such was his premonition, but he was uncertain who the enemy would be. Jamugha did not seem as though he would launch an assault, nor did To'oril Khan appear to be vigorously moving in his direction. Should it come to pass, it would be a problem for his own mind to fathom, and he had no idea at all where his own mind was moving for even the following day.

Temüjin's premonition became a reality half a year later, at the end of the sixth month of the year. News that an army from the state of Jin had crossed the Great Wall and attacked the Tatars reached him via a merchant from the Unggirads, Börte's people, and Temüjin immediately made the decision himself to attack the Tatars. Although Jin was also an enemy, the Tatars were a foe against whom the Mongols had long borne a grudge. Temüjin had never forgotten his father, Yisügei, saying, "Attack the Tayichi'uds, attack the Tatars!" Although he would follow this command in reverse order, he had to attack when the time for each was ripe. Were he to let this opportunity pass, he might not be able to conquer the Tatars and establish his predominance in the northeastern sector of the plateau for a long time to come. It was the chance of a lifetime.

Temüjin did precisely the same thing he had done ten years earlier when To'oril Khan hastily massacred the Merkids and departed.

Although previously, To'oril Khan played the main role, that part now fell to Temüjin. Just as To'oril Khan had called on Jamugha at that time, now Temüjin had no choice but to invite To'oril Khan to join the fray. This would both double the size of the attacking army and surely provoke criticism by other peoples.

Belgütei and his subordinates went on the mission into the Black Forest by the banks of the Tula River. By the time Belgütei was to return, Temüjin had his entire armed force prepared to move. When Belgütei did return, he reported that To'oril Khan had already left the Black Forest at the head of the entire Kereyid army. Temüjin sensed that such a vulturelike, quick-witted movement to launch an attack and acquire spoils was just to the liking of To'oril Khan.

Temüjin's army of 30,000 marched day and night to the northeast to reach the wilderness of the Mongolian plateau. On the tenth day, they met up with the army of To'oril Khan near the confluence of the Kherlen and Ulja rivers.

There, after the passage of ten years, Temüjin saw To'oril Khan, who was now over sixty years of age.

"My son," said the aged commander, facing Temüjin with the same frigid eyes and brow changed not a whit from before, "if we massacre the Tatars, we will have to kill every single male. We must split the women, possessions, and sheep in half. Any objections? The Tatars are an enemy you Mongols cannot detest enough."

"Agreed," replied Temüjin. Revenge had to be taken on the Tatars. The blood of Mongol ancestors had been spilled by them any number of times. Qutula Khan and his six brothers had lost their lives fighting the Tatars. Hambaghai Khan had been captured by the Tatars and delivered into the hands of the Jin. The latter nailed him to a wooden donkey, flayed him alive, and cut up his flesh into tiny pieces. "You must take revenge for me on this enemy, even if you wear down all ten of your fingernails and then lose all ten fingers." Even now Temüjin remembered this story and could hear the voice of old Bültechü who recounted it to him.

"My anda!" said To'oril Khan. "At sunrise on the third day following the division of the plunder, I shall return home with my army from the occupied area. And you do the same."

"Agreed." When Temüjin replied this time, To'oril Khan for the first time smiled at his sworn friend, who did not know if the other man might be his enemy.

Once they had agreed on the allocation of spoils and when mutually to withdraw, the attack would begin. From the northwest To'oril Khan and from the southwest Temüjin would launch the assault on the Tatars, who were engaged in battle with the Jin army and its superior equipment.

Facing enemies on three fronts, the Tatars were thoroughly annihilated at the end of seven days of mortal combat. Temüjin took a policy of not allowing a single enemy troop to live in battle. The Tatar chief, Me'üjin Se'ültü, was taken prisoner and brought before Temüjin, where they cut the crown of his head in half and he breathed his last. All the men taken captive were executed. The women were bound and assembled at one site, divided into two groups, and marched off respectively by To'oril Khan or Temüjin. When all of the valuable possessions had been stripped from the Tatar settlement nearby, it was burned to the ground.

To'oril Khan and Temüjin received thanks for their cooperation from the commander of the Jin forces, with To'oril Khan being given the title of "prince" and Temüjin the official post of "head of one hundred households." Quietly, Temüjin also accepted the strange and, as far as he was now concerned, substantively valueless title of "pacification commissioner." Although this did not appear entirely the attitude of To'oril Khan, Temüjin's feelings were more complex. From his perspective, the mighty state of Jin on the other side of the Great Wall was also an implacable enemy. Someday, he thought, he would like to return his "pacification commissioner" title to the ruler of the Jin. But at this point, Temüjin kept such thoughts to himself and could not give form to them in any decisive way. He still lacked the luxury of being able to think about what transpired on the other side of the Great Wall.

The withdrawal of troops was carried out as agreed with To'oril Khan. While both Temüjin's forces and those of To'oril Khan had several hundred vehicles loaded with mountains of plunder, there was a certain difference in their respective booty. Among Temüjin's, as among To'oril Khan's, were such items as silver baby carriages, large precious stones, and bedsteads with inlaid shells, but the majority of what they took was war chariots, weapons, and armor. Assembled here were all manner of things, some of course used by the Tatars and some formerly owned by the Jin army. Some things they took from the battlefield, and some they specifically purchased from the Jin.

There was one other odd item of booty. Qorchi, who joined the troops out of a sense of fulfilling a personal mission, got his hands on one infant orphan left in the Tatar encampment. He was wearing a waistcoat made of three-color damask lined with sable and with a gold ring attached as adornment. Although the baby eventually babbled a few words, his face bore signs of refinement revealing what appeared to be high birth. Having been so ordered, Qorchi had been able now for many years to fulfill Ö'elün's desire. This child was presented to Ö'elün, and she gave him the name Shigi Qutuqu. He was to be raised in Ö'elün's tent, so that this orphan of a Tatar black kite would become a Mongol falcon.

Upon his triumphal return to camp, Temüjin learned that a settlement under his control had been attacked in his absence by Seche Beki and Taichu of the Yürkins, several dozen people were stripped of their clothing, and a dozen or more were murdered. Temüjin had issued a mobilization order for the Yürkins in the now-completed battle against the Tatars. The Yürkins had not only failed to respond to it but also had the audacity to perpetrate this outrage while he was away at the front.

Temüjin quickly assembled an army to subjugate the Yürkins. This was a prime opportunity to wipe out Seche Beki, Taichu, and others like them. Their crimes were unmistakable. Without giving his relatives a moment to speak, Temüjin launched a surprise attack on the Yürkins along the Kherlen River, captured the brothers Seche Beki and Taichu, and decapitated them. He then had all the tents of their lineage moved to his own camp.

In the fighting, Qorchi found another orphaned youngster by the name of Boroghul, brought him back to camp, and presented him to Ö'elün.

"The Yürkins are the boldest among Mongols," said Qorchi. "Boroghul is destined to be such a one. By the time Temüjin becomes king of the Mongolian plateau, there will be numerous foundlings thronging this tent."

Qorchi had now begun to throw himself into the job of assembling orphans of conquered peoples. Ö'elün did not so much as wince at Qorchi's words. She remained steadfastly dedicated to raising these youngsters as Mongols. Küchü, Kököchü, Shigi Qutuqu, and Boroghul were all being reared as brothers in the same yurt.

With the Tatars now having disappeared from the Mongolian plateau, the three separate powers of Temüjin the Mongol, To'oril Khan the Kereyid, and Jamugha the Jadaran divided the 200,000 nomads of the plateau into three groups. In the thirty-ninth year of Temüjin's life, the allied armies of Temüjin and To'oril Khan would face Jamugha in battle, four years after the subjugation of the Tatars.

The decisive battle with Jamugha was to be a do-or-die, all-out confrontation for both Temüjin and To'oril Khan. Jamugha had gathered under his wings the Qatagin, Salji'ud, Ikires, Gorulas, Naiman, Tayichi'ud, and Oirat peoples, and he had completely absorbed settlements descended from the annihilated Tatars and Merkids. Even Börte's natal people, the Unggirads, were geographically connected with Jamugha's holdings.

Jamugha's forces began the battle. When news of Jamugha's march reached him, before he had even sorted out whether the report was true, To'oril Khan personally led his entire army to Temüjin's camp. Temüjin welcomed the old commander into his tent, and they elaborated a plan of operations to repulse the attack of Jamugha's huge army.

"Anda, before troubles erupt," proposed To'oril Khan, "we must each send out our best units in equal troop strength to the front."

"Agreed," replied Temüjin, and he then sent as advance forces the three units under Altan, Quchar, and Daritai Odchigin. For his part, To'oril Khan selected the units under commanders Senggüm, Jaqa Gambu, and Bilge Beki.

Although it was initially a fairly well-planned strategy, once the fighting commenced, both To'oril Khan and Temüjin continued sending powerful fighting units to the front as needed, irrespective of the personal sacrifices incurred. Temüjin was ultimately left at his base camp with only Jelme's forces, having already ordered those of Bo'orchu, Qasar, and Belgütei into battle. And To'oril Khan had done the same, ordering all but one unit to the front.

The battle lines spread across a frighteningly broad expanse of terrain. There was fighting along the upper and lower reaches of the Selengge, the Orkhon, the Onon, and the Kherlen rivers. From morning till nightfall, scouts conveyed news from the various zones incessantly. There were reports of victory and of defeat. On the fifth day after the fighting started, both sides saw a decisive battle forming. At the head of a large force, Jamugha began to move along the lower reaches of the Kherlen River.

When he learned this news, Temüjin turned to To'oril Khan and said:

"You stay here, old 'father.' I'll march ahead."

It was not in Temüjin's temperament to trust To'oril Khan. Despite his long past as hegemon of the north, To'oril Khan was well into his sixties. Although he might not be able to trust him, Temüjin would probably not have had any chance of success fighting Jamugha alone. Without an all-out battle, victory or defeat could not be determined. Win or lose, both sides had to be prepared, or so it seemed, to incur serious casualties. Yet Temüjin felt he personally would have to go into battle to gain peace of mind.

Responding to Temüjin's statement, To'oril Khan said:

"Little chicken, why do you take to the field by choice knowing that you may be wiped out? Jamugha is not your principal enemy. I'll go."

Temüjin tried to push his own plans further, but To'oril Khan, his slender, pallid face turning deep red, yelled:

"This is a decisive battle—we cannot lose it. Should I entrust it to you? You circle around to the left, and from there attack the Tayichi'uds on the left flank."

Temüjin had no choice but to yield to To'oril Khan the most difficult war front holding the key to victory. Leading a main force of 10,000 men, To'oril Khan headed toward the lower reaches of the Kherlen River. Temüjin was to command 10,000 troops in an attack on the Tayichi'uds who were trying to protect Jamugha and march toward the middle reaches of the Onon River where he was based.

For the first time, Temüjin was to join battle on an immense scale with his perennial enemies, the Tayichi'uds. Dividing his forces into several groups, he surrounded the Tayichi'uds' strongholds and then gradually tightened the noose around them. The fighting continued day and night.

During the battle, Temüjin was hit by an enemy arrow at sunset and suffered injury to a vein on his neck. Blood gushed out of the wound, but the fighting continued and with nightfall they were enveloped in darkness, so first aid could not reach him. The fighting ceased in the middle of the night, and Jelme sucked the blood from Temüjin's wound with his lips. Each time he sucked some blood, he spit it out, and with all his strength he sucked so that not a droplet of poison would remain in Temüjin's body. By morning, the surface of the earth around them was soaked in dark red blood.

The following morning two men from the surrounded Tayichi'ud settlement moved over to Temüjin's camp. They were Sorqan Shira, father of Chimbai and Chila'un, and a ruddy-complexioned young man of twenty-five or twenty-six. Temüjin owed Sorqan Shira a favor for having helped him once, and he thus protected the older man. As for the younger man, he launched an interrogation.

"What kind of fighter are you?"

"I'm an archer."

"Why have you surrendered to us?"

"I've run out of arrows."

"Do you know who the mighty archer was who broke the jawbone of my yellow steed and inflicted this wound on my neck?"

The young man seemed to be thinking for a moment and then replied:

"It was probably me. That was my arrow shot from the top of a hill."

"Knowing that, I can't let you live."

"Fine, kill me then!" he said.

Temüjin, though, was not interested in executing the young man. The radiance in the eyes of this ordinary soldier who, with no consideration for his own safety, responded truthfully reflected beautifully in Temüjin's own eyes. Parrying Temüjin's gaze, he refused to avert his eyes and yelled out:

"Cut off my head quickly then and be done with it!"

"Don't be in such a hurry to die," said Temüjin. "You can serve at my side. If I issue an order, you are to do whatever I say."

The young man remained silent, staring intently at Temüjin, who went on: "I shall give you the name Jebe," meaning weapon.

Now the expression on the young man's face changed, though he was still quiet. The name Jebe seemed appropriate to everyone assembled there. Not only was he an extremely capable archer, but also his mind was as sharp as an arrowhead. News arrived that evening from To'oril Khan's camp that Jamugha's main force had been destroyed and that they were pursuing Jamugha, who was now in flight.

Temüjin thoroughly mopped up the Tayichi'uds. His only regret was that they had been unable to capture their chief, Targhutai, but virtually every member of the lineage had been annihilated, so that the name Tayichi'ud would never again be mentioned by anyone on the Mongolian plateau. From Temüjin's perspective, the Tayichi'uds were relations of a sort, a people with the same ancestors, but he showed no mercy. Among the prisoners were many from the Borjigin line whose faces he had known from the camp they shared in his youth, and there were even a fair number of close relatives among them, but Temüjin regarded them all as mortal enemies. He accepted none of their appeals or defenses.

"For Tayichi'ud males," ordered Temüjin, "kill them as far as their descendants' descendants. Turn them into ashes to be blown away!"

And all men from the Tayichi'ud settlement were beheaded. The women and girls were assembled at a specific site and forced to clean up the execution grounds day in and day out. The only ones in the Tayichi'ud camp who were spared and allowed to join Temüjin's camp were Sorqan Shira, father of Chimbai and Chila'un, and the young man whom Temüjin had named Jebe.

From the time when the mopping-up operation was nearly complete, the troops began retreating from the battlefield. Bo'orchu, Belgütei, and Qasar returned from the front. Then a number of units under To'oril Khan's command returned. All of them had distinguished themselves magnificently on the battlefield. The last to return to camp was To'oril Khan's own unit that had forced Jamugha's main army into full retreat.

The section of the new battlefield still reeking from the stench of spilled blood was eventually turned over by Temüjin's and To'oril Khan's troops. The scene of innumerable warriors digging up the plains as far as the eye could see under a vast blue sky, as they climbed up a hillside, seemed to continually unfold like a luxuriously thick carpet.

On the third day following To'oril Khan's triumphal return, he and Temüjin went to the edge of a hill that had been prepared for their meeting. They both marched there with an ostentatious guard, but only the two men entered the tent provided for the meeting.

"It's all very cumbersome," said To'oril Khan with a forced smile. "Two men cooperate, bring down Jamugha, and notify each other of victories; why do they have to meet in this way?"

Temüjin also had a bitter smile on his face. It was precisely as To'oril Khan had put it. Yet both sides felt the need to do things in this manner.

For now Temüjin and To'oril Khan were the two rulers dividing the Mongolian plateau. What had once been divided in three with Jamugha was now simply divided in two. Although Jamugha was on the run, a large number of the troops formerly under his command had been disarmed by To'oril Khan and awaited judgment in their home settlements.

According to the pact agreed upon by the two men before the battle that had just transpired, everything belonging to peoples under Jamugha—men, women, sheep, horses, valuables, and weapons—was to be equally divided. Unlike after the destruction of the Merkids and Tatars, though, there was not much in the way of booty. The principal lineages were the Salji'ud, Ikires, Gorulas, Tayichi'ud, Oirat, Unggirad, and Naiman—small groups and settlements spread across the expansive Mongolian plateau. Dividing them up fairly was, as a practical matter, impossible.

"My son," said To'oril Khan, "I shall give you whichever lineage you wish. You choose first."

"But the defeat of Jamugha's main army was Father's accomplishment. I offer you to select first the lineage you wish," said Temüjin, conceding the privilege to To'oril Khan.

"The Unggirads," said To'oril Khan abruptly.

The Unggirads were the wealthiest people on the plateau. Of all the peoples, they were the one Temüjin wanted most, as his wife, Börte, was born among them, but there was nothing he could do now. Börte's father, Dei Sechen, had already passed away.

"Tayichi'uds," said Temüjin.

"Oirats," replied To'oril Khan.

"Salji'uds," continued Temüjin.

In this extremely rough method of division, the two conquerors one by one clearly took possession of the war booty spread over the plateau. In the end only the Naimans were left. The reason was that the only thing they had was their name, nothing substantive to take. They were of Turkic stock and the strangest people on the Mongolian plateau; there was no reason they should have been subordinate to Jamugha, To'oril Khan, or Temüjin in the first place. Although they lived on the same plateau, they were geographically isolated on a side facing the Altai mountain range. They were also economically self-sufficient. For some reason, then, they had responded to Jamugha's invitation, sending one small unit of troops to aid Jamugha in battle.

"We'll have to send a joint force of troops the long distance to the Naimans," said To'oril Khan.

"When?" asked Temüjin.

"Within the year probably. Until then we each have much that needs to be done."

As To'oril Khan indicated, much remained for them to attend to. It was certainly not going to be an easy matter to pacify the peoples now destined to fall under their control.

Once they had divided up the plunder, just between the two of them Temüjin and To'oril Khan exchanged toasts of congratulations on their victory. Under normal circumstances, they would have held a large banquet together with their many commanders, but they decided not to do so. The feeling in both of their minds was, for lack of a better way of putting it, that it was safer to avoid this line of action.

Temüjin understood full well that, while a joint operation with To'oril Khan against the Naimans within the year was fine, after the attack there would be a struggle between the two conquerors, whether or not they wished it. There had to be a single ruler over the Mongolian plateau. To'oril Khan and Temüjin could not rule jointly.

Promising each other that the next morning at sunrise they would return with their armies to their respective base camps, the two commanders rose from their seats. Then, just as they had arrived, they each withdrew to their bases with an ostentatious, armed military escort.

The following dawn the two military companies departed from the battlefield in opposite directions. After marching for a short while, Temüjin was suddenly overcome with a burning desire to launch a surprise attack on To'oril Khan's forces. His thinking ran as follows: To'oril Khan's army of 100,000 men, divided in thirds, had just then begun to move, marching like a linked chain; if he were to thrust a three-pronged attack in from the flank, bringing To'oril Khan down would not be that difficult. At the same time that Temüjin was pushing this ambitious desire aside, though, he sensed that To'oril Khan probably had the very same wish, and he issued an order to his entire army to lose no time in taking up battle formations. He wanted to be prepared on the off chance that To'oril Khan might launch an attack.

With his troops battle ready, they kept up a forced march. When they finally pitched camp, Temüjin was able to relax his vigilance.

After a march of several days, his forces returned triumphantly to base camp, but after only one night there, a unit of troops decamped again. They were taking appropriate measures toward the peoples who now came under Temüjin's control.

Temüjin entrusted the operation to two young officers. One was Jelme's younger brother Sübe'etei, and the other was Muqali. Both were young men who had joined Temüjin's camp with large numbers of others after he had withdrawn from Jamugha's camp. Sübe'etei was now twenty-eight, and Muqali was thirty-one.

These two men had fought with great distinction and on a number of occasions been the cause of victory. As a reward, Temüjin accorded them this important task, which came with a great deal of authority. After a night in camp with no time to rest, they set off with 2,000 men to occupy settlements of a number of conquered lineages.

After about two weeks' time, a group of Tayichi'ud women and an inordinately large number of sheep and horses were transported to them. Temüjin put the women to work as servants for his own people, sent the horses to be used for fighting, and released the sheep into joint pasturage.

From other conquered peoples, only young men to be incorporated into the military were sent in. No older folks, women, flocks of sheep, or valuable items arrived. Temüjin was pleased with all the arrangements made by his two young officers. Tasks that he had in the past given to Bo'orchu and Jelme, he now gave Sübe'etei and Muqali.

And not only these two men; Temüjin appointed numerous other young men to take up a string of posts. As a result, Bo'orchu, Jelme, Qasar, and Belgütei, who held important positions in Temüjin's camp, were able to absorb themselves in a variety of even more important and complex duties on various fronts. Temüjin and his key vassals were now extremely busy supervising the activities of nearly 200,000 people.

The following year, 1202, Temüjin turned forty. Word reached him at a new year's banquet that remnants of the Tatars, who had earlier allegedly been annihilated, had attacked a lineage under Temüjin's banner. He immediately brought the festivities to a close and decided to mobilize his forces for an assault on the Tatars.

Many reports claiming that the Tatars had begun maneuvering had arrived since the previous autumn, but out of regard for To'oril Khan, Temüjin hesitated to muster his army. Whenever a large army was assembled on the Mongolian plateau, it was necessary for Temüjin and To'oril Khan to have a mutual understanding. This was not because of a clearly delineated pact between them; rather, something on the order of a tacit understanding had emerged that necessitated this course of action. This was still more necessary in the case of the Tatars, over whom jurisdiction was still undecided.

In this instance, however, Temüjin developed a strategy without warning To'oril Khan. The time available to report to To'oril Khan was extremely limited, and he considered crushing the Tatars by sending troops with lightning speed. Not giving his rival time to so much as say a word, he could make the Tatar terrain his own.

Before departing for battle, Temüjin issued two orders. One prohibited all acts of looting in the occupied areas, and the other stated that, in the event of their forces being repulsed, they were to return to the initial site of attack to ambush the enemy there, and under no circumstances were they to flee of their own accord.

At the head of a force of 10,000 men, Temüjin traversed the wintry plateau. They were all cavalry, and both horses and soldiers marched through ferocious winds, making sounds like the incessant cracking of whips. Although the battle unfolded from Dalan Nemürges to the Ulqui River, it was over in only three days. Jebe performed brilliantly on the battlefield. The young man who had once broken the jawbone of Temüjin's mount and injured a vein in Temüjin's own neck was a stunning archer, but in hand-to-hand fighting he was even more powerful. Controlling his horse's torso with his legs and sitting up high on horseback, he was able to move his hands freely and manipulate his spear. In so doing, he attacked like a torrential storm, like something beyond human powers. Any opening of a line of assault was due to Jebe's abilities. He was an invulnerable steel arrow.

All of the men among the Tatar captives were assembled in one place and put to death. Temüjin had shown not the least compassion for either the Tatars or the Tayichi'uds. His younger half-brother, Belgütei, made a small blunder at this time. He informed one of the prisoners of the council's judgment that no men would be allowed to live. The Tatar captives thus rose in rebellion again, seized weapons, and put up a fortress. Another, smaller battle ensued in which several dozen of Temüjin's men died. Temüjin then for the first time fiercely reprimanded his younger brother and longtime right-hand man, and thereafter Belgütei was forbidden from participating in all council deliberations.

There was one further important incident that took place during this fighting. Temüjin's close kinsmen and military officers Altan, Quchar, and Daritai had violated military discipline and plundered precious goods for themselves. When he learned of this, Temüjin immediately sent Jebe and Qubilai Noyan [a "commander" not to be confused with the famous Mongol khan several generations later] and had them confiscate everything plundered—horses and valuables—from the three men.

While he was in the now emptied Tatar village, Temüjin divided up all the spoils among his entire armed forces, and he had his soldiers freely take one woman each. Temüjin selected for his own share two daughters of the Tatar chief: Yisügen and Yisüi. Temüjin's idea was that he would have every single Tatar woman, enemies of his ancestors for generations, give birth to illegitimate Mongol children. Temüjin himself pondered having his two new women from the purest of Tatar stock bear children who shared his own blood. In his field bed one night, he violated the two young sisters. This was the first time that Temüjin had personally made the women of a conquered people his own. He was fascinated by them—so that we can't say this was merely an act of revenge—for the bodies of these nubile young women of this alien people were so different from that of his wife, Börte.

Eventually Temüjin set out on the return trip. Groups of women, sheep, and horses were placed at the tail end of the long procession. This time the troops were not making fierce sounds in the wind, as when they set off for the front. Though there was no howling in the wind, the continuous wailing of the women at the end of the procession could be heard day and night. They were unwilling to be resigned to the sad fortunes visited upon them.

Shortly after Temüjin's celebratory return home, he learned that, just as he had attacked the Tatars and completely pacified them, so too had To'oril Khan dispatched troops to a Merkid area where their remnant elements were slowly becoming active and crushed them. Temüjin surmised that To'oril Khan's actions were a direct response to Temüjin's own—if Temüjin can do this, then I can as well!

The two men took no offense at each other's actions. When the light of spring began to shine, the Mongolian plateau once again returned to its early state of quiet. To'oril Khan and Temüjin were both busy building up their forces for the day, which everyone knew was coming, when they would be fighting each other.

Temüjin remained vigilant about training all of his men as soldiers. All of the lineages and peoples now under Mongol control worked in the pasturelands by turns, and when they were not with the flocks they received intense battlefield instruction. Maneuvers were consumed with group cavalry training. From high-ranking leaders Qasar, Belgütei, Bo'orchu, and Jelme to such first-rate fighters as Qachi'un, Temüge, Sübe'etei, Muqali, Qubilai Noyan, and Jebe all the way to Temüjin's son Jochi, they all dashed about the grasslands, bathed in dust and perspiration. They were all wolves now espying the mighty enemy To'oril Khan. At one point, Qasar addressed the assembled troops as their commander:

"March and spread out like the plains themselves. Take up your positions flowing out like the sea. And fight like chisels thrust into the enemy!"

Mongol soldiers were trained in the manner indicated by Qasar's words.

That fall Temüjin received a completely unexpected piece of
news, that Jamugha had affixed himself to To'oril Khan's camp.
After his defeat by the joint armies of To'oril Khan and Temüjin,
Jamugha had escape far to the north, but he had now reappeared
with a sizable body of men in To'oril Khan's camp. Instead of executing him on the spot, To'oril Khan welcomed Jamugha and his
followers as a fighting force under his wing.

Soon after hearing this report about Jamugha, Altan and Quchar
conspired to leave the Mongol encampment with the men under
them and take refuge with To'oril Khan. They were still angry at
the severe reprimand Temüjin had delivered for their violation of
military discipline. The defections of Altan and Quchar, though,
were not a matter of great importance for Temüjin now. Even had
they not rebelled, they were the germ of a disease that eventually
would have to have been extirpated. And thus, Temüjin sensed that
his conflict with To'oril Khan was slowly but surely emerging to the
surface.

In the spring of the following year, 1203, a messenger from
To'oril Khan's base arrived.

"My anda, my beloved son," he reported in To'oril Khan's
name. "The time has come to send an army against the Naimans.
At present, my army is making all preparations to cross the Altai
Mountains."

Temüjin soon sent his own messenger in response to To'oril
Khan's:

"My anda, my father. Mongol troops are prepared for an assault
on the Naimans and are standing by. We await father anda's order.
Anda, roar like a great tiger enraged! Cross the Altai Mountains!"

Temüjin knew that the attack on the Naimans would move to a
battle between the Kereyids and Mongols that would decide over-
lordship on the plateau. From the moment that the Naimans were
defeated, Kereyids and Mongols would see one another as the
enemy. Not only Temüjin foresaw this; To'oril Khan was at least
as aware of it as he. In this sense the declaration of attack on the
Naiman people that To'oril Khan and Temüjin exchanged was itself
a declaration of war against each other.

Less than one month later, the two armies acting in concert moved soldiers to the base area of this Turkic people holding sway over the western section of the plateau. Temüjin selected 30,000 crack troops and marched off himself at their head.

Temüjin had thought that To'oril Khan's troops would not be able to cross the Altai Mountains easily because of the deep, lingering snow there. And for his part, To'oril Khan had not thought that either his own or Temüjin's troops would be able to cross them. Nonetheless, both armies crossed the Altai chain at about the same time and surged into the camp of the Küchü'üds, who were the strongest soldiers among the Naimans. Wholesale carnage and plunder ensued.

Once they had attacked the Küchü'üd people, neither army remained long, but at about the same time regrouped. Although it was not apparent on the surface, both sides used the attack on the Naimans as a pretext to observe if the time was right to attack the other.

Soon after returning from the assault on the Naimans, Temüjin learned that the Naimans had retreated into the Black Forest by the Tula River and that To'oril Khan's forces had accordingly fought hard against them. Not one to miss an opportunity, Qasar argued that they should attack To'oril Khan now. Jelme and Bo'orchu both agreed, but Temüjin was hesitant. While this was clearly a prime opportunity to defeat To'oril Khan, such a victory seemed as though it would leave a very unpleasant aftertaste.

"Sixteen years ago," said Temüjin, "when we were extremely weak and about to engage in a battle without chance of success to retrieve Börte from the Merkids, didn't To'oril Khan come to our aid? We are what we have become today because of him. We shall save To'oril Khan one time and then have repaid the debt incurred. If we should save him right now, then I would surely have no regrets later. In the present battle against the Naimans, I sensed nothing in particular to fear from To'oril Khan's troops."

This was indeed an accurate reflection of what Temüjin was thinking. While he never would have said that To'oril Khan's troops were inferior to the Mongols in their fighting capacity, there was nothing extraordinary about them either. Their commanders were skilled on the battlefield and they always attained victory with minimal sacrifice, but in hand-to-hand combat in which a single soldier felled another, they seemed to reveal an unexpected weakness. By comparison, no matter how small the scale of combat, Mongol soldiers won by defeating their counterparts on an individual level. The Kereyid troops struck Temüjin as simply courageous soldiers, but the Mongol troops were wolves on the prowl for blood, with their long tongues hanging out, drooling saliva, panting.

When he had prevailed upon his commanders, Temüjin hurried to Baidaraq (Baidrag) River to assist To'oril Khan. There they came to the aid of To'oril Khan's son, Senggüm, who was in the midst of a difficult fight, and extricated his wife and sons who had been taken captive.

Soon after Temüjin returned to camp, To'oril Khan arrived there with a small detail of troops. It was an extremely bold move on his part. He had come to thank Temüjin for his assistance and to seek the establishment of a mutual pact. While the two men until this point in time had always spoken to each other as "my anda, father" and "my anda, son," they had not formally sworn an oath.

Despite this, the level of drive on To'oril Khan's part to seek such a pact was unfathomable to Temüjin. There was nothing that seemed meaningless or comical about the vow of friendship between the two men now. Temüjin responded to To'oril Khan's offer. He set up seats in the area before his tent, assembled several thousand of his followers there, and carried out the ceremony of exchanging vows of friendship with To'oril Khan.

Temüjin faced the old commander and raised a wine cup to him, but To'oril Khan retained the cold visage and frigid eye of his youth, and there was no indication whatsoever in him of a decline into old age. Although he had not a single strand of hair tied up on his head, there was a certain beauty and an eeriness shining in its silvery hue.

"I would like to give my daughter Cha'ur Beki to your son Jochi in marriage," said To'oril Khan. "This will strengthen the bonds between our two families. For if there is a serpent with fangs separating our families, there will be dissension between us."

Temüjin agreed. Although he had no inclination to take To'oril Khan at his word, he saw no need to brush off the older man's extended hand.

Soon after he returned to the Black Forest, To'oril Khan came back to invite Temüjin to a banquet celebrating the wedding of Cha'ur Beki and Jochi. While he continued to look upon To'oril Khan as his enemy, Temüjin thought at the time that this news was wonderful. To lure Temüjin into his camp, To'oril Khan first made the trip to the Mongol camp himself, without any guards. In so doing, To'oril Khan demonstrated his outstanding capacity to deal with a rival.

Temüjin had no desire at all to set off for the Black Forest of the Kereyids. To do so meant certain death. So he consulted with Qasar and Belgütei as to how to respond to To'oril Khan. He had to turn down the invitation, offering something that more or less resembled a valid reason.

As he reached this judgment, two servants from To'oril Khan's settlement by the names of Badai and Kishiliq arrived and announced that the Black Forest by the Tula River was teeming with armed soldiers. When he heard this, Temüjin's eyes suddenly became animated. *So this will be the final battle with To'oril Khan*, he thought. Temüjin immediately informed To'oril Khan's messenger that he would be overjoyed to accept the invitation to this congratulatory feast.

Once he had sent the messengers off, Temüjin issued an order for his entire army to mobilize. He had them take their best weapons and dress in their best armor. On the evening following their arrival at the Black Forest for the banquet, several tens of thousands of cavalry troops pitched camp. Then several dozen groups of soldiers and horses left camp and fanned out across the grasslands.

At dawn on the day of the celebration, To'oril Khan and Temüjin, each leading several tens of thousands of troops, spread across the plains known as the Black Desert. Both armies took up commanding positions.

After conferring with Bo'orchu, Jelme, and Qasar, among others, Temüjin arrayed members of the Uru'ud and Mangghud peoples, who were renowned among the Mongols for their great bravery, into the first battle formation. From his earliest years, Temüjin had heard how extraordinary these two peoples were on the battlefield. To this day, he remembered mention of these two ethnic groups by Börtechü, that old man with the phenomenal memory, when he recounted the Mongolian ancestors from the blue wolf and pale doe down through more than twenty generations.

—Among the sons of Qabichi Ba'atur was Tudun. Tudun had seven sons. The eldest was Qachi Külüg, who could ride a horse as fast as the wind. His wife was Nomolun, and they gave birth to your famed ancestor Qaidu. Qachi Külüg's six younger brothers bore the following names in order: Qachin, Qachi'u, Qachula, Qachi'un, Qaraldai, and Nachin Ba'atur, the youngest. Nachin Ba'atur had two sons who in the give and take of life loved the deity of battle more than even food, and they were the ancestors of the Uru'ud and Mangghud peoples, whom they did not know in their own lives—

It seemed that the blood of the god of war whom they loved more than food had been passed down unchanged to the Uru'ud and Mangghud peoples. In the battles thus far fought, their movements on the field were without peer. From an early age, they were trained in the use of the cutting ring and the spear. Their courage and gallantry were such that, when they switched battle arrays or when they adopted a circling-back strategy to attack the enemy in the rear, the black banners of the Uru'uds and the scarlet banners of the Mangghuds made their skill at advance and retreat seem perfectly exacting.

Temüjin summoned Jürchedei, a leader of the Uru'uds, a short, ruddy-faced, unprepossessing old man. Just as he accepted the order to serve in the advance troops, his eyes shone and he said in a low, hoarse voice:

"We accept your command whatever it may be. So, then, may I and my people devour the Kereyids."

Temüjin then summoned Quyildar, a leader of the Mangghuds, and conveyed to him the same order. Shy and stammering, Quyildar replied with embarrassment:

"We shall do as the Uru'uds, grab every single K-K-Kereyid, and d-d-devour them."

At the moment hostilities commenced, countless scarlet and black banners unfurled widely across the front. They had both cavalry and foot soldiers. Against them, To'oril Khan sent his crack cavalry of the Jirgins. The black and scarlet banners advanced, troops shouting out fiercely, though calmly. They pressed the assault, splitting the enemy cavalry into small clusters, and as the Jirgins looked on in blank amazement, knocked them off. They effectively did, just as their words indicated, gobble up the enemy one by one.

In the wake of the Jirgins, Tümen Tübe'en troops of whom To'oril Khan was extremely proud surged in like a tidal wave. The Uru'uds tried to tie them up and were put to rout, but the Mangghuds circled around from the flank and cut them off. The Tümen Tübe'en banner was "consumed" after ferocious fighting.

Then, a company with the banner of the Olan Dongqayid came out of the enemy camp in a quick attack. The Mangghuds were shattered and lost about half of their men, but the Uru'uds circled around the enemy's rear and dispersed them. Next, To'oril Khan's captain of 1,000 guard troops rushed in with clouds of dust to come to the aid of Olan Dongqayid. The Mangghuds defeated them, but Quyildar was stabbed by an enemy soldier and, pierced by a spear, he fell from his horse to the ground.

With an earth-shattering noise, 10,000 troops from To'oril Khan's main encampment now advanced. Temüjin's main force moved to the front to meet them. The scarlet and black banners of the Uru'uds and Mangghuds seemed to disappear in massive swarms of the enemy's immense army.

From then until evening, shouts, screams, and the neighing of military horses incessantly arose from the clouds of sand that covered the plains. When the crimson sunset, even more inflamed than usual, filled half the sky, the deadly fighting that had escalated all day long came to an end.

Protected by 1,000 bodyguards, Temüjin stood on a low-lying hillock. The battlefield was covered with corpses from both sides, and the banners of exhausted and wounded soldiers were planted at the top of small hills here and there, spread out in waves.

There was Bo'orchu's banner and Jelme's, and far to the north were those of Qasar and Belgütei next to each other. He also saw the banners of Qachi'un, Temüge, Jochi, and Jebe. Each of these had been planted on hills, but the number of troops around them had been sharply reduced, and a silence pervaded their facial expressions.

Although Temüjin had defeated To'oril Khan and forced him to flee, he did not issue an order to pursue. He had 1,000 bodyguards, but many of them had been seriously injured. Münglig, his face reddened with blood, had put together information based on reports sent in from troops here and there on the plain. The whereabouts of Bo'orchu, Temüjin's third son, Ögedei, and Boroghul, whom Ö'elün had raised as a foundling, remained unknown.

Each time he heard such a report from Münglig, Temüjin, his erect posture completely unaffected, ever so slightly moved the muscles of his cheeks. In fact, he moved them continually, as news of the deaths of so many Mongol warriors was being conveyed to him one after the next by Münglig.

Temüjin then issued an order to muster the entire army. Perhaps half, maybe a third of his forces were present. In the end, not a single man from the Uru'ud or Mangghud peoples appeared. It seemed as though they had been annihilated, gobbled up by the enemy.

Temüjin ordered his men to make camp there. When light began to shine on the battlefield the following morning, only Bo'orchu returned on foot, having suffered numerous wounds to his body. When he gazed directly at Bo'orchu's face, Temüjin's own face was wet with tears.

"Let it be known in heaven," he said, "that the Mongol warrior Bo'orchu has returned." Temüjin then beat his chest. Bo'orchu explained that, while pursuing an escaping enemy soldier, he fell from his horse. After waking from a long blackout, he walked straight through the night to reach camp.

Around midday Boroghul returned to camp, leading the seriously wounded Ögedei on horseback. When he took Ögedei down from the horse and handed him over to others, Boroghul said:

"The enemy took flight to the foothills of the Ma'u Heights in the direction of Hula'an Burughad, and there disappeared." The fearless young man had on him the blood of the Jirgins.

Temüjin did a roll call of his men. Aside from the wounded, 2,600 men remained with battlefield readiness. Leaving half of them at the field, he led the other half to take control of the settlements formerly under the now routed To'oril Khan. He linked up en route with 1,300 Uru'ud and Mangghud survivors who had earlier vanished from the fighting. The heroic Quyildar of the Mangghuds had sustained a serious wound, and soon after he met up with Temüjin, he died. Temüjin had his remains buried near the top of Mount Or Nu'u of the Qalqa River. This was a site at which, day and night, the wind howled as it slammed into the face of the rocky crags, a most appropriate spot for Quyildar's grave.

When he learned that there were Unggirads nearby, Temüjin sent the brothers Chimbai and Chila'un to encourage and receive their surrender. Temüjin marched farther and camped east of Tüngge Stream. From there it was but a half-day's journey to To'oril Khan's Black Forest.

Temüjin sent a messenger to To'oril Khan:

"My father, anda, I have not forgotten my debt to you. I therefore came to the assistance of your son Senggüm when he was in the midst of a bitter fight. Despite this, you have prevaricated and plotted to kill me. My father, anda, I shall before long attack you in the Black Forest. There we shall fight the last fight."

Temüjin did not spare much time before attacking the Black Forest of To'oril Khan. That night he ordered his entire army to charge into the forest. Although the wolves were injured, their striking power had not lost its force.

For three days and three nights, the decisive battle raged on. The deadly fight unfolded around every tree and stone. The scarlet and black banners ran day and night throughout the woods.

Late in the night of the third day, the final resistance of the Kereyids was smashed. Several hundred settlements now became prey to the Mongol wolves. The men were killed and the women were tied up. To'oril Khan's corpse was discovered four days later far to the north of the Black Forest. He had sustained an attack by another lineage and died. The corpse of his son Senggüm also turned up, and only the whereabouts of Jamugha remained unknown.

As was appropriate upon the death of such an extraordinary commander as To'oril Khan, Temüjin ordered all Kereyid males to follow their leader. One by one the Kereyid men were executed.

Temüjin then had one company of troops pitch camp in the Black Forest, where no men were left alive, and he himself took women and valuables as he joined the triumphal return home. There was now not a single force opposed to Temüjin on the Mongolian plateau. He had disposed of the Tatars, dispatched the Tayichi'uds, destroyed Jamugha's army, and annihilated the Kereyids, who had long taken pride in their preeminence on the plateau. Temüjin, though, was not seething with the feeling of a victor. He was rather overcome with the sensation that a long and painful internal discord had finally settled down.

On the second night of their march, Temüjin walked up the incline of the plain where the sick and wounded soldiers had camped late in the night. Several hundred tents were quietly lined up like so many graves. In every tent he looked into, his commanders and soldiers slept like the dead. Bo'orchu slept, as did Jelme and Muqali. All of them—officers and men alike—had the appearance of beggars.

When Temüjin returned to his own tent, Qasar woke and rose from his bed. Qasar, too, was wearing tattered armor and clothing.

"The army will rest this entire year," said Temüjin. "Next year we shall cross the Altai Mountains."

"And attack the Naimans?" asked Qasar.

"Yes, attack the Naimans," said Temüjin. "The Mongols' best fighters should be wearing fine attire, should live in stunning dwellings, and should have large water jugs and elegant beds. Our exceptional Mongol soldiers should have the best weaponry and should ride in the best war chariots."

Temüjin and To'oril Khan had crossed the Altai Mountains and attacked the Naimans, but it was only a brief invasion, hardly an attack at all. During that invasion, however, Temüjin had come to see the lifestyle of a people completely different from the impoverished

Mongols. They had musical instruments, elegant altars, stylish and sensible kitchens, writing that enabled them to record any and every event, temples where many people would gather, and homes that were fixed to the ground and did not move.

"With the new year we shall cross the Altai Mountains," said Temüjin. "We shall pacify the Naimans and make use of the new weaponry they possess as our own."

Not until this time did it first occur to Temüjin that he would have to fight against the Jin state of the Jurchen people. Since he had destroyed both the Tatars and the Tayichi'uds, the only enemy of his ancestors that remained was the Jin state, which would have to be attacked and defeated last. Temüjin revealed none of this to Qasar. Invading the Jin was still on the order of a fantasy in the minds of all Mongolian wolves, except Temüjin. And for the third time, he opened his mouth and spoke:

"We shall have to cross the Altai Mountains."

From that year into the next, Temüjin devoted himself to pacification of the conquered peoples on the Mongolian plateau and to rebuilding. He strictly forbade the wounding or killing of others under any and all circumstances. Anyone who injured another was to be executed. Theft was similarly dealt with severely. Anyone who stole a sheep or horse was put to the sword.

At the same time, all able-bodied men living in settlements on the Mongolian plateau received military training. The army was arranged with 1,000 men to a company, with a captain in charge, and beneath each of these were the heads of groups of 100 men and groups of 10 men. Temüjin stationed troops at sites all across the Mongolian plateau, enabling him to move warriors to any desired location.

He freely moved settlements of peoples and their flocks of sheep, and to open new grazing land, he gave them great leeway in their lives. He also gradually completed the placement of necessary settlements for his militarized state.

In the early summer of 1204, the year following his defeat of To'oril Khan, Temüjin raised an army of conquest against the

Naimans and, after sacrificing before the flag, set off. Earlier, the Küchü'üds of the Naimans had collaborated with To'oril Khan in their attack, but this time their adversary was the ruler of the entire Naiman people, Tayang Khan. Temüjin hoped to bring all the Naimans under his control. His troops followed the Kherlen River upstream, and when they crossed a branch of the Altai Mountains, they raided farther and farther into enemy terrain. Tayang Khan concentrated and deployed his troops along the lower reaches of the Tamir River, where he expected to meet the Naimans in battle. For Temüjin this was a battle unlike any he had fought to date. The enemy had several hundred war chariots, and archers clad in dignified uniforms and armor were placed in the area between the chariots as if embedded there.

Until the fighting actually began, the Mongol officers could not surmise how the battle would unfold. There were among the Naiman troops soldiers of different ethnicities, and they held their own new weapons, different from those of the Naimans.

There then rang out from the Naiman position the loud and magnificent sounds of drums and gongs. They reverberated across the plains all the way to Temüjin's camp, but hostilities did not begin so simply. That night numerous bonfires at random sites were lit up in the enemy camp.

The next day, the two armies faced each other, waiting for the time to strike, and on the morning of the third day Temüjin summoned his commanders and ordered them to start the attack at noon. Qasar, in charge of the front-line troops, asked:

"How shall we fight them?"

"Qasar," replied Temüjin with a smile, "shouldn't it be just as you put it: spread out like the plains themselves, take up positions like the sea, and fight ferociously like chisels thrust into the enemy! Is there a better way to proceed? Do you know any other way?"

And that was what Qasar proceeded to do. With shouts and calls, Mongol companies spread out dexterously like the plains and took up countless positions like the sea. A moment later, fierce fighting ensued like chisels thrust into the enemy. The battle, now advancing and now retreating, continued into the evening.

"Aha, four Mongol wolves have set off," said Temüjin, looking down from above onto the battlefield, the words slipping from his mouth unawares. Until just then, Jebe, Jelme, Qubilai Noyan, and Sübe'etei had been waiting for the right opportunity to advance to the front lines, possibly in compliance with Qasar's order; each led their company and rode at the head diagonally over the open field, which described a gentle slope. To be sure, these were the four wolves who had been let loose. In body and mind, they were made of iron. As necessity demanded, their mouths could become chisels and their tongues awls. In place of whips, they held cutting rings. They raced on, brushing off dewdrops, mowing down the grass, and riding on the wind.

Just as the four wolves rushed into the front lines, the enemy troops, as if this was some sort of signal, began all together to retreat.

"They're circling around," said Temüjin in distress. "The wolf cubs loosed early this morning seem to be circling around to suckle their mother's milk."

Then, out of nowhere, daredevil Uru'ud and Mangghud troops appeared at the front with complete surprise in pursuit of the re-treating enemy, and they circled the chariots, cut off the cavalry troops, and began to surround the foot soldiers. The Uru'ud and Mangghud troops had been sharply reduced in manpower by the earlier fighting, but they had incorporated even more dauntless sol-diers into their companies.

With their appearance, the enemy army began to retreat farther.

"Ah," called out Temüjin, "the giant python is moving. Shake your head, go forward!"

Qasar, commanding the front-line forces, appeared on the plains at the head of the entire army now under him. His small frame seemed to Temüjin like a large python three fathoms in length. The python opened its immense mouth to consume a three-year-old horse or ox, and now to devour the entire Naiman army, he began to dash around the great plain. The Naimans were forced to retreat yet farther, taking one battle position, then a second and a third, all in retreat.

Temüjin issued an attack order to the rear guard under his command. Riding down the hill slowly and waiting for his company to arrive, he stood in the front. Bending forward low on horseback, together with several dozen brigades to either side, he advanced as if he were going to outflank the entire plain. The Naiman troops crumbled and sought refuge on Mount Naqu behind them. The Mongol wolves pressed the attack and climbed to every spot near the foot of the mountain.

Temüjin surrounded Mount Naqu that night and pitched camp there. The attack could not be relaxed even at nightfall. Reinforcements were then sent into the mountains from the foothills. At dawn, the Naimans were cornered at the peak of the mountain and repeated a frantic counterattack. Only about one third of their troops escaped to the peak, about one third fell down into the valley, and the remaining third were captured by the Mongols.

On the day after the defeat of the Naimans' main force at the pinnacle of Mount Naqu, Temüjin's army captured Tayang Khan, ruler of the Naimans, and took control of the Naiman settlements scattered over the southern slopes of the Altai mountain range.

From the prisoners, Temüjin learned that Jamugha had come and joined the Naiman encampment. When he heard the name Jamugha, Temüjin was taken with a profoundly nostalgic sensation. This heroic figure who was once known as master of the northern wastelands had fled to To'oril Khan's camp after his own camp had been lost. Now that To'oril Khan had been defeated, he had cast his lot with the Naimans. The past three years had not been easy for him.

The image of Jamugha's face, always smiling, came into Temüjin's mind. He had completely devoted his life to fighting Temüjin and now, Temüjin thought, he might still be alive. Men of the Jadaran, Qatagin, Salji'ud, Dörben, Tayichi'ud, and Unggirad peoples commanded by Jamugha all came until the evening of that day to surrender at Temüjin's base. No one brought news of Jamugha himself.

Temüjin took Tayang Khan's mother prisoner, and when he noted that she still had a youthful appearance, he made her one of his concubines. Temüjin was gradually beginning to acquire an unusual interest in making women of conquered peoples his own. Beginning two years earlier, after pacifying remnants of the Tatars and making the enemy ruler's two daughters, Yisügen and Yisüi, his concubines, he had taken any number of young women in this manner. To be sure, he never laid hands on women of his own lineage, but when he discovered women of other, defeated lineages who struck him as even the least bit interesting, he peremptorily brought them into his personal service.

After a battle, when Temüjin saw numerous women tied up in a row being marched off as prisoners, he was always stirred by an indescribable, savage inclination. He remembered that both his mother, Ö'elün, and his wife, Börte, had been hauled off in this way. Although Temüjin would always select women who interested him from groups of captives and invite them into his tent, not one of them ever attempted to resist his advances and protect their bodies. Whether it was due to something he said or of their own free will, they never made a pained or saddened face.

Temüjin understood women not at all. While men were prepared even to die for a battle, women without exception were submissive to enemy men when their side lost. Temüjin could never trust women, and that included Ö'elün and Börte. The perception he had held on to since his youth had not changed in the least.

At one point in time, his younger brother Qasar had argued that the dividing up of captive women to the troops after each battle violated military discipline. Laughing, Temüjin had said loudly to him:

"When you win a battle, it's perfectly fine to spread enemy women over your bed and sleep with them as cushions. Impregnate them and make them give birth to Mongol children. Do women have any other purpose?"

Temüjin spoke in a rather disdainful manner, and Qasar was taken aback by the dark look on his face. More than twenty years had passed since Temüjin first entertained doubts about whether he himself bore Mongol blood, and he still had not been able to fully resolve the question. As in his own case, so too no definitive judgment had been reached on the blood of his eldest son Jochi. Some things about Jochi resembled his father and others did not.

Temüjin was now the sole power controlling the Mongolian plateau, and whether the blood coursing through his veins was Mongol or Merkid was not of major import, but he knew then, as he had hoped in his heart as a youngster, that he wanted to be a descendant of the Mongolian blue wolf.

Upon returning home from the Naiman conquest, Temüjin heard of a turbulent atmosphere prevailing among the remaining Merkids, and he decided to go and attack soon. When he had defeated the Merkids earlier, he and his forces had carried out a mass execution leaving no men alive, but with roots as strong as weeds, the Merkid remnants had somehow gathered together and were forming themselves into a lineage anew.

Temüjin took a merciless attitude toward the Merkids, as he had toward the Tayichi'uds and the Tatars in the past. He could not tolerate, from men who might have the same blood as his, that which he might have allowed from other lineages.

In the early autumn, Temüjin went to war against the Merkid chief Toghto'a and quickly defeated him. His forces then proceeded to despoil then entire region. At this time, a man by the name of Dayir Usun came forward with the following proposal: "I have the most beautiful woman, my daughter, of our people, and if you wish to have her, I would like to present her to you." Temüjin ordered that she be brought forward. When she learned what was about to take place, however, she ran away and hid from her father's view. Temüjin immediately ordered that troops be sent to search for her and bring her in.

She was discovered by the soldiers about ten days later. Her clothes were covered in mud, and her face and hair were filthy. Temüjin had her brought before him.

"What's your name?"

"Qulan." She spoke in a clear tone of voice, responding with eyebrows raised in a somewhat resistant manner.

"Where were you hiding for those ten days?" She replied by offering the names of a number of ethnic groups among whom she had been hiding.

"Why didn't you just stay in one place?" asked Temüjin.

"Wherever I went," said Qulan with an expression of anger on her face, "the young men of that lineage attacked me. Men are all barbarian beasts."

What Qulan said seemed to ring true. With the fighting having only just stopped, massacres ensued everywhere, and order had not been fully restored. Women who had no special protectors, when put in such a situation, knew without having to articulate it what fate awaited them.

Temüjin was overcome by profound antipathy for this young woman who was rejecting presentation of her body to him and had become a plaything for insurgents of other lineages. Rejection by a woman of an ethnic group he had himself conquered was a new experience for Temüjin. That by itself would have been more than enough to earn his wrath, but in addition, the fact that she had been raped by several other lineages seemed to him to be an act of spite directed solely at himself.

"You and the men who violated you," said Temüjin, as if issuing a manifesto, "will all be apprehended and executed." Qulan looked at him severely.

"I will not be raped. I have always defended against this with my life as my sword. If I am fated for such an experience, I shall choose death."

"What are you babbling about, Merkid female!"

Temüjin put no confidence in Qulan's words. He did not believe her capable of such things. But with a composure that only someone who has accepted death as inevitable could muster, she said:

"I am speaking to the deities. Only they believe me." Then she smiled, with her eyes glittering frigidly at Temüjin and her face covered with dirt. Temüjin had never seen a smile such as that adorning Qulan's face. Her face was filled with pride, and her voice reverberated with it.

"Tie up the woman!" Temüjin ordered a man at his side to escort Qulan to a room in a private home.

Two days later, he visited this room where she was confined. Qulan was sitting on a bed, but when she recognized the figure of Temüjin standing in the doorway, she got off the bed and braced herself:

"Don't you come in! You take one step in this room, and I shall end my life," she said sternly.

"By what means have you chosen to die?" asked Temüjin.

"If I bite through my tongue," she said, "death will come easily to me."

A sensibility was detectable here that only someone who had settled upon a matter in his mind would possess. Temüjin, who had made every race of people on the entire Mongolian plateau tremble, lacked such power as he stood before Qulan. And he hesitated before approaching her any further.

It seemed to him that Qulan was now different from the way she had been when they first met. The dirt had been cleaned from her face, revealing what could justly be called the finest beauty among the Merkids. She was not only, as far as Temüjin was concerned, a great beauty for a Merkid, but also arguably the most beautiful woman he had ever seen. He had once been enchanted by the glistening beauty of his wife, Börte, but the woman standing before his eyes now was much lovelier than she and, it seemed, much more intelligent. There was a darkness tinged with sorrow to her deeply notched face, like a work of sculpture, that Börte had no trace of. Her hair was half golden and her eyes had a slight touch of blue.

Temüjin left that day as he had come, but the next day and the one following he visited the home where Qulan was being held. The words she spoke remained unchanged, and Temüjin had to leave with the satisfaction only of having seen her face.

To pacify the Merkids, Temüjin remained in the Merkid settlement for two months, and during that time he called on Qulan any number of times. It was strange, to say the least, that Temüjin would be treated in this manner by a woman who was an enemy prisoner.

Had she not been Qulan, she would have been executed on the spot, but Temüjin could not bring himself to do this.

The night before his company was to depart for their triumphal return, Temüjin visited her again one last time and said: "I thought you were someone else."

He didn't believe such words could come from his own mouth and thus startled himself. Once the words were out, though, there was no way to retrieve them.

"I'd like you to serve in my tent," he said. Qulan then looked directly at Temüjin with her dark face and said:

"How can you say such a thing in all seriousness?"

"My words come from my heart," he replied. "Can you understand that?"

"What you say is probably true," she said with something of an intimate tone, altogether different from her usual manner. "Were it not so, death would already have paid me a call. Is what you feel for me now love?"

"Yes," he replied.

"You say it's love now, but is this love greater, deeper than you feel for all other women?"

"Much more so."

"Even more than for your wife?" asked Qulan. Temüjin was astonished and could not quickly respond. "If indeed your love for me is stronger and greater than for your wife, then you may take my body. If your love is not so strong, then no matter what means you may use, I shall not be yours. I am prepared for death at any time."

Rather than say something in reply, Temüjin took a step and then another into the room. He approached Qulan. She shrank back, but did not utter anything rejecting him. When he embraced her, Temüjin honestly believed that his love for her was stronger than he had ever felt for anyone.

Unexpected for Temüjin was the fact that Qulan had a body of perfect purity. When she had first been brought before him, she had proudly claimed that she had risked her life to protect her virginity, but Temüjin hadn't believed it. It hardly seemed likely for a young woman to have been able to do so, during ten days in the prevailing chaos. True to her word, though, she was still a virgin. As if some sort of evidence of how difficult this had been, a number of contusions had left black-and-blue marks on her white body: on her fleshy shoulder, between her well-formed, protuberant breasts, and at her neat and trim waist.

When he left Qulan's room the following morning, Temüjin thought that he loved this woman more than any other and that he would continue to love her his entire life. The vow he made to Qulan was surely not the sort of thing he was going to break.

Having pacified the Merkid remnants, Temüjin set off on his return home. In the evening he pitched camp at a site about one day's travel from his own settlement in the foothills of Mount Burqan, and before Temüjin entered his tent, he thought about informing his wife, Börte, of Qulan in advance. With his other women, Temüjin had not made a special point of notifying Börte. If he did not inform her, she would of course learn of Qulan; they would each ignore it, and somehow things would settle down. Börte surely did not believe that, over the course of such a long military expedition, Temüjin in the peak of his years would spend his time without female companionship.

The case of Qulan, however, was different, and Temüjin wanted Börte to somehow recognize her existence. It might be that Börte would require special treatment in future vis-à-vis his other concubines, and as best he could, he wanted to avoid the eruption of any troublesome quarrels with her.

Temüjin sent Muqali to Börte as a messenger. A commander eight years Temüjin's junior, he was known for his faithfulness on any matter whatsoever. He returned the following day and conveyed a message from Börte to Temüjin:

"Temüjin, ruler of our beloved Mongolian plateau. Should you return home triumphantly to the settlement, you will find a new tent decorated with new furniture next to the tent of your wife, Börte. I pray that the young Qulan who will live there will compensate for the areas in which I am insufficient and will be a wellspring for your extraordinary strength."

Börte's language struck Temüjin as altogether satisfactory. Whatever he might have anticipated, he really couldn't expect anything more agreeable. Börte would lose nothing of her dignity as the legal wife, and she had demonstrated magnanimity for the respect her husband was paying her.

Soon after his return from the Merkid expedition, a group of Merkids based at Mount Tayighar rose in revolt, and Temüjin immediately dispatched a punitive force. As commander, Temüjin appointed the son of Sorqan Shira, the short and big-headed Chimbai. Chimbai was a bold commander, perturbed by nothing at all, but this was the first time that he was assuming a post of such considerable responsibility. With a physique so small that, it was said, he could not ride a horse without someone offering a hand, Chimbai had suffered losses on the battlefield. In this expedition, though, he acquitted himself splendidly, compelling the enemy commander Toghto'a and his son Qudu to flee far away to the south.

Temüjin would not remain long in his own camp, though, for that year he was to lead his entire army across the Altai Mountains again to attack the Naimans. That winter the snows were heavy, and he could not hope to cross the mountains. He therefore had no choice but to pass the time with all of his forces stationed in the northern foothills of the Altai Mountains. He was accompanied on this expedition by Qulan alone.

Following the new year came spring, and Temüjin led his entire armed forces over the Altai Mountains for a third time to invade the Naimans once again. They battled a joint army composed of Merkid and Naiman remnants at the basin of the Buqdurma River and defeated them. The leaders of the remnant forces split into small groups and scattered in all directions.

Temüjin appointed Jelme's younger brother Sübe'etei, who had posted stunning achievements the previous year during the attack on the Naimans, to lead a combat chariot made of iron in pursuit of enemy remnant fighters. Having just turned thirty, Sübe'etei was a young commander, and Temüjin counseled him when he was setting off on his mission:

"Should the enemy escapees acquire wings and fly off at great speed into the sky, Sübe'etei, you shall become a great falcon and seize them. Should they dig deep into the earth to hide themselves, you shall become an iron hoe and bore into the soil after them. Should they become fish in the lakes and the sea, you shall become a net to catch them. You have already traversed high peaks and crossed great rivers. This expedition will last incomparably longer than before. Remember the great distances to be covered, and be compassionate to the war horses that they not grow too gaunt. Replenish your provisions before they are depleted. No matter how many wild beasts you encounter on your way, do not hunt them down to the point of emaciating the horses. Go, and may divine protection come to the brave Mongol warriors who carry out this mission to allow not a single enemy soldier to escape."

Sübe'etei then set off, and he acted as he was instructed. Defeated remnant troops hiding in the southern foothills of the Altai Mountains were attacked one by one, taken prisoner, and beheaded.

As Sübe'etei's thorough mopping-up war was continuing, Jamugha was brought into Temüjin's base camp, shackled to five of his subordinates.

It was a day when the sun was obscured by clouds and everything in nature was turning ashen in color. Temüjin stood face to face with Jamugha in front of his tent. Twelve years had passed since his bitter defeat in battle against Jamugha when each of them commanded some 30,000 men. And it had been four years since he had gone on to ally with the late To'oril Khan and defeat Jamugha. Many years had passed since Temüjin had seen this man in the flesh.

He stared fixedly at Jamugha's face. His mien had changed so much he resembled another person altogether. He had had a round face in the past, but now it had become sallow with prominent cheekbones. One thing remained exactly as it had been—he was smiling.

Before speaking to Jamugha, Temüjin grilled the five underlings who came fettered to him to ascertain facts. Jamugha had fought against Sübe'etei's forces and repeatedly been defeated until only these five subordinates remained. In the end, these men had the misfortune to be tied up to him. Asking why he should let men who had laid hands upon their master live, Temüjin had the five men fettered to Jamugha beheaded on the spot, right before Jamugha's eyes.

Temüjin lifted Jamugha from the ground where he was sitting and put him in a chair. He then said:

"My anda, Jamugha, we are friends. We once lived in the same settlement. Despite that, you separated yourself from me, and you were for a long time my enemy. But we are again together today. I clearly recall the day on which we swore our blood-brother anda pact by the Qorqonaq Valley. The commotion of the banquet still rings in my ears, and the color of the fire that night is reflected in my eyes even today. We swore our pact that day. We are still friends."

Temüjin did not have the heart to execute Jamugha. He thought of moral obligations from years past and wondered if he might spare the life of this now powerless man.

Jamugha then replied:

"Anda, Temüjin. I am your friend now, but what value do I have for you? I am not thinking that I lost to you. My defeat at your hands was heaven's will. To the extent that I am living, I wished and believed that the day would come when you fell. You should quickly put an end to me. If you have some feeling for me as your anda, then kill me without shedding my blood and bury my corpse on a hilltop."

"So be it, anda Jamugha," replied Temüjin with a minimum of words. "I would forgive you, but because of the embarrassment to you, you shall be put to death just as you have requested it." Then he turned to his aide and said:

"Execute him without shedding blood. Do not dispose of the corpse in front of me. And bury him with full honors." Temüjin then stood up from his seat. He remained shut up in his tent all day long.

Sübe'etei accomplished his mission fully in half a year and appeared before Temüjin with a sunburned face. He had captured all the sons of the enemy leaders and executed all of them, right down to the infants. The items taken from the Naimans were all rare and extraordinary for the Mongols. Precious stones, carpets, clothing, weaponry, and the like formed several immense piles at Temüjin's base.

Amid the stack of precious jewels, Temüjin tried to take one he wanted for Qulan, but she stared into his face and said:

"These beautiful things, rare objects, and valuable items you should send to Börte, who is taking care of things in your absence on the other side of the Altai Mountains. I don't need a single stone or a single piece of cloth. All I wish for is one thing. Henceforth, whenever you go out to take the field, please keep me by your side."

Temüjin agreed. The embroidery, carpets, precious stones, and furniture from foreign lands were all tied to the backs of horses, and under special guard went back over the Altai Mountains to be delivered to the yurts in the foothills of Mount Burqan.

4

Temüjin Becomes Chinggis Khan

TEMÜJIN'S TRIUMPHAL RETURN TO his camp following the conquest of the Naimans took place in the spring of 1206. The Naimans' defeat meant that he had now fully pacified all of the peoples who built their settlements across the entire Mongolian plateau. He was literally the sole power holder, the sole king, on the plateau.

Soon after his return home, Temüjin set up a great banner with nine white tails—nine being a divine number to the Mongols and white considered an auspicious color—outside their camp on the upper reaches of the Onon River. It was essential to declare to all the peoples scattered across the entire terrain of the Mongolian plateau that he, Temüjin, was now *khan* of all Mongolia. Of necessity the ceremony was both grand and extremely solemn.

From about one month before this ceremony was carried out, the entire area surrounding the encampment was a scene of unprecedented congestion and disorder. Foodstuffs and other goods sent in on horseback by many peoples for the glorious event were arriving on virtually a daily basis, and laborers sent by these peoples were hard at work building stands for the audience in the broad pastureland outside the settlement. And for many days prior to the event, women were preparing food. Several dozen cauldrons were lined up in rows, and several dozen racks on which mutton was hanging were built beside them. In addition, an extraordinary number of pots of fermented mare's milk were all laid out on the ground with a curtain covering them. With the ceremony only a few days off, the settlement was filled with the aromas of fermented mare's milk and lambs' fat boiling. Temüjin's tent was rebuilt so high that it seemed to soar right into the sky, and a window at the top, when looked up at from below, appeared distant and tiny.

The site of the event was to be in front of Temüjin's new, large tent. The immense banner with nine tails had been installed, and the May wind was gently blowing the white hairs attached to it.

The big day arrived. The several thousand people permitted to participate in the grand ceremony crammed into the open area before the soaring tent. In the stands built on several levels surrounding the ceremonial site, crowds numbering in the tens of thousands gathered from all over the plateau to observe.

At the appointed time, Temüjin assumed his appointed position. At his right side were his mother, Ö'elün, his wife, Börte, and his four children, Jochi, Cha'adai, Ögedei, and Tolui; behind them numerous concubines were arrayed. Only Qulan had been assigned a place in the front row, while Yisügen and Yisüi had been given seats in the rear. The alien foundlings raised by Ö'elün—Shigi Qutuqu, Boroghul, Küchü, and Kököchü—had all grown up into vigorous young men and were lined up in the rear as well.

To Temüjin's left were his younger siblings, Qasar, Belgütei, Qachi'un, Temüge, and Temülün, and by their side were his high officials, Bo'orchu and Jelme, as well as his commanders, Chimbai, Chila'un, Jebe, Muqali, Sübe'etei, and Qubilai Noyan, and the elderly Münglig and Sorqan Shira.

The great deliberative body comprising the leaders of the various Mongolian peoples—the Quriltai—was convened in an earnest, formal manner. The elders of all these peoples resolved to install Temüjin as ruler of all Mongolia, and at that point a thoroughly unfamiliar name was called out by all the elders:

"Chinggis Khan! Chinggis Khan! Chinggis Khan!"

This was the appellation for the *khan* or sovereign of Mongolia respectfully being offered to Temüjin. It bore the meaning of a magnificent ruler. From this time forward, all the settlements over the entire Mongolian plateau were united under the name of Mongolia.

Chinggis Khan stood up from his seat. Cheers rang out from the site of the ceremony as well as from the assemblage surrounding it.

"Chinggis Khan! Chinggis Khan!"

At the top of their lungs, one and all called out the name of Chinggis Khan. He responded by raising his hand. He was forty-four years old. His hair had already turned half gray, while his mustache and beard remained black. Unlike when he had been a young man, his torso was now corpulent and he showed signs of slowing down.

More than at any time in the past, however, Chinggis Khan's entire body was full to overflowing with his own vigorous will. Mongolia had now taken on the form of a state. Gradually it was preparing to contest its archrival, the Jin, on the battlefield, something heretofore almost unthinkable, though now not beyond all expectation.

Bathed in the cheering voices of the assembled crowd, Chinggis Khan tried to envision in his own mind the position in which he was now standing. This was not a small piece of territory, from beyond the Altai Mountains all the way to the Xing'an mountain range. From the area around Lake Baikal in the north across the barren terrain of the Gobi Desert to the south, it extended to the Great Wall of China. Nearly two million nomads were scattered over the great expanse of the Mongolian plateau. Representatives of all of its settlements had now gathered here and were hailing him as their khan, their great ruler.

Had he so wished it, Chinggis Khan would have been able to call together all the nomads and cross the Great Wall. Chinggis was coming to believe that he actually would do this. If he was indeed a descendant of the blue wolf, he had to do it.

The sky was wide, blue, and clear. From the moment when Chinggis stood up in response to the cheers of the crowd, the sunlight had gradually begun to grow stronger and sharper. Facing the multitudes over which the commotion was spreading, he attempted to make his first speech as great khan. To quiet the tumult of the crowd, he waved his hand furiously. No matter how hard he waved, though, the excitement continued to hold sway over the throngs of people.

"There was a blue wolf born with a destiny set by heaven. There was a pale doe who came across a great lake in the west. These two creatures mated and gave birth to Batachiqan, ancestor of the Mongols. Mongols are the descendants of the blue wolf. The twenty-one peoples who encamp on the Mongolian plateau have cohered as a single force today around this blue wolf. At your recommendation, I now have acceded to the position of khan. A pack of wolves, we must cross the Xing'an Mountains, the Altai Mountains, Mount Tianshan, and the Qilian Mountains. We must do this to make all the camps on the Mongolian plateau nobler and more respectable. We must make for ourselves richer lives, richer enjoyments, and richer work than we have ever imagined before. If we wish all this for ourselves, can we live in stationary homes and be able to follow the flocks of sheep without moving with them? Your new khan has been authorized to issue to you all manner of orders to achieve this. Have trust in me! Carry out the orders I give, my courageous and fierce wolves of the new Mongolian state!"

Chinggis then ordered the banquet festivities open. Food and drink were brought out not only at the site of the ceremony itself but as far as the gallery around which the crowds thronged. The din of the feast continued day and night. During the daytime, virtually every day, the distinctive martial arts of the twenty-one peoples and numerous lineages were introduced, songs were sung in altogether different melodies and languages, and dances were performed. At nighttime, almost every night, a glowing moon came out. Several dozen bonfires were lit in the open area before Chinggis Khan's tent, as the drinking and eating continued unabated. People were drunk, people were dancing, and people were singing. The festive mood was unrestrained with no sense of hierarchy among the revelers.

On the third night, Chinggis noticed some old women in shabby clothing dancing with strange hand movements. Their song and dance concerned driving the flocks of sheep, and they repeated it over and over again without becoming weary. Chinggis suddenly realized that the movements were penetrating his own body. The women were poor, unsightly creatures whose appearance in no way resembled the pale doe. His thought was they would have to have more attractive clothing, and far more songs and dances to perform.

Inside his tent, Chinggis continued to be unnerved by the revelry of the festivities. In the midst of it all, he was overcome by an acute sense that Mongol men needed to have ever more intense training like wolves and Mongol women needed to be adorned in finer clothing like does.

On the final day of the long celebratory banquet, Chinggis announced to his subordinates the distribution of rewards about which he had been thinking while the festivities had been under way. On that day Chinggis first ordered that 95 men who had worked with him for many years be named chiefs of 1,000 households. They included Bo'orchu, Münglig, Muqali, Jelme, and Sorqan Shira. It was expected that from these 95 would be selected chiefs of 10,000 households.

When he turned to passing out honors, Chinggis sent attendants to summon to his tent specific individuals certain to be present somewhere across the wide grounds. The first to be so called were Bo'orchu and Muqali. Temüjin grasped Bo'orchu's hand and said:

"Friend, until this point in time, I have not expressed my thanks to you. You are my oldest friend who has sacrificed everything to work on my behalf."

He remembered fondly the day when a young Bo'orchu helped him retrieve eight stolen horses.

"Friend, your father, Naqu Bayan, is a wealthy man. You have abandoned the position of heir to a wealthy family and traveled a difficult path with me to this point. Bo'orchu, you shall control 10,000 households in the region of the Altai Mountains."

This was a gift so generous that Bo'orchu himself was stunned. Chinggis continued:

"Muqali, you shall control 10,000 households in the region of the Xing'an mountain range."

The young commander remained expressionless and silent in the face of the extraordinary reward given to him. When Chinggis had attacked his relatives Seche Beki and Taichu, a man by the name of Kü'ün U'a came to join Chinggis's camp along with two young men—one of whom was Muqali. At the time of the attack on the Naimans, he had distinguished himself on the field of battle, but unlike other such young men, he had a sincerity of character that had won the confidence of all the men fighting under him. Chinggis had selected this young commander. While Bo'orchu's achievements were in the past, in Muqali's case expectations ran high into the future. Chinggis named the young commander to lead the subsequent attack on the Jin. All Chinggis said was:

"You shall soon lead one million wolves and cross the Great Wall."

Expressionless, Muqali merely bowed his head.

Third to be called was the old man Qorchi. This old-timer who had once predicted that Temüjin would in future become khan of all Mongolia had not taken part in the fighting, but having been relieved of military duties, he had spent the past ten years in utter idleness. Qorchi had not even been given a seat at the installation ceremony, but had set up a chair before his tent and watched the daily hustle-bustle of the banquet as a bystander.

Qorchi made his way before Chinggis on legs that had in recent years become dangerously infirm.

"Prognosticator Qorchi," said Chinggis with deep affection. He remembered clearly when this old man—at the most difficult time, when he too had left Jamugha's camp—stood before him one night with a bright red face. The prophetic words uttered by this old man that night had now come to pass. Chinggis understood full well just how mightily influential on himself Qorchi's forecast had been.

"At that time, you said that if I were to become khan of all Mongolia, you wanted thirty beautiful women. I shall now fulfill for you that promise. You are an extraordinary, lecherous prognosticator! Go ahead and select for yourself thirty beautiful women."

Qorchi slowly moved the muscles of his even more deeply wrinkled face and said:

"Qorchi has now grown old. However, with thirty beautiful women, perhaps I shall grow young again." A quiet smile appeared on his face.

"In addition to thirty women," said Chinggis, "you shall take control over 10,000 households combining the Chinos, Tö'ölös, and Telenggüd lineages of the Adarkins. And you shall take control over the People of the Forest who live at the delta of the Erdish River."

Slowly bending his knees, Qorchi sat down on the ground. Suddenly the weight of the people of 10,000 households resting on his slender shoulders left him unable to stand any longer. With help from two assistants on either side, Qorchi lumbered off to his own small tent among the assembled masses of people.

After Qorchi had departed from his presence, Chinggis clarified the nature of Qorchi's powers further:

"Without Qorchi's permission, the People of the Forest may not move eastward. In all affairs, they are to consult Qorchi and receive his orders."

Each time words emerged from Chinggis's lips, a din went through the multitudes assembled around the ceremonial site. Chinggis's words spread through the crowd from one person to the next in relay fashion, and cheers and shouts then flowed over the site like rippling waves. The next brave fighter to come before Chinggis Khan was Qubilai Noyan. He was a young, dauntless commander on a par with Jelme, Jebe, and Sübe'etei, and he had never lost a battle.

"Qubilai, you shall take charge of all affairs concerning the army."

Although thoroughly satisfied by the reward he received, for his part Qubilai wanted to be assigned a more vigorous posting, even if lower in rank, directly linked to fighting. To be sure, his thinking did not at this time go so far as desiring the wildly immense authority to be able to dispatch an army of one million strong to various foreign lands.

"Fight on! Fight on!" murmured this Mongol wolf. He was just over thirty years of age and was a bit dissatisfied as he withdrew from before Chinggis.

Then Jelme came forward. The young man who had descended from Mount Burqan together with his father, carrying a pair of bellows on his shoulders, was nearing fifty years of age. He was a trusted retainer to Chinggis, second only to Bo'orchu.

"Friend," said Chinggis, "it would take me many days to recount all your meritorious deeds. When I was born, your father presented you to us with swaddling clothes made of wolf's fur. I should now like to offer you a gift in return. Among all the peoples of the Mongols, if Jelme alone commits offenses nine times, he shall not be punished."

Chinggis had not yet decided on a position to offer this friend. Were he to give him a large piece of territory or an especially wide range of authority, it seemed too small for Jelme.

"Jelme," continued Chinggis, "as for the position you shall assume and the range of your powers, let the two of us think about this together."

At the moment, Jelme would have been satisfied with any reward at all. He wanted to ask for some time off. Although he was of unparalleled strength on the battlefield, his real forte was in handling all the many details of which others were unaware. From early that very morning, Jelme had been concerned with how properly to return all the personal effects borrowed from many peoples for the festivities. In addition, he had to offer an appropriate return gift for all the presents received from these peoples, but no one was using their brain to effect this, and he was becoming somewhat angry about it.

"Jelme," said Chinggis, and Jelme then jumped up shouting:

"Be careful of fires! Be careful of fires!" Just at that moment, he remembered that he had forgotten to make preparations for the cooks' handling of their fires.

Next, the seventy-year-old Sorqan Shira stepped forward. When Chinggis had been taken captive by Targhutai, chief of the Tayichi'uds, and attempted to escape, this old man came to his rescue, allowing him to spend a night in his home. At that time, Sorqan Shira was half-naked, churning fermented mare's milk, but the smell of the mare's milk was altogether different from that which had for the past few days permeated the banquet. Chinggis recalled the odor from Sorqan Shira's home, and said while sniffing:

"Sorqan Shira, father of Chimbai and Chila'un, what sort of reward are you hoping for?"

"If I were to be so bold as to speak frankly," the old man responded, "I'd like to settle down by the Selengge River on Merkid land, not pay rent, and freely use it for pasturage. And if I were to be favored even more, then please, great khan, you do what you think is best. I would be glad to take whatever you deem should come my way."

"Well then, old man," said Chinggis, "you shall make your camp at the Selengge River of the Merkids and you shall be free to make it pastureland. You shall be exempt from rent and taxes to graze your herds as you see fit. Like Jelme, you shall not be punished even should you commit nine offenses."

Chinggis still felt, though, as if he had not given Sorqan Shira quite enough, as he recalled that during his escape when he had hid himself at the water's edge, Sorqan Shira had purposefully ignored him so as not to attract others' attention.

"If in the course of battle, you have acquired valuables from the enemy, Sorqan Shira, you may keep all that you have acquired for yourself."

"Great khan," said Sorqan Shira, "I hope that I shall live to join the army in battle once again."

"If you do, I shall accord you special privileges. During the grand hunt at night, you shall be able to keep for yourself all the animals that you kill."

But Chinggis still felt as though Sorqan Shira had not gotten his due.

"Sorqan Shira, with arrows strapped to you, may you live every evening as a banquet. And, so, my friend Sorqan Shira—"

Sorqan Shira then interrupted Chinggis and said:

"Great khan, this is already too much. What more could I hope for? If there is anything I might wish for, it would be to have the armies of the great khan cross the Great Wall and enter the state of Jin."

Indicating that there was nothing further that he wished, Sorqan Shira crossed his arms before him and hurriedly withdrew from

Chinggis's presence. Sorqan Shira's words led Chinggis to think
that having put Muqali, the man who was to lead the attacking army
against the Jin, in charge of 10,000 households might have been insufficient reward. Chinggis again called for Muqali and said:

"I am giving you the title of prince of the realm. Hereafter, people are to refer to you as Muqali, Prince of the Realm."

Muqali's complexion blanched before such a major reward, and
he replied that, upon serious reflection about the propriety of his
accepting such an honor, he would respond as to whether he could
assume this appellation or not.

In this fashion, Chinggis gave out to Chimbai, Chila'un, Jebe,
and other meritorious commanders what they were due. Jebe and
Sübe'etei, those two intrepid Mongol wolves, became chiefs of 1,000
households. The announcement of rewards continued well into the
night, and it was unclear when it would conclude. On another day,
he planned to award positions and powers to his younger brothers,
his children, and his wives and concubines.

Although the banquet came to an end that day, from the following day announcements continued on a daily basis of the posts that
the officers and men of the entire army were to assume. Orders were
conveyed with great austerity to the places where all the commanders were arrayed, and Chinggis Khan himself articulated what each
of their responsibilities was to be, down to the minutest of details.

The first announcement was that of bodyguards assigned to the
tent of Chinggis himself. These watchmen were in principle to be
made up of the children of chiefs of 10,000, 1,000, and 100 households. In addition, a path was opened whereby those among the
sons of common folk who were especially attractive or talented
could join this force.

"Sons of the chiefs of 1,000 households shall come to serve with
10 attendants and one younger brother. Sons of the chiefs of 100
households shall come to serve with five attendants and one younger brother. Sons of chiefs of 10 households shall come to serve with
three attendants and one younger brother. Each of these attendants
must be selected from distinguished families."

Chinggis began to work first on organizing the guard at his camp, which was to be responsible to him personally. This personal guard was to comprise bodyguards and archers. Two unknown young men were appointed chiefs of the bodyguards and of the archers. Their names had not yet risen among Chinggis's troops. At every opportunity, in wartime or peacetime, Chinggis had been keeping a close watch over the actions of these two young men. Then, when he divided his personal guard of 10,000 into 10 units, he appointed a chief bodyguard of each group of 1,000. The majority of these men were the sons of meritorious officers.

Chinggis went on to describe the duties of the bodyguards and the archers on night watch:

—If anyone passes the camp front or back after sundown, they are to be taken in and questioned the next day. With the changing of the guard, the night guards must turn in their identification tallies.

—The night guards shall sleep around the circumference of the camp, and if anyone should enter at night, their heads are to be cut off immediately.

—No one shall sit in a seat above the night guards. No one shall ask the number of night guards. If someone should walk among the night guards, arrest him and tie him up.

—No night guard may leave the camp.

—Any incidents arising among the night guards shall be judged in consultation with Shigi Qutula.

Shigi Qutula was a Tatar orphan raised by Chinggis's mother, Ö'elün. By his own strange fate, he had grown into a young man with a serenity of mind that, no matter what transpired, remained unruffled. In a position most fitting to him, Chinggis installed this Tatar foundling with a perennially pallid face who was not much liked by others. A fair amount of time went into Chinggis's announcements on the organization and duties of the personal guard.

To his commanders who heard him, Chinggis Khan that day seemed a thoroughly different man from the Chinggis who, in the chaotic atmosphere at the time of the banquet, had been anxious to reward his men. The expression on his face, the tone of his voice, and the look in his eye were all those of an altogether changed person. Aside from a tiny group of his officers, no one had any idea when Chinggis had thought all of this up. With each passing day, the organization of military and civil administrations of a new Mongolian state was announced by Chinggis Khan himself. He and his top commanders had to stand for lengthy periods of time in the searing summer sun, and his face became deeply sunburned.

One day Qulan said to Chinggis, who had come to her tent:

"Great khan, shouldn't you soon offer rewards to relatives who share my blood? Even if it's just a simple stone, until they actually receive it, they can't properly think of it as their own."

"You needn't be concerned," he replied, smiling, "for soon we shall be dividing up rewards to blood relatives. Every princess will be able to take what she desires. What is it that you would like?"

"I wish for nothing that I do not already have," Qulan replied. "Are not the states of the Uyghurs, the Jin, and others in your mind now, great khan? I would like to see all those magnificent dreams come true together with you, great khan. When shall you cross the Altai Mountains for the fourth time?"

Chinggis silently stared into Qulan's face. The pale doe showed off a lithe figure as she stood next to him.

Soon after the founding of the Mongolian state, the most troublesome issue for Chinggis became that of Münglig and his seven sons. Fifteen or sixteen years older than Chinggis, Münglig was now already an old man of some sixty years of age.

He had given Münglig and his sons positions of considerable trust. He had placed Münglig in a post enabling him to sit on the highest council of elders, and his sons had taken up various and sundry positions of importance. Chinggis had invested such trust in them solely out of obligation to Münglig's father, Charaqa. Chinggis could never forget that, shortly after his father, Yisügei, had died some thirty years earlier, his household had fallen to the depths of misery, and when all the other families separated themselves from him, only one man, old Charaqa, came and gave his life for them.

At the time of Charaqa's death, the young Chinggis was profoundly moved by the singular fidelity of this older man, and throughout the following thirty years the emotions from that time lived on in his heart. In lieu of repaying Charaqa himself, Chinggis was rewarding his son Münglig and Charaqa's seven grandsons.

As for Münglig himself, Chinggis simply did not trust the man. Unlike Charaqa, he had abandoned Chinggis and his entire family and then had the audacity to return with his seven sons once Chinggis had become a grown man. But Chinggis overlooked all such matters when it came to Münglig and his sons. Whenever he contemplated them, Chinggis forced himself to replace the lot of them in his mind with the faithful Charaqa.

The most difficult thing about Münglig for Chinggis to endure was how intimate he had become with Chinggis's mother. When their relationship began was unclear, but Münglig had returned to his service at Chinggis's camp thirteen years ago, and probably it had started sometime soon thereafter. Ö'elün was now in her mid-sixties; thirteen years before, she would have been only fifty or so. For many years she had devoted herself to the painstaking work of raising her own five children, and it was certainly imaginable—and indeed permissible—for her to wish to spend her last years living as a woman again.

Chinggis, however, was unhappy to see Münglig at the tent of his mother. This may have been permissible for her, but not for Münglig. For this reason, he had for many years kept his distance from his mother's tent.

With Chinggis having adopted this attitude, the relationship between Ö'elün and Münglig was semi-officially recognized, and thus Münglig exercised a certain amount of latent influence. And not only Münglig but his seven sons as well; they hid behind their father's position, and they gradually began to commit more and more actions of an intolerable nature. Particularly egregious was his eldest son, the shaman priest Teb Tenggeri. This diviner had selected the name Chinggis Khan for Temüjin, and this too helped make Teb Tenggeri more arrogant. Chinggis allowed Teb Tenggeri to freely attend all council meetings as a spokesman for the divine, but the middle-aged soothsayer with his balding pate, dauntless and hawklike eyes, and dark skin manipulated his father's singular position and his own special privilege as an oracle who could control matters of both religion and politics. He worked diligently and oftentimes with unseemly behavior to extend the influence of his own relatives.

Just as Chinggis did not trust Münglig, he did not trust Teb Tenggeri. However, because Teb Tenggeri's predictions were uncannily precise, even if he despised the man, he could not expel the oracle whom he represented out of hand.

Toward the end of the summer in the year that Chinggis acceded to the position of khan, an incident came to pass. Teb Tenggeri was waiting upon Chinggis, seeking a private audience.

"I convey to you words from the deity of long life," he said by way of introduction, in a highly dignified manner. These were to be words that Chinggis could not ignore. His younger brother Qasar, claimed Teb Tenggeri, was plotting to depose Chinggis and become king. Chinggis could simply not believe this.

"Even if these are words of a deity," he said sternly to this unearthly diviner, "what sort of explanation is there for them? Upon what basis can you make such a claim? Go and ask the deity?"

Teb Tenggeri replied, with a ghastly smile coming over his face:

"The deity says to the great khan to go to Qasar's tent. The great khan will see something dreadful there."

Upon hearing this, Chinggis and several of his attendants left their tent and walked the roughly 200 yards to Qasar's tent. Twilight was just enveloping the neighborhood. There appeared to be some sort of celebration under way at Qasar's tent, and a banquet begun that day was winding down.

Chinggis stood in a corner of the open space before Qasar's tent. The people crowding the area were standing and causing a commotion. Many people smelling of alcohol were coming out of the tent and vomiting. At this moment, Chinggis noticed among the people there Qulan, accompanied by several maidservants, emerging from the tent. Although it would not have been unusual for Qasar to invite Qulan to a celebration, in the next instant Chinggis saw Qasar appear at the entrance to his tent, coming after her and trying to take her hand. Qasar was plainly drunk. Qulan tried twice to brush aside his hand, and surrounded by her maidservants, she walked through the crowd over to the opposite corner from where Chinggis was standing.

Chinggis was overcome with rage at Qasar. As Teb Tenggeri had said, he saw something dreadful. And, as Teb Tenggeri said, Qasar seemed clearly to be harboring treasonous intentions.

When he returned to his tent, Chinggis immediately sent troops to seize Qasar. A few minutes later, Chinggis proceeded to Qasar's tent. Qasar had been stripped of his girdle and sword and stood shackled before his bed. Furious with him, Chinggis could not bring himself to speak. Why was Qasar, who had been at his side since they were children and with whom he had shared every trial, now revolting against him? Chinggis stood silently, unable to decide what to do with his younger brother. Should he banish Qasar, execute him, or lock him in jail?

Just then, the curtain at the entrance to his tent flapped open roughly, and he saw his mother, Ö'elün, enter. She had recently begun to show a rapid physical deterioration, and her gait was precarious, as if she were suffering spasms. Ö'elün's appearance was for Chinggis a completely unexpected event. Someone, it seemed, had reported the pressing news to her.

Ö'elün walked right over to Qasar, untied the rope binding him, and returned his hat and girdle to him. When she finished, unable to suppress her rage, she sat down on the spot cross-legged. With a scowl on her face, she stared fixedly at Chinggis and said:

"Chinggis Khan, do you want me to expose my withered, drooping breasts to you? Do you want me to again take out these same two breasts from which you drank and Qasar suckled? You murdered your younger brother Begter. Are you now once again about to kill Qasar? Like a dog chewing its afterbirth, a panther rushing into a cliff, a lion unable to stifle its rage, a serpent swallowing animals alive, a large falcon dashing at its own shadow, a *churaqa* fish swallowing silently, a camel biting at the heel of its colt, a wolf injuring its head and mouth, a mandarin duck eating its young because it cannot keep up with them, a jackal attacking if one moves his sleeping spot, a tiger not hesitating to capture its quarry, and a wolverine rushing off recklessly, are you about to murder Qasar who has for so long served at your side?"

Unthinking, Chinggis took two or three steps back. Old Ö'elün was fuming with anger. His mother's wrath was greater even than when he had killed Begter, and the words that rushed out of her mouth, as if she were possessed, were more truculent than at that earlier time. Somewhat bewildered, Chinggis stared into his mother's face. Her visage was like that of a giant serpent that would swallow him, standing before her, alive. She had wailed at the time of the killing of Begter, but now not a single tear was to be seen. Chinggis took another two or three steps back.

"Qasar is free to go," he asserted. "Qasar shall remain at my side for many years to come."

Turing his back on his mother and younger brother, Chinggis left the tent. He walked along with a sense of helplessness under the high nocturnal sky inlaid with stars. Getting to the bottom of whether Qasar had harbored rebellious ambitions aside, it was a fact that he had tried to grab Qulan's hand, and that action alone could not be allowed. However, Chinggis had allowed it. For Ö'elün, who had borne all manner of difficulty in raising them, only for his irreplaceable elderly mother, Chinggis would excuse Qasar's action.

This was not the reason, though, that Chinggis now felt helpless. It was because his mother's eyes were those of the doe that seeks to protect her young from predators. For the first time, Chinggis felt that he and Qasar both equally had Ö'elün as their mother, but he also had to recognize that there was something other than Qasar between them. While Qasar was legitimately the son born of Ö'elün and Yisügei, Chinggis was a child born as a result of Ö'elün's being kidnapped by a Merkid marauder. Of this there was no doubt. Just as Ö'elün despised the Merkid invader who had caused his birth, perhaps she also despised him. It seemed clear to Chinggis that day that she was trying to shield both the secret of his birth and the person of Qasar.

In any event, for his mother's sake Chinggis abandoned the idea of punishing Qasar. But, inasmuch as he was not going to discipline Qasar, he would now have to exact punishment from Teb Tenggeri, who had jumped to the conclusion, via oracular revelation, that Qasar was a traitor. Chinggis slept not a wink that night because of his mother and the oracle. With the approach of dawn, he made up his mind for his mother's sake to kill this mouthpiece for the divine.

The next day when he saw Teb Tenggeri, who came to his tent, Chinggis immediately had his guards seize him and turn him over to three strongmen who had earlier received orders to this effect. The strongmen took Teb Tenggeri outside the tent, walked him a short distance, and then quickly broke his back. As soon as they saw that he was dead, they discarded him among the weeds.

An hour later, Chinggis went to the site to see Teb Tenggeri's corpse. His father and brothers, each accompanied by their minions, had gathered together to take charge of Teb Tenggeri's remains. Münglig came before Chinggis and said:

"I have been the great khan's comrade from the earliest days of our Mongolian people, but you have now murdered my eldest son."

There was a certain echo of haughtiness in his words, conscious as he was of being Ö'elün's partner.

"Münglig," roared Chinggis, his voice trembling. "Teb Tenggeri met his end without heaven's mercy as a sacrifice to the tyrannical behavior of you and your family. Would you all like to join Teb Tenggeri and line up your corpses together?"

In abject fear, Münglig and his sons left Teb Tenggeri where he lay and withdrew. On this occasion as well, Chinggis for his mother's sake desisted from taking Münglig's life.

Teb Tenggeri's body remained on the ground as if he were an immortal spirit, consistent with his shamanistic beliefs. Although people were frightened by the strangeness of this incident, Chinggis didn't take it to heart. On behalf of his mother, he had saved two people he had been eager to kill. That Teb Tenggeri's corpse should end up on the ground struck Chinggis as perfectly fine.

Thereafter Chinggis treated Qasar as if nothing had happened. For his part, Qasar resumed his valued position as Chinggis's right-hand man. The same circumstances prevailed in the case of Münglig. He continued as before, living with Ö'elün, and without any censure whatsoever he retained his privilege of attending meetings of the highest council of elders. With the death of Teb Tenggeri, though, the influence of Münglig and his family members was sharply curtailed, and their high-handed behavior ceased.

The following year, 1207, shortly after the founding of his state, Chinggis Khan set to work thoroughly mopping up surrounding areas in which there were people who had yet to acknowledge his authority.

First, he sent Qubilai Noyan to attack the Qarluqs in the early spring. Although Qubilai was the commander in charge of all military matters, he had specially requested of Chinggis to lead an army on this mission. The chief of the Qarluqs surrendered without a fight, and returning with Qubilai to camp, had an audience with Chinggis. The khan treated him warmly and promised to give him a daughter, a Mongol princess, in marriage when she reached her majority. A girl born to his concubine Yisüi was still only three years of age, making it a bit early to offer her in marriage yet.

Next, there were reports of unrest among the Naimans, and Jebe was sent on an expedition to crush it in the early summer. In half a year's time, Jebe had wiped them out, and he returned triumphantly in late autumn.

Soon after Jebe's return to camp, ambassadors from the Uyghurs, who lived in areas peripheral to Mongolian terrain, arrived and swore fealty to Chinggis. As tribute, they offered gold, silver, small and large pearls, silks, brocades, and damask—all highly valued items. Chinggis rewarded the Uyghur chief and promised him Princess Al Altun. She was the daughter of Yisügen and was only a few years old.

In 1208, Chinggis sent his eldest son, Jochi, as commander of an army against the forested region to the north. It was the first military action outside the borders of the state since its founding. If Chinggis were to be prepared for trouble with the Jin to his southeast, where they shared a border now, and if he were to engage the Uyghurs to the southwest in battle, he had first to eliminate any threat from the north. There was no powerful force in the north. A number of backward tribes were scattered in the area around Lake Baikal, and the north was severely cold wasteland where no one could live, Siberian terrain the Mongols had been unable to penetrate.

Jochi was twenty-one years of age. Born to his mother, Börte, for the purpose of enduring all the hardships of the Mongolian people, he had received rigorous training. When rumors of an expedition into Siberia began to spread, Börte asked Chinggis if this task might be given to Jochi for his first leadership role in battle.

"That land is interminable," said Chinggis. "After crossing Lake Baikal, I don't know how far one can go."

"Jochi's feet are stronger than the hoofs of a mountain goat," said Börte, raising her head.

"The next battle on Siberian terrain," said Chinggis, "will not be against other men. More likely it will be against nature."

"Since he was a baby, Jochi has been raised as a friend of the wind and snow," replied Börte. "He was not raised inside a tent."

"But in the next battle, ninety out of a hundred men may not return," said Chinggis, and with a stern look in her eyes, Börte responded:

"Was not Jochi born to face head on such an austere fate?"

For a moment, Chinggis continued staring at Börte, and eventually he said in a low voice:

"So be it, we'll send Jochi!"

Chinggis had been thinking that the leader of this battle in Siberia would have to be someone who had at least reached middle age and who could temper severity with leniency, and Jelme would be the perfect choice. Given Börte's earnest desire, though, Chinggis now made up his mind to give twenty-one-year-old Jochi, his eldest son, the task. Chinggis sensed in Börte's eyes a sharp look of defiance. She was challenging the father who had never fully believed that Jochi was his own son.

This was the first time Jochi was to be commander of an army. Leading several tens of thousands of wolves, he departed from the great Mongol encampment in early May, a time when the snow was melting in the north. They headed north along a tributary of the Selengge River.

Late that year, Jochi returned victorious. His achievements on the battlefield had been extraordinary. With Quduqa Beki of the Oirats, who first came to surrender before him, as his guide, Jochi went on to conquer in succession the Oirat, Buriat, Barghu, Urasud, Qabqanas, Qangqas, and Tuvan peoples. He then defeated the Kyrgyz, who were the most powerful people in this area, subdued the People of the Forest in the northwest region, and returned with a number of the Kyrgyz leaders. They presented to Chinggis Khan great quantities of large white arctic falcons, white geldings, and black sables. Quduqa Beki of the Oirats came with them.

As sovereign of the Mongolian people, Chinggis issued the following edict according high praise for Jochi's triumphs:

—Jochi went on an expedition to the barren terrain of the northwest, enduring a long and rocky path. Not harming the local inhabitants nor wounding the geldings, you have conquered the fortunate People of the Forest. As for the people and the land that you conquered, it is altogether fitting that these shall now be yours.

Chinggis had now to recognize something extraordinary that he had failed to notice heretofore about Jochi with the overly slender, rather delicate frame. Chinggis was now fully satisfied that Jochi bore the blood of the Mongolian people and had superbly proven himself a descendant of the blue wolf.

The day his decree hailing Jochi's accomplishments was announced, Chinggis received in audience the chiefs of the peoples living on the Mongolian periphery who had now become his subordinates. He was in extremely good humor. He proclaimed that day that Quduqa Beki, the first to perform meritorious service among them as reported to the throne by Jochi, would receive Princess Checheyiken, born to one of the khan's concubines. It was then noted that there was far too great an age difference between the forty-year-old Quduqa Beki and the five-year-old Checheyiken, and Chinggis immediately halted this reward midstream and decided that Checheyiken would instead go to Quduqa Beki's thirteen-year-old son, Inalchi.

"Quduqa Beki," proclaimed Chinggis, "tomorrow, be standing on the hillock north of the encampment. At that time, you may take from all of the flocks of sheep as far as the eye can see."

"Inalchi is my second son," replied Quduqa Beki. "My eldest son, Törölchi, I left back in our settlement."

When he heard this, Chinggis said:

"In that case, I shall give Holuiqan, daughter of Jochi, to your eldest son Törölchi."

When Quduqa Beki of the Oirats withdrew, next to appear was none other than the chief of the Önggüds who had participated in the fighting with them.

"Leader of the Önggüds," intoned Chinggis, "I shall give to you Princess Alaqai Beki."

Alaqai Beki had only recently been born to a concubine. Even if they were his own daughters or granddaughters, Chinggis did not have much respect for females. He saw no need whatsoever to keep the infant girl under his own care.

On the occasion of his giving this terrain to Jochi, Chinggis announced that he was also bestowing territory on his close relatives, to whom he had not as yet given anything. To Ö'elün and his youngest brother Temüge, he gave 10,000 people each. In Mongol society, family headship was inherited by the youngest son, meaning that Temüge was to acquire a greater portion than any of his siblings. Ö'elün remained silent, possibly displeased. Although he understood that his mother might have been dissatisfied, Chinggis had no plans to give the woman any more than this.

To his eldest son, Jochi, Chinggis gave 9,000 people; to his next son, Cha'adai, 8,000; to his third son, Ögedei, 5,000; and to his youngest son, Tolui, the same number of 5,000. To his younger brothers, Qasar and Belgütei, he gave 4,000 and 1,500, respectively. Although the rewards to close relatives were rather small, those to Qasar and Belgütei were especially so. As far as Chinggis was concerned, there was no need whatsoever to hurriedly hand over spoils to his family members. He perhaps should have given greater rewards to Qasar and Belgütei. That was all to transpire at a later date. For now, he had simply taken control over the Mongolian plateau as his own domain.

There was, in fact, one further reason for this distribution: a certain distance was beginning to develop between Chinggis and his younger brothers, Qasar and Belgütei. Qasar probably had a different father than Chinggis, and Belgütei clearly had a different mother. All three had endured many difficult years before the Mongols reached their present situation, and all had stood together as one in body and mind against every hardship and suffering.

Until now, Chinggis had thought that his two brothers had a valued and necessary place difficult to fill with anyone else. Now that the Mongols had risen to such prominence with their great state, Chinggis no longer felt that Qasar and Belgütei possessed any such importance. It was different in the cases of Bo'orchu and Jelme. While Qasar lacked the talent to rule over men, his capacity as a distinguished commander on the battlefield could not be denied. Belgütei, though, in the fighting against the Naimans had posted a string of defeats due to imprudence. He not only was incapable of leading his own troops but also lacked certain elements needed in a leader of men.

Chinggis had not forgotten to reward these two men, but in so doing there was a time and method to be selected. He had dreamed that he would give to Qasar the villages off in the unknown west and to Belgütei the unknown grasslands to the north, and then make them each rulers over their respective domains. Chinggis was not in the least moved in this instance by his mother's dissatisfaction. Ö'elün had thought that she no longer served any need. She would always be with him and with the Mongol people.

As the end of the year approached, Ö'elün suddenly became ill and after three days passed away. She was sixty-six. The funeral was a grand affair. Her corpse was carried on the shoulders of the four foundlings, all of different ethnicities, whom she had raised and who all had grown into splendid adults serving important functions—

Kököchü, Küchü, Shigi Qutuqu, and Boroghul—and she was laid to rest at a site with a beautiful view of the slope of Mount Burqan.

When his mother's body was placed in the grave, Chinggis for the first time wailed. His cries immediately spread to the surrounding peoples. Lamentations were heard from Chinggis's brothers too, of course, as well as from Börte, Bo'orchu, Jelme, Chimbai, and Chila'un. The two million people of the twenty-one Mongol divisions all spent the next month in mourning.

The greatest thing that Chinggis took from the death of his mother was the thought that the one person who knew the secret of his birth had departed this world. With the passing of the woman who had given birth to him, raised him, and shared all their great hardships, Chinggis suffered as the child with whom she had shared blood; apart from this, though, the person who at least possessed the knowledge to judge whether he was Merkid or Mongol was now gone, and he felt a deep loneliness, as if suddenly abandoned naked on the face of the earth. He hadn't been able to ferret anything out of Ö'elün, and he had no desire to do so; what was troubling him was the simple fact that the person who held the decisive information was no more.

With the death of his mother, Chinggis felt a certain sense of expansive freedom that he never would have predicted. It was the absence of a person who kept watch on what he was thinking. Chinggis had dreamed until now that he was the legitimate descendant of the blue wolf and the pale doe, but if he tried to believe this, he felt that Ö'elün was somehow always impeding his thoughts. While mourning his mother, Chinggis realized for the first time that he was now free to dream and to believe that he himself was the legitimate heir of the blue wolf—and he was able to enhance this point as self-knowledge.

The great state of Jin was now brought into close-up before Chinggis Khan: as an enemy to be butchered and as spoils to be greedily devoured.

A new year's banquet was not held in Chinggis's camp while the mourning continued, and in its stead he summoned on a daily basis his subordinates with many and sundry expressions on their faces. He placed the same issue before each of these trusted men and sought their response. Rarely one to express his own views verbally, Chinggis wanted to hear theirs. The proposition he laid before them was how the Mongols, soon after forming their state, could be put on the path to prosperity.

Over a period of about ten days, Chinggis was able to listen to the opinions of several dozen men and women. He learned the views of important officers such as Bo'orchu, Muqali, and Jelme; the thoughts of the elders of the various lineages; the points of view of youngsters training day and night for battle; and even the ideas of the women who tended the sheep. And in so doing, Chinggis learned that all strata of men and women who formed the Mongolian state, now only shortly after its founding, hoped for a more prosperous life that they might enjoy even more than the one into which they had been born. This aspiration coincided with Chinggis's own thinking. What the great majority of people reported to their great khan as the means to attain this hoped-for life was an invasion of the neighboring land—that, and a fair distribution of the spoils and tribute acquired through such an invasion.

Among those whom Chinggis queried for their views, two who held positions significantly different from his own were his commander Jebe and his beloved concubine Qulan. An audacious young man who once had taken a shot at Chinggis, Jebe seemed to come up with something, as effortlessly as one would pick up a pebble, of which none of the other Mongols had thought:

"The Mongolian people must abandon their sheep. As long as we keep the sheep, good fortune will never be ours." Jebe's words were filled with an almost unimaginable audacity.

"Better land on which to live than the Mongolian plateau," said Qulan, "without a doubt lies elsewhere. Can we not all leave this place with its ferociously hot summers and equally frigid winters and go there together? Great khan, pitching our tents at the foot-hills of mountains more beautiful than Mount Burqan and building cities along rivers clearer than the Onon are your affairs." What Qulan said was not the sort of thing any Mongol had ever mouthed before.

Chinggis understood that, although these two had expressed it differently, they were thinking exactly the same thing. Both were indicating that there was nothing on the ancestral soil of the Mongolian people that boded well for future prosperity. Chinggis would discuss what each had said on another occasion, but when they had finished speaking, he said the same thing to both:

"The Mongols may soon be doing this."

The only place rich in resources on which the two million Mongols might live, having abandoned their flocks of sheep, was the land of the state of Jin. If they were looking for beautiful mountains and clear streams, the only conceivable place was the Jin.

At the end of the first month of the year, Chinggis addressed the Mongol council of elders and expressed the words of Jebe and Qulan, albeit in altogether different language:

"The mission bequeathed by the heaven of the Mongol people is linked to our age-old enemy, the Jin. Our ancestor Hambaghai Khan was captured by the Tatars, transported to the Jin, and nailed to a wooden donkey. While he was still alive, his skin was peeled off. Both Qabul Khan and Qutula Khan were murdered in plots. We must never forget the bloodstained humiliations experienced throughout Mongol history. I expect that we shall commence our battle against the Jin this spring, and we must eliminate any state that hinders the path of the Mongol armies on their way against the Jin."

The state that stood in the way of the Mongol armies was the Xixia. Before he launched a decisive battle against the Jin, then, they would have to attack the Xixia. Two years earlier, the Xixia had brought tribute, and they now enjoyed peaceful ties with the Mongols, but Chinggis had never been satisfied with the arrangement. Whether or not he was justified, at some point he would have to take weapons in hand and subjugate, then destroy the Xixia. Those who were anxious about the Mongol posture vis-à-vis the state of Jin would all have to be eliminated.

A small incident took place before the arrival of spring. Qorchi, the elderly, lewd prognosticator who was given control over 10,000 households of people living in the delta of the Erdish River, was apprehended by the people in one of the settlements he ruled. Using the "special privilege" Chinggis had bestowed upon him, Qorchi had gone out hunting for beautiful girls among the local villagers, causing them considerable misery.

To save Qorchi, Chinggis decided to send Quduqa Beki of the Oirats, who had cooperated with Jochi in the previous year's fighting. Soon after, however, news reached Chinggis that Quduqa Beki had been captured.

To save both Qorchi and Quduqa Beki, Chinggis now decided to dispatch Boroghul with a small detachment of troops. When he was about to set out, Chinggis ordered him to resolve the matter peaceably as best he could, without resorting to violence. If anyone could succeed in this, he thought, Boroghul could. When Chinggis had attacked the traitors Seche Beki and Taichu of the Yürkins, Boroghul had been a five- or six-year-old whom old Qorchi had picked up in the camp, and that youngster had now grown into a strapping youth nearing twenty years of age.

From Boroghul's perspective, old Qorchi was his benefactor who had selected him, and Chinggis Khan had now presented him with the task of saving his benefactor from peril. It was not only because of this tie between Boroghul and Qorchi but also because Chinggis thought that Boroghul was the right man for the job. The young man had a sweet face like a girl that made a good impression, and he had a native talent in negotiations. He was able to move his counterparts to his own way of thinking without upsetting them, as though they were pieces on a chessboard.

Among the four foundlings raised by Ö'elün, Chinggis was particularly drawn to Boroghul and harbored great expectations for his future. Chinggis thought vaguely that at some future time when he would dispatch an ambassador to a major state, he would probably send Boroghul.

Sending Boroghul to the Erdish River delta, however, turned out to be a major disaster for Chinggis. About a month after leaving

the Mongol camp, Boroghul returned as a corpse. Chinggis was ap-
palled to realize that, because of some insignificant complications at
the frontier, he had lost an irreplaceably valuable person.

"This was my blunder," Chinggis said with a sigh. "I should
have kept Boroghul well within our encampment until it came time
to send him as emissary to the Jin capital."

A moment later, his entire face flushed crimson, Chinggis
screamed out:

"Burn down the entire Erdish River delta, every tree, every blade
of grass. Dörbei Doqshin, set an army on the march!"

Dörbei Doqshin was a commander who seemed to have been
born to commit mass murder against any group deemed an enemy.
After he left a place, it was said, not a tree or a blade of grass could be
seen. Bo'orchu and Muqali opposed the sending of Dörbei Doqshin
to handle a matter on Mongolian terrain, but Chinggis would not be
dissuaded in this.

A month later, Dörbei Doqshin, a small man with pallid skin and
reddish-brown hair, returned with old Qorchi and Quduqa Beki.
His troops were carrying a bizarre collection of weapons, hatchets,
adzes, saws, and chisels among them.

"The People of the Forest are all dead," reported Dörbei
Doqshin. "The trees of the forest have all been turned to ash."

He had accomplished Chinggis's orders to the letter.

In early summer, as planned, Chinggis mobilized an army on an
immense scale to launch an attack on the Xixia. The Xixia was a
state created by the Tangut people of Tibet, who held sway in the
area between the Mongols and the Jin. Insofar as the Mongols did
not control this area, they were prevented from attacking the Jin.
Were they to avoid the Xixia, they would run into the obstacles of
the Great Wall and the Xing'an Mountains, and it was virtually impossible for a large army to break through these impediments. The
only way to advance a great army against the Jin was to pacify the
Xixia and enter within the Great Wall from southern Xixia terrain.

Invading Xixia, though, would be quite an undertaking, for it
entailed Mongol armies crossing an immense desert in a march that
would require a number of weeks. At the end of May, Chinggis led

a massive force of well over 100,000 in crossing the vast wasteland of the Gobi Desert, heading straight for the Xixia capital of Zhongxing. In the desert they met the Xixia army, led by the heir to the Xixia throne of King Li Anquan. For the Mongol soldiers, this was their first battle with a genuinely alien ethnicity.

However, their own relative military superiority was amply apparent. The camels, horses, and troops of the Xixia army were quickly surrounded on all sides by bands of Mongol cavalrymen and stunned by an assault from which they were unable to recover.

Mongol troops repeatedly outstripped the defeated enemy army and continued on toward Zhongxing. En route Chinggis divided his men into three groupings respectively under the command of Jebe, Muqali, and Qubilai Noyan. The ferocious Mongol wolves pressed in on Zhongxing from the north, west, and south, and in short order they had the city surrounded.

Both Chinggis and his subordinates now saw for the first time the great turbid flow of the Yellow River to the west of the city, and also for the first time they saw the Great Wall, which engirded one mountain ridge after another like an iron corridor. The siege lasted half a year, and Chinggis had to lift it early because the Yellow River overflowed its banks. Ultimately, though, a peace was reached with the Xixia ruler and Chinggis compelled him to send tribute; with the ruler's daughter among them, Chinggis's forces withdrew.

The expedition against the Xixia bore unexpected fruit for Chinggis. Fearing the power of the Mongols, the Uyghurs who had built a state to the west of the Xixia sent an ambassador bearing tribute to them as well.

5

Attack on the Jin

WHEN CHINGGIS RETURNED TO his camp on the Mongolian plateau at the end of the year, he introduced into Mongol military training all the new knowledge he had acquired in the fighting with the first truly alien people of an alien state he had confronted, the Xixia. The group battle formation was largely altered, with military units all incorporated into the cavalry. As for weapons, they abandoned short spears and adopted longer ones, at the same time introducing the basilisk and cannon in place of bows and arrows. Day by day, battle training grew more strenuous and more strict. Aside from the very young, the old, and the infirm, all men were moved into military barracks and received military training. Those who did not receive such training were assigned to the production of weaponry including "willow leaf armor" and "encompassing armor," as well as the "ram's horn bow" and "sounding arrows." The women tended the flocks of sheep and sewed the clothing. Even when night fell on the Mongolian plateau, the flicker of lantern lights could be seen everywhere. These showed the movement of cavalry troops, torches in hand, in nocturnal military exercises.

Many roads were now being built within Mongolia, and post stations with robust troops and horses were established at strategic points along them. All news was transmitted from station to station, and conveyed to Chinggis Khan's camp with the speed of an arrow. Similarly, Chinggis's orders were conveyed like a surging wave to every remote site on the vast plateau.

Laws and punishments were reinstituted with even greater severity. Thieves had to return three times the value of stolen goods. In
the case of the theft of a camel, even just one, the thief would be
executed. There were even strict penal regulations concerning ar-
guments and the drinking of alcohol. All of these laws and penalties
reflected a situation in which the soldiers were out on expeditions
and the homeland was emptied of them, leaving only the women
behind.

Chinggis spent the entire year of 1210 in preparation for a military expedition against the state of Jin. He had not fully resolved in
his own mind, though, just when to attack. He had as yet no idea just
how immense was the might possessed by the great Jurchen state
of the Jin, as well as its military capacity and its economic clout.
Such preparations, having required years, now seemed to be nearing completion, as the Mongols had amassed considerable strength.

In the summer of this year, an emissary from the Jin arrived.
Around the time that the delegation appeared at the border, news
was transmitted immediately through a dozen or more post stations
to Chinggis's tent. Thus, Chinggis waited for several days for the
emissary to arrive.

The ambassador conveyed the news that the Jin emperor Zhangzong [r. 1189–1208] had died and his son Yinji [or Yongji, r. 1208–13]
had acceded to the throne. He came on this occasion to encourage a
renewal of the now long-abrogated Mongol tribute.

Chinggis treated the ambassador coolly from the start, adopt-
ing an attitude fully consistent with interviewing an embassy from
a subject state. The person who acceded to the Jin throne had to
be a brave and sagacious ruler, but Yinji, he had heard, was not a
man of such caliber. It was thus utterly preposterous that he be encouraged to send tribute to Jin. Chinggis said as much and stood
up. The emissary and his group had no choice but to return home
immediately.

Although news of the death of Emperor Zhangzong had actually
reached Chinggis's ears the previous year, he had been unable to
ascertain if it was true. The formal Jin embassy now enabled him to
know the truth. That night in a room in his tent, Chinggis decided

that the time was right to send his armies against the Jin. On the morning of the second day thereafter, he announced his decision to a group of the Mongol elders. The expedition was to commence six months from then, in the third month of 1211.

From the day he proclaimed the date for launching the expedition, military meetings were held on a daily basis in Chinggis's tent. Fierce debates ensued among the commanders—Bo'orchu, Jelme, Qasar, Muqali, Jebe, and Sübe'etei, among others—over the attack routes to take against the Jin. The western route passed through Xixia, and now that the Xixia had been subjugated, it seemed the most natural way. It was convenient in terms of logistics, and the road itself was generally clear. The eastern route crossed over one mountain range after another, and after breaking through a corner of the Great Wall, they would have to forge an assault route. Taking the eastern way had the two benefits of catching the enemy by surprise and being able to forge a road of invasion that followed a number of sites along the line of the Great Wall. The western route followed a narrow stretch of land through the southern terrain of the Xixia.

After listening to the opinions of his commanders, Chinggis ultimately decided to take the eastern route. Like wolves crossing a mountain pass on a moonlit night, the pack of Mongol wolves would have to cross the Great Wall at numerous points and surge en masse into Jin territory. For many years, a clear image of this had been in Chinggis's mind. Although there was no basis whatsoever for this necessarily to have been the choice, Chinggis wagered the fate of the Mongols on the vision he had harbored since his youth, an all-or-nothing gamble.

With the new year of 1211, groups of soldiers began to move all over the Mongolian plateau, gradually aligning and assembling at Chinggis's camp. A small number of such groups moved uninterruptedly farther and farther upriver to the Onon and Kherlen river valleys.

Early in the third month of the year, Chinggis announced the invasion of the Jin before the entire group of Mongol armies. From that day forward, decrees began to be issued virtually every day about realignment of military units. The broad grassy plain by Chinggis's camp now was deep in soldiers, camels, horses, and military vehicles. Countless sheep were also gathered in a corner of the field.

Mongol soldiers were all assigned to one of six large military units: three units under the command, respectively, of Muqali, Sübe'etei, and Jebe; the left army under the command of Qasar; the right army led by Chinggis's three sons, Jochi, Cha'adai, and Ögedei; and the central army under the command of Chinggis and his youngest son, Tolui. Remaining on guard at camp was a force of only 2,000 under the command of Toquchar.

Three days before the departure of the troops, Chinggis climbed Mount Burqan alone and at its peak prayed for victory. He tied a sash around his neck, undid the string around his clothing, knelt before an altar, and poured fermented mare's milk on the ground.

—Alas, god of eternity, because our ancestors have been insulted and injured by the ruler of the state of Jin, I have raised an army and shall avenge them. This is the will of the entire Mongolian people. If you approve of this, then grant us the heaven-sent ability to carry out our task. And, order the people, good deities, and demons of this world below to cooperate with and aid us.

On the eve of the army's departure, Chinggis assembled his sons Jochi, Cha'adai, Ögedei, and Tolui in his tent and to share a last dinner with their mother, Börte. Chinggis was now forty-nine years of age, Jochi twenty-four, Cha'adai twenty-two, Ögedei twenty, and Tolui eighteen.

"Börte," said Chinggis, "the four sons to whom you have given birth will all be heading out against the Jin as commanders. As you will be separated from your sons later this evening, so shall I be from them. From tomorrow, father and sons must each follow a different path into battle. The coming front will be different in its great breadth from all of those heretofore."

"Why should I be so sad," replied Börte, "to separate from my sons? Did I not marry you and bear you sons to give birth to the wolves that destroyed the Tatars and the Tayichi'uds? Now that those children have grown up, the Tatars and Tayichi'uds whom these children were set to destroy have all been annihilated by you, with even their corpses no longer remaining. The children are hungry. Give them the freedom to cross the Great Wall and seize and feast on the minions of the Jin."

Börte was a year older than Chinggis, and the golden locks that had glistened when she was young had all now turned to silver.

The dinner lasted well into the night. Chinggis and his four sons left camp late. When he departed from his sons in front of his tent, Chinggis walked toward the center of camp, and there handled a number of arrangements with Bo'orchu until the break of dawn. When all the arrangements were complete, the two men sat down facing each other. That night, when they would depart, he could not know when next he would see this commander, Bo'orchu, who had been assigned to the right army with three of Chinggis's sons and who since his own youth had shared every pain and hardship with Chinggis.

When he and Bo'orchu parted and left the tent, dawn was beginning to break on all sides. Chinggis walked directly to Qulan's yurt. The early morning air pierced his skin with its chill. Still wearing her night clothing, Qulan was sleeping with her young child. He was a three-year-old boy Chinggis had sired by the name of Kölgen.

As he approached her bed, Qulan awoke at the faint sound of his footsteps. When she recognized him, Qulan got out of bed and quietly stood facing him. Chinggis felt Qulan's large, wide-open eyes staring at him earnestly. He had drawn apart from her for a while recently under the great pressure of urgent military matters.

Qulan seemed to be waiting for Chinggis to say something, but he silently came closer to take a look at the child's sleeping face in bed. The boy looked like Qulan, and in his youthful face one could see Qulan's exact eyes, nose, and mouth.

Moving away from the child, Chinggis turned and riveted his eyes on the mien of his youthful beloved princess. Not a word had as yet been exchanged between them. Finally, Qulan, apparently unable to bear the silence any longer, said:

"Great khan, what is it that you are trying to say?"

"Qulan," he replied, "what is it that your ears wish to hear?"

"There is only one thing that I wish to know," she said. "But isn't there something beyond that which the great khan would like to say to me?"

"No. It's just that I've been very busy."

"The great khan hasn't told me anything at all about the army's departure for Jin and that it is to take place today. These things I knew myself. But I don't think I want to hear such things now from your lips."

"Tell me what it is that you do wish to hear," said Chinggis.

"Isn't that something that should come from the great khan? I've been waiting here every single day for the past month for this," said Qulan, with a bit of reproach in her voice.

Chinggis, of course, fully understood what Qulan wanted to ask. Until the moment of his departure pressed near, Chinggis had not wanted to tell her of this because he had not yet made up his own mind. Needless to say, there was the matter of Qulan accompanying him on this military expedition. Considering three-year-old Köl-gen, whom she could not leave, she would clearly have to remain behind with her child.

As to how all this resonated in Qulan's mind, though, Chinggis was wary of heedlessly rushing to speak. Although he was usually able to surmise what someone was thinking, man or woman, only in the case of Qulan was this never true. In his estimation, her mind was as unfathomable as innumerable lakes filled to overflowing with cobalt blue water and shut away deep in the Altai mountain range.

As he now waited anxiously for the appointed time, howev-er, Chinggis had to say something. Her eyes staring right at him, Chinggis scowled back and said:

"Qulan, you must come with me."

Having disgorged the words, he realized that he had blurted out precisely the opposite of what he had been thinking until this point. He was startled by his own words. At that moment, Qulan's expres-sion for the time softened.

"Great khan," she said softly, "had you just now uttered the very opposite of what you said, I believe I would have chosen death. Great khan, you have saved my life. What shall I do with Kölgen?"

Chinggis was no longer of a mind to be able to resist Qulan's will.

"Kölgen too must cross the Great Wall," he said.

When he finished speaking, Chinggis had finally made up his mind once and for all that Kölgen would accompany them. Although just a three-year-old, he was a member of the Mongolian wolf pack. In such a battle against the Jin, in which they were gambling everything, even if his four limbs had not yet fully grown, what possible objection could be raised before the descendants of the blue wolf to his coming on this mission?

Before Chinggis had finished speaking, Qulan took a step closer to him and gently extended her arm. Chinggis did not respond and his expression grew more severe:

"Do you know," he asked, "what it means to take Kölgen on this expedition?"

"I do."

"What?"

"Great khan, do you not understand my heart? When the princes born to Börte all march to the front, I want my son Kölgen to bask in this same good fortune. Although only three years of age, he must be able to join the army. Great khan, you have granted my most earnest wish. There is nothing else I seek. By joining the army en route to the front, Kölgen may be engulfed in the flames of battle, he may be abandoned among an alien people, but that would be his fate. I am not fearful of this in the least. I did not give birth to Kölgen so that he should become a member of the royalty. As a nameless member of the populace, he sets off, and I wish only that he live by cutting open his own road in life with his own might."

Qulan continued to speak in a calm tone of voice, but it was filled with an intense passion. Chinggis gazed at Qulan's magnificently glittering eyes. He had never loved her so much as he did at this very moment. He too hoped that Kölgen would live his life in such a manner. This was not the love of a Mongol sovereign but that of a father. A man had to make his way in life through great difficulties, like himself and Qasar and Jelme—this was how it had to be for a Mongol wolf.

From that day until the next, the military units under Chinggis's command began to deploy from camp according to a prescribed manner and timetable. The first units to set out were those under Jebe's command and then those under Muqali's.

When the right army under the command of his sons, Jochi, Cha'adai, and Ögedei set off, the day was almost over and darkness setting in. Following them, when Qasar's right army left the settlement in a long file, they were all soon engulfed in darkness. Finally, Chinggis and his son Tolui set off with the central army late in the night. Placing himself in the middle of his troops, Chinggis rode his horse in the bright moonlight.

And so, 200,000 Mongol troops, following the eastern route, headed for the state of Jin. After a journey of many days across the desert, they would cross any number of mountains and valleys and then be able to see their objective, the Great Wall, certain to mightily impede any invasion, a sight they had once seen earlier when they surrounded the Xixia capital of Zhongxing.

Occasionally Chinggis looked over his shoulder at the troops behind him to ascertain with his own eyes the overall order of the march. Their spearheads shone dimly in the moonlight, and the line of the light extended across the immense plain like the flow of a river. Somewhere in this flow, Qulan and three-year-old Kölgen were, he knew, in a yurt being pulled by a horse.

Chinggis had organized his army of 200,000 men invading the Jin in a unique manner. At the lowest level were groups of 10; these came together into military units of 100, 1,000, and 10,000, each of which at their respective levels was supervised by a chief. Veteran generals were assigned as leaders of these larger units of 10,000. Chinggis's orders could be transmitted to them at any time by his staff, and in no time at all the orders could percolate down from his generals to the many lower-level groupings.

Having set off from the base camp in the foothills of Mount Burqan, Chinggis's expeditionary force against the Jin marched south and advanced along the banks of the Kherlen River; after leaving the river route, which on the fifth day took a sharp bend to the east, they reached a corner of the vast wasteland.

On the day they left the Kherlen, Chinggis was overcome by emotion. He had departed from the Kherlen River two years earlier when they invaded the Xixia and crossed the immense Gobi Desert, but his present mood was altogether different from what he had felt at that time. Waiting for them on the other side of the Gobi was not Xixia but the state of Jin. With terrain many times the size of the Mongols' and with an army of many times the manpower, the Jin was a civilized state that had built numerous secure citadels and carried on a cultured life of the highest level. It was completely beyond his imagination how the battle would unfold. While he had a certain amount of confidence in victory and all preparations to that end were now complete, he could not sustain this feeling with a clear sense of conviction or surety.

The flow of the Yellow River, a name he had heard from his childhood, had crossed his line of vision only once, from the Xixia capital of Zhongxing, but that was only the farthest extreme of the most peripheral portion of this massive, living entity. Not a single Mongol soldier could so much as conceive a true image of the Yellow River, which, it was said, moved at the will of the gods over the surface of the earth itself. Likewise, they had once while in Zhongxing seen the Great Wall, which had since antiquity impeded the invasions of northern nomadic peoples, but that was only the westernmost edge of this great beast, fortified in its torso by earth and stone, from which fire arrows burst out everywhere when men approached. Of what was actually on the land surrounded by the Great Wall and the Yellow River, they had no knowledge.

When as a boy he had heard stories about the Jin from his father, Yisügei, he always imagined it as a huge vat, and in it something was boiling as if naturally. Everything in it was bubbling up because of unquenchable hell fires from ancient times. The best thoughts people had ever attained, technology, the inborn hindrances of men, ignorance, as well as wealth, poverty, warfare, peace, singing and dancing, splendid court ceremonies, wandering refugees, wine shops, theaters, mass slaughter, gambling, lynching, worldly fame, and ruin, any and everything altogether boiled to a pulp. Eerie bubbles appeared and disappeared continuously on the surface of this ghastly effervescent morass. And so did the Mongol khan Hambaghai, nailed to a wooden donkey and flayed while still alive. Almost every year from time immemorial, innocent Mongolian people by the dozens and hundreds had been kidnapped by soldiers of the state of Jin and tossed into this cauldron.

When they left the course of the Kherlen River, Chinggis himself could not say for certain if he would ever stand on its bank again. This was true not only of Chinggis but also of his 200,000 troops. Standing on a small bluff one morning, Chinggis caught the last sight of the Kherlen flowing at daybreak. He then issued marching orders to all the troops under his command. Although it was already the middle of the third month of the year, corresponding roughly to April, the region they were in was still trapped in a deep winter's sleep, and whenever they stopped the freezing weather pierced their skin and penetrated their bones.

At about the same time that Chinggis's troops were to leave camp, Jebe's forces set off, and then slightly later, on parallel courses, the forces under the commands of Sübe'etei and Muqali decamped. The day was about to dawn, but light from the torches still being held aloft by the soldiers could be seen here and there. The troop disposition of the various divisions differed slightly at the time of departure from camp. Innumerable sheep, camels, horses, and other livestock were absorbed among the cavalry, making the units that much larger. Camels had the task of transporting foodstuffs (primarily meat and milk) and weaponry, while sheep were brought along as a source of food during their trek across the desert. Although the horses served as remounts for the troops, they had a great number, from two or three to as many as six or seven per man. Accordingly, as far as the eye could see, numerous files of troops extending over the desert terrain had long bands of domesticated animals with them.

Each of the soldiers was wearing a leather helmet covering the majority of his head and leather military garb over his body. Each bore a long spear in hand and wore a sword and arrows at the waist, with his bow tied to his horse.

From that day forward, Chinggis rode in an immense yurt as he marched his troops. The yurt was moved on four wheels, drawn by several dozen horses. On either side he was protected by mounted guard troops, and numerous Borjigin banners enveloped the vehicle.

For several days the troops saw nothing whatsoever resembling a tree. All around them stretched a dry, sandy plain, and if anything broke the monotony of the scenery, it was a denuded hillside, the reddish-black hue of rust, or salt water lakes of varying sizes, which appeared from time to time en route.

Continuing their forced march for roughly two weeks, they emerged from the desert onto the plateau region and eventually pushed their way into a spur of the rugged Yinshan mountain range. From around the time they entered this mountainous region, the troops began whispering the name of the town of Datong—never so much as even stated before—among themselves. Until then they had mentioned the name of Zhongdu [Beijing] and had been primarily concerned with reaching it, but at some point the new toponym of Datong had replaced Zhongdu, frequently on everyone's lips. It made no great difference to the troops whether the object was Zhongdu or Datong. Both were names of unknown cities in an unknown country—they didn't even know what direction the two cities lay in.

After marching 430 miles, the expeditionary forces led by Chinggis entered a settlement of the Önggüd people, who held sway over the northern side of the Great Wall. Although the Önggüds were one of the nomadic peoples of the Mongolian plateau, they neighbored the state of Jin and were completely under Jin control. Thus, Chinggis considered them a separate ethnicity. The Önggüds had never seen such a huge army as now thoroughly enveloped their settlement, and in blank amazement had no idea what to do. The Önggüd chief pledged fealty to Chinggis and offered personally to lead the troops invading the Jin.

A number of Mongol battalions that had come together to form one powerful unit now split up and headed for discrete objectives. This, of course, applied to the units under Jebe, Sübe'etei, and Muqali; the right army led by Chinggis's three sons, Jochi, Cha'adai, and Ögedei, to which Bo'orchu had been attached in a guardian function; and the left army under the command of Qasar, to which Jelme had been added—they all proceeded from the Önggüd settlement with several days between them. Only the central army under Chinggis and his son Tolui stayed back at the Önggüd village.

At about the same time, war broke out in the mountains and fields to the north of the Great Wall. The scene on various fronts was conveyed on a daily basis by horseback to Chinggis's base camp. He ordered his armies to mop up Jin terrain north of the Great Wall, and forbid them to invade deep into the Jin state on their own.

In the middle of the sixth month of that year, news reached Chinggis's base that a great Jin army had left Zhongdu and was heading for Shanxi province. Chinggis had drawn out the main force of the Jin, and he destroyed it, and thence set a policy to begin a full-fledged invasion. He knew the time was drawing near.

He dispatched Jebe with an urgent message ordering the central army under his command to mobilize. On the eve of their departure, Chinggis summoned Qulan to his tent and asked her if she would remain there until the end of the battle against the main Jin force.

"Great khan," she replied, "are you about to cross the Great Wall alone and leave me and Kölgen here? If so, then how is that any different from discarding us at the camp by the Kherlen River?"

"Then go with me into the conflagrations of battle," said Chinggis. "From tomorrow, three soldiers will be attached to you and Kölgen. Death will swoop down on the two of you continuously. You will have to protect yourselves."

Chinggis then called upon three soldiers with whom he had made prior arrangements and presented Qulan to them. One was an older man, the other two young. Three-year-old Kölgen was placed in one of the leather saddlebags hanging by the side of the older man's horse and set off to join his unit.

The troops departing from the Önggüd settlement early the following morning immediately came upon mountainous terrain along the southeastern portion of the village. They were all organized into a cavalry force, and every soldier was leading a remount as well. Qulan too was wearing leather armor and helmet and had a remount, and sat astride a white horse amid her guards.

One the second day, the troops reached a point about a half day's journey from the Great Wall and there paused at sunset. The soldiers had by now filled up the valleys of the mountains that spread out in overlapping, undulating fashion. They took a short rest that evening, and then late at night resumed their march, listening to the chirping sounds of nocturnal birds. The fighting began in the middle of this night. Jin troops guarding the stronghold along the line of the Great Wall first launched an attack of arrows against them.

Although it seemed as though the troop strength on the stronghold was less than half that of Mongols, they were unable to advance their invading army to the Great Wall because of its impregnability. Chinggis spread troops out along the line of the wall in an effort to seize control over one corner of it, in any location. War cries arose in every valley and on every mountain peak, but were met everywhere with ferocious resistance.

The fighting continued for an entire day and night, and after nightfall the forces under big-headed Chimbai held fast to a point on the Great Wall, while losing over half of their men. For the first time, a Mongol flag flew atop a corridor of the Great Wall. From this point forward the fighting unfolded at both the corridors and the stronghold of the wall, and at a number of sites Mongol troops climbed up to the Great Wall's stronghold.

While the fighting continued, at a site several hundred yards to the southwest, the wall was substantially demolished. The reverberations of bows and arrows mixed with battle cries, and the sound of immense boulders tumbling repeatedly into the valleys below could clearly be heard.

Late in the night Mongol troops crossed the Great Wall through the breach thus opened and rushed inside. Atop the Great Wall the

wind was fierce. It seemed to howl as if being torn to pieces right up
to the moon. Astride his horse, Chinggis stood on top of the stone
corridor of the Great Wall and from there watched when the endless rows of cavalrymen crossed over the wall, one after the next.
The moonlit night revealed other stone corridors before and behind
where he stood that curved and meandered along a long line. In
front of him was a steep slope, as the corridor rose from one high
point to the next as if ascending into a corner of the sky. Behind
him it extended gently on level ground, but about thirty yards in
front of them it suddenly broke off and disappeared. A portion farther ahead abruptly abutted the summit of a rocky hill beyond two
smaller prominences. Although Chinggis couldn't see it from where
he was standing, there was an incline on the far side of that hill, and
the Great Wall's corridor swelled up immensely there like a snake's
torso after it had swallowed a frog. It was this site that formed the
stronghold where the deadly fighting back and forth had continued
since the previous night.

    To calm down his impatient horse, Chinggis continuously pat-
ted its head. There was ample reason for the horse to be impatient.
Unlike the outside edge of the Great Wall, the inside edge led to a
gentle sloping terrain, and the cavalry troops who had crossed the
corridor galloped down the incline as though they were releasing
all at once a force that had been held in check. The trees covering the nearby mountains were all bent low because of the wind,
and the troops dashing though them could thus be fully seen in the
moonlight.

    For a long time now, Chinggis had dreamed of the day when,
drenched in the moonlight, Mongol soldiers would cross the Great
Wall of China, and now this dream was coming to fruition before
his very eyes. Yet while the scene so long depicted in his mind's eye
was a rather quiet one painted in bluish hues, the crossing of the
Great Wall that he was now seeing was unfolding in a raging wind.
The defensive power of the stronghold, the pain at the time of its
seizure, and the forging of an invasion route through it after demol-
ishing a section of the wall, to say nothing of the fact that this was
all occurring under a moonlit sky as bright as midday, were all for

Chinggis precisely as he had imagined them to be. Exactly the same. Only the wind had not been pictured. He had not envisioned such a ferocious wind howling, pounding heaven and earth. The wind seemed always to howl here as it was now. This stone rampart severely obstructing both nomadic and agrarian peoples for hundreds of years, impenetrable, continued to resound in the forceful wind that had blown down from a corner of heaven for centuries as well.

Until dawn, Chinggis stood on the corridor of the Great Wall. A long period of time elapsed before a huge army of several tens of thousands of cavalrymen and a roughly equal number of horses and camels had completely scaled the wall. As dawn neared, Chinggis's guard troops were the final soldiers to surmount the Great Wall, and Chinggis was among them. Then, as all the other subordinate troops had done, he and his horse galloped down the steep mountain incline inside.

About ten days later, Chinggis ambushed and defeated a large force under the command of Ding Xue, a Jin general, in the first battle to be fought on the enemy's home terrain. As a result, the Mongols occupied the area of the two counties of Dashuiluo and Fengli.

A few days after the central army under Chinggis's command crossed over the Great Wall, a report arrived stating that the first army under Jebe had crossed at a different site and captured the stronghold at Wushabao [in present-day Hubei province]. As if to follow this up, about two weeks later, the news of a victorious massacre at Wuyueying arrived.

Chinggis learned that his own troops and those of Jebe had encircled en masse from two sides the strategic site of Datong in Shanxi province. Chinggis did not rush to attack Datong. He spent the hot days of summer calming the people's concerns in the area under siege and allowing his troops and horses a respite. With the fighting only just begun, Mongol troops had crossed the Great Wall and stepped foot only in a small corner of Shanxi. Clearly battles would be fought for years to come.

The two units under Muqali and Sübe'etei had been charged with capturing the fortresses north of the Great Wall. The role assigned them was the most laborious and had shown the fewest results. The steep hills that formed a natural fortification guarding Zhongdu and the numerous strongholds scattered around the region severely impeded the onslaught of these two commanders. Chinggis had given this most difficult of tasks to his two brave commanders. He received continual reports from both armies, and each communication included news of victory, but the pace of their advance was extremely slow. Every inch of terrain required a number of days.

Early in the ninth month of the year, Chinggis joined forces with Jebe's army and occupied Baideng to the east of Datong, as Mongol troops surged in to surround Datong. They pursued the escaping Jin army headed in the direction of Zhongdu and massacred the majority of it.

About this time Chinggis received news that Muqali had captured Xuande and Jebe had occupied Fuzhou. Now the two strategic sites defending Zhongdu north of the Great Wall and Datong, the most important point in Shanxi, had been occupied by Mongol forces in but half a year from the commencement of hostilities.

The next month Chinggis learned that two Jin battalions had begun an action aimed at recovering Datong. At the head of his armed forces, he led a raid against the vanguard Jin troops and defeated them, then launched a further attack against their base army, but the two Jin commanders rushed to beat a hasty retreat. Chinggis pursued the fleeing army to the banks of the Hui River and there delivered an annihilating attack. In this fighting the Mongol cavalry magnificently demonstrated their might and literally trampled the Jin infantry under their horses' hoofs.

Taking advantage of early victories, Chinggis ordered Jebe to attack the Juyong Pass, the northern defense of Zhongdu. Jebe and his troops advanced from Datong, marched the great distance to the Juyong Pass, and in no time at all captured it. Chinggis then ordered the right army under Jochi, Cha'adai, and Ögedei to seize complete control over the area north of the Great Wall in Shanxi province.

Reports continually came to Chinggis's base camp in Datong from his three sons, as if in some sort of competition, of the occupation or mopping up of Yunnei, Dongshengzhou, Wuzhou, Shuozhou, Fengzhou, Jingzhou, and elsewhere. Bo'orchu explained how the fighting progressed with great clarity to Chinggis, so that it was as if he had observed his three young sons in battle with his own eyes.

The following year, 1212, Chinggis reached age fifty in Datong. At the start of the year, he learned that Muqali had captured the two cities of Changzhou and Huanzhou. Following that, one by one the fortresses north of the Great Wall fell to Muqali.

It was at this time that Chinggis heard a report to the effect that the Jin generals He Sheli and Jiu Jian were leading an immense army toward Datong with the aim of recovering that city. At the head of an army, the great khan left Datong, confronted the Jin forces on mountainous terrain en route, defeated them, and sent the Jin reinforcements fleeing in utter defeat.

When Chinggis learned that all the land north of the Great Wall was now completely occupied and a path opened up to invade Zhongdu, he abandoned Datong as no longer of strategic value. Moving his entire army north of the Great Wall, he decided now to set his sights solely on Zhongdu.

In the eighth month of the year, for the first time in fourteen months since capturing the Great Wall, Chinggis crossed the Great Wall, moving this time from south to north. A ferocious wind was blowing on the wall at the time, and everywhere along the stone corridors a sandstorm blew up in the air like a whirlwind. The Mongol troops were altogether changed from those who had passed this way the previous year. They had several thousand Jin prisoners, and mountains of plunder that were being transported over the Great Wall from the south to the north. All the Jin prisoners of war were assigned to haul this booty, and it took a number of days for the groups of camels laden with cargo to traverse the wall.

Chinggis built his base camp at the Önggüd settlement once again, and decided from there to direct his various military units spread out at numerous sites. For the first time in several months, he welcomed to his tent his eldest son, Jochi, and his general Bo'orchu. They had come to coordinate the next battle strategy.

For having seized control over the local river valley region, Chinggis issued an edict to the effect that Bo'orchu was to be awarded high military honors. In taking control over six prefectures between the Yinshan Mountains and the Great Wall, Bo'orchu had had some help; Jochi's strategy had paid off handsomely, and therefore Bo'orchu petitioned that Jochi also be rewarded for his courageous actions.

Chinggis knew full well that on his first campaign Jochi had conquered a number of peoples living around Lake Baikal and had attained distinguished achievements on the battlefield. Judging from this, the recent successes, as Bo'orchu indicated, were perhaps a result of Jochi's maneuvers. Chinggis nonetheless offered no special treatment whatsoever.

As he looked at the dramatically more stalwart Jochi, covered in the dust of the battlefield, Chinggis felt that rewarding Jochi would gradually cause his son to lose something of his innate character. Staring at Jochi's face with its striking resemblance to his mother, Börte, Chinggis thought the eyes were burning with defiance. He knew that when Börte spoke of Jochi, her eyes showed a fiery light not seen at any other time. Now he thought he was seeing that same light brimming before him in the eyes of his own eldest son.

"Jochi," said Chinggis. "What should I give you as reward for your fighting on the field of battle?"

The young commander, just twenty-five years of age, replied:

"Give me orders without end full of the greatest of difficulty, and I will carry them out one after the next."

Jochi's eyes were fixed unmoving on those of his father. These were audacious words, to say the least. One might even understand them as a declaration of insubordination. This eldest son of his, Chinggis thought, whose blood he was not sure was his own, was effectively informing him that he was now a fully grown man with an individual personality. Staring right back into Jochi's gaze, Chinggis called out:

"Son of Börte, who has been raised splendidly and bravely, I shall not forget these words of yours today. Henceforth, you shall be obliged on my orders to stand up against every single difficult situation as it arises."

Chinggis then had arrangements made for food and drink and a short banquet held in honor of his son and his two honored friends who had come from afar. Jochi and Bo'orchu returned to the site where their troops were camped.

After Jochi departed, Chinggis recognized that his own agitation was rising with each passing day. He couldn't get a sense of the precise character of his feelings toward Jochi. There was both love and hatred there. Based on time and circumstance, these emotions formed a complex mixture in which one of the two would on occasion surface above the other.

When Jochi had earlier pacified the peoples living north of Lake Baikal, Chinggis had issued an edict of congratulations and rejoiced in Jochi's hard-fought victories as if they were his own, but for some reason, in the present circumstance he could not find such a straightforward emotion in his heart. For deep down, he could not deny his two other sons Cha'adai and Ögedei. Chinggis apparently wanted to avoid recognizing meritorious service on the battlefield for Jochi alone. Although a bit younger than Jochi, they had both participated in the fighting as army commanders, and Chinggis wanted to recognize their merit on the field as well.

For a number of days after meeting face to face with Jochi, Chinggis sensed from that encounter that Jochi had been instilled with a ferocious spirit. Just as Jochi had requested that Chinggis order him to face all the most difficult of circumstances on the field of battle, Chinggis would be making similar demands of himself. As Jochi was on the verge of becoming a Mongol wolf, so too Chinggis himself had to become a Mongol wolf. Having crossed the Great Wall once and defeated the Jin army, Chinggis could no longer just imitate the image of the blue wolf that he had continued to hold within himself since his own youth. He had to become that wolf.

That year, though, Chinggis did not move his troops. He placed all of the units under his command close together north of the Great Wall and bided his time, preparing to surge en masse onto Jin terrain at any moment. In the latter half of the year, he enjoyed a harvest so rich even he could not have foreseen it. Yelü Liuge, a descendant of the royal Liao house of the Khitan people, which had been destroyed by the Jin, led his Khitan kinsmen in opposition to the Jin dynasty in the northeastern sector of the Jin state. When he heard this news,

Chinggis immediately sent his commander Alchi as an emissary to forge an alliance with Liuge. For his part, Liuge swore an oath of fealty to Chinggis, and Chinggis promised to protect the Khitan nobility.

The Jin then sent a punitive force against Liuge. The expeditionary force was under the command of Wanyan Heshuo. Chinggis sent 3,000 support troops to aid Liuge, and at the same time he ordered Jebe to launch an attack on the strategic northeastern site of Liaoyang, one of the former capitals of the Liao dynasty. Jebe rapidly brought the city down, and with the approval of Chinggis, Liuge took the position of Liao king. During the fighting, not only the area north of the Great Wall but also the massive territory beyond the Yinshan and Xing'an mountain ranges—an area roughly corresponding to the entire Mongolian plateau—was now added to the Mongol sphere of influence.

When he completed the expedition to Liaoyang, Jebe left his troops there and alone returned to Chinggis's base camp. Chinggis greeted him with great warmth. Of all the Mongol commanders, Jebe made his name resound most loudly in the state of Jin. His capacity to deploy troops, using his men with great dexterity and never losing on the field of battle, was feared by all Jin commanders as virtually superhuman.

From beyond the Xing'an Mountains, Jebe pulled along several thousand fine horses and brought them into Chinggis's camp. Thus, the periphery of the Önggüd settlement was teeming with tall horses whose lustrous skin was of a blackish-brown hue. At his audience with Chinggis, Jebe said:

"I once fought as a soldier of the Tayichi'uds against the great khan and injured the great khan's horse. For some time, I have been thinking of presenting the great khan with a horse by way of recompense, but only now am I able to see that wish to fruition."

"What you injured that day," replied Chinggis in good humor, "was not just my horse. Your arrows felled the horse and struck and wounded me in the neck."

"To compensate for injury done to the great khan's body," said Jebe, "I must offer my life. Please send not only your son Jochi but me as well into difficult battles when the occasion arises."

Only at this moment did Chinggis realize that Jebe had seen through the subtle relationship he shared with Jochi and was delicately admonishing him for it. And not only Jebe, for it seemed certain that Jelme and Bo'orchu also understood; this had become something of a lamentable issue among those who had offered meritorious service in the inception of the Mongol state. At this point in time, Chinggis said nothing about this to Jebe. Chinggis was unable to properly explain his love-hate feelings for Jochi to this fierce and obstinate commander with a pointed skull like an arrowhead, nor did he feel so inclined.

The start of 1213 was the second new year on which Chinggis found himself in a foreign land. To a new year's banquet, he invited from their various war fronts Muqali, Bo'orchu, Jebe, Qasar, and his three sons Jochi, Cha'adai, and Ögedei.

When they all met, he consulted with them about the sweeping assault on the state of Jin. Less a consultation, it was more an opportunity to unilaterally issue orders. He announced that the three commanders Muqali, Jebe, and Sübe'etei would strengthen the rear, while everyone else in the other three armies would be committed to Jin terrain. He was referring, in other words, to the three forces of Qasar's left army, Jochi's and his brothers' right army, and Chinggis and Tolui's central army. He decided as well to reassign Bo'orchu, heretofore guardian with the right army, to his own central army as its highest officer. Accordingly, leadership of the right army was entrusted completely to his three sons.

"The three of you must deal with things as a single unity," said Chinggis to Jochi, Cha'adai, and Ögedei. "Jochi shall have highest leadership authority. Cha'adai and Ögedei, help your elder brother. These are your orders: Enter the low ground of Hebei from Shanxi and then gallop across all of Jin territory. Seize every settled area that you pass by. When you attack, you must precede your troops in scaling the walls."

"We shall obey your order, great khan, our father," responded Jochi, representing his brothers, "and carry to fruition everything as you have ordered it."

Jochi's face had turned a pale green. Whatever they might all have thought, these were orders nearly impossible to execute. A hushed silence fell over the entire group. Bo'orchu, Jelme, and Muqali kept quiet, uttering not a word. With the order given and Jochi having accepted it, there was nothing further to say.

Chinggis next issued orders to his brother Qasar:

"Attack the area west of the Liao River, north of the Great Wall until you reach the sea. When winter comes to that region, everything is frozen solid, and neither humans nor horses can move. Complete the fighting by winter, for you are not to lose troops or horses due to the cold."

"Understood!" replied Qasar in a slightly wild tone of voice. Qasar seemed a bit displeased at not being able to attack the heartland of the Jin state.

Finally, Chinggis issued the orders for his own units:

"Tolui and I will bypass Zhongdu, move into Hebei, cross the Yellow River, and attack Shandong. Bo'orchu, you will always be with me."

The mission for his three units was not particularly difficult, in his estimation. In the fighting over the previous two years, he had come to know the Jin troops' capacity on the battlefield and to see that not a single Jin statesman was present there. The defenses around Zhongdu were weak, morale low, and the possibility of civil strife erupting at any time high. The Mongol cavalry could become a sharp awl and break through any time.

Chinggis had not considered, though, whether all of those assembled there that day would be able to meet face to face without incident after the conquest of the Jin. In particular, he hadn't taken into account whether everything among his three young sons would run smoothly.

It had been Jochi's wish for Chinggis to give him the mission fraught with the gravest difficulties, and this was Chinggis's wish as well. "Jochi, you are to become a wolf!" Because he had assigned such a task to Jochi, Chinggis was sacrificing the children with whom he was sure he shared blood—namely, Cha'adai and Ögedei—and placing their fate together with his. Chinggis made appropriate arrangements so that he would not show any special feeling toward Jochi and so that he would understand what his commanders were feeling. In addition, he knew that this was necessary for himself. On behalf of his wife, Börte, whom he had left back in the camp at Mount Burqan and had not seen for nearly two years now, he had to treat the children she had borne him all fairly.

The new year's banquet with Chinggis at its center was a grand affair of unprecedented proportions. Women escorted from Datong and many other places came and went amid the drinking. Outside the tents, snow came fluttering to the ground, but inside the broad tents were outfitted with floor heaters, making it nice and warm.

The drinking lasted from morning till night. In the evening, Chinggis stood at the entrance to his tent and looked at the outdoors painted completely in white. In the distance he saw a group of soldiers moving toward a hillside far to the east. He called his guard and asked whose troops they were and what they were about to do. The young guard immediately conveyed the name of the unit and that they were marching out in the snow. Chinggis never tired of gazing at the narrow defiles of troops here and there. The name of their leader was new to Chinggis. They were a beautiful sight. To Chinggis they appeared like a pack of young wolves.

Chinggis then shifted his line of vision to the young soldier standing at attention before him. Falling snow was mounting on their caps and shoulders. He too was without a doubt a Mongol wolf.

Although he returned to the festivities, Chinggis sensed that Bo'orchu, Jelme, and Qasar all seemed to have aged. At some point in time, he and many of his meritorious followers had grown older, and half of their hair had turn to white. Only the middle-aged Muqali, Jebe, and Sübe'etei still seemed young. Chinggis was coming to realize that the era of Muqali and Jebe—and then the era of a group of young leaders as yet unknown to him—was about to dawn.

6

Fall of the Jin Dynasty

EARLY IN THE FOURTH MONTH OF THE YEAR 1213, when the falling snow had gradually tapered off and the spring sun had begun to shine, Chinggis issued orders to his entire army to cross the Great Wall a second time and invade the state of Jin. Messengers were dispatched to the camps of the various military units, as well as to those of Muqali, Jebe, and Sübe'etei, who were not going to start operations yet.

Over the course of the following half month, Chinggis's base camp was in a constant state of disorder as troops came together and set off on the march. Chinggis himself spent almost every day busily preparing for the central army that he and Tolui commanded to head out. One such day, he paid a call on Qulan, whom he had not visited for roughly two weeks, to see if she was engaged in preparations to take the field.

Qulan's tent was quiet. She was alone, sitting in a chair, green jade earrings dangling from her ears.

"We take the field in three days. Are you ready to march?" he asked.

"This time," she replied unexpectedly, "I think I'll remain behind in my tent. Once the weather has warmed up a bit, I will gladly join the troops, but in the present weather I fear for Kölgen's health."

As he listened to her words, Chinggis realized that his own complexion was changing.

"Qulan, my beloved princess! Didn't you accompany this expeditionary force because you wished always to be with me?"

Chinggis spoke in an unintentionally firm tone of voice with an irrepressible feeling. Until now, Qulan had followed the army through every battle, always placing Kölgen in the leather saddlebag of an aging, trustworthy soldier. Not once had she refused to join the march. It was as a result of her importunate request to join the campaign, while recognizing all the inherent difficulties, that she, together with Kölgen, had accompanied them. Chinggis didn't know what to make of her present attitude. Was she overcome with fright at seeing a ferocious battle? Had she come to hold her own and Kölgen's lives too dear?

It would be difficult to say that Jochi, Cha'adai, and Ögedei hoped to survive the coming battle. The situation was no different for their youngest brother, Tolui. Chinggis thought that Tolui, although only just twenty years of age, could be given a unit to command on the battlefield. He assigned himself to the same unit, but once they reached the front they might suffer different fates, each not knowing what might have become of the other.

Without answering Qulan, Chinggis left her tent. After returning to his own, he kept to himself for a long period of time, keeping everyone at a distance. If all four sons he had sired with Börte were to meet death on the field of battle—something entirely within the realm of the possible—then in what position would that leave Kölgen, the child born to himself and Qulan?

As a father, Chinggis of course loved his son Kölgen. This child was born when Chinggis was already older, and he was born to his beloved Qulan. Although Chinggis had not clearly expressed it, Kölgen was more precious to him than any of his other sons. The proposition that Kölgen, still a young child, might go off to the front just like his half-brothers and he alone survive was altogether different than the notion that he should not proceed to the front at all and survive in a settlement somewhere.

An image of Börte's face floated into Chinggis's mind. For so many years, she had shared his troubles, and now, as if she were with him, he was staring fixedly at a point in space where he saw the visage of Börte, his legal wife, whom he had left behind in her tent at Mount Burqan. Chinggis did not fear her, but he could not erase the image of her from before him.

Chinggis had once walked around inside his tent, not sleeping a wink the entire night, wondering if he should seize the shaman priest Teb Tenggeri or his own younger brother Qasar. Now, he had again shut himself up in his own tent since midday and did not leave until after it was enveloped completely in darkness. Late that night, Chinggis called to an aide and instructed him to summon Sorqan Shira, father of his two commanders, Chimbai and Chila'un. Eventually, the old man, now in his mid-seventies, brought his thin, weary body before Chinggis. Staring at Sorqan Shira's face, Chinggis said:

"Old man. When I was a lad taken captive by the Tayichi'uds, you saved my life. Will you do something for me one more time?"

"If the great khan orders it," he replied, "Sorqan Shira has no choice but to obey."

When the old man had spoken, Chinggis's own words emerged in brief phrases, the conclusion to his thinking from midday to nighttime.

"Sorqan Shira, go now directly to Qulan's tent and take Kölgen. Give Kölgen to some anonymous member of the Mongolian people to be raised as such. Under no circumstance must you reveal that Kölgen is my child."

Hearing these words, the color of Sorqan Shira's face, which never revealed an ordinary emotion, changed.

"Go to the princess's tent and seize the prince. Give the prince to a nameless member of the Mongolian people, to be raised. Do not inform anyone of the prince's identity," Sorqan Shira repeated in a low voice, as though rehearsing in his own words what the great khan had just said.

"And do not tell Qulan to whom you have entrusted Kölgen as parents," added Chinggis. "Do not tell me either. This will be something that only Sorqan Shira on this earth shall know."

Sorqan Shira again repeated his instructions, said, "Um" and groaned briefly, stumbling a bit under the weight of his assignment, and then left.

The next day Chinggis visited Qulan's tent. When the sound of his footsteps reached the tent, he called to her:

"Qulan, you will now proceed with me to the field of battle. Upon the invasion of the state of Jin, I shall give you the honor of being the only woman to be part of the army."

Qulan stiffened her pale features and replied in a low voice:

"I respectfully accept your command."

After this she said nothing, but she had been stunned by the immense impact the words she had uttered the previous day had unintentionally had, and was overwhelmingly shattered in body and soul. The indolence and cowardice taking root in her beloved Kölgen, who had so quickly and without any warning captivated her, had now visited a severe fate upon her with the seizure, equally without warning, of her adored son.

"Make preparations for departure quickly," said Chinggis.

"They are already made," replied Qulan. "Great khan," she added as she raised her dejected face, "you have thrown the child made by myself and the great khan into the vast sea. I may never see Kölgen again."

Her tone was rather subdued.

"If Kölgen possesses the superior qualities of a man," responded Chinggis, "he will surely grow up and become a Mongol wolf, surpass others, and make a name for himself—not because you have been treated as a Mongol princess or because you raised Kölgen as a Mongol prince. Qulan, you will be with me forever as my fine servant. Furthermore, we shall see to it that Kölgen will be reared on the basis of his own capacities as a son of the Mongolian masses."

As he spoke these words, Chinggis found that he too was stricken by an inexplicable emotion that made him shudder. He now understood for the first time the import of the cruel measure he had taken on behalf of Kölgen. Although he knew that he was desperately trying to protect both Qulan whom he loved and Kölgen whom he loved, unfortunately he had been unable to put that feeling into words to Qulan. There was really nothing he could do, he reasoned, if she did not understand the arrangement he had made.

No sooner had he spoken the words than she, who was like a precious gem, disappeared without a trace. From that moment until the day the troops began to march, no one saw her. Chinggis was absorbed in military business and had no time to visit Qulan's tent. When the troops departed from camp, Qulan was on horseback by Chinggis's side. For three days and three nights Qulan wept nonstop until her lachrymal glands were completely dried out and not another tear could be shed. Neither Chinggis nor Qulan thenceforth so much as uttered a syllable of Kölgen's name.

En route to the invasion of Zhongdu, the central army under Chinggis's leadership captured a number of citadels scattered along the way. All of them had earlier been captured by Muqali, and after the Mongol forces retreated, they fell back into the hands of Jin troops. Chinggis's forces attacked and seized Xuande and then surrounded Dexing. During the fighting, he put his son Tolui in charge of the Dexing army of occupation. Orders were strict. At the head of his army in a tough fight, Tolui and his men climbed up the city's ramparts and staked Borjigin banners along it.

Chinggis marched his army on and attempted to take the city of Huailai. On the way he came upon a huge army of crack Jin troops under the command of Left Army Supervisor Gao Qi, and after a ferocious battle lasting three days and nights, overcame them.

Without so much as a respite, Chinggis marched his troops on and pressed close to Juyong Pass, but he learned that a large Jin force was stationed there, and fearing heavy casualties, he changed direction and crossed the Great Wall far west of the pass. They proceeded to bring down a number of fortresses and inflict defeats on the Jin army. When they emerged on the Hebei plain, they promptly occupied the two walled towns of Zhuozhou and Yizhou. Zhongdu was but a stone's throw away. The Mongol cavalry continued its march amid gale winds and thunderclaps. Looking north, Chinggis deployed his troops for Zhongdu.

Chinggis met up at Yizhou with Jebe's forces, who had marched all the way from Liaoyang. Less than two months had passed since he had issued the orders to Jebe in the rear to invade Jin terrain.

Without resting, Jebe left Yizhou and led an attack on the Juyong Pass from within the Great Wall, and eventually his troops succeeded in capturing it. This was his second seizure of the Juyong Pass. Leaving Zhongdu alone for now, Chinggis advanced his forces to the Yellow River basin and overran the Shandong region.

During this period, the right army under the command of Jochi moved, as ordered, to fight in the mountainous area of Shanxi. They captured all of the walled towns in the province, moved on to the Hebei plain, and then appeared at will throughout Shanxi and Hebei. The cavalry unit of the left army under Qasar raced back and forth searching for the enemy on terrain west of the Liao River.

Thus, several hundred Mongol cavalry troops trampled Jin territory under their horses' hoofs. From this year through the spring of 1214, they despoiled ninety cities and planted Borjigin banners upon the walls of every one of them.

In the fourth month of the year, Chinggis issued orders to his entire army, spread out across various sites on Jin terrain, to coalesce on the outskirts of Zhongdu. On a virtually daily basis thereafter for over a month, Mongol horsemen from both south and north of the Hebei plain, as well as from the east and west, raised a blinding sandstorm from all directions and emerged in the middle of it. The plain to the west of Zhongdu was densely covered with Mongol troops. Numbering 200,000 when they had set out from the Mongolian plateau, they had grown to more than twice that now. Half of them were surrendered Jin troops.

Chinggis and his commanders met for the first time in fifteen months in a corner of the plain overlooking the city of Zhongdu. Like a small island in the great sea, Zhongdu alone had escaped being captured and lay there before their eyes. Within this city, there was ceaseless strife, with apprehension inviting further apprehension, continual assassinations, and power holders changing one after the next.

Chinggis dispatched two emissaries to this last Jin city whose life was hanging by a thread. A signed letter to the Jin emperor was entrusted to them:

—All of your territory north of the Yellow River has now fallen into our hands, and all that remains is Zhongdu alone. It is heaven that has caused you to be reduced to such weakness. Should I press closer to you? I fear that I would incur heaven's anger. I am about to pull my troops back. You should provide my troops with comfort and thanks, which will calm the hostility of my commanders.

Although the tone was intended not to injure the honor of the Jin emperor, the letter was nonetheless plainly advice to surrender. When Chinggis selected the messenger to carry the letter, he much regretted that Boroghul, the foundling his mother Ö'elün had raised, was no longer alive. Chinggis felt again the long-dormant sorrow of Boroghul's loss when he was sent to rescue Qorchi.

In reply, the Jin emperor conveyed his acceptance of Chinggis's offer and the will to conclude a peace. Commander Muqali and Chinggis's eldest son, Jochi, proceeded to Zhongdu as representatives of the great khan and discussed peace. It was called "peace," but it was in substance surrender by the Jin.

Chinggis demanded a royal princess but nothing else. There was no need. With the 200,000 Jin troops incorporated into his army came enormous quantities of items collected in the 90 cities aside from Zhongdu—weapons, agricultural implements, horse gear, and clothing and related ornaments. Had something been sought in Zhongdu just before the fall of the city, it would have been a princess. In place of carpets and bedding, Chinggis had to spread over his bed a woman of the imperial house of the great Jin state. Revenge for the gruesome manner in which Hambaghai Khan had been murdered would be borne by a single young daughter of the Jin emperor.

Several days after the peace discussions came to an end, Hatun, a daughter of the former Jin emperor Wanyan Shengguo [Taizong, d. 1135] was sent to Chinggis's camp together with an immense quantity of gold, numerous valuables, 500 boys and 500 girls, and 3,000 horses.

Gathering up this extraordinary booty, Chinggis ordered his entire army to withdraw from the Jin. At the head of his troops,

Chinggis started from Juyong Pass to the vast north. On this day
the wind was blowing fiercely at the Great Wall, and the trees along
the corridors of the wall were rustling and shaking, being torn to
pieces. When he brought his horse to a halt at the corridor, Chinggis observed his long line of troops, who never knew how long they
would march, and said to Jebe, who was serving at his side:

"We'll be able to cross more comfortably at Juyong Pass, because of you." The commander who had attacked and taken Juyong
Pass twice, once from the north and once from the south, made a
watchful eye and said, laughing:

"I wonder how many more times Jebe will have to capture the
Juyong Pass?"

Chinggis laughed as well. Their laughter immediately vanished,
usurped by the wind, and neither's voice reached the other's ears.
As Jebe had said, Chinggis did not believe that he had brought the
immense apparition known as the state of Jin under his personal
control for all time. Chinggis himself could not say if he would be
able completely to conquer the Jin.

Grand Councilor Wanyan Fuxing of the Jin came to escort the
invaders as far as north of the Juyong Pass.

After three full years, the Mongol officers and troops were now able
to return to the Mongolian plateau in triumph. When he arrived at
his tent on Mount Burqan, Chinggis remained a short while and
then moved his base camp to Lake Yur of the Tatars. It was still necessary to keep a watch on the movements of the Jin, and he felt that
it would be wise, before anything untoward transpired, to defend
against any friction between Börte and Qulan.

In addition to Qulan, Chinggis brought Princess Hatun from the
state of Jin into the former Tatar base area. Although the number
of stunningly beautiful women Chinggis had acquired at various
sites on Chinese terrain had become considerable, he had them all
work in service to Qulan and Hatun. Hatun was taciturn, quite un-
attractive, and short. Although he considered her a princess, Ching-

gis soon stopped summoning her to his own tent. He did, however, continue to treat her as befit royalty.

Shortly after the victorious return of the Mongol armies to the Mongolian plateau, Sorqan Shira, the oldest member of their armed forces, died. Twice during his own lifetime, Chinggis had been in life-threatening danger, and on both occasions this old man had saved him. He now rewarded Sorqan Shira with the rites of a state funeral. On the day of the ceremony, Chinggis and Qulan went to the gravesite and dropped a few clods of earth onto the coffin. Both Chinggis and Qulan grieved that, with the death of Sorqan Shira, the only man who knew where Kölgen was living was now gone. Chinggis, though, said nothing about Kölgen, and Qulan never so much as mentioned his name. Sorqan Shira's coffin was lowered well into the earth before their eyes, and they would never see him again.

As Jebe had anticipated at the Juyong Pass, the day the Mongol armies would have to cross the Great Wall again arrived earlier than expected. A report was delivered to Chinggis's base camp to the effect that the Jin emperor had moved capitals from Zhongdu to Bianjing (modern-day Kaifeng) at the end of the sixth month, shortly after the Mongol armies returned home.

When Chinggis learned that the Jin had no peaceful intentions, his indignation at this frightful betrayal burned like a raging fire. Chinggis immediately issued marching orders against the Jin to the cavalry units of the Salji'uds, who had fought so outstandingly in the early battles with the Jin, and to the Jurchen cavalry units, who had massacred the enemy so brutally and tenaciously. Sammuqa would command the former and Mingghan the latter. His orders on this occasion were merciless to the extreme: take the city of Zhongdu and destroy everything in it completely.

At the same time, Chinggis ordered Commander Muqali to proceed to Liaodong. He had heard from the Khitan Prince Yelü Liuge that Jin troops were about to try to retake the region, and he wanted to put a stop to it. When he set out, Chinggis instructed Muqali, this man of incomparable achievements as fighter and statesman:

—I entrust to you governance of the land to the north of the Daxing Mountains. Conquest of the land to the south of these mountains is the responsibility of the army.

Chinggis had thought to have Muqali pacify the Jin and take over governance of the great Southern Song dynasty beyond it. In his estimation, Muqali was up to the job, but the latter was something that Chinggis felt he had to do himself. An attraction was beginning to surface in Chinggis's mind at this time, more than toward China: toward the unknown lands farther west where people had different skin and eye colors.

He saw off the two expeditionary forces—Muqali's army set to conquer the Jin and those of Sammuqa and Mingghan—from his base near Lake Yur. It was the seventh month of 1214; the peace with Jin had collapsed after only three months.

From the end of this year through the spring of the next, Chinggis interviewed the messengers who came almost every day to his tent with reports on the movements of the expeditionary forces. He thus had a thoroughly clear understanding of the operations of these two armies in China. The actual fighting led by Sammuqa, Mingghan, and others aimed at capturing Zhongdu began early in 1215. The expeditionary army enveloped Zhongdu, cut off the city's contact with the outside world, and gradually defeated the Jin military moving north by destroying them one by one. It seemed to Chinggis, waiting impatiently, to take an excruciatingly long period of time until news of the fall of Zhongdu arrived. Why, he wondered, were they taking so long? To both lose no time in receiving news of a victory and avoid the heat of summer, he moved his base camp to Huanzhou. The long-awaited seizure of Zhongdu transpired in the sixth month of the year, and word of it reached his tent in Huanzhou about ten days later. The camp was all astir with this news, and for three days and nights a grand and completely unceremonious banquet ensued among all the officers and soldiers. Reports of further victories from the front continued to reach the banqueters.

—Zhongdu is now being burned to the ground.

The messenger's statements were always the same. Almost every day for over a month, Chinggis listened to the message that Zhongdu was being consumed by flames. Other than the fact that Zhongdu was continuing to burn, he learned that the enemy's Grand Councilor Wanyan Fuxing had died after taking poison on the day the city had fallen.

Chinggis had known the Jin commander Fuxing. They had met on the battlefield any number of times, and when they negotiated a peace settlement they had again met when he came as a Jin emissary. He was an extraordinary commander of exemplary personal character. Although Chinggis knew that the great city of Zhongdu was burning down and that countless precious items trapped within it were being reduced to ashes, only the loss of Commander Fuxing struck him as regrettable. Had he surrendered, Chinggis had thought of making him a subordinate and sending him to protect the city of Zhongdu.

Fuxing's act of suicide was incomprehensible to Chinggis. It was common knowledge from ancient times among nomadic peoples that when a commander's sword was broken or arrows expended and his forces lost in battle, there was absolutely no stigma attached to surrendering to the enemy. Upon surrendering, one would be either forgiven or put to death, a verdict in the hands of the former adversary. Although he had now captured innumerable cities, every one of the commanding officers had ultimately surrendered at the bitter end. Chinggis had accepted their surrender and either forgiven or executed them. Fuxing's case, though, was altogether different. With the city burning, unwilling to surrender, he had taken his own life.

The more he thought about Wanyan Fuxing, the less strange the fact that the city of Zhongdu would continue burning for over a month seemed to Chinggis. He thought he could see the color of the flames burning Zhongdu to the ground in his mind's eye. It was different from any color he had hitherto seen in burning cities.

Summoning men of the Jin and the Song dynastic states, Chinggis asked if the histories of their countries had any cases of commanders who had committed suicide besides Fuxing. Both the Jin and the Song men answered in the same manner:

"Many famous commanders whose names have come down to us in history did precisely the same thing when their cities fell."

Among the many things that he acquired in the capture of the Jin, perhaps most important was the knowledge of how their military men behaved under such circumstances. This was something alien to the Mongolian people's tradition and absent from their present practice. No matter what their training or expertise on the battlefield, suicide was unacceptable.

Chinggis had ordered his army attacking Zhongdu that all those in the city without distinction who survived the fighting—whether soldiers or members of the general population—were to be assembled in a corner outside the city walls. In this instance, Chinggis adopted a somewhat different method for dealing with the captives. In every case to date, he would select women when a city fell and have them tied up and escorted to his base camp. This time, he postponed dealing with the women, and ordered first a selection of men who had particular skills or who had received some education. He paid strict attention so that in dealing with such men there would be no judgments made on the basis of personal feelings. No matter how hostile their sentiments toward the Mongols, those with special training or education were to be brought to his camp.

He picked Shigi Qutuqu, the Tatar foundling to whom Chinggis had given highest responsibility for juridical affairs, to handle them. Having never lost his icelike frigidity in every situation he faced, Shigi Qutuqu twisted his expressionless, pale face and left the very day he received Chinggis's orders for Zhongdu. About one month later, Chinggis learned that Shigi Qutuqu had successfully completed his task in full. Almost every day, together with precious objects, Jin men of various and sundry appearance were escorted out of Zhongdu. Some were farmers, some blacksmiths, some astrologers, some officials, some scholars, some military commanders, and some ordinary foot soldiers. All manner of professions were contained among them.

At his base camp, Chinggis had another investigation made of their special talents and a report brought to him. Scarcely any women were brought out of the city. Those few were astrologers or shamans with haunting eyes in a pallid and bloodless face.

"Won't there by any more women coming out?" asked Chinggis of the man in charge.

"None will be," replied the clerk, and Chinggis imagined the bitter smile on the face of Shigi Qutuqu.

One day, Chinggis received a report that among the captives brought out of the city was a Khitan man by the name of Yelü Chucai (1190–1244), who had served in a number of high-level positions for the Jin imperial court in Zhongdu. Chinggis quickly ordered that this man be brought before him. When he arrived, he appeared to be unusually young, with a long beard and an extremely broad frame.

In his mind Chinggis lined up the members of his entourage next to this man, but they only reached his shoulders. This uncommonly large fellow had a fine set of black whiskers from his cheeks to his jaw and a calm disposition without so much as an iota of nervousness.

"Tell me your age," said Chinggis.

"I am twenty-six," he replied. His low voice conveyed a sense of considerable importance easily detected.

"You are Khitan?"

"Most certainly."

"Your homeland, the Khitan kingdom, was destroyed by the Jin, and you were pressed into a position with this present small state. I have now conquered the Jin and taken revenge against the enemy on behalf of your homeland. You should thank me as great khan of the Mongols."

"My family," he replied to Chinggis in a dignified manner and without the least trace of hesitation, "has served the state of Jin for generations and received a stipend accordingly. I am a vassal of the state of Jin. Why should I be happy at its misfortunes?" Even after he finished speaking, Yelü Chucai's lustrous voice reverberated pleasantly, penetrating deeply into Chinggis's mind.

"In what areas of learning are you accomplished?"

"Astronomy, geography, history, strategy, medicine, and augury."

"Are you really learned in the ways of augury?"

"That is my most accomplished field."

"So, divine my future. What fate awaits the Mongol blue wolves?"

"Divining the future of the Mongol people should be done with methods used by the Mongolian people. Give me a ram's scapula."

In response to his request, Chinggis had a ram's scapula brought to Yelü Chucai, who then exited the great khan's tent, built an earthen oven, burned the bone there, and investigated the cracks in it. He announced to the great khan:

"New war drums can be heard beating to the west. The time is approaching for the great khan's armies to again cross the Altai Mountains and invade the state of Kara Khitai. Such a time will surely come within three years."

"And what shall I do," replied Chinggis to this audacious prognosticator, "if your predictions prove inaccurate?"

Yelü Chucai looked directly into Chinggis's eyes and said:

"Do what the great khan wishes. If the great khan so wishes it, death."

Everything Yelü Chucai had said found an agreeable response in Chinggis's mind. It seemed to him that he had never before met such an extraordinary man. Chinggis decided to have him serve him at his side from that day forward.

Although a number of important officials expressed opposition to employing Yelü Chucai in this way, Chinggis ignored them. Their reasons were that they could not understand what he was thinking and found him suspicious of nature.

"I once selected Jebe from among the captives, and he had injured both me and my horse. Should I now have the least hesitation about placing at my side this civil official of the Jin who has never inflicted any harm upon me? I gave that young prisoner the name Jebe (arrow). Perhaps I shall give Yelü Chucai the name Utu-Saqal (long beard)."

Soon thereafter, the large diviner with the full, lengthy beard began to serve at Chinggis's side.

When they brought down the city of Zhongdu, as a second step in the process, Chinggis made Sammuqa commander of an army of 10,000 and sent him to attack and capture the new Jin capital. Chinggis had Sammuqa traverse Xixia territory, heading toward Henan province in China. In the eleventh month of the year, Sammuqa's forces marched on the Jin for the third time, crossed Xixia terrain, and entered the Chongshan mountain range. Hindered by rugged topography, they suffered through numerous hardships before reaching Henan and attacking the new capital at Bianjing. Not wishing to overexert his entire army, Sammuqa was forced to withdraw in defeat in the decisive battle with the Jin army.

Successive reports of the defeat arrived from Sammuqa, and a messenger from the Jin emperor, as if chasing after him, soon arrived at Chinggis's camp, suing for peace. Chinggis consulted with Bo'orchu, Jelme, and other senior members of his staff and offered the extremely severe conditions that all Jin territory north of the Yellow River be relinquished to the Mongols and that the Jin emperor abandon that title, to be replaced with "King of Henan."

The Jin emissary departed, and a response to these demands was never forthcoming. Inasmuch as he had thought that the Jin might not accept the conditions, Chinggis had no emotional reaction at all to their silence.

In the spring of 1216, Sammuqa led his defeated and wounded troops back to Chinggis's camp. Chinggis called Sammuqa in for a meeting to explain the reasons for his loss on the battlefield. When Sammuqa finished his report to the great khan, Chinggis said:

"Sammuqa, I shall give you one chance to vindicate your honor from this defeat. As before you shall lead an army of 10,000, and in the midst of frigid winter weather, you shall march off to invade and capture Henan once again. Once again, you shall go through Xixia terrain, climb over the deep snows and steep precipices of the Songshan Mountains, enter Henan, and seize the capital of Bianjing."

Sammuqa's face changed complexions. Even with twice as many troops as he had earlier, given the great difficulty of marching through the mountain passes, he did not believe that he could capture Bianjing. He had no choice, however, but to accept his orders.

Chinggis observed thereafter the ferocious battlefield and marching drills that Sammuqa imposed on his men, twice the training of others. Chinggis truly loved this young commander whom he had himself selected. As Bo'orchu, Jelme, and Qasar were aging, Chinggis was trying to train a second stratum of military leaders in their twenties to continue the work of the first stratum of Muqali, Jebe, and Sübe'etei. Sammuqa was one of this second group.

In this same year, Chinggis evacuated his Huanzhou base camp and returned his army to the Borjigin camp, where his mother's grave was located in the foothills of Mount Burqan and over which his wife, Börte, had been keeping watch. The great majority of officers and soldiers had not set foot here for five years since their departure in the third month of 1211.

After the peace talks with the Jin were completed in 1214, Chinggis and a group of his men had set foot on their native soil briefly and then quickly repaired to the Lake Yur area, but on this occasion they were returning in triumph and en masse.

Not joining the return were Muqali and the men under his command, who were moving the front to Liaodong and Liaoxi, as well as a small number of troops stationed in the Zhongdu area after the seizure of that city. Although Chinggis had not taken the new Jin capital at Bianjing, the majority of the territory north of the Yellow River now fell under his dominion, and using a relatively small number of Mongol officers and men, he gained overall control of the organized military units, including those of the Jin, in these areas.

The Mongol military groupings were not altogether different from what they had been at the time of the 1211 expedition. Among the various units were those formed by Jin soldiers, Khitan soldiers, and Chinese of the Song dynasty. There were also groups without weapons. At times, such alien units alone continued for several dozen miles. There were vehicular units stacked high with treasures, and camels and horses laden with weaponry and agricultural implements. Numerous women and children from the state of Jin who were being used as servants and laborers also formed long lines.

Thus, the Mongol forces comprising all sorts of different elements set out from Huanzhou, crossed the desert, came to the bank of the Kherlen River, and from there marched farther and farther upriver. They were welcomed at every settlement along the way. Almost every day, the army units passed among happily excited peoples.

The region at the foothills of Mount Burqan was thrown into an unprecedented confusion. By the Tula River bed and on the banks of the Kherlen River, hundreds of new settlements had come into existence, and several new cities seemed to have suddenly taken shape on the grasslands.

Celebrations of the military triumphs were carried out across the entire Mongolian plateau on a grand scale. Unlike when Chinggis was installed as great khan, Mongolia was now a large state with a control structure and had demolished the Jin dynasty; its once nomadic people were now the citizens of the Mongolian state, differentiated by classes. There were numerous shops lined up at the camp by Mount Burqan in which all manner of items were sold or exchanged. Among them were wine shops and food stores. Different restaurants featuring Chinese, Jurchen, Khitan, and Xixia food were there, and even horses, lambs, and camels were for sale. There were as well both the heads of settlements made up of servants from the Jin and women costumed in the Jin style.

Chinggis walked among the markets on the grasslands. Although he made his way with only a few attendants, there was no insecurity in the least. During the long war with the Jin, there had not been any disorder on the grasslands run almost entirely by women who remained behind, and there had been no hostility or bickering among divergent groups. The bustling villages remained as before, but now the festivities that allowed for limitless eating and drinking and for dressing up and sauntering around without having to attend to work were coming to an end after ten days.

In order that his officers and men not be too relaxed from their state of alert, Chinggis set out on a small expedition and battle. Remnants of the Merkids who had been chased from their settlement had quietly built another settlement in the Altai Mountains.

They retained their antipathy for Chinggis, and they were slowly becoming a force once again.

Chinggis had come to his present position of predominance by pacifying all of the peoples on the grasslands, but the treatment meted out to the Merkids, unlike instances involving other peoples, had been extremely severe, aimed at thoroughly liquidating them. Given this attitude on his part, it made perfect sense that Merkid resistance was itself ferociously pertinacious. Like weeds they survived, and like weeds they grew unchecked wherever Chinggis's line of vision did not extend, all the time keeping an eye out for an opportunity to exact revenge.

Soon after the festivities ended, Chinggis issued orders to his eldest son to subjugate the Merkids. He summoned Jochi and said to him:

"Destroy all of the Merkid remnants."

"Understood," Jochi replied in somewhat formulaic language. "I shall move in accordance with the great khan's orders."

Whenever he set out to suppress the Merkids, Chinggis gave the task to Jochi, but there was something in this a bit unsatisfying both to Chinggis himself, who had issued the order, and to Jochi, who accepted it.

When it came to the Merkids, Chinggis found it difficult to fathom his own emotional twists and turns. He could not allow them to exist, because they might be kinsmen with the same blood as his own. Their very existence might negate the fact that he was a Mongolian blue wolf. The crime committed by this race in abducting and raping his mother Ö'elün could not be permitted to go on forever, in the name of the Mongolian blue wolf.

This was not only true for himself; Jochi shared a similar fate. He very much wanted to say: "Jochi, if you are indeed a blue wolf, you must destroy by your own hand that which threatens the legitimacy of your blood! Your mother, Börte, was hauled away and violated by them—you must not allow this crime to go unpunished!"

Of course, Chinggis never explained his thinking to Jochi. Jochi did not know how to assess Chinggis's attitude on this matter, but words could not pass between them in this instance of the father-son bond. As had been the case earlier as well, Chinggis saw a cold flash in Jochi's eyes, full of something like resistance.

Chinggis decided to assigned the young commander Sübe'etei to Jochi and to have them meet the enemy jointly. Jochi and Sübe'etei immediately took charge of their forces and made their way deep into the Altai Mountains. This war of subjugation ended in early autumn. Having slaughtered the younger brother of the Merkid leader defeated earlier and the brother's two older sons, Jochi returned with the third son, Qodu Khan, as prisoner.

Jochi begged for clemency in this case, stating that the young man, the sole survivor of the Merkid people, was a famed bowman, and in fact his first arrow would hit the target and his second would pierce the first arrow's shaft—a technique rarely seen.

"Not only is Qodu Khan a fine warrior, but he is also a man of genuine sincerity. If the great khan spares his life, he will surely serve you."

"His life can't be spared. Execute him immediately," ordered Chinggis simply.

Jochi seemed to say something, but no words came from his mouth. And with his own hands he put Qodu Khan, the young Merkid commander, to death.

Early in the eleventh month of the year, Sammuqa set out from the camp at Mount Burqan, as he had been ordered, at the head of an army of 10,000 men. After about two months' time, Chinggis received his first messenger from Sammuqa, and from that point on the messengers arrived at ten-day intervals. Although he was able to gain only a fragmented sense of the movements of Sammuqa's forces, by stitching the pieces together he was able to follow Sammuqa's troops.

—The troops have cut across Xixia terrain.

—The troops have captured Tongguan, the fortified city on the southern shore of the Yellow River.

—The troops have seized five cities, including Ruzhou.

—The troops are closing in on the western environs of Bianjing.

After this last one, messages from Sammuqa ceased. Owing to insufficient troop strength, he had been unable to surround Bianjing and was again unable to take the capital of the Jin, perched on the edge of utter collapse. Sammuqa camped at a site not far from Bianjing and did not move. Chinggis sent a messenger, praising his hard work and his decision not to recklessly attempt a siege of Bianjing. Sammuqa remained encamped where he was.

In 1217 Muqali made his way to Chinggis's camp to report on the culmination of major battles in Liaoxi and Liaodong. He had been gone since setting out from the encampment at Lake Yur in 1214. Aside from a brief three-month period at the Lake Yur camp, ever since Muqali began fighting against the Jin in 1211, he had spent day and night in fierce battles, and now at long last he had brought the expansive terrain of Liaoxi and Liaodong under his control. Muqali was a man of preeminent qualities both as a warrior and as a statesman.

Chinggis had all of his high officials in attendance as he offered Muqali the highest honors. He rewarded him for his extraordinary achievements, gave him the title of prince of the state, and accorded him all authority as director of the armed forces in China. The long and bitter fighting on foreign soil had caused the young commander to age any number of years, his expressionless face remaining unmoved. In addition, the dust in the air made his complexion so ruddy that he did not look like someone born on the grasslands.

Less than 10 days later, Muqali headed once again to his post. Under his command were 23,000 troops organized into Mongol, Khitan, and Jurchen units. Muqali's posting now was the state of Jin, in which the royal Jin house teetered on the edge of extinction, and his jurisdiction as the new prince of the state was immense.

Having defeated his old enemies and gathered the great majority of their terrain under his control, Chinggis spent the period from 1217 through the spring of 1218 at his camp by Mount Burqan. The lives of the Mongol people had completely changed. With agricultural tools introduced from the Jin, the grasslands were gradually opened to cultivation, and in the southeastern sector people adopted a semiagricultural lifestyle. With the technology acquired from the Jin, wells were dug everywhere, and large amounts of pastureland were improved for farming.

On almost a daily basis, innumerable caravans from east and west now assembled at Chinggis's camp. Chinggis liked being able to see men of every race, with different skin colors and eye colors, coming together and spreading out with camels and horses laden with merchandise.

On Chinggis's orders, it was standard practice for caravans that had made their way from the distant west to present themselves at the great khan's tent soon after unpacking their wares in the market. Chinggis treated them with cordiality and never took their merchandise without compensating them.

Among such caravans, those that most impressed the great khan were from the Muslim state of Khorazm. They brought beautiful utensils and handicrafts that Mongol expeditionary troops had never seen before, even on Jin terrain. That included glass items and all manner of precious stones, as well as personal ornaments of exquisite craftsmanship. They also had rugs so magnificent that one could scarcely imagine how they were made. For these stunning items, the Mongols exchanged goods obtained from the Jin: silk, cotton cloth, writing brushes, paper, ink, inkstones, paintings, and antiques.

Chinggis put in special orders with the caravans from Khorazm for weaponry and for paraphernalia related to religious rituals. He sought such items from an unknown state at the suggestion of Yelü Chucai, whose education, knowledge, and character Chinggis so admired. This large man with the long beard had won the great khan's affection and offered his own distinctive views on all matters of policy.

Chinggis expressed a surprisingly strong desire that Yelü Chucai learn about these unknown things, and thus all caravans had to answer the latter's questions, often for a considerable period of time, at the tent of the great khan.

When Chinggis queried Yelü Chucai closely for his opinion, it was always centered on what the Mongols should do to become stronger. Yelü Chucai's response was always the same. They had to continue to preserve an abiding interest in a high level of culture, with a burning ferocity like that of red-hot steel. There was always the opposition between honoring culture and honoring military might.

"Although the Jin state was destroyed by the great khan's military strength, it still had a far higher level of culture," said Yelü Chucai. "The great khan must now study many of the artifacts from the Jin. You should govern the people of Jin wisely and act in a manner that encourages them to contribute all that they possess."

"Although it attained a high level of culture," replied Chinggis, "the Jin state fell under our rule, did it not, because it had inferior military capacity?"

"When the great khan says 'rule,' what do you mean? If one morning General Muqali withdraws from Jin, what sort of 'rule' will remain? Military force can only hold down an opponent. It cannot rule him. To the extent that they do not yet have a high level of culture in their own land, Mongol officers and men cannot fully rule the state of Jin. At some time, they will, to the contrary, be absorbed into the Jin and ultimately be ruled by the Jin, as it were."

Yelü Chucai always made Chinggis fall silent. The Mongol khan enjoyed being persuaded by his young advisor and retreating into silence. Whenever he felt compelled to say nothing further, Chinggis incorporated into policy in one form or another the views of his interlocutor.

Chinggis learned from Yelü Chucai that the greatest force for concentrating the people's minds as one was love of their own ethnicity and religious belief, not fidelity to the powerful. Thus, Chinggis prohibited any alien people's beliefs from entering his settlement freely and causing harm. For his own Mongolian people, he encouraged belief in heaven, as Mongols had held from time immemorial, as evidence for their distinctive qualities. He did not, however, enforce this belief on lineages other than the Borjigin.

Chinggis never relaxed the ironclad regulations even a little bit, and at the same time he accepted Yelü Chucai's idea and instituted moral education—such as rejecting theft and murder—for his nomadic people. For the Mongols, the theft of sheep meant death, but now he was gradually planting among them an altogether new concept that one had to avoid theft because it brought unhappiness both to oneself and to others.

One thing Chinggis completed ignored was that the young man possessed Khitan blood. This first cropped up early in 1218, when Chinggis suddenly ordered troops under his command to invade the Xixia. Although he subjugated the Xixia, he also felt the need to encamp Mongol troops on their terrain. The fighting arose all of a sudden, without provocation. A Mongol cavalry unit enveloped in clouds of dust attacked the Xixia capital and forced the king to flee for Xiliang in the west. Chinggis thus effected an occupation of Xixia by a powerful Mongol battalion.

For a number of days before and after this battle, Chinggis would not face Yelü Chucai. At such times, however, the latter never reproached Chinggis. Indeed, he never so much as mentioned the topic.

Chinggis's real objective in marching against the Xixia was not to cause, through a Mongol occupation of the area, the least unsettledness in the neighboring Uyghur state. The Naiman King Küchülüg, once an enemy who had managed to escape in the fighting, had now, with his own state destroyed, usurped the throne of the Kara Khitai (Western Liao) king and held it for six years. It was thus a foregone conclusion for Chinggis that before long he would have to attack. When they were ready to move against the Kara Khitai, given its geographic proximity, he would have to march through the neighboring state of the Uyghurs, which would then fall under Mongol control.

7

The Destruction
of Khorazm

IN THE SUMMER OF 1218, Chinggis placed Jebe in command of an army of 20,000 men and had him march on the kingdom of Kara Khitai. The divination performed by Yelü Chucai with a ram's scapula at the time of his first audience with Chinggis, indicating that there would be war drums in the southwest, was now becoming reality. The objective of invading Kara Khitai was to bring down the Naiman King Küchülüg, and by taking over his territory, establish a border with the state of Khorazm, with its highly esteemed culture. Chinggis maintained friendly relations and a high volume of trade with Khorazm, and in so doing he sought to acquire many things theretofore unknown to him.

When Jebe invaded Kara Khitai, he immediately announced that there would be freedom of religion and freed the adherents of Islam who had suffered under Küchülüg. Muslims rose in rebellion at numerous sites and saw Jebe as their ally. Jebe defeated the forces of Küchülüg at many places and captured the walled cities of Hami, Kashgar, Yarkand, and Khotan. He pursued Küchülüg himself, who fled as far as the Pamir plateau, where he was attacked by local people and killed. Jebe sent his head back to the great khan along with 1,000 horses raised by the people of the region.

The pacification of Kara Khitai was accomplished at great speed; in the space of roughly three months, Jebe had brought under Mongol rule an immense state that spread north and south across Tianshan. In the fighting, the Mongols formed two huge wings to the left and right of the army's main body. Led by Muqali and Jebe, a thorough mopping up was under way.

Chinggis issued a proclamation for his distinguished commander Jebe that both recognized his stunning accomplishment and warned him against being overly boastful about it.

Although the invasion and capture of Kara Khitai were effected to promote trade with the great unknown kingdom of Khorazm, Chinggis acquired something else of enormous importance. Altogether new agricultural and industrial technologies, which even the state of Jin had lacked, now streamed onto the Mongolian plateau, like water running to lower ground. Fruits, carpets, wines, and numerous handicraft products, the likes of which the Mongols had never seen before, crossed the wastelands and the Gobi Desert, arriving daily on the plateau.

Chinggis Khan was now autocrat over an immense stretch of territory. He resolved to send his first caravan to Khorazm and to enlist caravan members from among his relatives. In short order one or two candidates from his own family and from among his commanders stepped forward, and a company of 450 men was organized. There was some concern that every member of the company should be a Muslim.

The caravan set out from Chinggis's camp, and when it reached Otrar on the banks of the Syr Darya, they were arrested by Ghayir Khan, the officer left in charge of the region, and all the merchandise they had brought along was plundered. Ghayir Khan then reported to Muhammad, shah of Khorazm, that the caravan was all Mongol spies and that he had executed all 450 of them.

Chinggis was completely unprepared when he learned this news, and it gave rise to a fierce antipathy in him for this large, unknown land. The goodwill he had shown toward Khorazm was now completely turned to enmity.

The land of Khorazm was entirely unfamiliar to Chinggis, to Yelü Chucai, and to many of his staff members in terms of both the conditions prevailing there and the sensibilities of the people. With the small amount of information gleaned from caravans, they knew that it was a large Muslim state with phenomenal wealth. What sort of state organization and what level of armed forces it possessed were unknown. Chinggis consulted Yelü Chucai about sending troops against Khorazm in retaliation.

"What we know about Khorazm," said Yelü Chucai, "is that it is unified by the Muslim faith and that large groups of Muslims make up the state. Religion is the steel that binds them together, but the Mongols have nothing comparable to this. Judging by the goods that the caravans have brought, their cultural level is unfathomably high. Might it make more sense to postpone the dispatching of troops?"

Chinggis also consulted with the older leaders, Qasar and Jelme, but neither agreed with the idea of sending troops.

"All we know about Khorazm," said Qasar, "is that their soldiers wear steel armor. Compared to our leather armor, it's difficult to immediately say which is better or worse, but clearly our weapons cannot penetrate their armor. One thing's for sure: fighting with them will take on an altogether new form, unknown to us so far."

"It seems to me that Khorazm is like the great sea," continued Jelme. "For caravans from Khorazm come speaking all manner of languages and practicing all sorts of customs. The only thing they share is the Islamic faith. It strikes me that the great khan ought not toss crack Mongol troops into a bottomless ocean."

Chinggis went on to consult with many of his other commanders, but in everyone's estimation Khorazm seemed to be an eerie religious state whose actual form remained largely unclear. No one thought it a good idea to act aggressively and send troops.

Finally, Chinggis summoned Jochi to his tent. When he appeared before Chinggis, Jochi immediately said:

"Why should I fear an attack on Khorazm?"

Chinggis had not decided on that course of action, and when he proceeded to consult with Jochi, the latter replied:

"Because a peak is high, can Mongol wolves not dash over it? Because a valley is deep, can we not make our way through it? Great khan, make me and tens of thousands of troops under my command dash over that peak and cut through that valley."

Looking into Jochi's eyes, Chinggis did not feel that he was for certain a Mongol blue wolf.

"They say that Khorazm is like a great sea," said Chinggis. "If you destroy one state, another will appear. Although I am prepared to lose Jochi and those under your command, I am concerned that I would have to throw all of Mongolia into the great sea."

"Is this not what all Mongol soldiers were born fated to do?" answered Jochi. "The great khan did not wish that, as a result of the conquest of Kara Khitai, we would have an enemy, but we Borjigins have always had enemies, from the time our grandfathers and great-grandfathers were born until we die. Having enemies is what makes us Borjigins. Blue wolves must have enemies. A wolf with no enemies is not a true wolf. Because of frauds like Yelü Chucai, the great khan is on the verge of implanting us with the spirit of the Khitans. Now is the time to get rid of Yelü Chucai and take your revenge instead. Fill the lives of the Mongol people with battle, as our ancestors did."

"Young Mongol wolf." Chinggis opened his mouth quietly to speak, having listened silently to Jochi's words. "Are you suggesting that I have ceased to be a wolf? When we come up with a plan for dealing with Khorazm, I shall give you the glory of leading the attack, and the main body of my troops will step over your corpse and march on."

After he dismissed Jochi, Chinggis's attitude began to improve greatly. Although he had no desire to accept his eldest son's proposal as offered, for the first time in a while he was inspired by the spirit of invasion and attack his son elicited.

Chinggis once again solicited the opinion of his wife, Börte, in her tent. A year his senior, she now had white hair and a portly torso, and was a venerable woman covered with precious stones. Her movements had slowed with age, and the glitter in her eye had dimmed with each passing year.

Börte had only rarely spoken over the previous four or five years, but when asked by Chinggis about the advisability of invading Khorazm, she said with a light smile:

"Send the army, if the great khan so wishes. Don't move the army, if the great khan does not so wish it. The great khan has managed affairs these few years without consulting my views."

"It may transpire that every Mongol soldier will be wounded," replied Chinggis. "Is that acceptable?"

"Great khan," said Börte with a smile, "when have you ever been so covetous? Other than your now aging wife, what sort of subordinates have you had?"

Listening to his wife speak, Chinggis realized that this was precisely the issue: she was not terribly satisfied with their present circumstances, in which they wanted for nothing. For Chinggis this was bizarre, beyond the bounds of ordinary understanding. As he was steadily rising to be ruler of a great state, Börte was gradually being buried in a deep snow of dissatisfaction with her surroundings. The reason was not clearly identifiable, and Chinggis left Börte with a feeling of profound frustration.

For the last opinion, Chinggis visited Qulan's tent. Unlike Börte, Qulan was a woman still in her prime. Her face still shone with limitless radiance, and she carried herself with the dignity of the most beloved consort of the ruler.

"The great khan," said Qulan, a charming smile lighting up her face, "has the love and affection of 3,000 widows focused on himself, and that is still not enough. Will you now mount the princesses of Khorazm on elephants and bring them to your tent?"

Whenever he came before Qulan, Chinggis felt as if enveloped in a sweet luxuriousness, and in the reflection of her radiance, he felt himself exposed to stunning ideas. This, however, by no means meant that Chinggis trusted the beauty and lustrousness that Qulan possessed.

Although they had not spoken of it since he had entrusted their beloved son Kölgen to Sorqan Shira, she had, it would seem, not forgotten this incident. Qulan often softly criticized the fact that Chinggis had numerous concubines, but it never harmed her pride in the least, because she believed in her heart of hearts that the leader of the Mongolian people loved her more than all the others. When Chinggis asked her in all seriousness for her views on attacking Khorazm, Qulan advised him with an enthusiasm greater than that of anyone he had thus far consulted to send an armed expedition.

"The great khan must attack Khorazm," she said, "for Khorazm is far wealthier than Mongolia and far more advanced. The fruits of such a battle will be immense, and the fighting will be equally intense. Cast all of the Mongolian people into the crucible of war. I for one would like to live with the great khan on the field of battle in that foreign land.

"Take away everything I have. Precious stones, beautiful clothing, all my extravagant personal effects—take it all away from me. Then see to it that I am always in the midst of war cries. Amid the sharp reverberations of arrows, I shall make sure of only one thing with the great khan and wish to speak of only one topic.

"I may have taken the great khan to task in the past for his many concubines. I may have demanded treasures and land of the great khan in the past. Not once did I ever believe that all of this stuff in my tent surrounding me was really mine. I was merely borrowing it to adorn myself. When I abandon this tent, these things here will cease to belong to me.

"Great khan, see to it that I am with you in the fierce battles to come with Khorazm. Give me the opportunity to say just one thing."

"What is that one thing you wish to speak with me about?" asked Chinggis, thinking it all a bit strange.

"It is something that can only be spoken of at the time. At that time, heaven will reside in my body and instruct me as to what to say."

These were the divergent—similar, though dissimilar—words elicited from Jochi, Börte, and Qulan concerning Chinggis's decision about sending an expedition against Khorazm.

Although he was resolved to go to war, his plan did not take shape immediately. He had to treat the appeal of Yelü Chucai and many other commanders opposing such a war with respect, and he had to take their views into account, albeit in an utterly different form from the ways they were articulated to him: in military movements against this unknown religious state.

Chinggis revealed his battle plans to no one and worked extremely hard to gather, by every means at his disposal, information about the state of Khorazm. He traveled around the settlements on the Mongolian plateau, working to drum up morale among the troops who would be under his command.

At the end of 1218, Chinggis convened the Quriltai, the Mongolian council of elders, and for the first time consulted with his close relatives, high officials, and senior advisors concerning the attack on Khorazm. It was less a consultation than an announcement; Chinggis declared his plan unilaterally at this time and had those present at the meeting approve it. It was decided further that, while Chinggis was at the front, in his stead his younger brother Temüge would rule over domestic affairs. All of Chinggis's relatives, as well as his high officials and senior advisors, were to depart for the war, and of all his concubines, only Qulan was permitted to join him on the march. Yelü Chucai was also ordered to follow the army to battle.

A messenger was immediately sent to Xixia, now a subservient state of the Mongols, to join the battle. Xixia, however, unexpectedly refused to dispatch relief troops. This led Chinggis to realize that Xixia saw Khorazm as bigger and stronger than the Mongols and were avoiding antagonizing the state of Khorazm.

Chinggis led a force of 200,000 men in the spring of 1219 from his camp in the foothills of Mount Burqan. It was movement on a grand scale of wolf packs dressed in armor. The troops crossed the Altai Mountains at the height of summer, marched west to the plains and mountainous regions in the northern foothills of Tianshan, made their way to the Chui River, and camped there. Inasmuch as he had no idea how strong Khorazm was militarily, Chinggis decided to wait for his opponents to move first. From summer through fall, he and his entire armed forces engaged in massive-scale hunting expeditions over the course of weeks. To keep his troops in readiness, as well as to keep the horses trained for battle and to acquire fresh provisions, hunting was a necessity for the units of Mongol troops.

At the same time, Chinggis was devoting himself to gathering reports on domestic affairs within Khorazm. He was able to glean that it was an amalgam of numerous ethnicities, which, of course, meant that it possessed many weak points as well. The weakest element was the fact that, in preparing to face the Mongols, Khorazm had amassed a force of 400,000, but it lacked a single superior leader who exercised control over this army made up of many different ethnic groups. Although Muhammad, shah of Khorazm, was the ruler of a Muslim sphere, he could not serve as the man in charge of a large military force. The army was spread among several dozen walled towns dotting a massive expanse of terrain. They filled up all of these walled sites and adopted a strategy from the start of evading open-field warfare with mounted troops and long lances, which was the Mongols' great strength.

In mid-autumn, Chinggis abruptly discontinued the hunting and issued orders to his entire army for the invasion of the borders of the northwestern state of Khorazm. The Syr Darya, which starts in the Tianshan mountain range and empties into the Aral Sea, cut off the forward movement of the Mongol armed forces, and all along it fortresses had been placed here and there. Before they advanced farther, Chinggis divided his entire army into four units. He put his eldest son, Jochi, in charge of the first army and sent him toward the lower reaches of the Syr Darya, and he entrusted the second army to his second son, Cha'adai, and his third son, Ögedei, and decided that they should lead their forces to attack and capture Otrar along the middle reaches of the Syr Darya. The third army he placed in the hands of three young commanders, Alaq, Soqtuu, and Taghai, and he ordered them to pacify the upper reaches of the Syr Darya. Tolui, his fourth son, was placed in command of the fourth army, and he decided that this force would cross the Syr Darya and attack Bukhara, a major stronghold of distant Khorazm's army.

Chinggis made it clear to the warriors under his command that this fight was to crush the entire army of Khorazm and to continue until its sovereign, Muhammad, was put to death. His extremely rigid orders were that those who surrendered would be allowed to live, but all who resisted—be they soldiers or civilians—were to be massacred. In Chinggis's mind, this was a war in which all Mongo-

lian strength was invested, on which he was staking the very existence of his people.

As he had when he waged war against the state of Jin, Chinggis
gathered all of his relatives and high officials at his tent and held a
send-off feast as if it were the last time they would see one another.
At the time of the Jin invasion, this had taken place at his tent in
the foothills of Mount Burqan, but now it was being held at his tent
in the wilderness on foreign terrain, some ten days away from the
Erdish River.

On this occasion, Chinggis announced who among his four sons
was to assume the position of sovereign, should he die. This was,
to be sure, the most important matter of concern not only for these
four sons but also for all of his ministers and senior advisors, and all
the officers and soldiers of the Mongolian people as a whole. In everyone's estimation, Chinggis loved his youngest son, Tolui, most.
From time immemorial, the Mongolian people had practiced a system of ultimogeniture, so Tolui was due to inherit Chinggis's own
personal property, but Chinggis's love for Tolui did not derive from
a special relationship the two men shared.

Chinggis profoundly admired Tolui's bravery and his brilliant
flash on the battlefield. In every expedition to date, Chinggis had
placed himself in the same unit as Tolui. While this indicated that
he was a supporter of the youngest son, it was not that alone that
sealed the case, because he was pleased as well by the manner in
which Tolui deployed his forces and the way they fought. There
was something deeply refreshing about a twenty-six-year-old commander in whom Chinggis found so many admirable qualities.

All those in attendance thought that Chinggis would either name
his eldest son, Jochi, by virtue of his glorious military exploits, about
which there was no debate whatsoever, or Tolui, who had earned
his deepest love. The name that emerged from Chinggis's mouth,
however, was altogether different.

"Ögedei."

Everyone heard the name of Chinggis's third son. The moment
they heard it, everyone doubted their own ears. Before long, though,
they perforce learned that their ears had not failed them.

"Jochi, what do you think?" said Chinggis. "Speak!"

"I have no objection whatsoever," he replied, "to Ögedei's name being put forward. Together with my younger brothers Cha'adai and Tolui, we shall work to help Ögedei. It is splendid that Ögedei shall be heir to our father, the great khan."

With a pallid expression, Jochi had responded with few words.

"Cha'adai, what do you think? Speak!"

"Just as Jochi has put it," he replied, "together with my brothers, I shall work to assist my father as long as he lives and to assist Ögedei after Father passes away. Should any man defy us, we shall strike out and kill him. Should any man flee, we shall track him down and thrust daggers at him from behind. Ögedei is the most gentle and sincere of the brothers. Ögedei has the talents best suited to being ruler of all Mongolia. It is altogether fitting, then, that Ögedei receive the position of heir to the great khan."

There was far more fervent emotion in Cha'adai's words than in those of Jochi.

"Tolui, what do you think? Speak!" Chinggis fixed his gaze on his youngest son.

"Standing before my elder brother whom Father has named," he answered, "should he forget something, I shall remind him. When he is asleep, I shall shake him to wake up. We shall march off together to the battlefield, always to be the whip of pacification. I shall never be absent from troop deployment, marching on every lengthy expedition and fighting in every severe battle."

After nodding his head in satisfaction, Chinggis finally said:

"Ögedei, do you have anything to say? If so, speak!"

Understandably, Ögedei could not hide his excitement, but as was his wont, he quietly composed himself and replied:

"Do I have anything to say? Just that whenever Father has orders, I obey whatever they may be. I would just fear that my own children may be weak and unable to accede to the position of great khan."

All in attendance were hushed, listening to this exchange between Chinggis and his four sons, but by the time they finished speaking, everyone was beginning to come to the view that Chinggis's designation had been a wise one. Although all present had only just became aware of this selection, it now appeared to them that there was no better person than Ögedei to lead all the Mongolian people as their sovereign after Chinggis.

Ögedei lacked the kind of ferocity that each of his three brothers possessed; he was a gentle man by nature, a deeply kind man, a man who took responsibility for everything, never resorting to trickery or artifice. He was a modest man who did not stand out among his brothers, but by the same token, when he made up his mind, he dauntlessly moved to action with alacrity. This was a strength befitting the successor to the great khan, in which he excelled everyone.

When it was clear that no one harbored any objection to his choice, Chinggis said:

"The land before us is expansive without limit, the rivers flow to infinitude, and the fields of grass continue without end. The dwelling places that I shall divide among Jochi, Cha'adai, and Tolui will thus be immense."

Only Jochi's pale mien would always remain in Chinggis's eyes. The bravest commander among the Mongolian people, Jochi was a warrior with a will of steel who never flinched in the face of imminent death, a man who amazed even Chinggis himself. He had no peer among the entire Mongolian nation when it came to carrying out great deeds. In fact, Chinggis had vacillated about who should be his successor, Ögedei or Jochi. Who was more suitable was a subtle issue, extremely difficult to resolve. Ultimately, he selected Ögedei. That Jochi's face had paled at the news was not altogether unexpected to Chinggis.

Chinggis and all those before him raised their wine cups to the coming desperate battle. For everyone but Jochi, it was a gesture of parting perhaps to an unknown fate, but for Jochi it bore a somewhat different meaning. It seemed to Chinggis that for Jochi this was a moment of estrangement. Chinggis had thought about this a great deal. Had something unusual occurred, it would not have been unexpected. He forcibly pushed the thought aside as insignificant. In his mind, he called out to Jochi:

"'Guest' of the Borjigin, you still haven't proven yourself to be a true descendant of the blue wolf, just as I haven't. Go off now!

Take a path of great difficulty far, far away. You must fight and win innumerable, fierce battles, just as I must. Jochi, if you are indeed a shining Mongol wolf, you must seize your dwelling place by force with your own strength."

Chinggis then saw Jochi, who had walked over and was standing before him. He raised his wine cup to his son and said simply:

"I have heard that there is a poisonous scorpion along the lower reaches of the Syr Darya. Be mindful of that!"

"Yes, my father and great khan."

Staring back at Chinggis without defiance, Jochi replied with few words of his own in an emphatic tone of voice.

The four Mongol units descended upon the Syr Darya at approximately the same time. Jochi's forces set their sights on the city of Jand, the armies of Cha'adai and Ögedei laid siege to Otrar, and the soldiers under Alaq, Soqtuu, and Taghai moved toward Fanakat.

Chinggis and Tolui led the main army and pitched camp on the Syr Darya, and soon news of victories repeatedly reached them from their various military units. They crossed the river with the entire army and headed for the city of Bukhara, deep within Khorazm's terrain, precisely as planned. With the main army advancing toward Bukhara, communications between the main force of the enemy and the fortresses along the Syr Darya were naturally severed.

Chinggis marched over the desert and the plains region for over a month. Eventually reaching the city of Zarnuq, Chinggis sent a messenger who called out at the city gate:

"As sons of heaven, we are defenders of the Muslim people. By order of the great khan of the Mongols, we are here now to save you. The great Mongolian army presses upon your gate. Should you so much as resist even slightly, we shall without a moment's notice destroy your strongholds and homes. If you surrender, you shall escape with your lives and property."

The city dwellers immediately came out. Only the young men were commandeered into the Mongolian military, while the others were allowed to return to their homes.

Plundering the city lasted for three days. All items of importance were confiscated by the troops. When the fortress strongholds were destroyed, Mongol soldiers set off on a dangerous route toward the city of Nur. Over a month later they reached the walled settlement, and Chinggis had them promptly open the city gates, bring the residents outside the walls, and plunder the city over the course of several days.

Although Chinggis forbid his men from injuring the city folk, the pillage was thorough. As a result, foodstuffs had to be secured, and the most valuable possessions—as the natural right of the victors— had to be transformed into a part of Mongolian national strength.

Mongol cavalry units greeted the new year of 1220 while en route to Bukhara. When they reached the outskirts of the city in the first month of the year, they camped by the banks of the Sughd River. Around them stretched extraordinarily fertile fields. After allowing his forces sufficient respite, Chinggis had his immense army surround the city. Within the walls was a besieged army of 20,000 that did not respond to the advice to surrender, and a fierce battle attacking and defending the city ensued over the following days.

One night, the besieged troops suddenly flung open the city gates and launched an attack. They broke through the Mongol encirclement and escaped in the direction of the Amu Darya. Chinggis had his men pursue them as far as the Amu Darya and slaughtered every one of them. The riverbed was filled with corpses, the river's surge turned red from all the blood. For the first time, the soldiers under Chinggis's command witnessed such a great flow of blood, which made them maniacal.

The following day Chinggis entered the city through the main gate. Shops, temples, and homes filled the interior and bespoke, at a glance, a city of great wealth. Men and women of various ethnicities crowded around him through the streets and neighborhoods. Four hundred soldiers who had not attempted to surrender remained within. When he entered the city gate, Chinggis quickly gave orders to attack the interior, and the moat soon filled up with city dwellers holding weapons.

It took the Mongol soldiers 12 days to bring down the 400 enemy troops. Many Mongols died, as did many urbanites who were chased away. With catapults and batteries, they finally broke through the city walls, and Mongol soldiers poured in.

After capturing Bukhara, Chinggis expelled the residents from the city with nothing more than the clothes on their backs. Mongol troops then proceeded to enter the city and plunder it as they pleased. Anyone who failed to comply with this decree and hid something was summarily executed. Of the city dwellers assembled at a site outside the walls now, the women were divided up among the troops. All the virgins were taken off. The men were compelled to admit where they had secreted possessions, all of which were confiscated, and then were drafted into the Mongolian army.

When Chinggis departed from Bukhara, he issued orders to have the vacant city set afire and reduced to ashes. By this example, Chinggis indicated what fate awaited a city that moved in any fashion to treat him as their enemy.

As Bukhara was engulfed in flames, Chinggis set off with his men in the direction of Samarkand, a city even greater in size than Bukhara. They marched for five days, during which time the Mongol soldiers, already baptized in blood and cruelty, were transformed into wild animals with glaring eyes. They differed from wild beasts only insofar as their advance was held in check by strict military discipline. When the blue moon appeared each night, the marching soldiers cast black shadows on the desert hillocks. During this harsh forced march, many of the numerous young men with blue eyes whom they had brought along with them from Bukhara collapsed en route, and all those who collapsed were killed on the spot.

After they had marched over desert, wasteland, and rocky hills for several days, the city of Samarkand on the low ground below their line of vision suddenly loomed before them. Even in the eyes of crazed Mongol troops, Samarkand was more beautiful than they had ever imagined. The area outside the city walls was lush with an unbroken view of fruit trees and flowering plants. The groves of fruit trees continued all along the banks of the Sughd River that flowed around the city. This immense metropolis nestled in such beautiful natural surroundings was encircled by a stone wall several levels thick, which had been specifically reinforced to withstand an impending attack by Mongol forces.

Before Chinggis pressed the assault on Samarkand, he sent two detachments to two cities that lay between Bukhara and Samarkand. While the main force of his army camped at the Sughd River, news of the capture of these two walled towns arrived.

Garrison troops were stationed on all four sides of Samarkand, led by the finest commanders in Khorazm's army. Chinggis did not begin the assault precipitously but refined the attack strategy while in camp. Soon after he arrived at the banks of the Sughd River, three units that had earlier gone to capture fortresses along the Syr Darya completed their mission, and after several days arrived to join forces with his main army. First came the unit under Jochi's command. About six months after setting out, Jochi had captured the city of Sïqnaq, plundered three other nearby cities, taken the city of Jand, and placed the lower reaches of the Syr Darya under his control. All those who fought against the Mongol forces were put to death, the greatest number in the city of Sïqnaq, where the majority of the residents were butchered by Mongol soldiers.

About ten days after Jochi's unit arrived, that of Cha'adai and Ögedei appeared. They had received orders to attack and take Otrar because Chinggis's earlier delegation seeking amity had been slaughtered, the immediate cause of the present war. After fighting for five months, Mongol troops took the city, and after another month of fierce fighting within the city walls, they quelled it. Half of the residents were executed, and the remaining half escorted under guard to Samarkand together with the lord of the city, Ghayir Khan. Chinggis would not meet him and simply ordered his execution. Shackled, Ghayir Khan saw at his side a silver bar melting and boiling hot. He asked a soldier what he was planning to do with it. "We're going to pour it in your eyes and ears," replied the soldier. And indeed, Ghayir Khan met his end in this fashion.

Another 10 days later, the units under the three young commanders arrived. They comprised a force of only 5,000, but all were dauntingly courageous. They had quickly captured the city of Fanakat, expelled the residents, and put all the troops holding weapons to death. They then had moved upstream along the Syr Darya and attacked the fortress of Khojend that had been constructed in the river. A long battle ensued with the garrison commander, Temür Malik, and ultimately they attacked the city with war boats. The sole error committed by these units was to allow Temür Malik to escape.

The numerous captured troops and voluminous plunder were brought into each unit's ranks. Hence, one now saw soldiers of many different ethnicities at the Mongol encampment by the Sughd River. The Mongols thus first became aware at this time of the multitude of different peoples in the world.

When the three units came together, Chinggis organized them into two brigades to pursue Muhammad, shah of Khorazm, who had promptly abandoned Samarkand and disappeared in the direction of the Amu Darya. One brigade was to be led by Jebe and the other by Sübe'etei. Chinggis issued the following orders to these two commanders, in whom he invested the greatest of trust:

"Like two arrows shot from this starting point, your two brigades will each set out from here and proceed in two directions. Your task is the same. Seize Muhammad's unit, hem them in, and exterminate them. Should you see that they have large numbers of troops, then avoid a clash and link up with an allied force. If they retreat, do not even stop to catch your breath but attack. A city that submits will be allowed to do so, but all resisters must be mercilessly annihilated."

Soon that very day, two large brigades departed camp. At a distance of about half a mile from Samarkand, the two files of troops split apart like two arrows.

The attack on Samarkand began at the end of the third month of the year. Chinggis stood at the head of troops of different ethnicities who had come along from a variety of locales, and he saw to it that they followed behind the Mongol infantry. Khorazm's army fought largely in cities. The majority of its garrison troops were Qangli, of Turkic origin, while others, a minority, were Persians. After a fierce battle lasting seven days, Chinggis took control of the city except for its innermost area, and he succeeded in getting the Qangli troops who had surrendered out of the city. The attack on the inner city commenced on all sides. It was set aflame, and 1,000 Persian troops fighting to the bitter end were all butchered.

This battle was extremely chaotic, and numerous Samarkand residents burned to death in the fire. Thirty thousand noncombatant Qangli who had surrendered were also massacred in one night.

The night that Samarkand burned was like a scene from a dream for Chinggis. Orange flames singed the jet-black sky, and all manner of human screams filled the night for what seemed like a hideously long stretch of time. When the white rays of dawn began to float onto the horizon, Chinggis could see that only those people blessed with good fortune who had gathered in certain places outside the city walls had survived the inferno. There were 30,000 laborers carrying the tools of their trades, 51,000 captives, a small number of women, and 20 elephants.

Having reduced Samarkand to ashes, Chinggis moved to a site between it and the city of Nakhshab, where he stayed from spring through summer. He had to allow his men and horses a rest until the autumn period of fighting arrived. The encampment was on an ideal site for grazing the horses.

All cities located north of the Amu Darya were now in Chinggis's hands. Unlike during times of war, Chinggis strictly forbade his Mongol troops from injuring or plundering the local populace. The troops loitering about, like devils looking for blood and women and valuables, gradually reverted once again to human beings. At the same time, green grass was growing on land that had been soaked in quantities of blood, and cities that had been destroyed were slowly coming back to life. Even in places that seemed to have been permanently transformed into uninhabited ruins, people began returning as if unaware and picking up their lives again.

Chinggis sent Mongol officers to such cities, and as a basis for observation, had them establish a political system run by present inhabitants selected from the Muslims. He placed occupying forces at sites where there was the least danger to public order. Then they built wide roads to facilitate movement of large military units between cities. In the expansive lands between the Syr Darya and the

Amu Darya, there were grasslands and desert, and laborers from the resident populace being guided by Mongol troops were visible everywhere.

During this time, a succession of messengers, like fiends with bodies drenched in blood, came from the expeditionary units under Jebe and Sübe'etei. They had taken the city of Balkh, which had not resisted, with injury to no one there, whereas in the city of Zava, which had resisted, every single resident was slaughtered. One by one, the units attacked and captured all of the cities until they came to Nishapur, the central base of operations for Khorazm. A place that did not resist the Mongols was left as is, but if it resisted even a bit, it was reduced to ashes. Mongol troops entered the city of Nishapur without bloodshed at the beginning of the sixth month of the year. The two units pursued Muhammad, who left and headed for a succession of cities along the coast of the Caspian Sea, and nothing was heard from him thereafter. In the capture of Muhammad's armies, the two Mongol units had the mission of hunting down Muhammad himself wherever the trail led them.

When the period of pasturage from spring to autumn came to a close, Chinggis learned that Muhammad's heir, Jalal al-Din, had established his base in Khorazm's capital of Urganch. He placed his three sons Jochi, Cha'adai, and Ögedei at the head of a great army and dispatched them to attack and take it.

The walled city of Urganch was a large metropolis built to span the Amu Darya where it spilled into the Aral Sea. Mongol soldiers attempted to destroy the bridges connecting the two districts of the city, but this resulted in 3,000 deaths of their own and failure. Defense of the city was firm and garrison troop morale high. The siege lasted for six months, and they were unable to bring the city down. Every time the Mongols launched an attack against the city, it resulted in numerous deaths on their side.

Realizing that the number of dead and wounded was needlessly high and that the reason they had been unable to attain a swift victory was the antagonism between his two sons Jochi and Cha'adai, Chinggis issued orders that Ögedei was to take over command of the army. Not unexpectedly, Ögedei tried to reach an understanding between his two elder brothers, and he then set off to attack the capital of Khorazm. The resistance within the city was fierce, and to take one section of it, they literally built a mountain of corpses. In the fourth month of 1221, Mongol troops seized full control over Urganch. Of the residents and soldiers, only 100,000 craftsmen were absorbed into the Mongol army, and everyone else was put to death. Although Mongol troop strength stood at 50,000, every soldier had to kill 24 members of this alien people. In body and spirit, the troops were literally dyed red in all the blood.

When this great slaughter was over, the Mongol army destroyed the dikes on the Amu Darya, causing an inundation of water into the city piled high with dead bodies that washed away all the homes and possessions there. Because of the length of this brutal war, everything in the city was drenched in blood, and the Mongol troops could not bring themselves to plunder it. They had, however, been unable to capture the brave leader of the enemy, Jalal al-Din.

After receiving news of the capture of Urganch, Chinggis made camp in the grassland region along the banks of the Amu Darya. After a six-month absence, Cha'adai and Ögedei returned to Chinggis's camp, but after the occupation of Urganch, Jochi separated from his two brothers and led his own military unit north to the Syr Darya to pacify that region. This action went beyond Chinggis's orders. When he heard reports from Cha'adai and Ögedei, Chinggis felt a rage burning within, but he said nothing and showed nothing on his face. While Jochi's action was reproachable for going beyond his orders, the strategy he adopted was wise, and had Jochi not done this, Chinggis would have had to order someone else to do so. For this reason, Chinggis forced himself to swallow his anger.

Chinggis now gave his troops—whose numbers had swelled several dozen times with numerous soldiers of different ethnicities—a respite in camp to enjoy life as normal men. He deprived his youngest son, Tolui, of a rest, though, and sent him deep into Khorazm's terrain to track down Jalal al-Din.

At the end of summer, Chinggis again moved his military operations to cities along the northern bank of the Amu Darya, capturing a few walled settlements and placing his headquarters at a

pastureland by the river. Following Jalal al-Din's footsteps, Tolui
seized a number of cities at which the former had been based, but
he was unable to capture him. Shigi Qutuqu, the foundling raised
by Ö'elün, had fought against Jalal al-Din at Parvan and lost. This
was a terribly hard blow to the Mongol troops on expedition. Shigi
Qutuqu returned to Chinggis's base, having lost the majority of the
men under his command. He awaited judgment as the man responsible for this defeat. Chinggis, though, did not blame him:

"Shigi Qutuqu, you have become accustomed to always win-
ning. You now know the severities of fate. Make good use of this
first taste of defeat!"

That was all the great khan said. He wasn't shielding Shigi
Qutuqu, just demonstrating respect for his mother, Ö'elün, who
had raised him.

Soon after Shigi Qutuqu's defeat, Chinggis learned that Muhammad, who had escaped in the second month of the year to a small
isolated island in the Caspian Sea, died there of illness. Jebe and
Sübe'etei, who had been sent to capture him, now found the object
of their mission gone and sent a messenger to the camp of the great
khan. They were seeking his approval to take up a new task and
march off in that direction. They hoped to be able to cross the Caucasus Mountains with their armies.

These two exceptional Mongol commanders could not think of
camping their troops in the area straddling the Black Sea and the
Caspian Sea until permission arrived from Chinggis. The messenger returned, but Chinggis could not imagine that he caught up with
them.

They had not forgotten that Chinggis had sent them off with orders to advance like two arrows. Two arrows shot out of a bow must
cut straight through the air until they hit the ground. Although he
had been angry at Jochi, Chinggis showed not the least unhappiness
with Jebe and Sübe'etei, although they had similarly acted beyond
their orders.

When early that winter Chinggis received a report that Jalal al-
Din had appeared with a great army in the Kashmir region, he personally led an army riding over a long distance in the direction of

Kashmir. En route he captured a string of cities, and in every case he used the same tactic: in cities that did not resist, all of their troops were assimilated into his forces unharmed; in those that resisted, every person and building was completely destroyed. In the fighting, they faced numerous difficulties. Mongol soldiers surrounded the city of Bāmiyān in the heart of the Hindukush Mountains, and in the combat one of Cha'adai's sons was killed by a stray arrow. Chinggis deeply loved this grandson of his who died in battle, and his orders for the seizure of Bāmiyān were extremely severe.

"Attack, attack, and destroy—and don't leave a single tree or blade of grass standing! This city will remain uninhabited for the next hundred years!"

Chinggis thus forbid plundering anything whatsoever from this city. It eventually fell, all of its people perished, and the city disappeared from the face of the earth without a trace.

Cha'adai did not know of his son's death, and when he returned from another battle to his father's camp, Chinggis, his face crimson with rage, asked him in harsh words:

"Will you follow my orders?"

Stunned, Cha'adai replied: "I would choose death before repudiating the orders of the great khan, my father."

Chinggis listened and then continued: "Listen, Cha'adai. Your son died in the fighting. I forbid you to grieve."

Thus, Cha'adai was unable to lament the death of his beloved son before the great khan.

Chinggis then went on to India in pursuit of Jalal al-Din, shifted the scene of fighting a number of times, and eventually captured his troops on the banks of the Indus River. Able to restore Shigi Qutuqu's honor for his earlier defeat, Chinggis himself stood at the head of his entire armed forces. At the end of his tether after a fierce fight and exhausted, Jalal al-Din leaped with his horse from a 20-foot precipice, and with his shield on his back and bearing a flag in his hand, attempted to cross the great river. Mongol troops showered him from behind with innumerable arrows, but Chinggis, demonstrating esteem for this courageous enemy commander, called a halt to them.

Chinggis found himself camped early in the year 1222 in the
northern foothills of the Hindukush Mountains, covered in a thick
snow. He dispatched his commanders to cities within Jalal al-Din's
sphere of influence with orders to mop them up completely. Cities
south of the Amu Darya that had until then not been laid waste in
warfare were one after the next subjected to Mongol attacks and the
majority of their populations slaughtered. Messengers bearing news
of bloody victories from military contingents on various fronts
were arriving in camp almost daily, and one day early in the fourth
month of the year a visitor with a somewhat different complexion
also appeared. This was the Daoist priest Changchun (1148–1227),
who had traveled, at Chinggis's invitation, the great distance from
Shandong province in eastern China.

Just a year earlier, Chinggis had learned the name of this Daoist
master, a man with the highest authority within the Daoist world
who had gathered around him a number of followers. Chinggis had
Yelü Chucai draft an edict summoning him, and then with a twenty-
man escort, he sent Liu Zhonglu as a messenger to Changchun's
home. The main reason Chinggis wished to meet Changchun was
to ask him about techniques for attaining immortality. At some point
in the helter-skelter of war, Chinggis had turned sixty years of age,
and he was becoming aware of his own declining physical strength.

No sooner had he welcomed this guest from afar than Chinggis summoned him to his tent. The great khan watched as the old
man with bent back, enfeebled by age, merely stooped forward, not
bowing down, and then, with arms folded, approached the khan.

"You responded to my summons from a distant land," said
Chinggis through an interpreter. "And having acceded to my request, you have traveled thousands of *li* in coming here. I am extremely pleased."

"I received your decree and came," replied the old man. "This is
all in accordance with the will of heaven."

Changchun did not actually see Chinggis's face. As if there was,
in fact, no one standing before him, the short elderly man cast his
unfocused gaze at a point in space.

"Perfected one who has come from afar, do you possess any kind of elixir for longevity? If you do, can you provide it to me?"

"I do have a way of protecting life, but no elixir to extend it."

Chinggis watched the old man's mouth move and heard the words emerge from it, but there was no emotion whatsoever in his expression.

"Is there then really no medicine for immortality?" asked Chinggis again, this time in a louder voice.

"I do have a way of protecting life," said the old man again in precisely the same words, "but no medicine for prolonging life."

Although he felt somewhat betrayed, Chinggis thought it was certainly good to have summoned this old man. Their conversation was carried on entirely through an interpreter, but there was nonetheless a certain freshness to their exchange of words. For Chinggis it was the first time in quite a long while that he had met anyone who did not take his every word as a direct order.

"The people call the Daoist master a celestial being. Do you call yourself that?"

"That is merely something other people say of me. I cannot vouch for that which is given to me."

Master Changchun said nothing beyond replying to queries addressed to him by Chinggis.

For the next two or three days, a number of poems written by Changchun over the course of the long voyage to the Mongol camp were offered to the great khan in Liu Zhonglu's transcription. These poems spoke of Samarkand, Luntai, various settlements in the desert, and many other places. Chinggis gave them to Yelü Chucai and asked him for the poems he'd written while accompanying the army, so they could be given to Changchun. Chinggis thought that although one was young and one old, these two extraordinary individuals in whom he placed such trust certainly seemed to have reached a mutual understanding.

Several days later, Chinggis attempted to ask Changchun what he thought of the quality of Yelü Chucai's poems. The Daoist master answered that they were fine specimens, but when asked if he might like to meet the man, he replied that he had no special desire to do so. Finding this suspicious, Chinggis summoned Yelü Chucai and asked him the very same question. The young man with the full beard responded in his always resonant voice full of pride:

"I think these are excellent poems. But why must I meet this old man?"

"Hmm, Changchun replied in the same manner about you," said Chinggis with a smile.

He nonetheless could not understand why these two men had no interest in meeting each other. When he mentioned the point to Yelü Chucai, the latter replied:

"Probably the master looked down on the fact that, while I follow the great khan's armies and am always by his side, I do nothing for the great khan."

"But why do you have no curiosity about the Daoist master?" asked Chinggis.

"Because, despite the fact that the Daoist master traveled an immense distance to come to the great khan's camp, there's not a thing he can do for the great khan."

"What do you mean by 'a thing'?" asked Chinggis.

"I am making sure that the name of the great khan will not be erased from history in the future," answered Yelü Chucai, "and he can do nothing to help me."

Chinggis's expression quickly hardened as he said:

"Why do you say that my name may be erased? My name and that of the Mongols are indestructible in the realm of history."

Betraying not the least timidity, the young man responded:

"I believe, unfortunately, that the name of the great khan will not be preserved in history, for the great khan's subordinates have committed untold acts of butchery."

When he heard this, Chinggis's expression changed, and trembling with rage, he stood up. He walked into the adjoining room but soon returned and said in utter seriousness:

"I should have you put to death for this, but any punishment would be too light for what you have just said. Until I can come up with an appropriate punishment, I shall desist from having you executed."

Then he blurted out with a smile: "You really can be terribly rude!"

Yelü Chucai's words had left no significant unpleasantness for Chinggis, but in any case he did not intend to punish this young man of whom he was so fond.

Several days later, he again summoned Yelü Chucai and said to him:

"I shall soon learn the Way from the Daoist master. You will serve me at that time."

This may in fact have been his punishment. As unofficial emissaries, Dian Zhenhai, Liu Zhonglu, and Alixian took down the words of the Daoist master. As official representatives, three court attendants did the same. Yelü Chucai was under orders to be in attendance at this meeting as well.

However, Chinggis's plan to place these two extraordinary, defiant intellectuals together had to be put off for six months because of a sudden Uyghur uprising. To crush it, Chinggis mobilized his own army, and he fixed the day to listen to Daoist master Changchun speak of the Way to a propitious date in the tenth month of the year, some six months away. Changchun requested to spend the time until then in Samarkand, and he moved with a guard of over 1,000 cavalry to that lovely city to the north some 20 days' journey away, which was now recovering from the depredations of war.

When Chinggis set out at the head of an army unit, neither Changchun nor Yelü Chucai was there. Numerous Uyghurs lived in the cities of Khorazm, and no small rebellion led by them could cover its own traces. For Chinggis, those who so much as harbored the idea of rebelling against him had to be eradicated from the earth, as one pulls grass out by its roots. The city of Herat was attacked by one of Chinggis's commanders, its walls burned to the ground, and all of its residents massacred. The city of Merv came under attack a second time, and only a handful of its residents survived.

It was early summer when Chinggis's forces attacked the city of Ghazna. He was looking for a new camp to escape the summer heat of the Hindukush. A messenger arrived at his new tent from the two units under Jebe and Sübe'etei, with whom contact had for a time been severed. He reported to Chinggis:

—The two army units circled around the southern shore of the Caspian Sea and crossed the Caucasus Mountains. They defeated the allied armed forces of the Kipchaks, the Aas, and the Rus, advanced farther west, and were about to enter Bulghar.

The messenger was reporting on the movements of the expeditionary army six months previous. About one month later, separate messengers arrived from each of the army units.

—We have defeated the Bulghar army everywhere, destroyed their cities, and turned to take the road into Russia.

This particular messenger was able to arrive comparatively quickly, and thus was reporting on military actions of only three months earlier.

The tracks taken by his two units seemed even to Chinggis to bear something of a dubious, almost haunting aspect. This was no longer the will of Chinggis but the wills of Jebe and Sübe'etei being carried out. Like arrows that had to continue cutting through the air until they fell to the ground, the two Mongol wolves had perforce to chase after the enemy, as if this were the ultimate will of their people. There was no respite from this and hence no end. They simply continued running until they expired.

According to the messenger's report, the operations of the two army units were like a fire burning over a prairie. After they passed through, nothing remained. Cities that resisted were turned completely into ruins, with no city walls, streets, people, or even trees and shrubs remaining intact. Iraq Ajemi, Azerbaijan, Kurdistan, Georgia, Syria, Armenia, Kipchak, and Bulghar were all territories over which the blue wolves passed, and all of their important cities were sacrificed to plunder and slaughter.

On the day he received the messengers from Jebe and Sübe'etei, Chinggis twice sensed the impossibility of forestalling their movements on his own. It seemed to him that he could only assist them. By contrast, he had not even received a report from his eldest son, Jochi, who had marched north from the Syr Darya. Chinggis issued an edict congratulating his two commanders Jebe and Sübe'etei for their exploits on the battlefield. To Jochi he issued orders to complete his campaign on the Kipchak plain with alacrity, head north of the Black and Caspian seas, subjugate the peoples living there, and then join up with the forces of Jebe and Sübe'etei.

A messenger arrived regularly every few weeks from Muqali, who was continuing with the overwhelming task of pacifying the state of Jin. Although this campaign had no conspicuous developments, Muqali worked vigorously to conquer the northern portion of Jin. The cities in this area had come under Mongol dominion and then reverted to the Jin after Chinggis's withdrawal. The present attack on these strongholds was being carried out by Muqali's forces alone. Chinggis issued a respectfully worded edict of appreciation to Muqali for his efforts every time a messenger reported his accomplishments in camp.

At the end of the eighth month of the year, Daoist master Changchun returned to Chinggis's camp from Samarkand. Chinggis, though, had decided to lead his entire army to the north and had moved in that direction. On the way toward Samarkand, the propitious day in the tenth month came on which it had been agreed he would listen to Changchun discourse on the Way. On this day, Chinggis had a splendid curtain installed, abstained from contact with women, and adorned his room with lustrous candlelight.

Although Chinggis had Yelü Chucai serve him on this occasion, Chucai and Changchun merely bowed silently to each other and did not exchange a single word. Three or four days later, Chinggis again invited Changchun to speak about the Way. On this occasion as well, Yelü Chucai was in attendance, and again the two men said not a word to each other.

"The Way gives birth to heaven and nurtures the earth. The sun and the moon, the stars in the sky, demons and goblins, men and animals—all come from the Way. Some men know the greatness of the Way and some do not. The Way first spawns the creation of heaven and earth and only then gives birth to mankind. Only when men were born did the light of the divine shine forth and move as if in flight. For food they ate everything alive. With the passage of time, their bodies became heavy, and the light of the divine flickered out. This is because their passions grew deeper.

"Originally, the great khan was a celestial being. Heaven is using the great khan to defeat tyrannical, violent men. When you overcome these grave difficulties and accomplish this task, the great khan will perforce ascend to heaven and become a celestial being once again. While you remain on earth, your tone of voice must drop, your appetites must diminish, you must restrain from slaughter, and you must peacefully protect your body. If you do all these things, long life will naturally reside in the great khan's body.

"The divine is pure. He who follows the Way and obtains it will act with prudence and discretion day and night. If you act with goodness and pursue the Way, you shall rise to the level of heaven and become a saint.

"The way for the great khan to train is to promote secret charities without and strengthen the mind within. Having compassion toward the people, protecting the lives of the masses, and bringing a great peace to the world are to be your external practices; protecting the divine is your internal practice."

These words poured forth from Daoist Master Changchun. Chinggis listened attentively to the master's words from start to finish on these two occasions, but both times when "great khan" came dashing out of Changchun's mouth, frequently he felt he was being cut short. For what Chinggis was actually doing was entirely in contravention of the Way. Yet the time spent listening to Master Changchun was quiet, austere time such as Chinggis had to this point never experienced. Although punctuated by the sounds of cracking whips outside, listening to these words of the Daoist master was by no means unpleasant.

Chinggis pitched camp outside Samarkand and did not enter the city. The area in and around the city had already revived completely from the conflagrations of war, and all manner of peoples lived there, pursuing their lives in a peaceful manner. The majority of residents were Uyghurs, and above them Han, Khitans, and Tanguts employed a great number of Uyghurs. Among the local officials were numerous Turks, Iranians, Arabs, and countless others with eyes of differing shades. And walking amid all these different peoples were Mongol soldiers.

Mongol troops, whether high or low in status, all enjoyed a luxurious life, frequenting restaurants and drinking establishments with women of different ethnic backgrounds and walking among the orchards on the outskirts of the city. Although corpses had been strewn all over this city and hell fires had been lapping at its buildings, after only two years, one could not even imagine those bygone days, looking at the prosperity of the city now.

Among the cities of Khorazm that the Mongols had attacked, Samarkand was the first to return to peace, and with the passage of a few more years, all the cities of Khorazm would follow this path. And not only Khorazm, for all the states of the Caspian and Black Sea regions, as yet unknown to Chinggis, which had been conquered by Jebe and Sübe'etei, would follow a similar pattern. In this sense Samarkand proved to be a model for many other cities in the future.

For some reason, though, Chinggis had no interest whatsoever in entering the revived Samarkand. There was a grand detached palace with luxurious pavilions and gardens that had been prepared for him, and if he had so desired, he could have released peacocks and elephants brought there from other conquered states. All of the officers and troops of his military units hoped to go into Samarkand, but Chinggis was resistant to doing so.

Chinggis pitched his camp at a site two days away from Samarkand and remained there until the eleventh month of the year. At that time, he announced that they would again move south for the winter months. As he had done since his youth, as his ancestors for countless generations had done, they had to fold up hundreds of tents, form themselves into large groups, and move, following the flocks with the seasons.

Chinggis decided that they would spend the winter at Buya Katur, in the mountains of northwestern India near the Indus River valley. Several days after he arrived at the new camp, Chinggis's third son Ögedei, his entire body reeking from the stench of blood, came with his Mongol troops, who had spent many years in open warfare and who had eyes like those of wild animals, mountains of plunder, and Indian captives in a number roughly equal to that of his own troops. The Indians wore white cloths around their heads, so when seen from afar, Ögedei's soldiers had appeared like troops with snow upon their heads.

When the New Year's festivities for 1223 came to an end, Chinggis announced the return of military units to Khorazm, as they had expected. He was unable to have peace of mind unless he was back on the field of battle, or failing that, moving with his yurt.

The Mongol base camp and with it the principal military units once again marched through mountainous and desert regions toward Samarkand. Without entering the city, they moved the great distance to the upstream area of the Syr Darya and there pitched camp. While on this march, Chinggis listened on several occasions to Changchun discourse on the Way. Some of it he understood and some he did not, but he clearly enjoyed listening to Changchun speak on the subject.

While in camp on the bank of the Syr Darya, Chinggis often passed the time hunting. On one occasion, when he was in the midst of a hunt and in his last spurt in the attack on a group of raging wild boars that had run amok, he fell from his horse. Although he suffered no painful injuries, he could scarcely believe that he had actually fallen off a horse. At that point in time, Changchun said to him:

"The great khan has already reached an advanced age. The great khan's fall was an exhortation from heaven. That the wild boars did not attack the great khan was a result of divine protection. Should you not reduce the number of hunts?"

For Chinggis, tumbling from his horse was a great blow. He had no choice but to follow Changchun's words. Shortly after this incident, Changchun sought Chinggis's permission to return home.

"Three full years have now passed since I left my home village by the sea. Originally, I responded to the great khan's summons for a three-year period. The heaven-ordained time for my return has now arrived."

Changchun had already asked twice for permission to return home, but Chinggis had not allowed it. Now, however, when he heard the Daoist master say that the "heaven-ordained time had arrived," he saw no reason to detain him any longer.

Early in the third month of the year, Changchun left Chinggis's camp, with Alixian as imperially designated emissary and Menggutai, Hela, and Bahai, among others, as vice-emissaries. Chinggis had a Mongol battalion guard Changchun on his journey to the east.

Soon after the Daoist master's departure, Chinggis personally sensed a great change of heart. The desire to return to the foothills of Mount Burqan suddenly began to burn fiercely in his breast. He revealed this desire first to Qulan. Although five years had passed since they had left his home, Qulan had remained at his side the entire time.

"Should it be the wish of the great khan," she said, "how could anyone oppose you?"

"Don't you find the Mongolian plateau to your taste?" he asked.

"Why, do I have my own taste? My mind has always been one with that of the great khan. Even when the great khan lies in this very bed with concubines of other hair colors, my mind is one with that of the great khan."

Qulan's health had suffered while living on foreign soil for so long and always serving at Chinggis's side, and she had for the past two years not shared a bed with him. Although she had once had a stout and radiant body, Qulan had grown emaciated, completely unlike her former self. Her skin, though, retained its tenacious luster like alabaster, and her eyes were even colder than before. Her grace, which was difficult to ignore, appeared along the lines of her tense cheeks, so that one could not say that her personal appearance had declined to any degree whatsoever.

"If the great khan so desires, who am I to interpose an objection? Were I, however, to describe my own self-serving wish—" Qulan cut off her words midstream and stared directly at Chinggis.

"What?" he asked. "If you had a wish, what would it be?"

"I have heard that on the other side of the Himalayas there is a great and as yet unconquered kingdom. It is a hot land in which immense elephants live. It is the land where Buddhism arose, where men wear white turbans on their heads, and where women cover their heads in white cloth. It is a bit strange to me that the great khan does not want to bring this land under his dominion. What's more, they say it is a strong land with a mighty army that holds untold wealth."

"Perhaps I do not fully understand you, Qulan. You do not want the land on the far side of the Himalayas, but you do seem to want the ferocious battle that will ensue there."

"To be sure," replied Qulan, "I have lived together with the great khan through great difficulties. Neither a khan who would be king nor a khan who would sit upon a gem-bedecked chair in the Jade Palace did I wish to be with at all. Great khan, there is no task too difficult for you. Mongol troops now ride freely over the whole world. If there were a task that the great khan found difficult, then it might be crossing the Himalayas, traversing the Indus River, and confronting in battle large herds of elephants covering the surface of the earth, shaking as they came, and the soldiers guarding them."

"Qulan, would your health be able to endure this? The Indus River is immense, and the snow covering the Himalayan peaks continues without end."

"Great khan, was not the river to which we abandoned our son Kölgen greater than the Indus? And greater than the expanses of snow on the peaks of the Himalayas? I have gone as far as throwing Kölgen into it. I have no fear whatsoever about throwing my own life in."

Chinggis remained silent for a moment, but eventually he said:

"Fine, I shall grant your wish. You shall be with me when we invade India."

Chinggis thus decided to adopt Qulan's idea, which had gotten under his skin in a manner altogether different from the words of Daoist master Changchun or Yelü Chucai. The desire to return home disappeared for a time from Chinggis's mind, and in its stead a violent urge filled his entire body.

Chinggis felt compelled to follow Qulan's suggestion because he knew that she wished to give up her own young life to his hege-

monic conquests. Although she did wish to see Mount Burqan,
Qulan had no desire for a triumphal return there. That was something for Börte and the various descendants to whom she had given
birth. Qulan sought to invest the meaning of her life as a concubine
in an altogether different place.

Chinggis soon set to work on preparations to invade India again.
His plan, though, could not soon be realized. Cha'adai and Ögedei
had left Chinggis's main camp the previous year in the region near
Bukhara and were carrying out a separate strategy. Chinggis had
had to send a messenger to tell them to return posthaste to the encampment along the Syr Darya. Messengers were also sent to his
eldest son, Jochi, on the Kipchak plain and to the base of Jebe and
Sübe'etei, the two leaders of the possessed Mongol wolf pack, ordering them all to return.

Cha'adai and Ögedei arrived within about three weeks with
their forces, but the return of the detachments under Jochi, Jebe,
and Sübe'etei, located far away, required considerably more time.
Chinggis set summer for Jochi's return and the end of autumn for
Jebe and Sübe'etei's.

Chinggis spent the summer season hunting in the mountainous
region to the north. This was needed both for the continued training of his troops and to keep up morale. At summer's end, he again
moved camp to the bank of the Syr Darya. One day a messenger
from Jochi arrived to report that not a single wild animal was left
on the Kipchak plain and he was pursuing them farther upstream on
the Syr Darya as a memento for the great khan.

Although he had not seen or held Jochi's gift in his hands, Chinggis was extremely pleased. Half a month prior to the predetermined
day, Chinggis dispatched about 30,000 troops to the upper reaches
of the Syr Darya to receive Jochi's present. In early autumn they
had hunted wild boar, horses, oxen, deer, and all manner of other
animals in fields by the Syr Darya. There was a herd of several
hundred head of wild animals and a large drove of wild rabbits fill-
ing the fields like ground beetles, making an extraordinary sound.
Chinggis was duly stunned as never before by Jochi's performance,
ranging over thousands of miles.

Hunting was unfolding on a grand scale heretofore unknown, a virtually daily war between man and beast across the upper reaches of the Syr Darya. When the hunt was over, though, neither Jochi nor any of his men were to be seen. Two messengers arrived to report that Jochi had fallen ill during the hunt and had withdrawn to his Kipchak camp. Chinggis immediately dispatched a messenger with orders for Jochi to return to base camp despite his illness. Chinggis now became furious that, in spite of such stark instructions, not one man had returned to service.

That autumn Chinggis received news that Muqali, commander of the expeditionary army against the state of Jin, had died unexpectedly at the age of fifty-three. Chinggis felt as though his own right arm had been suddenly torn off. Having given over responsibility for pacifying the Jin to Muqali, Chinggis had not had to be the least bit concerned on that front, and he had been free to devote his energies to the attack on Khorazm. His dismay was thus great.

He had his entire army fall in line by their barracks and there announced Muqali's death. He ordered all officers and men to observe one month's mourning:

"Commander Muqali, in whom I held the greatest trust, has died. Had he had but six months more, Muqali might have been able to replace the Jin with his own kingdom."

Unable to speak further, Chinggis stepped down from the podium. He had planned to praise Muqali's achievements, but he felt as though these great deeds could not be sufficiently esteemed in words. That day Chinggis summoned only commanders Bo'orchu and Jelme to his tent, and together they grieved over Muqali's death. The import of this was that he and Bo'orchu and Jelme were the only men who appreciated how great and fine a man Muqali had been.

At sixty-one, Bo'orchu was the same age as Chinggis; Jelme was sixty-four. Two years earlier, Jelme had become paralyzed through half of his body, and his speech was not at all clear. Bo'orchu had been sick since the previous spring, his spirit weakened as well. As he stood before Chinggis now, tears welled up in both of his eyes.

When Chinggis said that they were ultimately the only ones who knew of Muqali's greatness and after them it would all be buried and gone, Jelme waved his hand furiously as if to disagree and said something, but neither Chinggis nor Bo'orchu could understand him clearly. Several times, Chinggis held his ear close to Jelme's mouth, and finally he was able to comprehend what Jelme was trying to say:

"No, it's not just the three of us. Muqali's greatness is known to everyone in the state of Jin."

Late that year, messengers from Jebe and Sübe'etei arrived at Chinggis's camp near Samarkand.

"The two army units have invaded Russia, dealt a crushing blow to the allied princes of Russia at the Kalka River, turned southern Russia into a battlefield with fire and flowing blood, appeared at the Dnieper River, and then ridden on farther to the coast of the Azov Sea."

While clearly Mongol soldiers themselves, the messengers had an odd appearance. They were wearing narrow pants clinging tightly to their legs and neckerchiefs around their heads. Wine and extraordinary items made of glass were to be found in their saddlebags. Several dozen crosses taken in plunder were attached to their saddles. They merely reported on the movement of troops but had no response at all to Chinggis's orders for those troops to return to camp.

8

Return to
Mount Burqan

IN EARLY 1224, CHINGGIS ANNOUNCED to his entire army his plan to launch an attack against India. The grand design was to traverse either the Hindukush or the Qara-Qorum range, enter India, conquer the major Indian strongholds, and when the fighting came to an end, attempt to return to the Mongolian plateau by way of Tibet. Neither Chinggis nor any of his commanders could surmise how many months or years it might take to achieve these ends.

When the forthcoming battle was announced, a number of army units began to organize themselves into heavy and light units. Numerous captives of many different ethnicities were ordered to work from morning till night for a month to turn unhulled rice into polished rice and to repair armor. To cross over great mountain ranges and immense rivers, Mongol soldiers had to work daily at new exercises involving the felling of trees, fording of rivers, and building of bridges.

In early spring the Mongol forces divided into several units and set out from the Syr Darya camp. Prior to departure, Chinggis sent couriers to Jebe and Sübe'etei, who had not followed his orders and were marching far away on foreign terrain, and to his eldest son, Jochi, who had similarly ignored his orders and remained on the Kipchak plain. The task of these couriers was to inform them all of the new battle plans and to convey orders to the effect that they should bring whatever fighting they were presently pursuing to a close and return home.

After the Mongol armies had marched for over a month, they could see in the distance the apex of the Qara-Qorum Mountains, like the blade of a saw, which they would have to traverse. After roughly another month or more, they pushed their way through the mountains. These rugged mountains soared into the sky, and dense forests grew luxuriantly around them. When the soldiers had crossed these endless forests, they came to snow-capped peaks, and after they had crossed the peaks, more densely wooded areas obstructed the view of their objective. In only a short period of time, men and horses alike were thoroughly exhausted.

While the troops were camped in a small village in the mountains, Qulan passed away. Chinggis knew full well when they left the banks of the Syr Darya that she did not have long to live. When he received news that Qulan's condition had become grave, Chinggis visited her yurt. She lay with her thin, waxen, almost transparent arms and legs spread across her bed. As he approached, she opened her closed eyes as if she had been waiting for this moment. Her eyes struck Chinggis as much larger than he remembered. Although there was a fire burning inside the yurt, the cold of the dead of winter filled the air. Qulan was near death. A low, clear sound resembling nothing like a human voice emanated from her lips:

"Under the ice."

After she had said this, a faint smile floated over her face as she tried to reach her hand in Chinggis's direction. The hand, though, had to abandon its effort midway. Chinggis swallowed and then watched as this woman, whom he had loved more than any other and who had given him her love in a way no other woman had ever expressed it, was about to breathe her last before his eyes.

Qulan's last words, "under the ice," seemed to Chinggis to mean the site she wished for her burial. As he had once forbidden his son Cha'adai from mourning his own son's death, Chinggis would not allow himself now to mourn the passing of Qulan. He had so ordered himself days and weeks prior to her actual death.

Soon thereafter Qulan stopped breathing, and when her death was announced by a Persian doctor, Chinggis left her yurt. Inasmuch as he forbid himself from mourning, it would not do for him to show sadness at her death. He would carry out her funeral and have her remains buried beneath the glacial ice. This would be the final act he performed for his beloved who had now departed. He decided that night to have an altar erected in her yurt, convey the news of her death to his top commanders, and have them attend at the ceremony bidding her farewell.

That ceremony was carried out in the cold, when it seemed as if dawn itself was frozen. Before the night had given way to light, the coffin had been removed from the campsite. Some thirty commanders who had known her well carried the coffin in turns, with roughly an equal number of soldiers joining in the funeral procession. That day the procession passed through low, densely grown shrubbery, and gradually by nightfall they reached a desolate ravine shut off by snow and ice, where one could not see a single tree or blade of grass.

The following day soldiers found several dozen cracks in the ice over the ravine, and this information was reported to Chinggis. Chinggis inspected every one of them himself and selected the largest rent in the ice for Qulan's grave. Tilting it to the right and left, four young Uyghurs slowly lowered her coffin to a considerable depth in the frost. When the cord they were using to hold and lower the coffin ran out, the young men opened their hands in which they had been holding it. Did the coffin stop somewhere on the way down, or did it sink to some unknown depth? They heard a single cold, grating, metallic sound and nothing thereafter.

With the coffin now under the ice, the entire party, fearing a change of weather, immediately left the grave site. About halfway back on their return, they completed their nonstop descent of the mountain as the wind began howling.

Despite the ban he placed on himself from mourning Qulan's death, Chinggis could do nothing about the blow he felt in his heart. As they marched through mountainous terrain that would continue for an indefinite period of time, Chinggis no longer understood why they were invading India. The invasion had been planned at the suggestion of Qulan, and from his perspective, he set out with a desire to find for her a place to die.

Chinggis had no choice but to station troops in the village where Qulan died for a month to carry out the appropriate religious rituals for his beloved concubine. During that time, he had a most extraordinary dream. It took place at daybreak, and in it Chinggis saw a deerlike animal appear at his bedside. At first he thought it was a deer, but on close inspection he saw that it was not, as its tail resembled that of a horse, its hair was green in color, its head had a single horn, and it spoke human language. As the animal bent its forelegs and sat down by Chinggis's bedside, out of the blue it said to him: "You must lose no time getting your army together and return to your own land." Having spoken, the animal stood up and left the tent. Although it was clearly a dream, the genuineness of the animal's deportment and the way it entered and left his tent made it seem very real.

The following day, Chinggis summoned Yelü Chucai and asked him what the dream might have meant.

"The animal," replied Chucai, "is known as a *jiaoduan* in Chinese, and it is conversant in all languages. It ordinarily appears in a chaotic period full of the horror of bloodshed. The *jiaoduan* probably appeared before the great khan at the will of heaven."

Chinggis's usual practice was not to take Yelü Chucai at his word. He listened silently to what this young man of learning whom he so liked had to say, but never simply accepted what he heard. This occasion was different.

"Then," said the great khan, "we shall obey the words of the *jiaoduan*."

The light in the *jiaoduan*'s pupils seemed to Chinggis to resemble the light in Qulan's eyes. Perhaps, he thought, Qulan had transformed into the animal known as the *jiaoduan* and come explicitly to warn him.

That very day orders were issued to form up ranks in the army, and two days later the Mongolian military units set their sights on Peshawar. All of his commanders had understood that the invasion of India would be a fight that would require great effort and bring few results. Therefore, a change in plans was met happily by all.

Chinggis went through Peshawar, crossed the Khyber Pass, and pitched camp for the summer at Baghlan. While encamped there, he came to the firm decision to return his entire army to the Mongolian plateau. Once before Chinggis had made such a mental decision, but it had been cut short by the Indian campaign. Since breaking camp at Mount Burqan in the spring of 1219, Chinggis had spent five years treading over foreign soil. It was time now to enable his men who had been fighting throughout these years to set foot on their native land and to give solace to their rough and hardened minds.

At the end of the summer, Chinggis set off from Baghlan in a northerly direction. His aim was to assemble his troops at Samarkand and from there begin a proper march back home. When passing near the city of Bukhara en route earlier, he had learned of the rebellious sentiments of the populace there. Chinggis sent a military unit in to slaughter them. The troops forded the Amu Darya several times and entered Bukhara, the first city in the state of Khorazm that Chinggis had had burned to the ground to show that any hostile actions against his army would incur serious consequences. The great majority of the men had been murdered, and those who survived had been drafted into his army. All of the virgins had been abducted, and the city, emptied of its people, had been set ablaze and literally reduced to ashes.

In the more than four years since then, Bukhara, just like Samarkand, was beginning to form into a new city and prospering. Just as before, people thronged it, and all manner of men and women were buying and selling goods, calling out, eating, and moving around in all directions. Only the ruins of the former city walls encircling it remained now, as remnants from a nightmare of several days' duration.

The large Mongol unit took a long time to march straight through the city from south to north. There was no look of fear on the faces of the inhabitants. There was no expression of warm greeting to the Mongols either. Most faces betrayed no emotion at all. As had been the case in Samarkand, Bukhara had now become home to a wide mixture of ethnic groups. These included Han Chinese, Khitans,

Tanguts, Turks, Persians, and Arabs, and mixed in among them all was a small number of occupying Mongol soldiers.

In Chinggis's eyes, even the Mongol soldiers—his subordinates, to be sure—bore exactly the same expression, inasmuch as they were now mixed with these many different ethnicities. There was no hint of exuberance in welcoming their own kinsmen, just apathy. Chinggis was thus unable to feel the least sense of victory here. These thronging young men and women were not a conquered people. They were neither enemy nor ally. Should he feel concerned in the least that they were a threat to his life, every one of them would instantly turn into his enemy. Chinggis realized that, even with a great massacre, there were some things that he had been unable to change. Killing a large number of people to no purpose and destroying a walled city merely scattered unhappiness and sorrow.

Chinggis and his troops marched another five days from Bukhara to Samarkand. He planned to spend the winter there and the following spring proceed to the Mongolian plateau. Thus, the four winter months they were to stay became in effect the last Mongol military encampment in the state of Khorazm. In fact, it was less than an encampment, for only a small number of troops could actually be placed within the city. The residents overflowed and lived in close proximity to their neighbors, with the population now several times more numerous than before the great massacre. There was simply not enough room for the Mongol armies.

A number of units set up camps in the areas adjacent to the city. The soldiers, both Mongols and those from many foreign lands who had been taken captive, went into the city when they had free time. With its throngs of people and resultant chaos, Samarkand was like a beehive of activity.

During this period, Chinggis only rarely set foot in Samarkand. Whenever there were banquets, he held them in his tent, and whenever he wanted to see shows, acrobatic performances, or theatrics, the performers were summoned to him. Next to his own camp, Cha'adai, Ögedei, Tolui, Qasar, Belgütei, and others pitched tents, but he never put in an appearance there. Only once, though, on a whim he made a round of inspection of them all.

In every tent, Chinggis saw spectacles he could scarcely believe. Although their living quarters were shaped like yurts, firm buildings constructed on the inside with brick and stone had been built, with fancy stoves, luxurious beds, and magnificent chairs and tables for visitors. Amid this stunning furniture were bottles of wine and crystal glasses. Some had green grass plots inside and beds of flowers blooming everywhere. In addition, numerous ponds had been built with spouting water.

All these furnishings and conveniences were not mere ornamentation—the continual coming and going of guests had made them almost necessities. The officers were paying frequent calls on one another and often received wealthy guests from other ethnic groups. This trend was not only apparent among his top commanders; even the clothing and possessions of ordinary soldiers had changed. It had become all the rage among the troops to play strange songs on bizarre instruments.

Chinggis, though, said nothing faultfinding about any of this. He had instructed himself to remain silent on this score. It seemed to him a dream come true that he had given to all Mongol men and women such a life for their relatives. Chinggis recalled that when he had assumed the position of great khan and the ceremony of several days' duration was carried out, he felt deep emotion watching in front of his own tent a group of filthily attired old women dancing to a simple step and repeating the same tune over and over. At that time, he vowed to relieve the Mongol people of such sadness and poverty so they might contemplate enriching their lives. Was this, in fact, what he was now witnessing? This transformation had affected the conquering officers and troops and was undoubtedly happening in the tents by Mount Burqan as well. The lives of the women and old folks who had been left behind had undoubtedly changed to an unrecognizable degree. Wasn't this, after all, what he had been seeking all along?

The evening he walked around to the camps of his kinsmen, Chinggis recalled that he had chosen to live in the dark Mongol-style camp as of old because he so liked it. But he couldn't force anyone else to do so. Nor could he blame the others who did not share his views or his desired lifestyle. Chinggis sternly instructed himself to this effect, but even as he thought about it, he could not in his heart of hearts acquiesce in this incomprehensible behavior. That night he did not return to his sleeping quarters until late and thought about his beloved Qulan. For the first time since her death, he was overcome with a profound sadness that she was no longer alive, a sadness that tore into his heart. Qulan who had sought to share all of his hardships with him, Qulan who had so admirably been able to bear his having relinquished their son, Kölgen, to the nameless masses, this Qulan had been extremely rare and precious to Chinggis.

On another occasion, Chinggis made an inspection of the city of Samarkand. The Mongol soldiers he saw there did not understand what it meant to be a Mongol, insofar as they made no attempt to be attentive to it. Some wore Persian garb, while others decorated their bodies with Turkish objects.

That day Chinggis went to inspect a shop making military clothing and weaponry that had been set up in a corner of the city, but at the shoemaker's shop there he found the long shoes worn by Turks. The young officer serving as Chinggis's guide explained proudly that these were both beautiful to the eye and comfortable to wear on the march—and they were durable. Chinggis merely nodded and listened that day, but in his heart he wondered if anyone wearing such shoes was really a Mongol soldier. Was it conceivable that a wolf of the Borjigin lineage would ever don such footwear? Could they even fit on the paws of the wolf packs as they ran over snowy plains, crossed mountains, and raced across ravines? Although he wanted to say all this, he persevered quietly.

When he returned to his tent that day, Chinggis again thought about Qulan. It was strange that he should have remembered her under these circumstances.

Since stationing troops at Samarkand, Chinggis had sent messengers any number of times to the quarters of his commanders Jebe and Sübe'etei and to his eldest son, Jochi, to convey orders for them to return immediately to Samarkand. Whether the dispatched messengers had reached their objectives or not, not one of them had returned. Every time the messagers would set off and then all news of them vanished.

Late in the year, after nearly a year's passage of time, a messenger returned from Jebe and Sübe'etei. On this occasion, it was not just a messenger but a unit comprised of 100 Mongol soldiers and 500 non-Mongols bearing large quantities of booty to be delivered to Chinggis's camp. There was a mountain of valuable items: weapons, furnishings, art objects, and religious sculptures. Several hundred camels came laden to great heights with all this plunder. After affording them two days to recuperate, Chinggis had a group of the soldiers return to their bases to inform Jebe and Sübe'etei, their commanders, of the orders to congregate at Samarkand. Chinggis also saw to it that all the presents from Jebe and Sübe'etei were soon transported to the camp in the foothills of Mount Burqan.

When the end of 1224 drew close, the messenger Chinggis had earlier dispatched returned with a single soldier from Jochi's camp on the Kipchak plain. The latter offered the following message from Jochi: "For the past three years Jochi has been ill and unable to take part in long marches. He cannot return home with Chinggis; however, he shall return to the land of the Mongolian plateau at the first possible opportunity—please accept this explanation."

Chinggis felt violent anger at hearing this. He had sent out countless messengers, but no news whatsoever had been forthcoming until eventually this answer arrived—he was behaving as if he'd severed all ties to the Mongolian people. When an expeditionary army was to withdraw together, what did it mean for a single person to remain behind? That very day Chinggis sent a messenger out from Samarkand with orders to Jochi:

—No matter what, the entire army must assemble immediately in Samarkand.

The year 1225 began, and Chinggis planned new year's festivities with his commanders and decided that they would set out from Samarkand late in the fourth month to return home. He also decided to keep it a secret from the officers and men until the first week of that month.

Early the previous month, Chinggis had unexpectedly received news that Jebe and Sübe'etei's units were on their way to Samarkand. After the first messenger arrived, messengers began coming on a daily basis with information on these units' movements. These reports seemed to indicate that, since the time when these two units set out from the city to track down Muhammad, they had multiplied their strength several times. Two units comprised of Bulgarians and Russians had been completely integrated into the Mongol fighting brigades.

The day that Jebe and Sübe'etei returned to Samarkand after cutting off their four-year campaign, Chinggis had his entire army arrayed before the city gate to greet them. The advance forces of the returning army had followed the course of the Sughd River flowing to the north of the city and appeared first. They approached the city in a long procession and situated themselves in a corner of the prearranged open area. By the time all the troops had taken up positions in this area, a considerable amount of time had elapsed.

Although Bo'orchu and two or three other commanders first approached the returning army, eventually a band of a dozen or more men from that army headed in Chinggis's direction. Chinggis was overjoyed to greet his two commanders whom he had not seen for so long and strode over to them himself. When he met the band of returnees coming toward him, he stopped, as did they. One commander from this group approached him with a calm gait. It was Sübe'etei.

Sübe'etei appeared to Chinggis as if he had grown much larger. He was just over fifty years of age but showed no weariness from the campaign at all, if anything seeming younger and more fearless than before. Sübe'etei briefly reported their return. The names of a number of lands and a number of mountain ranges, as well as rivers and lakes, all passed his lips, but the great majority of these were new to Chinggis.

Chinggis was satisfied. He was waiting for the appearance of one other, Jebe. But for some reason, no matter how long they waited,

Jebe did not appear. He was not among the group standing a short way away.

Chinggis was about to ask about Jebe, but he oddly felt himself extremely ill at ease. Still standing right before him, Sübe'etei remained silent. What had happened to Jebe? *Why is this commander with the head like the tip of an arrow not appearing before me?* Staring hard at Sübe'etei with a stern face, Chinggis suddenly moved away from where they had been standing. *I'll go find him myself,* he thought.

Chinggis walked by himself among the countless troops packed together. When he strode before them, the soldiers tightened up their formations at the orders of their leaders. Chinggis walked among the narrow defiles between the units. What had happened to Jebe? *That youngster, Jebe, many years ago with a single arrow broke the jawbone of my yellow war horse and injured me in the neck.*

Chinggis marched on. His piercing eyes wide open, he headed toward more troops. If Jebe was there, he had to show himself. The arrow, the arrowhead. But Jebe did not appear. Chinggis now took in what he had never seen before, units of non-Mongol soldiers, one after the next. There was one unit with shockingly white faces and another with black. Different orders rang out, all manner of military formations, and Chinggis for the first time saw it all with his own eyes.

Having given up on finding Jebe himself, Chinggis returned to his earlier position, where Sübe'etei was still standing like a post, and stopping right in front of Sübe'etei, he said:

"Did Jebe die of illness or on the field of battle?" His voice bore a snapping, fierce tone.

"Jebe died neither on the battlefield nor of illness," replied Sübe'etei, also with a fierce tone. "He died after using up the years allotted to him. He breathed his last in a village to the southwest of the Sea of Aral. He now rests on the back of a hillside by that village."

After he had replied, perspiration began pouring off Sübe'etei's head. One sharp arrow had spent its allotted years and broken in two. Chinggis nodded and forced himself not to grieve for Jebe. If he could bear the passing of Qulan, then he had to endure the passing of Jebe as well.

At the end of the fourth month, the entire army set out from Samarkand. Chinggis waited until the very day of departure for Jochi's return, but his forces never arrived. Having dispatched any number of messengers to the Kipchak plain, he once again did so, with orders this time to meet up with the main army in the coming year at Buqa-Sökekü on Naiman terrain.

On the day before leaving Samarkand, Chinggis had the empress dowager of Muhammad, once ruler of this land, and her ladies-in-waiting, as captured hostages, line up on the city ramparts and bid the state of Khorazm farewell. Carrying them off with him to the Mongolian plain, he had no desire ever to return to this place again.

From spring to summer and on to autumn, the immense Mongol army big enough to cover the surface of the earth slowly moved back toward its homeland. They passed numerous towns and cities where they had once shed much blood with their own hands. They would camp at certain sites for a few days and pass through others without stopping. They crossed the Syr Darya and many of its tributaries. They skillfully built bridges with techniques unknown to them four years earlier, and over countless bridges their long ranks marched for days with no end in sight. Troops from every ethnic group had been assimilated into their military files.

At the beginning of autumn, Mongol forces reached the Chui River, where the units camped for a short while before continuing on. The Chui River was different in color from the Syr Darya or the Amu Darya they had crossed so many times. Those rivers flowed west into the Sea of Aral. The Chui River flowed far to the north, no one knew whence. By mid-autumn, the armies crossed the Altai Mountains.

When the Mongol forces arrived at the Emil River, the old frontier between the Naiman and Uyghur peoples, Chinggis met a unit of 1,000 men who had come from the camp to greet him. Among the welcoming party were his son Tolui and the young faces of Chinggis's grandsons, eleven-year-old Qubilai and nine-year-old Hülegü. Chinggis planned a hunt for these imperial grandchildren. It was their first hunt, and Chinggis himself thus carried out for them the inauguration ceremony for their participation. In a custom aimed at bringing them good fortune, his old, large hands grasped meat and fat, and he rubbed the tender, sproutlike middle fingers of the two boys.

Looking at the faces of Khubilai and Hülegü with throngs of men and women waiting on them, Chinggis could not but think of Kölgen, who was being raised as the son of some unknown Mongol family. Kölgen, who was abandoned without a trace by the late Sorqan Shira at the time of the second Mongol invasion of the state of Jin in 1213, would now be seventeen years old, if he was still living. And a fine soldier he would have been.

Chinggis, though, never regretted giving Kölgen over to a cruel fate. *Kölgen, I shall never rub your middle finger with meat and fat. You can do it yourself. No one did it to me. If you have the strength, you must live by your own might—just as I have done.*

When Chinggis looked at Qubilai and Hülegü, his face with its large ears, penetrating eyes, tight lips, and white beard filled with tranquility and calm. When he thought about Kölgen, the expression on his face ran to extremes of severity. In the same manner, his heart now was filled with love, but the expression on his face was altogether different.

On the Buqa-Sökekü plain, about two days' journey from the banks of the Emil River, Chinggis held a banquet of thanks for his entire army for all the hard work over many years on foreign terrain. They were now standing on a section of the Mongolian plateau. The banquet lasted for several days on a grand scale. Virtually every day, his three sons Cha'adai, Ögedei, and Tolui, his three younger brothers Qasar, Belgütei, and Qachi'un, and his commanders Bo'orchu, Jelme, Sübe'etei, Qubilai Noyan, Chimbai, and Chila'un all gathered at Chinggis's tent and drank wine together while inhaling the aroma of their native soil. Absent were commanders Muqali and Jebe and his son Jochi.

When he left Samarkand, Chinggis had dispatched a messenger to Jochi with orders to meet at the site of their present festivities, but as before, he had no response. Aside from this one incident, Ching-

gis had been completely satisfied with Jochi. The banquet was now
reaching boisterous proportions. It was intended to be a party after
which they would not bring back to their home tents the bloody
stench of the battlefield. All violent and bloodthirsty behavior was
to be dispensed with here.

Troops of many different ethnicities from across the wide expanse of Central Asia were getting drunk, yelling, singing, and
dancing. And the revelry continued day and night. Children of
mixed blood formed groups, several dozen each, and put on enter-
tainment with women, their mothers, who had attached themselves
to certain lineages. One Kankali woman with mixed blood from an
altogether different ethnicity was dancing by herself. Her dance
under the moonlight struck everyone as mysterious and beautiful,
as her stout body, unlike that of any Mongol woman, swayed and
trembled.

"I alone," said Chinggis, joking, "have the characteristics necessary to be greeted by women on the Mongolian plateau."

He alone was wearing Mongolian clothing and shoes, and he
alone knew what it meant to live according to Mongolian custom.
Even old-timers Bo'orchu and Jelme had discarded their military
garb and were attired in clothing from Khorazm sewn with gold and
silver thread.

When the great banquet came to a close, the Mongol military
units moved gradually from the northern foothills of the Altai
Mountains toward the heart of the Mongolian plateau. The scenery
of their home terrain, which they had not seen for some time, suf-
fused the hearts of the Mongol officers and troops.

Chinggis did not have his eye set on the camp at the foot of Mount
Burqan. In every settlement en route, they were given a grand welcome, and Chinggis would stop at each for several or more days. He
rewarded the troops native to each settlement by demobilizing them
and allowing them to remain there with their families.

In early winter the Mongol military units reached the camp
at the Tula River next to the camp by Mount Burqan, which was
now the effective political and economic center of the Mongolian
state. Once a Kereyid settlement, this place was unforgettable for

Chinggis, despite his best efforts—the site of the Black Forest where To'oril Khan had once held authority. After a fierce battle lasting three days and three nights, they had defeated To'oril Khan here, and he remembered that battle as if it had been fought the day before. When he thought about it, he realized that over twenty years had since passed.

Chinggis set up camp here and demobilized on a huge scale all units except for his personal guard, enabling them all to return to their respective settlements. Chinggis remained for the next three weeks, walking around the Black Forest redolent with memories for him and carrying on hunts by the Tula River. Knowing that a grave had never been established for To'oril Khan, his onetime friend and later enemy, Chinggis had a stone monument placed at the site where he had lost his life, north of the Black Forest. The inscription read in Uyghur script: LORD OF THE BLACK FOREST, HERE RESTS THE INDOMITABLE SOUL OF TO'ORIL KHAN.

Once the stele for To'oril Khan had been erected, Chinggis held a grand memorial service for him. To'oril Khan had been his benefactor, and in the extremely difficult days of Chinggis's youth, he had been able to escape persecution by the Tayichi'uds and somehow carry on protecting the Borjigin banner primarily because of To'oril Khan's assistance. It was he who had forged the alliance with Jamugha and he who later worked with Chinggis to bring Jamugha down.

In the end, Chinggis met To'oril Khan in mortal combat and defeated him, but Chinggis felt no pain about this whatsoever. Fate had made it inevitable that he and To'oril Khan would meet in battle, and it was a principle of nature that one of them would have to win. If the dead are mindful, then To'oril Khan would have understood all this well, and he, more than anyone else, would undoubtedly have been happy at the triumphal return of Chinggis and his men from foreign terrain.

Although Chinggis never developed a liking for Jamugha, he admired the skinny old man's intrepid spirit. But at no time in his battles against Khorazm did Chinggis ever feel confronted by an opponent as strong as To'oril Khan.

From the Black Forest by the shores of the Tula River to the Borjigin settlement in the foothills of Mount Burqan, they marched so slowly that it took three or four days to cover this short distance. Chinggis, though, was in no hurry. Time and again, he was urged by one or another of his commanders to have his palanquin move on farther east, but he did not respond.

"If I die, I shall rest here," he replied on one such occasion. "Why do I need to rush while I am still living?"

After he had thus spoken, no one made any further suggestions of this sort.

Chinggis had not seen his wife, Börte. Insofar as she herself had not come to the Black Forest to greet him, Chinggis was not overly interested in continuing on to the camp by Mount Burqan to see her. Börte might have asked: "The entire army has returned, but why has only Jochi not done so as well?"

In this matter, Chinggis lacked the confidence that she would understand the words he would use. Even as truth, they would undoubtedly be unacceptable to her. Chinggis waited for Jochi at the settlement by the Tula River. Clearly, the fact that Jochi had not been selected as his successor was a concern for Börte, and the fact that Jochi alone had not returned would surely give her cause to believe that something untoward had arisen in the relationship between Chinggis and Jochi.

For his part Chinggis was not interested in quarreling any further with Börte. If possible, he would wait for Jochi without seeing her. He wished to avoid as best he could any ill feeling between himself and her. Messengers arrived in his camp from every direction on a daily basis. Although he hoped that each new one would be from Jochi, he was disappointed every time.

Although he was waiting for Jochi to make contact, there were limits. Ultimately, Chinggis had to make his triumphal return to the homeland of his people. When he broke camp by the banks of the Tula River, he announced that he had given up on Jochi's return and would now advance with his palanquin to his home by Mount Burqan. With numerous Borjigin banners enveloping his retinue, a long array of his personal guard, foot soldiers, cavalry, and pure

Borjigin officers and troops, the true descendants of the blue wolf, marched upstream following the course of the river.

In the afternoon of the third day, the form of a mountain so dear to his heart came in view: Mount Burqan, where the spirits of his people rested. That afternoon, the troops reached the upper reaches of the Kherlen River and continued farther against the course of the river. They reached the Borjigin camp at nightfall, when the western sky was burning bright crimson and the magnificent evening glow was visible in a corner of the sky. Börte, attended by countless ladies-in-waiting and personal guards, greeted Chinggis at the entrance to the settlement. She was now sixty-four years of age. Her legs had grown corpulent and made it difficult for her to walk. She actually was transported to the spot seated in a chair.

When he came before her, she stood up slowly from the chair. Her pure white hair, like a snow-capped peak, retained a distinctive brilliance, just as when she was young. Her facial expression remained unchanged. With the weight of the muscles in her relaxed face, it seemed to tremble a bit. Chinggis saw large ruby earrings dangling from Börte's ears and a large jasper necklace around her neck. He only noticed the chair in which she was sitting when she stood up; it was inlaid all over with fine precious gems, stunningly radiant to the eye.

"Great khan," said Börte, and nothing more. She relaxed after a difficult breath and then regulated her breathing in order to speak further:

"What a great day today is. It is both the day of the great khan's victorious return home and the day on which news of the Mongol guest has become known."

Börte still was referring to Jochi as the "Mongol guest," as his name denoted in their language, and not as "your son." Chinggis had no idea what she meant by news of Jochi arriving. He paid no attention to her now, though, as throngs of people from the settlement crowded around when he entered.

The following day, Chinggis hosted a dinner at his tent for Börte, Cha'adai, Ögedei, Tolui, and all their children. He had already met Tolui's sons, Qubilai and Hülegü, but his now more than twenty grandchildren had grown so much he could hardly recognize them. On this occasion he tried to confirm with Börte her words from the previous day about Jochi.

Because of her breathlessness, Börte summed up briefly what she wanted to say. It had been reported to her a year or so earlier that Jochi had not returned to camp, and countless rumors were flying as to why. Although Börte was much pained by all this, the previous day a traveling merchant from Khorazm conveyed to her the news that Jochi was still alive and well and enjoying his hunting on the Kipchak plain.

When he heard this, Chinggis felt the blood draining from his head. If this rumor were true, he was thinking, then Jochi's actions were impermissible. In solicitude to his aging wife, Chinggis did not allow the anger to show on his face, but when the dinner ended that evening, he immediately ordered one of his guards to find the traveling merchant whom Börte had met.

Several days later a middle-aged Persian was brought to Chinggis's tent. When he met the man, Chinggis grilled him fiercely. He was able to learn that Jochi had established a position for himself as sovereign of the Kipchak plain, and while living as its ruler, he was hosting hunts and continuing to train his troops.

Chinggis was burning with anger such as he had never felt in his entire life, for numerous messengers had been sent, but Jochi had ignored them all; and Jochi had paid no attention to his orders as great khan. In consideration of Börte, Chinggis continued waiting daily for contact from Jochi. He was also indignant at having his paternal worry completely betrayed. Anyone at all who violated his orders had to be executed. The fate endured by many cities of Khorazm that harbored rebelliousness would have to be that of Jochi as well.

Within 10 days' time, the Mongolian plateau was again seized with an uproarious atmosphere. Soldiers from all the settlements converged on the camp in the foothills of Mount Burqan. With 300,000 troops under them, Cha'adai and Ögedei were given command of a Kipchak expeditionary army.

When the force against Jochi set out, that alone did not calm Chinggis's worries. Before long he mobilized troops a second time.

He placed Tolui in command and joined the army himself. This second force, though, did not set off immediately, because Bo'orchu and Jelme opposed Chinggis's mission against Jochi. But Chinggis would not be dissuaded from his plan. No one was able to placate the great khan's anger. Because of Jochi, the Mongolian plateau was once again empty.

Chinggis had no intention of showing Jochi the least mercy. He and his entire military unit would have to be slaughtered and the Kipchak plain transformed into a desolate wilderness of rubble and stones. His anger would never subside until these tasks had been achieved. If he failed to act in this manner, then he would have failed to show proper authority over the numerous foreign peoples as well as the officers and men of his own Mongolian state. Chinggis did not see Börte. He left camp with Tolui and moved to a Kereyid settlement. Numerous men and horses had already taken the field in an area of the Black Forest by the banks of the Tula River.

Two or three days after Chinggis pitched camp in the Kereyid settlement, a dispatch courier arrived with news from the units under the command of Cha'adai and Ögedei. He was accompanied by another messenger from the Kipchak plain. Both men were wearing a black belt around their waist, a sign that they were in mourning. They were escorted into Chinggis's tent.

—Prince Jochi has been in bed sick for the past three years, but in the eighth month of 1225 his illness took a serious turn, and he passed away in a settlement north of the Caspian Sea on the Kipchak plain. It was his dying will that in the coming spring his entire military force and his remains return to camp.

Once the messenger from the Kipchak plain conveyed this report, Chinggis just stared blankly at him. The messenger from Cha'adai and Ögedei, confirming the veracity of this communication, reported that Jochi had died after a long period of illness; early in the fall of 1223, when they had rounded up the wild animals from the Kipchak area by the Syr Darya, Jochi was already ill and could not take part, but, conscious of Chinggis's concerns, he had concealed his illness at the time.

Chinggis ordered the messengers to take a respite and then sealed himself up in his room by himself. He was profoundly irritated with his own gullibility for believing the groundless report of the traveling merchant. All alone, Chinggis was overcome by an intense fit of lamentation. He had been able to forbid himself from grieving at the deaths of Qulan and Jebe, but when he learned that Jochi had been so long bedridden with illness and then died far from home, Chinggis simply could no longer bear the sadness of his son's death. Tears flowed from the large eyes with which he had overpowered everyone who faced him, fell to his pale cheeks covered with brown spots, and soaked the white whiskers covering his jaw. A low moan like that of a wild beast came from Chinggis's throat in bits and snatches as he walked back and forth in his quarters.

Stopping himself from crying, Chinggis called out for a guard and ordered that no one was to approach his room. If someone were to see him there, he would be taken out and promptly executed. The guard accepted the order respectfully and departed. Once alone again, Chinggis burst into tears. As if rocked by a tidal wave, the old Mongol sovereign resigned himself to the great sorrow overpowering him.

Chinggis now knew. He had loved Jochi more than anyone else. Like Chinggis himself, Jochi was born of the womb of a ravaged mother, and he shared the fate of that young man to prove that he was a descendant of the Mongol blue wolf. Chinggis loved him more than anyone.

The next day Chinggis issued a proclamation announcing the death of Jochi:

—Prince Jochi died in a corner of the Kipchak plain. It was by the shores of the sea where in antiquity the blue wolf and the pale doe, ancestors of the Mongolian people and born by order of heaven, came. It is now called the Caspian Sea. Prince Jochi was courageous by nature. He faced many battles and was always a model for Mongol officers and troops alike. He attacked and conquered 90 citadels, 200 cities, and the state of Jin; he defeated Khorazm and established the Kipchak kingdom, becoming its first sovereign, north

of the Aral, Caspian, and Black seas. May Jochi's descendants long
rule over the Kipchak kingdom. May the armies that followed him
maintain the conquering exploits of their founder on the plain.

Using the expression "Kipchak kingdom" was the only reward
Chinggis could give Jochi at this point. The edict was drafted by
Yelü Chucai.

Chinggis then issued a proclamation to Börte expressing grief at
the death of her son:

—Empress Börte, I offer my condolences on the death of Prince
Jochi, the son you bore and nurtured. It is something you and I both
shall mourn. Jochi was, just as his name indicates, a guest. He was a
guest bequeathed to the Borjigin lineage from heaven. He has now
returned to heaven.

Several days later Chinggis began to overcome his grief. When
he regained his composure, he called a meeting with his officers to
plan an attack on Xixia. He issued orders to all military units to mobilize for the invasion, and he instructed the units under the command of Cha'adai and Ögedei already on the field in Khorazm to
advance immediately on Xixia.

The attack on Xixia was to be a decisive battle for three reasons.
First, when the Mongols attempted to invade Khorazm, the Xixia
king had refused to come to their aid, and punishment had not yet
been administered; second, although the assault on the state of Jin
after the death of Muqali was a task Chinggis felt he had to carry out,
the thorough subjugation of Xixia took priority; and third, the blow
Chinggis suffered from the death of Jochi could not be healed except
through the launching of a great military campaign. Chinggis hoped
to fill the remaining years of his life with the dust of battles attacking
Xixia and Jin. He had not yet definitively proved to himself that he
was a descendant of the Mongol blue wolf. Like Jochi and Jebe and,
to be sure, Qulan, his life had to be enveloped by the battlefield. To
that end, Chinggis had to make himself into the blue wolf itself.

As all Mongol military units were to join in the attack on Xixia,
they broke camp by the Tula River in late 1225, only some ten days
after the proclamation on Jochi's death had been issued.

The first month of 1226 found the Mongol armies on the great wastelands of the Gobi Desert. It was still the mourning period for Prince Jochi, necessitating cancellation of new year's festivities. The troops all prayed to the eastern sky, and that day they marched southward all day long through a cold, blowing wind mixed with sand. The march was more difficult than any the Mongol units had experienced before. From the middle of the month they were assaulted daily by a driving snow, and the number of men and horses felled or smitten by frostbite increased steadily.

In the middle of the second month of the year, the Mongol units finally reached Xixia territory. Chinggis waited for the arrival of the forces under Cha'adai and Ögedei. They merged and set off with a strategy to invade Xixia on all fronts. Fighting began immediately in an area of northern Xixia. From spring through summer, numerous northern cities, beginning with Heishuicheng, fell into Mongol hands one after the next.

Chinggis regrouped all of his units at the Hunchui Mountains, endured a period of ferocious heat, and then launched another campaign in the autumn. In short order, they attacked Ganzhou and Suzhou [not the homophonous city in the lower Yangzi River delta region] and then advanced to take Liangzhou and Lingzhou. In this campaign as earlier, Chinggis completely mopped up all those cities that opposed his forces. After Mongol units passed through such places, only corpses covering the emptied cities and fields remained behind.

In the second month of the following year, 1227, Mongol forces pressed in on the capital at Ningxia. Chinggis had one unit split off and surround the capital, and he himself led another to cross the Yellow River. Once they crossed the river, the movements of the Mongol unit were just like that of a band of devils. Coming and going like the wind, they sacked Jishizhou, Lintaofu, Taozhou, Hezhou, Xining, and Xindufu. They butchered the resident populations, destroyed the city walls, and burned down the cities.

In the fifth month of the year, Chinggis built his base camp at Longde to the west of Pingliangfu and sent emissaries to the court of the state of Jin, demanding its surrender. Having completed the subjugation of Xixia beyond the capital at Ningxia, he was now ready for the invasion of Jin at any moment. While in camp he received a delegation of surrender from Li Xian, ruler of Xixia, who was in Ningxia. Li Xian sought an extension of one month's time to turn over his city to the Mongols, and Chinggis allowed it.

While awaiting the capitulation of Ningxia, Chinggis worked out the grand scheme for the invasion of Jin. He realized that he himself would now have to take up the task of subjugating Jin, which his late friend and colleague Muqali had sadly not lived to see through to fruition.

In the seventh month, Chinggis received in camp an emissary from the Jin emperor bearing items of tribute. Most extraordinary among these gifts was a great tub brimming with innumerable precious stones. Chinggis, though, was looking not for precious stones but for the Jin territory, which had once fallen under the hoofs of Mongol horses. Chinggis divided up most of the gems among his officers and threw the rest on the ground. For some reason, there appeared to be several thousand precious stones abandoned by Chinggis. What had at some point been only a few dozen stones in the tub now seemed virtually numberless, and they seemed to cover the entire area of the courtyard of the base camp.

Chinggis covered his eyes with his hands and after a moment pulled his hands away. The gems were still there spread over the earth. He summoned one of his guards and asked if gems were in fact covering the ground. The man quickly replied in the negative, and Chinggis then realized that he had fallen terribly ill. About a month earlier he had experienced a similar phenomenon on the Yellow River plain. At that time it wasn't gems but human bones. The skeletons of twenty or thirty Xixia soldiers killed in the fighting the previous year appeared in Chinggis's eyes to be innumerable human bones covering the plain.

That night Chinggis called to his tent Ögedei and Tolui and told them that his remaining days were few. When he died, he instructed them, they should save the mourning period until the entire army returned home. That night Chinggis retired to his sick bed.

In a few days the illness took a sharp turn for the worse. In dim consciousness, Chinggis called out the name "Jochi," his departed son.

When he realized that Jochi was already dead, he called out the name "Qulan," his late beloved concubine.

When he realized that his beloved was lying in a box beneath a glacier that covered a ravine in the high mountains of the Hindukush, he called out the name "Muqali."

Next, he called out the name "Jebe." All the people he wanted to see were dead. Other than Qulan's, all of their graves were unknown to him, and he could no longer picture them in his mind's eye.

Finally, he called out the name "Tolui." Tolui immediately replied, and at last Chinggis had come to the name of someone not dead.

"The best troops of Jin," he told Tolui, "are massed at Tongguan. Tongguan has a line of mountains to its south and a large river to its north. You should be able to break through quickly. Once you have invaded Jin, go on and take the road toward the state of Song. Send troops to Tangzhou and Dengzhou in southern Henan province and attack the capital at Kaifeng all at once. It is a thousand *li* after you leave Tongguan, and you will have no reinforcements from there. Tolui, you must do as I say."

Once he had conveyed to Tolui his dying will for the invasion of the state of Jin, he closed his eyes. A short while later, he said to no one in particular:

"If Xixia does not offer up their city by the promised deadline, move ahead with an all-out attack, kill the Xixia ruler, and massacre every one of Ningxia's residents."

Some thirty minutes later, Chinggis breathed his last.

The ruler of Xixia did in fact break his promise to Chinggis, and when the time for capitulation came, he did not relinquish the city of Ningxia. A huge Mongol army pressed in on the city, attacked from all four sides, and brought it down. Li Xian was brought out and put to death, as were the great majority of the residents. About a month later, all Mongol units massed on the banks of the Yellow River, abandoned the front, and returned to the Mongolian plateau.

As had been decided earlier, Ögedei took control over the entire army. Chinggis's death was known to only a small number of central commanders and was not revealed to the troops.

Braving the great heat, the Mongol units crossed Xixia terrain and emerged on the Gobi Desert, and then they headed due north for Mount Burqan, the source of the Onon and Kherlen rivers. They marched quietly. A coffin was laid out among the troops, borne aloft by a dozen or more soldiers. Although everyone knew that the remains of someone important were in the coffin, no one thought they could be Chinggis's.

Just before this unit set out, they killed every one of the villagers who had seen them on the march. Young, old, male, and female, all met the same fate. Rumors of this spread rapidly, and soon no one appeared where this unit marched. Even when they cut through a village, it was completely emptied out.

The troops bearing Chinggis's remains reached the Borjigin camp at the end of the ninth month. At the entrance to the camp, Tolui announced to all the troops for the first time that Chinggis had died. The evening the units broke up and pitched camp nearby, but other than the sound of horses' hoofs and soldiers' feet, not a human voice was heard. Chinggis's coffin was placed inside Börte's camp, and only the highest officers served at its side throughout the night. Under the night sky like a thick carpet studded with countless stars, the Borjigin camp did not, as it had in the past, bring numerous people together to spend a quiet night with innumerable troop tents spread out.

The day after Chinggis's coffin was placed before Börte's yurt, it was moved to the tent of Yisüi, then in succession, day by day, to Yisügen's, to Jin Princess Hadun's, and then to the tents of some dozen or more important concubines. Finally, it was placed in Chinggis's own yurt.

At the announcement of his death, people from all the settlements on the Mongolian plateau gathered, and they kept coming for two or three months. As a result, the Borjigin settlement was filled with men and women of all ages for a long period of mourning. After half a year's time, Chinggis's remains were buried in a corner of the great forest in the mountains by Mount Burqan. On the day of his interment, a fierce wind lashed the whole area of Mount Burqan, and the woods surrounding his grave made a rumbling sound as they shook in the wind. For a time, the funeral ceremony had to be postponed.

The woods in which Chinggis was buried grew luxuriantly over the next two or three years, becoming a dense forest. Before two or three decades had passed, no one could say any longer with any surety where Chinggis's grave was located. He lived for sixty-five years, and his rule lasted for twenty-two.

Author's
Afterword (1960)

IN 1924 A BOOK BEARING the long and ponderous title *Chingisu Kan wa Minamoto no Yoshitsune nari* (Chinggis Khan was Minamoto no Yoshitsune)[1] was published and then immediately reprinted eleven times in the same month, fast becoming a best-seller for that year. The author was a man by the name of Oyabe Zen'ichirō (1867–1941). In the spring of the following year, a dozen or more scholars took up their pens to contest the ideas laid out in this best-seller in the journal *Chūō shidan* put out by the National History Institute. The eminent scholars Kindaichi Kyōsuke (1882–1971), Ōmori Kingorō (1867–1937), Fujisawa Morihiko (1886–1967), Miyake Setsurei (1860–1945), and Torii Ryūzō (1870–1953) were among them.[2] This number of *Chūōshidan* appeared as a special supplement, and judging from the fact that the words "Chinggis Khan was not Yoshitsune" were on its cover, it was clearly dedicated to attacking the book *Chingisu Kan wa Minamoto no Yoshitsune nari*.

I was only in middle school at the time and knew nothing either of this book or of the scholars' responses to it. When I entered senior high school in Kanazawa, I had a friend who passionately argued that Chinggis Khan was indeed Minamoto no Yoshitsune (1159–89). During these years, then, Oyabe Zen'ichirō's best-seller was still holding its own and evidently was being read by a certain portion of Japanese youth.

I got my hands on a copy of the book in college and, interested in what it was actually all about, I tried reading it but found it extremely tedious. That said, though, aside from what I may have learned in middle school, it was this book and the scholarly rebuttal in *Chūō shidan,* which I later obtained, that sparked my own interest in the great Mongolian hero Chinggis Khan.

Late in the war years, I bought a copy at an Osaka bookstore of *Chingisu Kan jitsuroku* (The veritable record of Chinggis Khan), known to me as a famous work compiled by Professor Naka Michiyo (1851–1908).[3] It was a lovely book with a deep blue cover, but shortly after the war I parted with this and another book at a used bookshop.

In 1950 or 1951 I came across the same work in a used bookstore in the Kanda section of Tokyo and purchased it.[4] The deep blue color of the cover on this copy was utterly faded, and the words in the title were defaced to the point of illegibility. It had been published by Chikuma shobō in 1943 and seemed no more damaged than was usual at that time. I could only imagine that it had barely survived a fire during the war.

Chingisu Kan jitsuroku was a historical text secretly kept by the Mongol Yuan dynasty, as its original title, *Yuanchao mishi* (Secret history of the Mongols), indicates. It was originally written in Mongolian using the Uyghur script, but in the early years of the Ming dynasty (1368–1644) it was rewritten into Chinese characters; at the time the translators used Chinese characters as phonograms and rendered Mongolian words by sound. Beside each Chinese character, Naka added Japanese syllabaries, and he included as well an outline of the text in literary Chinese.

This work is like a Mongolian version of the *Kojiki* (Record of ancient matters), the quasi-mythical history of ancient Japan. When both historians and biographers discuss this or that fact about the life of Chinggis Khan, this is the one text they can never ignore. Particularly for the era of Chinggis's youth and young adulthood, there is no other source.

It was only when I got my hands on it a second time that I read the book. I was completely smitten by the lively account of the development of the Mongolian people in the form of epic poetry and the high tone. More interesting to me at that time than writing about

Chinggis Khan was to be able to write about how the Mongols grew to such enormous strength and rose to such great prominence, like a mighty river. And the title of my novel would, I thought, have to be *Aoki ōkami* (The blue wolf), for the opening of the *Secret History of the Mongols* recounts how the progenitor of the Mongolian people, by a decree of heaven, was born when a blue wolf crossed a vast and beautiful lake in the west and mated with a pale doe. On the cover of my thin university notebook, I wrote the title "Aoki ōkami" and was preparing to write the book. In any event, I have been ready with this title for a long time.

Since then, little by little, my bookshelves have filled up with books and pamphlets related to the Mongols. These include: the journal *Mōko gakuhō* (Mongolian studies, July 1940–April 1941) put out by the Mongolian Studies Institute; *Gakujutsu hōkoku* (Scholarly reports, 1909) published by the Research Department of the East Asian Association; *Mōko kanshūhō no kenkyū* (Studies on the customary law of the Mongols, 1935) by Valentin Aleksandrovich Riazanovskii and translated by the East Asian Economic Research Association of the South Manchurian Railway Company; and many similar works that appeared at the time of the Greater East Asian Co-prosperity Sphere.[5] Whenever I happened upon such works, I bought them. As I look back now, many were of no utility whatsoever in writing this book.

In writing about Chinggis Khan, though, I knew there were books that I would have to read, and I began collecting them once I had decided to write on him in earnest. Among others, these included the following Japanese translations: Constantin d'Ohsson (1779–1851), *Mōko shi* (History of the Mongols);[6] Boris Iakovlevich Vladimirtsov (1884–1931), *Mōko shakai seido shi* (History of Mongolian social institutions);[7] Owen Lattimore (1900–89), *Nōgyō Shina to yūboku minzoku* (Agricultural China and nomadic peoples);[8] and Grigorii Nikolaevich Potanin (1835–1920), *Seihoku no Mōko no dōwa to densetsu* (Tales and myths of northwestern Mongolia).[9] I had these in hand about a year before starting to publish *Aoki ōkami* serially in the journal *Bungei shunjū*.

Although I was initially taken with the desire to depict the rise of the Mongolian people, I focused more closely on the lone personality of Chinggis as I became aware that the rise of the Mongols was due largely to the singular efforts of this extraordinary figure. Had Chinggis never appeared in this world, Asian history would certainly have been altogether different. Napoleon once reputedly said: "My life is not nearly so grand as that of Chinggis Khan." It was he who turned the impoverished Mongolian people, scattered all across the Mongolian plateau and constantly involved in small battles between settlements, into descendants of the blue wolf. Only with his appearance were the Mongols reborn as a thoroughly different and exceptional people.

Once I had decided to write about Chinggis, though, I had no interest in writing some sort of heroic tale of a man who in a single generation built an immense state straddling Europe and Asia. Nor, for that matter, did I want to write a history of the military campaigns of Chinggis Khan, the invader of unprecedented brutality. Of course, in writing about the years of his life, I would certainly have to touch on these topics, but what I wished most to depict was the secret of the origins of his overwhelming—indeed, unfathomable—desire to conquer. The circumstances were completely different from, for example, Hitler's ambitions to dominate the world. The states surrounding the Mongolian plateau were themselves totally unknown entities to Chinggis in size, topography, and ethnic sensibilities. It was like groping in the dark when he came upon them.

Before he had fully subjugated the great state of Jin (ruled by the Jurchens in north China), he sent troops against the Xixia and Uyghurs, ultimately entered the realm of the Islamic states farther west, and from the Caspian Sea dispatched an army as far as Russia. The desire to conquer must have emerged from the determination of one man alone, but this is not the sort of subject that can easily be resolved by saying it was all due to the will to dominate with which one person was born. I, of course, do not know the answer to such things, and it is precisely because we do not know that I thought I might write in such a way as to fill the gaps in our knowledge.

Thus, my desire to write about this historical figure arose out of the difficulties I encountered in trying to understand him. When it is difficult to comprehend anything and everything, then no desire to write ever arises in the first place, but by the same token, when everything is known about a person, that too is unlikely to lead to any such wish. The reason I thought I might write about the life of Chinggis Khan was that, while I understood something about the man, there remained unsatisfying points that I did not comprehend: the root of his ambition to conquer and the mysteries surrounding it.

Among the biographies and creative works about Chinggis that I have looked over are the following works: a play by Kōda Rohan (1867–1947) and a novel by Ozaki Shirō (1894–1964), both entitled *Chingisu Kan*;[10] Ralph Fox (1900–37), *Genghis Khan*;[11] Yanagida Izumi (1894–1969), *Sōnen Temujin* (Temüjin in the prime of life);[12] Michael Prawdin (1894–1971), *Tschingis-Chan, der Sturm aus Asien*;[13] Harold Lamb (1892–1962), *Genghis Khan, the Emperor of All Men*;[14] and Marcel Brion (1895–1984), *La vie des Huns*.[15]

All of these works depict Chinggis through his middle years, based on the account given in the *Secret History of the Mongols*. I too had no other text from which to draw. To put it more precisely, no matter how one goes about writing, the image created of Chinggis in these years never measures up to the *Secret History*. My sense was that there was nothing we could add to the portrayal in that source. But, inasmuch as I was writing a biographical novel about Chinggis, I had to write about him in this period. As many biographers of Chinggis have undoubtedly felt, I had no choice but to base my Chinggis of that time on the *Secret History*, although I realized that I was writing a work of fiction.

Together with the *Secret History*, the old text known as the *Menggu yuanliu* (Origins of the Mongols) is regarded as peerless in Mongolian literature. The latter work contains numerous ancient tales of the Mongols, and its author, Ssanang Ssetsen (mid-seventeenth century), was a descendant of Chinggis, as well as a historian, military man, and prince of a Mongolian settlement. Using his exquisite imagination, he composed a history of the Mongolian people from the inception of their state until the middle of the seventeenth century. Originally "True Draft History of the Origins of the Khans," the title was changed to its present form on orders of the Qianlong emperor (r. 1736–96) of the Qing dynasty. One further text worth noting is the Mongolian chronicle, *Altan Tobči*. It contains ancient Mongolian traditions as well as religious stories, and thus should be arrayed next to the *Secret History* and the *Menggu yuanliu*.

We have a Japanese translation of the *Menggu yuanliu* by Gō Minoru (1904–89) and of the *Altan Tobči* by Kobayashi Takashirō (1904–87).[16] The historical facts recounted in both works are confused, sometimes according with depictions given in the *Secret History* and sometimes twisted. These are, however, all we have for the Mongolian people, and as long as we continue to ignore them, we will remain trapped in a realm of fuzziness. Therefore, I have kept these two works, together with the *Secret History*, always at my side.

Chinggis unified the settlements on the Mongolian plateau, became sovereign over them all, and conquered the state of Jin, but afterward when he invaded Central Asia, we have no accounts concerning the conquering Mongol armies aside from those by men living in the Western lands that were invaded. I used the aforementioned renowned works by d'Ohsson and Vladimirtsov, which were written using these other texts, and I only had a chance to peruse the latter's *Chingis-Khan* as I was working on the final portions of my own *Aoki ōkami*.[17] I perforce used these works to trace the movements of the Mongol armies, and thus to surmise the activities of Chinggis and others.

Two extremely welcome texts that provide information on Chinggis's movements while resident in Central Asia are *Zhanran jushi ji* (Works of a retired scholar at ease) by Yelü Chucai (1190–1244) and *Changchun zhenren xiyou ji* (Account of travels to the west by Daoist master Changchun).[18] At Chinggis's summons, Changchun (1148–

1227) traveled to the great khan's tents in the Hindukush to explain the methods of achieving long life. Yelü Chucai was a close advisor to Chinggis and was always by his side; after the great khan's death, he served his son Ögedei, making significant achievements as political, economic, and cultural advisor for the Yuan dynasty.

In addition to being accounts of Mongol history, these two works contain materials from the Chinese side that are highly salutary to biographers of Chinggis Khan. The meeting between the famous Daoist master Changchun and the great mass murderer Chinggis would be interesting in and of itself, but in the exchanges between them recounted in the *Changchun zhenren xiyou ji*, we find invaluable information on Chinggis the man.

The most problematic element for me in writing *Aoki ōkami* was the place names on the Mongolian plateau. In the *Secret History*, names of mountains and rivers crop up in inordinate abundance, and I couldn't even imagine where many of them were located. They are, of course, different from their present names, making investigation all but impossible. Chinggis was born in a place in the foothills of Mount Burqan where his people pitched their camp from his birth through his youth. But which mountain is this Mount Burqan? Even today we do not know with certainty, nor for that matter do we know where he was buried.

Given this situation, I have little idea about the mountains and rivers. By chance, though, I once received a four-volume work bearing the title *Introduction to China*, compiled by about a dozen French missionaries, from the Isseidō Bookstore in the Kanda section of Tokyo.[19] It was published in Paris early in the eighteenth century. It includes numerous woodblock-printed maps and has the names of everything from the tributaries of small rivers to hillocks in the middle of the desert assiduously transcribed in the section labeled "Tartary." When I tried to find the names of places, mountains, and rivers in the *Secret History*, I was able to locate the majority of them in the roughly twenty old maps in this collection.

Chinggis died in the borderland between Jin and Xixia terrain. His last words were instructions to proceed with an invasion of Jin and to keep his passing a secret for a certain period of time. The dying words of Takeda Shingen (1521–73) were orders to his men to plant their military banner at Seta the next day and keep his death a secret for three years.[20] As heroic figures and warriors, the two men were on a totally different scale, but their dying wishes were nonetheless similar. One died en route to the capital in Kyoto, the other died with the pacification of the great state of Jin before his eyes. The Japanese warrior and the Mongol invader differed in that, while soon after Shingen's death the Takeda house perished, in Chinggis's case his extraordinary sons and grandsons persevered in his will, lived out his ambitions 100 percent, and wrote numerous pages in the history of Eurasia.

NOTES

None of the information given in these notes can be found in Inoue Yasushi's text. I have added it here as explanatory material for the interested reader or specialist. —JF

1. (Tokyo: Fuzanbō, 1924).
2. Kindaichi was a scholar of Japanese linguistics generally and the Ainu language in particular; Ōmori of Japanese medical history; Fujisawa of ethnography and mythology; Miyake was one of the most widely published and read cultural critics of his long life; and Torii was a pioneer anthropologist.
3. (Tokyo: Dai Nihon tosho kabushiki gaisha, 1907). Naka was a noted historian whose many works included *Shina tsūshi* (Comprehensive history of China), the first modern history of this sort in any language and written in literary Chinese. It ends with the Song dynasty, because Naka did not believe he had enough raw data for the next section on the Mongol dynasty. He thus devoted the next period of years to securing a copy of the *Secret History of the Mongols* in Chinese and translating it; *Chingisu Kan jitsuroku* is that translation. He is also famous for having coined the term *Tōyō* (East Asia).
4. The Kanda section (referred to by many also as Jinbōchō) is home to numerous used bookstores.
5. *Mōko gakuhō* appeared only twice, volume 1 in July 1940 and volume 2 in April 1941; it was published by the Zenrin kyōkai. *Gakujutsu hōkoku* was

published in 1909 by the Tōyō kyōkai chōsabu and reprinted in 1967 by the Tōyō bunko in Tokyo. Riazonovskii's work, originally titled *Obych-noe pravo mongolskikh plemen* (Customary law of the Mongolian people), was translated by Yonemura Shōichi (Tokyo: Tō-A keizai chōsabu, 1935). The Greater East Asian Co-prosperity Sphere was the euphemistic term for the lands occupied by or sympathetic to Japanese expansionism in the 1930s and 1940s.

6. Translated by Tanaka Suiichirō (Tokyo: Iwanami shoten, 1909; 1936–38); it is a translation of his *Histoire des Mongols, depuis Tchinguiz-Khan jusqu'a Timour Bey ou Tamerlan* (Paris: Firmin Didot, 1824; La Haye: Les frères Van Cleef, 1834–35; Amsterdam: F. Muller, 1852).

7. Translated by Gaimushō chōsabu (Research Department of the Foreign Ministry) (Tokyo: Gaimushō chōsabu, 1936; Seikatsusha, 1941). It is a translation of *Obshchestvennyi stroi Mongolov, mongol'skii kochevoi feo-dalizm* (Social structure of the Mongols, Mongolian nomadic feudalism) (Leningrad: Izdatel'stvo Akademii nauk SSSR, 1934).

8. Translated by Gotō Tomio (Tokyo: Seikatsusha, 1940; reprint, Seoul, 1997). It is a translation of "The Geographical Factor in Mongol History," a speech given on December 14, 1936 and subsequently published in *Geographical Journal* 91 (1938): 1–20; it has been reprinted in Owen Lattimore, *Studies in Frontier History, Collected Papers 1928–1958* (London: Oxford University Press, 1962), 241–58.

9. Translated by Tō-A kenkyūjo (East Asian research group) (Tokyo: Ryōbun shokyoku, 1945). It is a translation of part of *Tangutsko–Tibets-kaia okraina Kitaia i tsentral'naia Mongoliia* (The Tangut–Tibetan border-lands of China and Central Mongolia) (St. Petersburg: Tipografia Suvori-na, 1893; reprint, Moscow: Gosudarstvennoe izdatel'stvo geograficheskoi literatury, 1950).

10. Ozaki: (Tokyo: Shinchōsha, 1940).

11. (London: John Lane, 1936); Japanese translation: *Chingisu Kan*, by Katō Asatori (Tokyo: Takemura, 1938).

12. (Tokyo: Taikandō, 1942).

13. (Stuttgart, Berlin: Deutsche Verlags-Abstalt, 1934); Japanese transla-tion: *Chingisu Kan, Ajia no arashi*, by Hamanaka Eiden (Tokyo: Fuzanbō, 1940).

14. (New York: R. M. McBride, 1927).

15. (Paris: Gallimard, 1931).

16. Respectively: *Mōko genryū* (Kyoto: Gō Minoru, 1940; Tokyo: Kōbundō shobō, 1940); *Mōko ōgonshi, Mōko minzoku no koten* (Golden history of the Mongols, a classic of the Mongol people) (Tokyo: Seikatsusha, 1941).

17. Vladimirtsov, *Chingis-Khan* (Berlin, Petersburg: Z. I. Grzhebin, 1922; reprint, St. Petersburg: Lan', 1998); English translation by D. S. Mirsky, *The Life of Chingis-Khan* (Boston: Houghton Mifflin, 1930; London: Routledge, 1930; reprint, New York: B. Blom, 1969); Japanese translation from the English by Kobayashi Takashirō (Tokyo: Nihon kōminsha, 1936; Tokyo: Seikatsusha, 1942).

18. The former has been published in fourteen fascicles (Taibei: Shijie shuju, 1988) and earlier (Shanghai: Shangwu yinshuguan, 1922?). The latter was written by Li Zhichang (1193–1256), who accompanied his master, Changchun, on the voyage; recent editions include: (Shanghai: Zhongghua shuji, 1934); (Lanzhou: Lanzhou guji shusian, 1990). We have an English translation by Arthur Waley (1889–1966), *The Travels of an Alchemist: The Journey of the Taoist, Ch'ang-ch'un, from China to the Hindukush at the Summons of Chinghiz Khan* (London: Routledge, 1931).

19. Inoue must be referring here to: Jean-Baptiste Du Halde, *Description de la Chine* (Paris, 1735) four volumes, with a famous set of maps done by D'Anville (1736). The full title is *Description géographique, historique, chronologique, politique, et physique de l'empire de la Chine et de la Tartarie chinoise: enrichie des cartes generales et particulieres de ces pays, de la carte générale & des cartes particulieres du Thibet, & de la Corée & ornée d'un grand nombre de figures et de vignettes gravées en taille-douce.*

20. Takeda and his clan form the central figures of Akira Kurosawa's 1980 epic film, *Kagemusha* (The shadow warrior).

Dramatis Personae

Note: The following is a list of the more important characters in the novel. Unless indicated as fictional (f), all characters are historical figures.

ALTAN: son of Qutula

BATACHIQAN: offspring of blue wolf and pale doe, ancestor of the Mongols

BEGTER: one of Temüjin's younger paternal half-brothers

BELGÜTEI: one of Temüjin's younger paternal half-brothers

BO'ORCHU: selfless friend to Temüjin, son of Naqu Bayan

BOROGHUL: foundling adopted and raised by Ö'elün

BÖRTE: Temüjin's wife

BÜLTECHÜ BA'ATUR (F): old raconteur of Mongol history

CHA'ADAI: second son to Temüjin and Börte

CHANGCHUN: Daoist priest summoned by Chinggis to his camp in the Hindukush

CHARAQA: father of Münglig and faithful to Temüjin and his family

CHA'UR BEKI: daughter of To'oril Khan, wife of Jochi

CHILA'UN: second son of Sorqan Shira and early friend to Temüjin

CHILEDÜ: Merkid leader

CHIMBAI: eldest son of Sorqan Shira and early friend to Temüjin

CHINGGIS KHAN (*see* TEMÜJIN)

CHOTAN: mother of Börte, mother-in-law of Temüjin

DARITAI ODCHIGIN: Temüjin's uncle

DAYIR USUN: a Merkid and father of Qulan

DEI SECHEN: leader of the Unggirad lineage, Temüjin's father-in-law

DÖRBEI DOQSHIN: commander under Chinggis Khan

GHAYIR KHAN: Khorazm military officer

HAMBAGHAI: second khan of the Mongolian people

HATUN: Jin princess given to Temüjin

HÜLEGÜ: grandson of Chinggis, son of Tolui

JALAL AL-DIN: heir to Muhammad as leader of Khorazm

JAMUGHA: leader of the Jadarans, onetime ally of Temüjin

JARCHI'UDAI: father of Jelme, whom he swore to offer in service to Temüjin at birth

JEBE: archer who nearly kills Temüjin and then becomes his trusted follower

JELME: sworn to Temüjin, trusted aide for many years

JOCHI: Temüjin and Börte's first-born son, lit. "guest"

JÜRCHEDEI: leader of the Uru'uds

KÖKÖCHÜ: Tayichi'ud orphan adopted and raised by Ö'elün

KÖLGEN: only son of Temüjin and Qulan

KUCHU: Merkid orphan adopted and raised by Ö'elün

KÜCHÜLÜG: Naiman king

LIU ZHONGLU: emissary sent to summon Changchun to Chinggis's camp

MUHAMMAD: shah of Khorazm

MÜNGLIG: Temüjin's Borjigin relative; son of Charaqa; father of Teb Tenggeri

MUQALI: valiant young commander under Temüjin

NAQU BAYAN: father of Bo'orchu

Ö'ELÜN (sometimes also spelled HÖ'ELÜN): mother of Temüjin (later Chinggis Khan)

ÖGEDEI: third son of Temüjin and Börte

QABUL KHAN: first khan of the Mongol people, great-grandfather of Temüjin

QACHI'UN: one of Temüjin's younger brothers

QADA'AN: daughter of Sorqan Shira, sister of Chimbai and Chila'un

QASAR: one of Temüjin's younger brothers

QO'AQCHIN: maidservant to Ö'elün

QOCHAR: Temüjin's cousin

QODU KHAN: young Merkid commander

QORCHI: old soothsayer originally of the Ba'arins

QUBILAI: grandson of Chinggis, son of Tolui

QUBILAI NOYAN: commander under Chinggis

QUDUQA BEKI: Oirat leader who surrenders to Chinggis and joins his army

QULAN: Chinggis's beloved concubine

QUTULA: third khan of the Mongolian people

QUYILDAR: leader of the Mangghuds

SAMMUQA: commander under Chinggis Khan

SECHE BEKI: Temüjin's cousin, brother of Taichu

SENGGÜM: To'oril Khan's son

SHIGI QUTUQU: Tatar foundling adopted and raised by Ö'elün

SORQAN SHIRA: maker of fermented mare's milk and early friend to
      Temüjin

SÜBE'ETEI: originally a Uriangqan, joins Temüjin's camp early on

TAICHU: Temüjin's cousin, brother of Seche Beki

TARGHUTAI: leader of the Tayichi'uds, onetime ally of Temüjin

TAYANG KHAN: ruler of the Naimans

TEB TENGGERI: shaman, son of Münglig

TEMÜGE: one of Temüjin's younger brothers

TEMÜJIN: founder of the Mongol empire (later Chinggis Khan)

TEMÜLÜN: younger sister of Temüjin

TOLUI: fourth son of Temüjin and Börte

TO'ORIL KHAN: leader of the Kereyids

WANYAN FUXING: grand councilor of the Jin

WANYAN HESHUO: Jin commander

YEKE CHEREN: Altan's cousin

YELÜ CHUCAI: Khitan prince, advisor to Chinggis Khan

YELÜ LIUGE: royal Khitan descendant, supporter of Mongol assault on Jin
      dynasty

YISÜGEI: father of Temüjin (later Chinggis Khan), fourth khan of the Mon-
      golian people

YISÜGEN: daughter of Tatar chief, taken by Temüjin as concubine, sister of
      Yisüi

YISÜI: daughter of Tatar chief, taken by Temüjin as concubine, sister of
      Yisügen

WEATHERHEAD BOOKS ON ASIA

Weatherhead East Asian Institute, Columbia University

LITERATURE (David Der-wei Wang, Editor)

Ye Zhaoyan, *Nanjing 1937: A Love Story*, translated by Michael Berry (2003)

Oda Makato, *The Breaking Jewel*, translated by Donald Keene (2003)

Han Shaogong, *A Dictionary of Maqiao*, translated by Julia Lovell (2003)

Takahashi Takako, *Lonely Woman*, translated by Maryellen Toman Mori (2004)

Chen Ran, *A Private Life*, translated by John Howard-Gibbon (2004)

Eileen Chang, *Written on Water*, translated by Andrew F. Jones (2004)

Writing Women in Modern China: The Revolutionary Years, 1936–1976, edited by
    Amy D. Dooling (2005)

Han Bangqing, *The Sing-song Girls of Shanghai*, first translated by Eileen Chang,
    revised and edited by Eva Hung (2005)

Loud Sparrows: Contemporary Chinese Short-Shorts, translated and edited by Aili Mu,
    Julie Chiu, Howard Goldblatt (2006)

Hiratsuka Raichō, *In the Beginning, Woman Was the Sun*, translated by Teruko Craig
    (2006)

Zhu Wen, *I Love Dollars and Other Stories of China*, translated by Julia Lovell (2007)

Kim Sowol, *Azaleas: A Book of Poems*, translated by David McCann (2007)

Wang Anyi, *The Song of Everlasting Sorrow: A Novel of Shanghai*, translated by
    Michael Berry (2008)

Ch'oe Yun, *There a Petal Silently Falls: Three Stories by Ch'oe Yun*, translated by
    Bruce and Ju-Chan Fulton (2008)

HISTORY, SOCIETY, AND CULTURE (Carol Gluck, Editor)

Takeuchi Yoshimi, *What Is Modernity? Writings of Takeuchi Yoshimi*, edited and
    translated, with an introduction, by Richard F. Calichman (2005)

Contemporary Japanese Thought, edited and translated by Richard F. Calichman,
    (2005)

Overcoming Modernity, edited and translated by Richard F. Calichman (2008)